D0110846

PRINCE OF THE CLOUDS

PRINCE OF THE CLOUDS

GIANNI RIOTTA

•

TRANSLATED FROM THE ITALIAN BY

STEPHEN SARTARELLI

•

ILLUSTRATIONS BY MATTEO PERICOLI

•

PICADOR USA
FARRAR, STRAUS AND GIROUX
NEW YORK

•

PRINCE OF THE CLOUDS. Copyright © 1997 by Gianni Riotta. Translation ©
Stephen Sartarelli. Illustrations © Matteo Pericoli. All rights reserved. Printed
in the United States of America. No part of this book may be used or reproduced in any manner whatsoever without written permission except in the case
of brief quotations embodied in critical articles or reviews. For information,
address Picador USA, 175 Fifth Avenue, New York, N.Y. 10010.

www.picadorusa.com

Picador® is a U.S. registered trademark and is used by Farrar, Straus and
Giroux under license from Pan Books Limited.

For information on Picador USA Reading Group Guides, as well as ordering,
please contact the Trade Marketing department at St. Martin's Press.
Phone: 1-800-221-7945 extension 763
Fax: 212-677-7456
E-mail: trademarketing@stmartins.com

Library of Congress Cataloging-in-Publication Data

Riotta, Gianni.
    [Principe delle nuvole. English]
    Prince of the clouds / by Gianni Riotta ; translated from the Italian by
Stephen Sartarelli.
        p. cm.
    ISBN 0-312-42015-3
    I. Sartarelli, Stephen, 1954– II. Title.
PQ4878.I52 P7513 2000
853'.914—dc21   99-055335

First published in Italy under the title *Principe Delle Nuvole*
by RCS Rizzoli Libri SpA

First Picador USA Edition: December 2001

10 9 8 7 6 5 4 3 2 1

TO MY COUSINS

Margherita Fundarò and Saverio Altavilla

AND MY FRIENDS

Maurizio Flores d'Arcais and Paola Cusumano

Jesus said, "If you bring forth what is within you,

what you have will save you.

If you do not have that within you,

what you do not have within you

[will] kill you."

Gospel of Thomas, 70

PRINCE OF THE CLOUDS

" 'I ASK but one favor of God: to have commanded my last battle at Waterloo. Always having to fight is a terrible destiny. At war, [when] shouting orders, I forget human feeling. Once the battle is over, the anguish begins. The soul and reason wear themselves out; there is no thinking of glory. At the moment of victory, I lose myself. Believe me, dear friend, besides losing a battle, the worst misfortune that can befall a man is to win it. My hope is not to fight. Ever again.' So said Arthur Wellesley, first Duke of Wellington, in confidence to Lady Shelley, thirty days after the decisive, victorious battle against Emperor Napoleon Bonaparte at Waterloo, June 18, 1815."

Colonel Carlo Terzo stopped reading and looked up at the sun, awaiting a reply. But Lieutenant Amedeo Campari, his feet firmly planted in the sand of a Maremma beach, gazed in silence at the horizon of sea and thrust his fencing foil at infinity. As light flashed from the blade, the southwest wind bent the tops of the pine trees and spilled white waves of foam onto the shore. It was fifteen minutes before noon on May 27, 1940.

Shuffling the manuscript pages as if they were playing cards, Colonel Terzo tried reading a second anecdote. " 'On the eve of the attack to liberate Pavia from the siege of François 1, Fernando d'Avalos, Marchese of Pescara, carefully considered what orders to give the Spanish infantry. Hungry for pillage, two courtiers burst into the tent to hurry him up: "Order the attack at once, My Lord!" Pescara listened to them in silence, then said: "May God grant me one hundred years of war, but not a single day of battle. We shall attack tomorrow, gentlemen, but only because there is no other choice." ' Are you convinced yet, Amedeo?"

The lieutenant removed his uniform jacket with the insignias of the Novara Lancers, folded up his shirt and, now bare-chested, resumed his duel against an invisible enemy. From the corner of his mouth dangled an Edelweiss cigarette. When only the butt was left, he mimed a jab and said: "We've been working together since '35. I'm not about to convert to your theory now." He leaped elegantly onto a brine-whitened tree trunk and tried out a new move.

Terzo had an idea: "Would you be able to close a single hand around the trunk on which you are standing?"

Surprised, Campari lowered his guard: "What do you mean?"

The colonel weighed his pages down with a small alabaster stone, so that the wind wouldn't blow them away, then took the foil out of his friend's hand and with the tip began to illustrate an ancient battle in the sand. "Obviously you can't close your hand around a tree trunk. Napoleon teaches that one should never try to surround a more powerful enemy with meager forces. And yet against all common sense, that is precisely what Hannibal Barca did at Cannae, on August 3, 216 B.C., dealing Rome her bloodiest defeat: seventy thousand dead. Left standing were Consul Paulus, who had tried in vain to postpone the conflict, twenty-nine military tribunes, and eighty senators. Some died trampled in the mêlée and some, just to avoid falling into enemy hands, choked themselves by swallowing clods of trodden earth. A tragic shambles, won in defiance of military strategy. Hannibal cut down the majestic tree of the Roman legions with his hand. The Romans drew up an extraordinary front along the banks of the Ophantus river, row upon row of legionaries. They wanted to destroy the Carthaginian army, to have done with the African invaders. Imagine their surprise when, once the mists of dawn had lifted, they saw Hannibal leave the Carthaginian veterans at the flanks and pack the center with Spanish and Gaul-

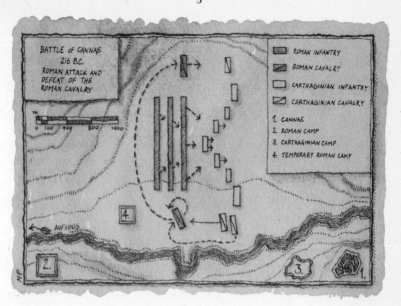

BATTLE of CANNAE
216 B.C.
ROMAN ATTACK AND
DEFEAT OF THE
ROMAN CAVALRY

ROMAN INFANTRY
ROMAN CAVALRY
CARTHAGINIAN INFANTRY
CARTHAGINIAN CAVALRY

1. CANNAE
2. ROMAN CAMP
3. CARTHAGINIAN CAMP
4. TEMPORARY ROMAN CAMP

AUFIDUS

BATTLE of CANNAE
216 B.C.
DESTRUCTION
OF THE ROMAN ARMY

HANNIBAL

ish mercenaries, soldiers who fought for pay, unreliable men, ready to flee to save their own skin. His armor gleaming, Hannibal took the field amid this riffraff, accompanied by his younger brother, the brave and noble Mago. Against the Romans' straight line," said Terzo, tracing the formation of the republican legions, "the Carthaginians formed a convex front." And the foil drew a precise semicircle among the seashells.

"Nobody before that," proclaimed Terzo, with the rapt air he used to assume when lecturing at the Modena Military Academy, reducing to silence even the unruliest cadets, "had ever entrusted the heart of the battle to unskilled, untrustworthy troops. Invoking the gods' protection, the Romans attacked. They hurled their lances and javelins, twirled their gladii, and pressed forward with their shields, breaking through the fragile front line of mercenaries. The Gauls and Spaniards retreated and fell back but, heartened by the cries and the example of Hannibal and Mago, they did not disband. They gave ground, step by step, avoiding chaos, all together, until their formation became concave." Terzo erased his first drawing with his hand, and then retraced, with the tip of the foil, the exact position of Hannibal's mercenaries.

"At the flanks, the Carthaginian veterans valorously held firm, but the Romans could smell victory. The front line of mercenaries would not last long against the fury of the Republican infantry. Ruin would follow. In this desperate moment, Hannibal sprang his trap. At his signal, the heavy African cavalry returned at a gallop from a diversionary raid, and the pincer was closed. Carried away by their brutal ardor, the Romans were caught in the Carthaginians' circle, with no room to retreat, like mice in a sack. They would fall one by one in the fray." Terzo's blade closed the front in a perfect circle. A wave a little longer than the rest wet his feet, dissolving Hannibal's perfect plan in a mass of little bubbles.

"And what lesson for living does your theory draw from this carnage?" Campari asked skeptically.

"Hannibal won by embracing his own weakness. He turned problems into weapons. Let the Romans line up their powerful legions. He would break them by relying on the worst of soldiers. He turned the strength of his adversaries against them. Isn't there a valid moral in this for us, too? Bear in mind that the coming war will be fought by civilians in uniform, not by professional soldiers. Aerial bombings will put women and the elderly on the front lines. We shall all have to use our frailty to surround and defeat enemies who think themselves all-powerful."

"And what about Wellington at Waterloo? Or Fernando d'Avalos at Pavia? Do you derive a moral from them, too?"

"Wellington and d'Avalos understood that there is no aspect of the human spirit—strength, courage, intelligence as well as cowardice, horror, cruelty—that is not revealed in battle. To win, Wellington must think the same thoughts as Napoleon, and know how to act like him. He must become his brother in order to strike him down, as Cain did Abel. Why are you surprised that d'Avalos talks of a hundred years of war without a single engagement? The Chinese master, Sun Tzu, teaches that 'the virtue of the strategist lies not in winning one hundred battles. The summit of virtue is to defeat the enemy without a fight.' One thousand years later, the Byzantine general Belisarius would say exactly the same thing: 'The only happy victory is the surrender of the enemy, with no suffering of one's own army.'"

Campari picked up the foil, now wet with seawater, and began wiping the sand off it. Colonel Carlo Terzo and Lieutenant Amedeo Campari had ended up working together only thanks to the logic of military life, which always mixes men and responsibilities at random. Born in Turin in 1901, Terzo had joined the army as a boy. At the Officer's Training School, General Augusto

Pimentel, happy finally to have a pupil willing to study, had assigned him to research the strategy of Prince Eugene of Savoy, "the little abbot." Terzo found documents and antique maps at the Florence museum, and his essay was eventually translated throughout Europe. Once he had completed War School, he was assigned to the Historical Office of the General Staff of the Royal Army. In collaboration with the architect Cosenza, a reserve officer rumored to have Marxist sympathies, he revised the translation of *On War*, the work of the Prussian strategist Karl von Clausewitz, later published by Generals Bollati and Canevari.

Amedeo Campari, from Milan, ten years his junior, was instead relegated to Archives, thanks to the actions of his favorite horse, the bay Malvino. It was hard to imagine two more different officers: Terzo forever bent over papers and ancient tomes, Amedeo busy taming colts, fencing, and courting beautiful women. There wasn't a single lady who didn't feel weightless when floating in his arms in a courtly dance. Married and unmarried women pined for him, but Campari, unflappable, simply smoothed his black moustaches and waited. He was waiting for the war. He had missed his chance for Africa, in '35, because Malvino had reared up at the river-leap, the final test in the National Championship, and he had woken up the next day in the hospital with a fractured cranium. With an order, on his bedside table, to report for service at the Historical Office, "to Colonel Carlo Terzo."

The collaboration between the dashing lieutenant and the erudite colonel soon matured into friendship. Restless when studying, Campari got excited only during on-site investigations, such as the one Terzo had persuaded him to carry out in the Maremma region of Tuscany, in search of Mago's encampment. On such occasions he would take advantage of the situation and bring along his foils, turning fields and footpaths into fencing boards. During their excursions, while Terzo was measuring the perimeter of a trench, and the aged archivist, Marshal Puntoni, was panting as he wrote down telemetrical data, Campari would cheerfully stand aside, smoking and practicing his fencing. And as time passed, he managed to infect the colonel with the same passion.

That day, too, he was placidly tanning himself while Terzo, a strict observer of protocol, kept on his jacket and cap. Their dispute had been dragging on for years, with the colonel convinced that "from the teachings of war one may derive a precise method for action in everyday life," and the lieutenant certain that "war is the domain of Fate, like hunting. You shoot instinctively, and you hit the fox. Galloping along at full speed, you fail to see a hidden branch and you're done for."

With Italy ready to declare war on France and England, they had to resolve their dispute once and for all. The time for debates was over. Colonel Terzo wanted to publish the *Manual for Strategic Living*, a book summarizing his method, and he had only that morning left to refute Campari's objections. Once back in Rome, they would receive their mobilization orders; the war would send them to faraway fronts. Terzo, fearing that Pimentel would force him to stay in Rome to do research, had turned to General Federico Marlin in the hopes that the general would assign him to Cyrenaica in North Africa as an aide-de-camp. He didn't much like Fascism, being one of those monarchist officers who turned up his nose at Mussolini. But he had been studying war all his life and now he wanted to see it, after hastening to complete his *Manual* before he left. He was convinced that the battles would validate his theories for the world. Campari was a happy warrior; he knew no other destiny than war. During these days of waiting, however, his disenchantment concealed, with one cigarette too many, the fear that his old fracture would lead some bureaucrat to declare him "unfit for combat." "I will not wither between the pages of Clausewitz," he had vowed to the young Laura d'Attimis, kissing her after a reception. In this spirit Colonel Terzo and Lieutenant Campari thus confronted their dispute one last time: Were war and life the domain of Fate, or was there a rule by which one might seize victory?

Having cleaned his foil, Campari took a swig of Frascati from his canteen, which he kept cool with a wet cloth. Wiping his mouth with his hand, he asked: "Care to fence?"

Terzo was no longer listening to him. As if pressed for time, or as if the imminent war had stripped him of his scholarly discipline, he took his friend by the arm and said: "My *Manual* ponders life the way the great strategists pondered their campaigns. By managing good luck and bad, victory and defeat, without losing heart or taking pride, we can live our lives believing there is always hope. I teach people how to find, in their despair, a hidden way of escape. If the enemy forces you to flee in confusion, you must retrieve a weapon and prepare an ambush. On every field of battle, on every occasion in life, we can find the courage, inventiveness, and luck to defeat enemies much more powerful than we are. As long as we are prepared to suffer and think, even confusion, even our inner disorder, can be turned to advantage. Take for example the battle of Rosebeke, November 27, 1382—"

"I want to live, and I want to fight. If I must die, let it be in war, not of boredom retracing the order to attack of fucking Philip of Artevelde at the fucking battle of Rosebeke." Tired of waiting, Campari tossed a foil to his companion.

"Don't underestimate Rosebeke," answered Terzo, unruffled. He doffed his cap and jacket, put up his guard. "A decisive battle," he continued, "with poor Philip ending up crushed by the French columns. If the Flemish had prevailed, the other cities would likewise have rebelled against the king, anticipating the French Revolution by more than four centuries. With a different outcome at Rosebeke, we wouldn't even be here . . ."

"Would there be anything wrong with that?" rebutted Campari, his weapon glinting in the sunlight. "I intend to fight this war, Carlo. I'm not going to stay behind and study. If your teaching is correct, I'll send you proof of it from the front. Today, though, it's my turn to teach you something. This duel will prove that you're wrong."

They were both good fencers: Amedeo a natural talent, fiery, always on the offensive, Terzo less athletically gifted but rational, and capable of spending three hours in front of the mirror practicing a move. Behind them, the dense Tuscan pine forest, cut only by a narrow path of red earth, abutted a seaside resort still closed but recently repainted for the coming season. The restaurant terrace stood atop the sheer promontory, conjoined to the beach below by a steep stone stairway. There the sea deepened, the water changing from green to blue. For the entire morning, Colonel Carlo Terzo had been fascinated by the borderline between the two colors: soon the vacationers would be arriving, swimming cheerfully in familiar waters, keeping their distance from the cobalt abyss over which two albatrosses now glided, looking for incautious prey.

BARELY POKING EACH OTHER with the tips of their foils, the two officers continued their discussion, becoming quickly hoarse from the effort, panting between thrusts and parries. "There is a foolproof rule for winning, dear Amedeo, in war and in our everyday lives, and I will prove it. I have been contemplating a statement by the Greek historian Xenophon, who had fought in the rout of Cyrus's mercenaries: 'The strategist must know how to make the enemy imagine that he is absent when he is present, and present when he is absent.' Just fifty years before him, in 400 B.C., the master of Chinese strategy, Sun Tzu, wrote: 'Warfare is the art of deceit. Therefore, when able, seem to be unable; when ready, seem unready; when nearby, seem far away; and when far away seem near.' Identical statements, written just a short time apart, in two remote places. How is it possible that

Xenophon and Sun Tzu arrived at the same conclusions? How did Sun Tzu foreshadow the words of General Belisarius? All three, you see, had learned, in battle, the secretive style of fighting. The warrior's precept is to be everywhere, resigned to hardship, decisive in conflict. Isn't a precept that can save us in war also useful in peacetime? This, in short, is my method."

Campari made a trial thrust, then a feint at his companion's shoulder, then advanced: "Have you also got a strategy for this duel?" he exclaimed. "First defense, then attack, because no battle is ever won from a defensive position alone. So says Clausewitz, right?" He leaped up onto a rusty gasoline drum, trying to pin down his adversary, then instantly jumped down, but the colonel parried him low, then high, faltered once, twice, then regained momentum and began to climb the stone stairs. Terzo's fastidious defense was wearing Campari out. Every masterly stroke of his was met with a parry, thrust, or turnabout learned during hours of tiring exercise. This day, however, he was sure. "I will win. And I will teach you something your books don't tell in the footnotes. I will run you through, and show you that even Alexander the Great can't turn chaos into a weapon. We are naked in the face of chaos: *that* is the warrior's great fortune. If you win the duel with your strategy, I will resign myself and admit you're right. But if I win, then you will give up shuffling papers. Agreed?"

"Agreed," replied Terzo, carefully testing the stairs beneath his feet before taking each step.

"You think that, by studying the battles, you've discovered the rules for winning. Correct?" Campari struck with the point of his weapon, but Terzo didn't bite at the feint and continued climbing the stairs. Ten more steps and he would reach the terrace above the rocks. There he would tire Campari out, inducing him to drop his guard. Being too competitive to ignore his provocations, his friend would overextend himself and end up defeated, like Prince Louis-Ferdinand of Prussia, who in 1806, at Saalfeld, charged thirty thousand veterans of Napoleon all by himself, dying a useless death.

Now Amedeo Campari, too, lightly climbed the final step, and they overwhelmed each other in a flurry of blows and shouts of "There!" "Aha!" "Parry" and "You're dead!" on the terrace of the resort. Carlo Terzo felt his arm grow heavy and was glad, because usually, at this point, he won. Having exhausted his repertoire of moves, Amedeo would redouble his assaults, lose concentration, and get caught in a mistake. The colonel was now bearing down on his adversary, driving him back against the void.

"You think you know every stroke?" shouted Amedeo, scattering the ash of his Edelweiss.

"Every one. I've done my homework."

"So you think you can fence with any opponent?"

The blades clashed violently, drew apart, and the two officers returned to measuring each other, knees flexed. Terzo had backed Campari against the railing over the sea. Now he had only to attack. Leaving his adversary with the sun in his eyes, he would feint toward the groin and then strike him in the chest.

"I WILL TEACH YOU the final secret, and I hope you will bear it in mind. In war and in peace. Your strategies have one invincible adversary. Do you know who he is?" asked Campari in all seriousness.

"You, I imagine," replied Terzo, straining in the effort: two more thrusts and he would deal the winning blow.

"No. The madman." And with a somersault, Amedeo Campari vaulted over Terzo and landed on his feet on the low wall surrounding the terrace. The sand that had flown from under his boots sifted down into the blue water after falling some fifty feet through the air. There in thin air, the lieutenant challenged his friend: "What now? What strategy do you suggest against the madman?"

Terzo dropped his foil: "Give me your hand. You're going to kill yourself." The waves were washing over the rocks, and the seagulls, disturbed by the cries of the duelists, hovered around Amedeo, whose left foot was over the green water of the beach, his right over the deep dark blue.

"The madman. Strategy calculates the risk faced by a normal person, however courageous and bold he may be," Campari recited. Down by the shore a small rowboat lingered, the fisherman attracted by the spectacle of a swordsman precariously teetering over the rocks. "You calculate the risks and prepare to attack. But what if the enemy is a madman, a lunatic, *un fou,* a joker, someone who doesn't give a damn about conventional strategy and is ready to be pulverized in order to win? Or rather to stand and philosophize at the edge of the abyss? What then, Colonel Terzo? What becomes of your all-powerful strategy in the face of someone willing to burn himself to a crisp for nothing? The happy warrior who values life no more than death?"

"Give me your hand, Amedeo, come down."

"To your level? To the ingenuity that knows everything, but dares nothing? Never." Amedeo dived into the air, landed in front of Terzo and administered him a violent, lashlike blow across the chest. "I win," he said, dripping with sweat. "And remember: you can learn how to live from Alexander the Great, but even Alexander had no protection against the madness of chaos." They embraced, laughing. Feeling that wiry torso against him, in the strong southwest wind, Colonel Carlo Terzo felt strangely moved.

"The war will decide who is right," he said. "I don't deny the power of life, Amedeo. I want only to teach people how to control it . . ."

At that moment, a car stopped on the path cutting through the pine forest. A captain stepped out and, having spotted the two officers, crossed the beach with measured steps. He climbed the stairs with small, puppet-like leaps and then gave an impeccable salute, hand to his visor. "Colonel Terzo?"

"That's him. The master strategist," replied Campari sarcastically.

Without smiling, the corpulent officer stood suddenly at attention. "Captain Nasca, Colonel. I've got orders for you. I'm to bring you back to Rome. I've had more than a little trouble finding you." He held out a yellow envelope, stamped "Ministry of Foreign Affairs, Cabinet of His Excellency Count Galeazzo Ciano," and shook the sand from his boots. Campari unceremoniously took the letter and, ignoring Nasca, who protested, "I have explicit orders to deliver the letter in person to Colonel—" he tore it open, pulled out a white card, and read aloud:

" 'Colonel Carlo Terzo must return, with all urgency, to Rome, for a private audience with the minister. Mission confidential.' There's even a postscript by Ciano himself, in nice black ink: 'Pardon the haste, but this is no time for etiquette. Cancel all engagements. I have an important announcement for you.' "

Campari slid the missive into Terzo's pocket and leaned forward, smiling. "I can't imagine what that windbag wants," he said, blowing the smoke of his Edelweiss into Nasca's face, "but leave me out of it. This is my war. I am going to the front, you malingerers. Understood?"

Captain Nasca accompanied the colonel to the car, quite miffed: "That young man is insolent. I will make a report . . ." But Terzo silenced him with a gesture, gathered up the pages of his manuscript, forgotten under the stone, and got into the car. As the driver was turning around, he gazed at his friend, slim and tan, the muscles lithe under the skin. Having returned to the beach, he had extracted a steel harpoon from his olive-green sack and was getting ready to go fishing. *All wars*, thought Terzo, *from the Trojan to the one about to break out, have been fought by boys like that, thin-chested, with a rebellious tuft of hair on the head and a proud, naïve gaze. May God grant us a hundred years of war without a day of battle, as He never did to the Marchese of Pescara, the Duke of Wellington, and so many armies of poor devils.* He opened the window and called out: "If we don't see each other again in Rome, Amedeo . . ."

But Amedeo Campari, lieutenant with the Novara Lancers, without a worry in the world, was chasing his shadow, brandishing the shiny harpoon against the abyss, in the sky and wind of the last springtime of peace.

IN HIS EXCELLENCY'S ANTECHAMBER there sat a tall lady, dressed in black, with ash-blond hair. On her knees she held a bureaucratic-looking brown leather portfolio, rather incongruous for a *femme* so apparently *fatale*. She looked at Terzo and smiled, sizing him up attentively, as if cataloguing face, place, and date of encounter. She didn't say a word or make a move, but simply bent slightly forward, ready to get up and vanish into the meanders of the ministry. At exactly half past seven p.m., a white-haired clerk opened the inner door, ushering out two diplomats who muttered *"Danke . . . Danke . . . Auf Wiedersehen . . ."* He turned to Terzo to excuse himself: "I am sorry about the wait, Colonel . . . Your turn will come." With a formal air, but cautious and without ceremony, he gestured to the woman: "You, madame, may come in now."

"The colonel has waited long enough. And I am curious to meet him. Come with me." She then took the embarrassed Terzo's arm and led him into the minister's office. "Don't you think the colonel's been too patient, darling? Why do you want to keep him waiting? Go ahead and talk to him. I'll wait," she said, addressing Ciano in a confidential tone. She dropped down onto a purple sofa, pulled a cigarette out from her clerical portfolio, slipped it into a black lacquer holder, and stared at Terzo, waiting.

"I'm sorry, signora, I don't smoke."

His Excellency Galeazzo Ciano, Count of Cortellazzo and Il

Duce's Foreign Minister, fired up his gold lighter. "As you wish, Emma. In any case, no secret in Rome ever escapes you. Delighted to meet you, Colonel. Please sit down over here. Let's talk," he said obligingly.

The light of the Roman sunset filled the so-called Hall of Victories. Some military maps, unfolded on top of one another on the large, paper-cluttered desk, looked like bedsheets in need of ironing. Among the various telephones was a logbook labeled "Troops on Alert, May 27, 1940. Confidential." The war preparations were slowly taking on the scent of the lady's perfume and light-blue smoke.

"Time is running out, Colonel. You are a man of arms, and the moment for taking up arms is almost upon us. Italy is going to war: Il Duce has made up his mind. I had my doubts, but with France on her knees, I've become convinced. We shall fight. General Pimentel has spoken very highly of you. I asked who would be the person best suited for the mission I have in mind, and he said without hesitation: 'Colonel Terzo.' "

Ciano studied the effect of this flattery, but Terzo merely adjusted his collar, embarrassed. In a more solemn tone, Ciano added: "I want you to serve, during the coming conflict, as the official historian of our armed forces. I have obtained the authorization of the Historical Office of the General Staff and the consent of the Propaganda Office of the Ministry of War. You will be free to choose the collaborators and premises you deem most suitable and necessary to carrying out your duty." Ciano crossed his arms.

"I . . . ," Terzo ventured.

"I understand. Pimentel and I have already discussed this. You are a reserved, studious man. You don't like honor and sinecures. That is precisely why I've chosen you. I'm not asking you to play the bookworm while the world is at war. I have something very different in mind. Look," he said, and he opened a massive safe that stood to the right of the desk, moved a pile of bound agendas, extracted a military map and spread it out. "We'll be fighting in the Mediterranean, but it will be a world war, a planetary war. You've also studied abroad, correct?"

He's been well informed, thought Terzo. He could only nod: "Yes, Your Excellency. I studied strategy in Germany, military tactics and history at Oxford and Paris. I was supposed to go to America as well; I was invited by Princeton University to give a course on Hannibal's Italian campaign. But now——"

"A man with international experience, that's what we need. I know the British consider you an authority. I'm told Liddell Hart himself wrote to you for your opinions, after his trip to Italy."

"Routine exchanges between scholars, Your Excellency. But I——"

"Pimentel sent me your book, *The Great Strategy of the Little Abbot,* the biography of Eugene of Savoy. Apparently the Prince of Piedmont liked it, too. Why do you dwell so long on the battle of Belgrade?"

This was the final test. Terzo was tempted to flunk it, to talk nonsense so that he might obtain authorization to go the front. But the historian in him prevailed, and to his surprise, he heard his own voice fill the office: "Eugene was up against two hundred thousand Turks, led by the ferocious janissaries. At his own command, back then in 1716, he had only fifty thousand men. He was already old and tired. Many others would have been overcome with panic. He instead took stock of the situation. Many years earlier, at Turin, he had laid siege to the French when they thought they were besieging him. At Belgrade he attacked at night, with bayonets, in total darkness, ordering his soldiers not to shoot until they were directly in front of the enemy positions. This was a tactic never used in that period; the custom was to fight in daylight. Caught by surprise, the Turks defended themselves with their artillery but were forced to surrender. And Belgrade fell."

"The moral?" asked Ciano.

"Never do what the enemy expects of you, either in war or in everyday life. I believe that in the coming war as well, in this regard, we Italians——"

"I am told you are preparing a *Manual*, deriving the rules of victory from the experience of war. What is it about?" Ciano interrupted him, his curiosity aroused.

Marshal Puntoni, the talkative archivist, must have told him this, too, thought Terzo. But he didn't have time to answer the question because the minister once again turned to the safe, this time extracting an ancient map bordered in fine gold. "Isn't this beautiful?" he asked. Before he closed the heavy door with the combination lock, the lady handed him a yellow envelope, which Ciano placed inside on top of the agendas.

"Very beautiful," said Terzo, studying the map in the red evening light. "It's the battle formations of Marengo, June 14, 1800."

"Could you help me to locate the French positions? I'm afraid I'm unable to do so alone," said the minister, his eyes lighting up, black hair slicked back with pomade. He looked like a little boy asking his father to explain some new, fascinating game: war.

"Yes, of course," replied Terzo. "But there's something I must tell you first."

"Yes," said Ciano, irritated by the request.

"If there is to be a war . . . I've already asked to be sent with a combat unit. If there is to be a war, Your Excellency, I want to go to the front."

"To the front?" The minister seemed annoyed. "Of course, to the front. I, too, have assumed the command of a bomb squadron at Pisa. I'm wearing the uniform, you see? Indeed, I understand and share your admirable enthusiasm. But I have a very unusual mission in mind for you. You will in fact visit the front: you'll have an airplane at your disposal for reconnaissance.

It's a magnificent idea and you're the only man who can help me. Even the Germans are interested in your studies. Win or lose, this war will be a decisive one for Italy and the world. It will determine the fate of the planet until the next millennium. I'm not asking you to shirk your duty. If you have to risk your life, then you'll risk your life. But you shall do so carrying out a mission without precedent in any war or country. For every battle fought, for every city captured or lost, for every conflict on land, at sea or in the sky, you will draw up a parallel with the past. We shall measure ourselves against history. From Marathon to the Spanish civil war—do you see what I'm getting at? I want the dynamics, the statics, I want to understand why we won or why we lost. To know how much the weapons and generals mattered, how much the field of battle and the will of the people mattered. You will have an expense account, you can conduct research in archives and visit theaters of conflict. We'll take care of everything; I'll give the necessary orders. If we win, as we certainly shall, the *Official Encyclopedia of Battles* by Carlo Terzo will become a canonical text for generations. Yet even if we were to lose—for we soldiers, amongst ourselves, cannot hide the fact that every battle is up for grabs—your effort will have been even more important. It will become the record of the past; it will tell us why Italy lost. The history of a world war, told in terms of the wars of history. Just think!"

Terzo pressed his hands onto the trousers of his uniform: "Your Excellency, I've never seen a dead man."

Ciano, who had leaned forward to write something, stopped his pen in mid-air and repeated: "A dead man?"

In his embarrassment, the colonel made a gesture as if to stand at attention: "A dead man, Your Excellency. I joined the army as a boy and I'm forty years old now. In 1935 I hoped to fight in Ethiopia, and instead I had to prepare a digest of battles lost by colonial armies against natives, to prove that the Italian defeat at Ardua was not unique. I cited the 16,500 British and

Askars killed in 1842 by the Afghanis of Akbar Khan; the ambush at Little Big Horn in 1876, when the Cheyenne and Sioux
of Sitting Bull and Crazy Horse overwhelmed George Custer's
Seventh Cavalry; the two thousand Englishmen massacred by
Zulus at Isandhlwana in 1879; Gordon Pasha, killed at Khar-
toum by the followers of the Mahdi, in 1885; the slaughter of
twelve thousand Spanish soldiers in 1921 by the Moroccan rebel
Abd-el-Krim, in the battle of Anual. Indeed, there is no battle I
can't reconstruct for you." The lady had approached the table,
struck by his sorrowful tone. "Or for the lady, of course," continued Terzo, politely. "But I have never seen a dead man, Your Excellency. War, for me, is an abstraction, an infinitesimal calculus.
Until I have seen a man die, until I myself have risked my life,
what kind of warrior am I? Am I a coward or a fighter? I have
vowed to put myself to the test before I die, and that is why I put
in a request to be assigned to an operational unit. Are you familiar with the battle of Cold Harbor? American Civil War, June 3,
1864."

"Not directly," admitted Ciano.

"The night before Cold Harbor, the Union soldiers of General U. S. Grant sewed handkerchiefs onto their blue jackets, on
which they wrote their first and last names in blue pencil, to
help the gravediggers recognize their corpses. And they were
right to do so: General Lee's Confederate musketry divisions
struck down more than seven thousand Union soldiers at dawn.
Why does one go into battle with full knowledge that one must
die? What does one think about the night before, when preparing one's own shroud with a handkerchief? It is not out of pride,
or vanity, that I ask to fight. I know that war is horrific. But how
can I ever judge a soldier's valor or fear if I've never seen combat? Please let me go . . . I beg you."

"Request denied, my dear Colonel. I am making you chief of
the Section of Comparative Military History. You will be sent all
allied and enemy war bulletins; I've already alerted the em-

bassies of the neutral countries. I shall personally mark, with an X, the battles I want you to compare with past ones, but I am also counting on your own initiative."

The colonel put up strong resistance: "General Marlin had me in mind as an aide-de-camp in Cyrenaica. I am subordinate to him in the immediate chain of command. He's very keen on it."

Ciano picked up the telephone. "Furzi? Where is that imbecile? Furzi! Get General Marlin for me. At once." He put the receiver back down and resumed taking notes, ignoring his company. When the telephone rang, without waiting to listen, he said: "General Marlin? You're well, yes? Yes, I am, too, as well as one can be these days. We're making ready, eh? Listen, General, I have here with me Colonel Carlo Terzo. I plan to entrust him with an extraordinary mission, which I am sure you will appreciate and which he himself can explain to you. I've already spoken to Il Duce about it, all we still need is the authorization for Terzo. Il Duce is very enthusiastic, but I would like to observe normal protocol. What do you say? It seems like a good idea, even though you don't know what it's about? Excellent. Terzo will tell you about it himself. Good evening, General, thank you."

It's useless, thought Terzo. *There's no point insisting, in this sort of uneven, frontal clash; you always lose in any case. I'll have to agree to it, do a bit of research, hoping all the while he'll forget about me. Then I'll resubmit the request and leave for the front. Ciano's reputed to be fickle.*

Terzo stood at attention again and said nothing. Ciano handed him the sheets of paper he had covered with miniscule handwriting. "Give these to Furzi, my secretary. He'll draw up the orders for you in detail and indicate the detachment." The telephone trilled again, and the secretary's white head appeared inside the door.

"An urgent call, Your Excellency. It's Berlin . . ."

Count Ciano turned around, toward the wall, speaking in a low voice into the receiver. Terzo could not leave: he had not been dismissed. Furzi, on his way out, had lit a lamp on the desk, and now Ciano's shadow fell dark on the white wall. He was murmuring: "Yes, that's fine for Ribbentrop, too, but Tirana remains open: Serrano Suner . . ."

The colonel smelled the lady's strong perfume nearby again and turned around. "Galeazzo hasn't even introduced us," she said to him. "I am Princess Emma Svyatoslava, of fallen Russian nobility. Somewhere up my family tree is the Duke of Kiev who waged war on the Byzantines. Unsuccessfully, or so, at least, my grandfather told me. Do you know anything about his battles?"

Colonel Terzo was not very familiar with women at the time, nor, for that matter, would he ever become so. For his fellow-soldiers, girls were generally classifiable with the same swiftness with which they calculated, or pretended to calculate, the caliber of a cannon shell: prostitutes, serving girls, and *chanteuses* for seducing when possible, noblewomen for falling in love with, respectable young ladies for marrying. He, however, confused the different types and ended up feeling ridiculous with all of them. Once in a while, when shut up in his room, it had occurred to him that there were certain analogies between seducing a woman and planning a battle. Ensuring supply lines, keeping the length of the front line short enough to avoid exposing oneself, covering one's flank with natural obstacles or cavalry, concentrating the offensive on a limited front and, most important, acting boldly. Having never succeeded in making these insights concrete, however, he had always remained alone.

Princess Emma, who had a slender waist and small breasts, looked at Terzo with impudence. A shock of blond hair fell onto her forehead, and she did not move it. "I want you to illustrate a battle for me," she said, smiling brazenly, as if saying, "Dance with me!" to a total stranger.

"A battle, Princess?" said Terzo, casting a desperate glance at

Count Ciano, who was still muttering on the phone—"Let Pavelich stew in his own juices . . . See what Attolico and Sir Loraine say . . ."—and still facing the wall.

"Emma, just call me Emma, and forget all this 'Princess' business. Nobility has brought me nothing but trouble. And don't pretend you don't understand: I want to see a real battle, right here on this table. Are we or are we not on the eve of the greatest war in history? It's time I, too, learned a few things. Understand, my dear Colonel?" said the Princess. "You boasted you could describe any battle. Well, please do so. For two days now, Galeazzo has been filling my head with: 'That Terzo is a genius. Ribbentrop wants the manuscript of his *Manual for Strategic Living*. He's even sent an agent to photograph it.' So, this map represents the battle of Marengo? Come here." And without respect for the dossiers, Princess Emma cleared off the table, throwing the portfolios onto the leather armchairs. Holding the antique document in her hand like a teacher about to correct somebody's homework, she said, in a serious tone: "I won't ask you to describe the battle of my ancestor Svyatoslav; you looked puzzled when I mentioned it, and I wouldn't want to ruin your reputation. We'll return to that another time. For now, I am happy with Marengo. And don't try to fool me; I will check what you say on the map . . ."

 TERZO DIDN'T KNOW what to do. The princess looked impatiently at the large, dark tabletop, which shone in the twilight, stripped of objects. Turning slightly around, Ciano covered the receiver with the palm of his hand and whispered: "Do as she says. Russians are very stubborn."

"I'm a Cossack, you'll never get that into your head. Let's go, Colonel; not even a rough soldier like you has the right to make a lady wait so long." She sat back down in the armchair, crossing her legs, and pointed to the field of battle. "Come on, there's a good boy."

Amedeo, thought Terzo, *would have survived a situation like this with some witty remark, without making a fool himself. But I haven't got his nonchalance.*

He only sighed: "Marengo?"

"Marengo," replied Emma, unyielding.

How many times had he discussed this battle with his students at the Academy? Didn't he know it by heart? So why was he hesitating? Because of the unusually languid feeling he was getting from the smell of the princess's perfume? Because of the disappointment of again being denied the experience of battle? Because it depressed him that the death of so many good men, his studies, and the search for meaning in horror, all came down to this parlor game? Or perhaps because, on the eve of a brutal war, Italy was preparing between telephone intrigues and social frivolities? The minister still had his back to them, his elegant silhouette projected by the lamp. Terzo quietly coughed, looked at the ceiling as if to pray, and began.

"Returning from the controversial Egyptian campaign, Napoleon Bonaparte pulled strings in Paris and got himself nominated First Consul. He was thirty-one years old. Looking for successes to consolidate his power, he turned his eye to northern Italy, which was occupied by the Austrian troops of General Michael von Melas—"

"The battle, Colonel . . . ," said Emma, already growing bored.

"One cannot understand battles without understanding why wars are fought, signora," Terzo interrupted her, immediately overcome by his passion for teaching. "The Austrian general, Baron von Melas, was an extraordinary man, a strategist of the old school. He prepared very well his defense against the French army of that dandy whose name he pronounced in the Italian fashion: *Buonaparte*. With his men he blocked the Alpine passes, laid siege to Genoa, established a strategic command along the Po River. He was ready for anything. Ready, as often happens in life, for anything except what actually lay in store for him. Napoleon had his army march in five columns through the Alpine passes, to prevent the Austrians from guessing what the final objective of the invasion might be. An ancient Mongol tactic, called the 'branch plan.' But the Saint Bernard pass proved deadly." Then, in a cold voice that used to be able to hold the attention of even the unimpressionable Campari, he quoted: " 'We are fighting snow, ice, blizzards, and avalanches. We have brutally violated the St. Bernard pass, and now it is avenging itself and making life impossible for us.' So wrote Napoleon on May 18. He was probably trying to add some luster to his endeavor in the eyes of the Parisians, but he needn't have bothered. Soon there would be no need for exaggeration. For on June 14, 1800, the adventure of Napoleon Bonaparte was in danger of coming to an end."

Colonel Terzo moved the lamp, the only object left on the table, further enlarging Ciano's shadow. "Let's say this lampshade is Marengo. It is less than three miles from Alessandria to Marengo. Napoleon arrived one hundred forty years ago, on June 13. Baron Melas didn't expect the 'dandy' to attack him. Old-school, yes, but not stupid: he let Napoleon believe he had only the advance guard with him, making it appear as if the main body of the army was quartered in Turin. But in fact, at six a.m. on June 14, at Sant'Eliseo, thirty-one thousand Austrian soldiers, ready to attack, forded the Bormida River." He used a leather bookmark to represent the river. "Under fire from eighty Austrian cannons in array"—and here Terzo grabbed a few small jars of glue to mark the position of the heavy artillery—"the twenty-three thousand Frenchmen began to falter. Impeccable in their white jackets, Melas's infantrymen attacked for five hours. To the northeast, the French were under the command of General Jean Lannes"—Terzo folded a copy of *L'Osservatore Romano,* the Vatican daily, to mark Lannes's position—"and to the south, under that of Claude Perrin Victor," represented by the periodical *Defense of the Race.*

"General Victor fell back around midday. Napoleon, still convinced it was only a feint and that the backbone of Melas's Austrian troops was in Turin setting a trap, did not assemble his forces. Instead he ordered General Louis Charles Desaix to continue the march beyond the Bormida, in pursuit of a phantom army, as the Austrians massacred the French. Imagine that: he sends six thousand cavalrymen away from the battle, having misunderstood the reality of the situation. At fourteen hundred hours, pressed from three different directions, Lannes also begins to retreat. Worried, Napoleon sends his last reserves into the fray. It's not enough. The French are forced to withdraw some four miles. At three o'clock in the afternoon, the Austrian whitecoats enter the village of San Giuliano." A framed photograph of the minister's wife, Edda Ciano, became San Giuliano.

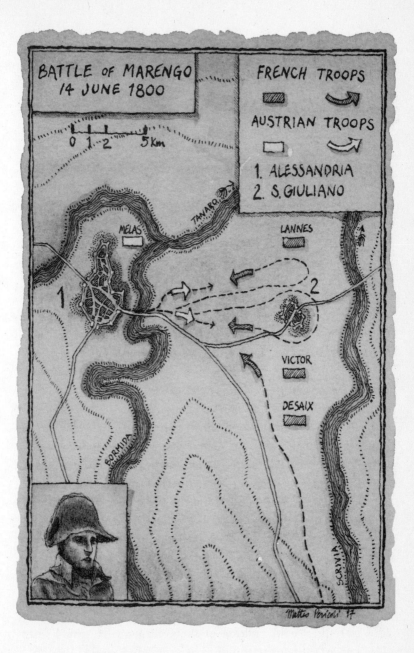

BATTLE of MARENGO
14 JUNE 1800

0 1 2 5km

FRENCH TROOPS

AUSTRIAN TROOPS

1. ALESSANDRIA
2. S. GIULIANO

TANARO

MELAS

LANNES

1

2

VICTOR

DESAIX

BORMIDA

SCRIVIA

Mattes Voricoli 97

Here, as he always did when lecturing, Terzo paused. The princess looked at him with renewed attentiveness, and he resumed artfully: "Napoleon had lost the battle of Marengo. Despite the exceptional crossing of the Alps, despite the miracles worked by the Genius's officers in fording the Dora Baltea under fire from Austrian artillery, despite the audacity of the 'branch plan,' the battle was lost. History would remember Napoleon as an ambitious strategist, capable of defying military convention, only to end up defeated, at age thirty-one, by a prophet of the old school. Baron Michael von Melas, already assured of victory, returned to Alessandria to rest, leaving his aides-de-camp to organize the mopping up."

Princess Emma had followed his narrative, now and then pointing her slender fingers on the map and sliding the red fingernails first along the Scrivia River, which was the black telephone cord, then along the bookmark of the Bormida. In silence Terzo looked up, but remained entirely engrossed in himself. The sun had set over Rome, the last magenta light falling onto the office battlefield and the agitated shadow of the minister, who was now yelling: "*I told* Sir Loraine, but he keeps talking about suffering and I don't know what else . . . "

Speaking as if to himself, Terzo continued: "History would indeed have been harsh on poor Napoleon. To send away the valiant Desaix from a battle barely begun, in pursuit of a mirage of an army . . . However—" and Terzo delicately picked up a silver trinket and placed it beside the battlefield, "General Desaix, poor, great General Louis Charles Desaix, had audacity and wisdom to spare, though he was only thirty-two. Riding along the Scrivia River, which was swollen with gray water and sand, he reflected on Napoleon's strange order: 'Follow the Austrians to the southeast, race toward the Apennines.' In no way convinced that Melas's attack was a feint, Desaix sent a dispatch-rider to request confirmation of the command. He could hear the Austrian cannons in the distance; the wind carried the muffled cries of the battle over the ripened wheatfields. 'No,' thought General Desaix, 'that is not a feint, dear Napoleon, that is battle, a pitched battle, which your genius cannot see.' Instead of hurrying off in pursuit of ghosts, Desaix hesitated on the riverbank. The other officers looked at him bewildered.

"The messenger returned at a gallop: 'Napoleon reconfirms: march away from Marengo, the bulk of Melas's forces is hidden, the battle is a trick.' He cannot disobey. Reluctantly, Desaix rides away from the fray."

"What? I thought Napoleon won at Marengo . . . ," said the Princess, surprised.

Terzo was no longer listening to her. Lifting the trinket that stood for Desaix, he moved it on the table, following an exact line. The silver gleamed in the lamplight. "Desaix had understood correctly. Melas was back there, wretched old man with his whitecoats. Desaix was noble by birth, Louis Charles Antoine de Veygoux. He sympathized with the Revolution, but did not approve of the beheading of Louis XVI. Since he couldn't keep his mouth shut about it, he ended up in jail. He wiggled out at the last minute and became an officer of the Republic, with the democratic name of Charles Desaix. He fought at Strasbourg, Mainz, Mannheim, and in Bavaria. He led the retreat through the Black Forest and was wounded crossing the Rhine in 1797. Then he sailed off to command a division at the battle of the Pyramids. While occupying upper Egypt he clashed with the Mameluk warriors of Murad Bey, descendants of the troops that had humiliated the Mongols at Ain Jalut, and studied their tactics. On his way back to France, he was made prisoner and wrote a magnificent diary, the *Journal de voyage,* published in 1907 by Chuquet. Napoleon then recalled him to lead two divisions on the Italian front. And so, on that afternoon, Desaix pranced about on his horse, following orders, but without much conviction. He watched the banks engulfed by the river in spate and took advantage of this to slow down the march. Then he turned back, toward San Giuliano and Marengo, ignoring the cavalrymen who wanted to speed up the march. From time to time he stopped, waited, looked at the sun in the sky to calculate the hour: 'Almost three, damnation.' Suddenly, he hears a gallop. Or is it the rumble of the muddy Scrivia? No! A French light cavalryman, bent over his horse's mane. A last Austrian bullet whistles behind him. Another messenger? Why on earth? What does Napoleon want now? A counterorder! General Desaix reads the message with his heart in his throat. 'Desaix: I wanted to attack Melas, but it's Melas who's attacking me. En masse. For heaven's sake turn back, if you still can. Bonaparte.' "

Terzo kissed the silver trinket and placed it back along the black cord that marked the course of the Scrivia River. "If Desaix had hastened to carry out his orders like a zealous little soldier, Napoleon's story would have ended at Marengo. Instead, Desaix slowed his march and thus still had time to turn back, to follow the counterorder. He forced his cavalrymen to gallop at a brutal pace. Run the men and animals to the ground, leave the mule trains behind: on to Marengo! Forget the compass and telescope, the map of Italy be damned . . ." The princess, spellbound by Terzo's enthusiasm, let the precious map fall to her legs, which it wrapped like a skirt. "General Louis Charles Desaix's cavalry advanced merely by following the white smoke of the cannon fire, the approaching cries of the wounded, the clanging of the bayonets, the shouts of the sergeants trying to stop the French troops on their way from San Giuliano and La Mandrina.

"General Desaix was the first to arrive. Napoleon, more disheartened than he would ever be again, even at Waterloo, barely manages to tell him: 'Melas struck early, while we were still divided and uncertain. The surprise worked. Now the Austrians are pressing hard, with their great superiority in infantry and cannon. They want to destroy the Army before nightfall and conclude our expedition in disaster.'

"Desaix watches the Austrian whitecoats. The final offensive, no longer urged on by Baron Melas, proceeds without haste. Enemy officers are seen advancing carefully through the smoke, certain of victory, wary of rifle shots, already thinking of where they might find a bit of supper.

"'What time is it?' asks Desaix.

"'Fifteen hundred hours,' says Napoleon, perplexed.

"'This battle is lost. But there's still time to win another,' says General Desaix, untroubled. He spurs his horse and orders the soldiers to charge."

Terzo marked the direction of the French cavalry by lining up a red and a blue pencil. "The Austrians are surprised. 'What?' say the whitecoats, continuing to fire, but already with less vigor than before, 'Wasn't the day already won? Haven't we advanced five miles? Won't that *Französe* fop give up?' The officers at the most advanced positions try to resist, but lose ground in the face of the carousels of Desaix's hussars. Unsure, they fall back to seek advice. Who had ever heard of an enemy starting to fight a lost battle all over again, as if they wanted to win it? Whatever happened to the logic of the field of conflict, codified by the Greeks at Marathon—the unity of time, place, and action, as in Aristotle's notion of tragedy, where whoever wins by evening triumphs and whoever loses dies? Baron Melas arrived in Alessandria, satisfied with his success, ready for a nap and then some supper, already tasting the honors that would brighten his later years. The aging general was aglow with the pleasure of having humiliated Napoleon, that arrogant boy who wanted to drive him mad with his Italian escapades, exposing him to the ridicule of military circles. But while the Baron was savoring the victory of fifteen hundred hours, General Desaix was fighting the second battle of Marengo. Under the young general's leadership, the French front was showing signs of recovery. The extremely youthful officer François Etienne Kellermann, without even waiting for orders, saw the vehemence of the counteroffensive and launched a cavalry charge against the Austrian flank. His father, Marshal François Christophe Kellermann, had led the soldiers of the Revolution against the Prussians of Karl Wilhelm Ferdinand, the Duke of Brunswick; in the fog and under artillery fire, Kellermann *père*'s boys, at Valmy, September 20, 1792, had saved the newborn Republic. Now it was the turn of Kellerman *fils*. So Desaix was acting as if the battle was not lost? Well, then, Kellermann would also attack. Marmont's gunners, exhausted, took fresh heart, returned to their cannons, and the French batteries began to hammer the increasingly ruffled whitecoats."

With his hands, Colonel Carlo Terzo swept the table clean, removing all the now useless objects: "The second battle of Marengo, the one desired by General Desaix after Napoleon had lost the first one, was won. At sunset, the Austrians retreated, leaving behind 9,402 casualties in the field. The French dead numbered 5,835. Baron Melas, overwhelmed, accepted the armistice the following day and withdrew to the east of the Mincio river. Bonaparte was master of northern Italy. Rejoicing, Paris celebrated his military genius. The uncertainty of the battle is recorded in the libretto to Puccini's *Tosca*. First, news of Melas's victory reaches Rome, and the cruel Baron Scarpia orders the *Te Deum* of thanks for Napoleon's defeat. Then the truth is announced: *'Bonaparte è vincitor. Melas? Melas è in fuga.'* The destitute Republican painter Mario Cavaradossi sings *'Vittoria . . . Vittoria . . . L'alba vindice appar che fa gli empi tremar . . .'"* Terzo sang the lines out loud with a half-tenor's voice, as he used to do when lecturing, to the applause of the students. He had forgotten he was still in the Foreign Ministry.

"And what of Desaix?" asked the princess.

"General Louis Charles Desaix, once lord of Veygoux," Terzo

replied solemnly, holding the silver trinket in hand, "fell in the attack just a few minutes after fifteen hundred hours. He was right; the second battle could be won. But he died immediately, struck down by a bullet. He had succeeded in the most difficult endeavor imaginable, in peace and in war, for armies and for individuals: not accepting the reality that others impose on us, but rather knowing how to transform it, in our own way. There is no greater virtue, signora. Whoever said you can fight only one battle in one day? It may seem like a geometrical truth, but Desaix did not accept it. General Desaix understood, before Napoleon did, that Melas's offensive was not a ruse. He resumed fighting when the French were resigned to being routed. He inspired Kellermann, saved the day, and gave Napoleon back to History. In all modesty, I am convinced that had General Desaix lived, *he* would have become the real leader of the French people. He had as much military genius as Napoleon, he had 'the courage of two o'clock in the morning,' the courage you must call upon when they wake you in your tent with some terrible news, and without thinking, still half asleep, you must give the right orders. Desaix would never have gone off to Russia to starve and freeze to death, because, unlike Napoleon, he knew when to move and when to hold still. He was motivated by calm, not by anxiety. And he fell at Marengo, a rare example of a strategist capable of winning even when dead."

"What an incredible story. I had never heard of General Desaix."

Terzo shuddered. It was the voice of Galeazzo Ciano. Having finished his telephone call, he had been listening spellbound as the evening breeze cooled the room. Embarrassed, the colonel concluded: "Napoleon dictated his war bulletins, pretending he had deployed his troops shrewdly, reassembling them finally, like a great pincer, at the fateful hour. In reality he had lost a battle fought according to his model of 'audacity at all costs.' If Paris had known just how close he had brought the army to defeat, his myth would have been shattered. When victory and the death of Desaix were announced, simultaneously, to Napoleon, he exclaimed gloomily: 'Why am I not allowed to weep?' Melodramatic, yes, but for once, sincere, too." The colonel picked up the antique map, which had slid over the princess's ankles, and looked at the minister. *And I even sang!* he thought, blushing.

Ciano realized the man before him was different from the rest. *No officer in the General Staff has so much culture*, he thought, *such a sense of destiny. It is as though he can read, in the wars of the past, the very future that we, due to laziness or stupidity, cannot see. To our detriment.*

In his summer aviator's uniform, the minister felt the sting of the breeze like some sinister omen: "Tell me, Colonel, what does your doctrine foresee for the coming war?"

Terzo, worried for months over the lack of strategy with which Italy was approaching the conflict, was excited to have the opportunity to forewarn Ciano. At that very moment, however, shouts of "War! War! War! War!" echoed in the office. It was the young men of the University Students for Fascism, dressed in black shirts and demonstrating in the street below. That grim, happy chorus brought the minister to the window. Raising his arm to salute the cortege, Ciano was not listening as the colonel explained, sorrowfully: "Our military tradition has always neglected the study of Clausewitz's theories. I fear that in this war, too, as in the Great War, we shall suffer the consequences, unless . . ."

III THE WAR came and went, and Terzo never saw Amedeo Campari again. The evening of his meeting with Ciano, upon returning home, the colonel had found a note under his door: "My dear friend: I'll not be cheated: I am going to the front. Forgive my desertion. I promise to provide you with material for your research. With affection, Amedeo." They sent him first to France, with the Armistice Committee. From there, on July 10, 1941, Campari rejoined his cavalry regiment, the Novara Lancers, and left with the Italian Expedition Corps for Russia. He traveled by train for twenty-seven days, toward the Carpathian Mountains. He was among the first to reach the Dniestr, fought at the fall of Stalino, at the Nikitova pipeline, and in the tragic Christmas battle. After the defensive battle of the Don, when the majority of the IEC veterans were sent back to Italy, Campari hooked up with the new arrivals of the IAR group, the Italian Army in Russia. With the Carloni Column he took part in eleven days of battle, during a long, 220-mile march. Then General Monroy sent him, as a liaison officer, to the Stalingrad front. On December 10, 1942, the Russians broke through at the bend in the river at Werk Mamon. The IAR began their painful retreat. Terzo from time to time would send Puntoni to the ministry to get the lists of those killed in battle, and they would go over them together. Finally one day they read the words: "Captain Amedeo Campari. Missing in Action. Nikolayevka. January 1943."

Ciano he met only one more time, a few days before learning

of Amedeo's fate. While he was alive, however, the minister never forgot the official assignment he had given Terzo. He found him an office with a view of the great park of Villa Ada, had Puntoni the archivist transferred there, and managed to allocate generous funding for the *Official Encyclopedia of Battles*.

After three years without success, the Allies surrounded the Axis powers and prepared to strangle them. From his office, Terzo catalogued battles and worried. When Marshal Graziani entrenched himself in the desert, at Sidi el-Barrani, Terzo blew up at Puntoni: "But how can anyone be so asinine? How can anyone be so ignorant of the dynamics of a war? What does he want to do, take the Suez Canal by himself? O'Connor's Nile Army will run him through from Marsa Mastruh, from the south and west. We have no trucks." He was brandishing an old copy of the *Reflections* of the Marqués de Santa Cruz, nervously leafing back and forth, pointing his index finger at certain lines and quoting: " 'Nothing is more *un*certain than the outcome of a battle, no matter the numerical advantage. One must never attack if in an unfavorable position, or if one is not well familiar with the enemy's forces.' "

Carlo Terzo knew too much about martial theory to respect the Fascists, who used armed conflicts for propaganda purposes. It appalled him to see so many fellow soldiers fall in a string of howling blunders worthy of a red-marked cadet's essay at the Military Academy. "Is it possible there was no way for the Duke of Aosta to draw up a formation a little less resigned to defeat?" he inveighed. "And anyway, why didn't the Duke take the field with the Allies, like de Gaulle in France? Hadn't anyone in the Balkans ever heard of Sun Tzu's motto: 'Know your enemy and yourself'?" The bulletins listed the defeats, masking them in strategic grease-paint, while Terzo kept on cataloguing battles and tormenting himself: "And yet I told Ciano: it's all there, already written down, in Clausewitz and Sun Tzu."

On July 25, 1943, Ciano voted against Mussolini at the Great

Council of Fascism and was executed at Verona; civil war engulfed northern Italy. General Pimentel was tortured to death by the Germans. Terzo was captured by the Americans in Palermo immediately after the invasion. He had been unceremoniously dispatched to Sicily by Ciano, with the excuse that he had to verify the position of a Carthaginian encampment during the second Punic War. He drafted his reports with no attempt to hide his disillusionment: "Fighting without being able to move—like the Italians, who have no trucks, planes, or ships—is madness. Hannibal made a shambles of the immobile legions because of the war of movement. As Napoleon wrote, 'War means marching ten leagues a day.'" The colonel's imprisonment did not last long. A certain Captain Paul Gawain, who had studied his books at West Point, had him freed and introduced him to General Eisenhower. "Colonel Terzo is a master of war," Gawain told the future president. "Thank God Mussolini wouldn't listen to him." And so Terzo went back to Rome, to take orders from his former commander, General Marlin.

Marlin was sitting at his desk, eyes cast down. He listened to Terzo's report, then said: "Continue compiling your *Manual*. Augment it with the data from Ciano's *Encyclopedia*. That way, at least, something worthwhile will have come of our war." And he went back to staring at the table. The General Staff forgot about Colonel Terzo and his research. He was still protected by the autonomy Ciano had granted him; the subsidies from the bottomless wells of the bureaucracy kept on coming, and he and Puntoni resumed their work. On the wall of the Records Office, the Marshal had hung a photograph of a handsome Amedeo Campari, his moustaches well curled, his Edelweiss lit. When Campari worked with them, Puntoni used to grumble at him: "Smoking is not allowed in the Archives, Lieutenant!" But ever since he'd been listed under "C" in the Official Missing in Action File, the archivist would look at the photo and say affectionately, "Go ahead and smoke, Lieutenant, smoke, the mil-

itary life be damned!" Whenever a contingent of prisoners returned from the Russian front, the two would race down to the
station. To no avail.

Theirs was a typical military situation, one that would have
gone unchanged who knows how long, if Puntoni's son, a clever
boy, hadn't read in a ministry bulletin that both had earned the
right to an early retirement. "It's too sad carrying on without
Campari," Terzo acknowledged, and so they filed a formal request, asking "in the meantime where to submit the documents
obtained for the *Official Encyclopedia of Military Battles*." The
country had other things to think about in those first months of
peace, and no reply was forthcoming. Puntoni went to live with
his son, Colonel Carlo Terzo moved to Palermo, Sicily, where his
wife had a small villa. A few days after the Americans' entry
into Rome, in fact, Colonel Terzo had taken half a day off from
his comparison between the first communications of Hitler's
Russian campaign and those of Napoleon's campaign in 1812, a
topic Captain Gawain had asked him to research, with the
promise of submitting it to Eisenhower. "The differences prevail over the similarities: the French won the war, but failed in
their political objective since, even after Moscow fell, the czar
would not surrender. The Germans didn't even win on the field
of battle, and with their brutality succeeded only in consolidat-
ing the Stalin regime. A classic example of the wrong strategy:
instead of bending the enemy's will, one seeks only victory by
arms, and reaps only defeat." During that half day of freedom,
Colonel Carlo Terzo had gotten married. To Princess Emma
Svyatoslava.

When he asked his wife, "But how is it a beauty like you
went to the altar with an unglamorous man like me?," she
laughed.

"I spent time with too many people who are no longer fash-
ionable," she said. "The Fascists consider me a traitor, the Communists a spy, and everyone else a whore. Some are convinced I

have untold amounts of money, countless gold ingots vanished from the port of Valona and left to me, as a pledge, by Ciano. As if they would ever let me have such stuff. You're a good man, sweet and intelligent. By marrying you, I can drop out of circulation and get some rest. Long ago my mother bought a house in Palermo, which we used to use in the days of the czar. 'When you breathe the air of Villa Igea, you remain young for life,' she used to say, 'but beware. The Sicilian aristocracy is fatally boring.'" The nobles, it's true, also seemed dreadful to Terzo, whose ideal of a pleasant evening was a glass of brandy and the *Kurtzer Beqriff aller militärischen Operationen* by the Austrian Count Khevenhüler. They gladly lived without the gossip that passed for a "social life" at the Circolo dei Nobili. But the tranquility of their existence was not to last.

Emma, that is, had smoked too many of those thin Greek cigarettes and contracted lung disease. Dr. Pantera, of the Civilian Hospital, frowned when he saw her and gave her a few months to live. "I'm telling *you*, Colonel. In private. You decide how to break the news to your wife."

Back at home after the hospital visit, Terzo saw his wife staring at rose-colored Mount Pellegrino, Utveggio Castle rising sheer out of the sea, the palm trees with their swallows' nests, the green, lemon-scented gardens and, in the distance, the white, shell-strewn beach of Mondello. Emma had lost weight. The locks of hair still fell down onto her face as before, and also as before, she would blow at them with a wisp of light-blue smoke.

Terzo drank a glass of water and cleared his throat, but Emma cut him off: "Don't bother. While you were with the doctor, I got the nurse to talk and she told me everything. Just think of me as a war casualty. There have been millions of us, my mother in Berlin, your friend Campari in Russia. Don't waste your time feeling sorry for me. I'll go away and you can resume your work on the war, even without that poor fool Ciano around.

You will publish it, and on the first page you will write: 'To my wife, Emma, whose ancestor Svyatoslav fought in a battle long ago, which I, with all my learning, know nothing about.'"

"I haven't got the papers with me anymore, dear. The documents are in Rome. I prefer to spend time with you."

"We'll end up boring each other. I married you to escape, and because—I can't help it—I am fascinated by the idea of a warrior with no war, who lives on paper. Do you want to watch me die? Please don't. You work, I'll smoke, and we'll keep each other company. As long as it lasts. All right?" She held out her hand to him, squeezed and kissed him. Colonel Terzo loved Princess Emma. He loved the idea that he had saved her from who knows what real or imagined dangers. He loved her silences, her fragrant step, her songlike voice: "Terzo? Colonel Terzo?" If she wanted him to go back to his research, he would work himself to death. But the papers . . . He tried to explain to her:

"Emma, I left the documents in Rome. The ministry doesn't know what to do with them. The history of military battles and my *Manual* are there. I can't resume working without my materials."

"Nonsense," she said, pointing her cigarette holder at the glass door to the study. It was an ancient villa, with floors made of flagstones mounted on flexible reeds. Terzo walked with the cadenced step of a military man, and his heavy shoes made the floors shake to and fro. He sprang up, opened the door, and saw, in front of the small Russian writing table that Emma had given him as a wedding present, dozens of brown crates decorated with the stamps and emblems of the Military Archives, Historical Office, General Staff. He opened one with a paper-knife and recognized his own handwriting on a discolored sheet of paper: "Notes on el-Alamein. Why did we lose? Rommel realized he had lost before General Navarini did: You cannot win when you set out from so far away. 'The two-thousand-mile retreat of

Rommel's Panzer Armee Afrika from el-Alamein to Tunis was one of the outstanding performances of its kind in military history,' noted the Englishman Liddell Hart."

"How did you do it?" he asked Emma.

"I still have a few friends. The son of your archivist Puntoni is carving out a career for himself with the new politicians. Listen to what he has written to you." From her purse, that same bureaucratic-looking briefcase she always had with her, she took out a pair of small glasses and read aloud:

Dear Colonel,

At the request of the princess, I am sending you the archives of your research, which you compiled with the late Lieutenant Campari and my father. As it is not easy to pry documents away from the Italian government, I have had to pull a few strings. A friend of mine persuaded Marshal Badoglio to speak to Professor Ettore Musco, and with a signature here and a signature there, the authorities have created the Amedeo Campari Institute for Comparative Military History, with a branch office at the home of Colonel Carlo Terzo, in Palermo. I attach hereto the statement of enfranchisement, on letterhead with all the required stamps. They're even going to give you a subsidy, however reduced compared to what you received before. My father provided me with a copy of the letter General Eisenhower wrote you in his own hand, thanking you for your report on the Russian campaign, and that signature has worked miracles. The papers, therefore, are yours again. In any case, you are the only person who knows what to make of all this scribbling. Politics is my concern, and I'm hoping to win a candidacy in the next administrative elections.

Respectfully yours,
Giulio Puntoni

P.S. Papa sends you his very best wishes. He goes to the Red Cross every day to look for news of Campari, but without much hope.

Excited, Terzo broke open the seals of the crates. "Leuthen, a decisive battle" read the first file, in Campari's nervous hand. Then: "Report on the on-site investigation conducted at Cannae to verify the area of the battlefield"; and "Report on the Mission to France for telemetric readings, 1914 campaign." And then the index cards, one per field general, one per battle: Montecuccoli, Sun Tzu, Frederick the Great, Maurice d'Orange, Jena, the Somme, the taking of Paris. He turned to Emma, but she had disappeared onto the terrace. The fresh sea breeze carried her voice indoors, through the white, fluttering curtains: "Go ahead and work, darling. I won't be much bother as I die. You're so adorable when you invent those battles of yours. If I don't go too soon, I'll end up falling in love with you. How could I ever forget the officer who sang *Tosca* in front of Ciano? Oh, by the way, there's something else. Our gardener has told me how much he wants his grandson to be admitted to the Military Academy. You know how nice he is with me: he brings me orange-blossoms for the night and honey for this nasty cough. He thinks you could help the boy prepare for the admission exam. He's a war orphan; his father died in Africa, and he lives with his widowed mother. I volunteered your services. Who knows military history better than you do? You start tomorrow. It'll relax you, you'll see."

"The exam for admission to the Modena Academy is scholastic, mostly mathematical," Terzo pointed out. "There's very little strategy and military history, unless the boy is interviewed in person by General Moscardelli."

"It won't hurt him to study with you. You'll feel like you're back at the Academy."

Thus, in an unknown city, with a beloved, dying wife and his home transformed into a Historic Institute dedicated to a friend who hated history, Colonel Carlo Terzo resumed his formidable work and prepared to teach the classical principles of strategy to the young Salvatore Dragonara.

 COLONEL TERZO got up at six o'clock in the morning, shaved, and went out on the terrace to drink the caffè latte he always had, along with bread and fruit, for breakfast. The sheets hanging from clotheslines between the railings billowed against the blue sky, buffeted by the shore breeze and snapping like sails in the wind. Signora Astraco, an early riser, leaned out the window and with some effort pushed the line forward with a bamboo reed. Ever so slowly, she moved the sheets away, raising the curtain on the city below.

The sea was flat, but crossed by currents that traced a network of roads, watercourses, streams, and paths around the calmer, oily areas, the dark-blue sea-pools. In the distance, where a fishing boat still lingered, whitecaps dotted the water. Terzo had not yet grown accustomed to the city where his wife had convinced him to move. Everything in their marriage, including the very idea of marrying, had been decided by Princess Emma. It had never occurred to the colonel to say no. Palermo seemed to him the perfect place for disappearing after a useless life. He didn't know anybody, and he seldom set foot inside the Officers' Club. He spent his days looking for traces of ancient battles. He had located a well at the center of Piazza Edison, formerly known as Piazza Littorio, and was convinced that on that very spot Hasdrubal had camped with his elephants during the First Punic War, in his attempt to storm the city and its Roman defenders. Terzo knew that Consul Lucius Caecilius Metellus had drawn the elephants into a trap, a ditch at the gates of Palermo, where Via della Libertà now stood, and he searched for traces of the battle among the art nouveau villas, measuring the sidewalks with a tape measure, to the amusement of the ladies out strolling.

The ruins of the center city, testimonies to Anglo-American aerial might, were visible even from the terrace: a horrific but winning strategy: that of sowing terror to break the enemy's will to fight. In the ancient port, the rubble was piled up on the sides of the streets; open-roofed noble palaces, between mullioned windows, framed fragments of blue sky. One building in particular attracted Terzo. It had, in front of the main entrance, a statue of Emperor Charles V, victor over the Turks in 1535. The emperor's bronze finger was raised, but who the object of that accusing gesture might be, Terzo couldn't say. Was he pointing his index finger to the clouds, now exposed to view by the RAF's bombs, or was he wagging it at the feeble resistance of the Italians, who had been unable to defend the city?

That open sky, framed by ruins, bothered the colonel. With his mania for cataloguing everything, he had got into the habit of listing, on a sheet of paper, its varying colors during the day and at night. "On mornings of scirocco the sky in this city becomes a Leaden Gray, when a band of hot steam descends and makes it impossible to breathe. But the Gray on high, at the Zenith, remains very beautiful, bright and opaque. It looks like the corridor to God. That, I imagine, is what the knights must have thought in the heat of the battle of Visby, on July 27, 1361, when 2,000 Swedish paladins were buried with their precious armor still on, because the air was so muggy the victors couldn't be bothered to despoil them. At daybreak, in clear weather, the sky instead turns a Dawn Rose, not the pale pink of Rome or the even softer shade of northern Europe. It is a color that promises strength, sensual and decisive. As the day progresses it takes on the hues of Good Friday Purple and Cloud Azure, condensing later to Italian Blue and Navy Blue, before turning to Cobalt Blue at night. Under such a sky Scipio fought at Zama-Naraggara, and the brave Duke of Aosta lost to the British at Amba Alagi. It's a crisp color, one that defines the ruins to perfection, as if it was the sky itself, and not the bombs, that had created them. A demanding color. Living in it forces one to be rigorous, to make the effort to understand. I am afraid of it. Afraid that this shadowless light will reveal to me the ruins of my life, with the same cruelty with which it illuminates the tufa blocks scattered at Cassaro. Imprisoned there, according to Signora Astraco, are Baroque putti and cherubs with broken wings, along with lead-lined panes, pots, books, and corpses. When the heat became stifling, the soldiers of the anti-aircraft units had no choice but to bury the wretched bodies, pouring quicklime into the rubble. Just like at Visby. The mistaken war plan Ciano had in his safe on that evening in 1940 leads to these broken stones under the sky. I tried to suggest to him that to go to war that way was madness. I told him about Clausewitz, about suffering, but he wouldn't listen. I could have shouted, implored him, made him hear me out. Instead I played at toy soldiers and Marengo, in front of poor Emma. And when I decided to explain to him what fighting and suffering were about, it was too late. I have never felt this terrible regret in other cities. Only here, where my wife is dying, in a city I will never know. Even the strategic plan of my life has been wrong. I thought I could foresee and understand everything, make myself invulnerable to pain and Fate, by studying war. Now my war is lost and Emma is sick. I have never seen combat, nor shall I ever. Destiny has unveiled the secrets of victory to me, without ever allowing me to fight. And it has split me open and exposed me to the sun, like the yellow stones of the buildings."

Down in the port, an American warship, painted gray, white star at the prow, started to maneuver. Terzo entered his study, opened a desk drawer, and took out a pair of German naval binoculars, a gift from Campari. From the terrace he tried to decipher the ship's model and weaponry. It was a formidable instrument, which Campari had won at poker from a Lieutenant Nicholas Walter, a German Catholic he would later meet again at Stalingrad. Terzo could make out the sailors in their white uniforms and the light cannons covered by waterproof tarps. He distractedly began to reconnoiter the sea all the way to the horizon. The wind had dropped and the fantastic routes traced by the currents became like the crossroads of an aquatic city.

If the sea were a magic battlefield, he thought, *two armies would now rise up, one facing the horizon, the other the city. The current flowing from Capo Gallo would be a river and General Horizon would use it to support his right flank. General City would choose the Island of Women as his stronghold, to allow reserves to flow along the brackish current there below. Then the battle. From the lower depths of the lagoon, the first charge. The froth of the waves was the smoke of the cannons.*

Following General Horizon's imaginary attack, Terzo scanned the sand banks where General City was barricaded. He measured the length of the nets and floats set out by the fishermen, sea-trenches extending all the way to Acqua dei Corsari. From the Emiro Giafar seafront promenade, General Horizon would launch his final offensive, taking care not to let himself be surrounded by the reserve troops hidden in the Addaura grottoes. Terzo heard some tapping on the tiles and turned around. It was Signora Astraco, curiously watching his frantic movements up and down, right and left. She timidly gestured toward the door with her inevitable bamboo reed: "Someone's here for you, Colonel." Her husband, captured by the English at Bardia, was still a prisoner in India, and while awaiting his return Signora Astraco had assigned herself the task of watching the life of the neighborhood from her window.

Terzo aimed the binoculars down to the street and immediately saw, enlarged by the German lenses, the face of an angel.

Golden curls, with slightly tawny shades, large, naïve green eyes, a cherub like those shattered by the bombs: "My name is Salvatore Dragonara, Colonel," the boy called up to him. "I'm here for the lesson."

It was eight o'clock. He lowered the entrance key in a wicker basket and opened the front door. Emma lay in the master bedroom, breathing softly. Her body, already emaciated, made scarcely a rise in the thick white eiderdown. A rectangle of clear sky filtered through the shutters and Terzo, though very sad, marveled at the power of life.

 "'THE MAIN PRINCIPLES of strategy are:

    1. Gather your forces.

    2. Find your enemy's principal strength.

    3. Defeat it.

4. Force the enemy to accept your conditions, to the point of occupying his land.' So said Napoleon Bonaparte, considered by many, but not by me, the greatest strategist in history. That is how you would expect me to begin my lesson. Right?"

Salvatore Dragonara looked at his new teacher, saw a swallow fly by like a black crescent over the terrace, and did not answer: he had no expectations at all, but the polite thing to him seemed to be to nod. With a slight bow, Terzo resumed: "Wrong. Actually, my first lesson of strategic history and criticism will be simply to get you to think, as I used to do with the students at the Academy, about the theme 'To win or to die? Chance in classical strategy.' For the true principles of strategy are different from those set forth by Napoleon. The cornerstones of strategy and battle are the two questions: Why does one win? and Why does one lose? Or rather, the infinity of answers we attempt to give to these questions. In your everyday life, as in the fiercest of battles—say, Hastings, October 14, 1066, or Omaha Beach, Normandy, June 6, 1944—we can find details, invisible at first glance yet clear as day if carefully studied, that explain how one wins and how one loses, how ephemeral the line between victory and defeat really is, and how, for the slightest thing, we end up crossing it. So many great victories in the field have been transformed into defeats because one can always take hold of a desperate situation and turn it into an advantage. Are you ready?"

Dragonara opened a black notebook, the first pages already covered with writing, and sighed.

"Good," said Terzo, perplexed. He hadn't yet succeeded in capturing the pupil's attention. At the Academy, they usually all pricked up their ears the first day, convinced they would soon become so many Alexanders the Great. This boy, however, remained unresponsive. "Every battle contains a symbol," he explained, intent on winning him over, "and it is up to us to recognize it. Do you know how one wins, in war and in life?"

"No, sir. I have no idea."

"By adapting to reality intelligently and boldly, at the crucial moment, by daring to make an original move. A move that the enemy cannot even imagine and that even your own soldiers would never dream of, a move—take note, Salvatore—that even you, when setting off to war, had no idea you could ever pull off. You defeat your enemy if you can defeat yourself, if you can overcome yourself, by proving yourself to be patient, wise, and tenacious. By suffering as you had never thought you were capable of suffering. Morale, that's the key word. Take the case of Alexander at the battle of Arbela-Gaugamela. Two years earlier, at Issus, in 333 B.C., Darius had let himself be squeezed into a narrow field by Alexander, leading to a disastrous defeat. Let us try to reason as he might have done. Remember: in war, he who thinks best and fastest, he who succeeds in thinking like his adversary, to the point of manipulating his actions, wins. You win by conquering the enemy's mind, not his army, as Hitler believed.

"Darius reasoned as follows: 'Why did I lose at Issus to that young Macedonian demon Alexander? Because I crowded my army into a little patch of land, where I was able to deploy neither chariots nor cavalry.' And do you know what the Persian monarch did to seek revenge? He adapted the new situation to his needs. He gathered slaves and soldiers and had them level the fields of Arbela-Gaugamela. Hours of labor spent breaking up the land, until there was not a single stone, tree stump, mud ditch left, no obstacle to movement whatsoever, smooth as a billiard table. Darius arrayed his army across this vast parade ground: 250,000 men (other sources exaggerate and speak of a million), two hundred scythed chariots equipped on the sides with deadly metal blades, fifteen war elephants. This time he felt truly invincible. Upon examining the situation, Alexander immediately realizes that Darius's front will be twice as long as the front formed by the forty thousand foot soldiers and seven thousand horsemen of the Macedonian army. Are you following me?"

Salvatore gave a start, and to show his interest, he politely asked: "Is it dangerous when the enemy's front is longer?"

"Dangerous?" said Terzo, horrified. "Do you know what a longer front means? It means that Alexander was certain to be surrounded and massacred before sundown on that artificial dance floor. How can you defeat an enemy capable of encircling you at any moment? Try to follow me. Darius, up to this point, has not made any theoretical mistakes. He has chosen the most suitable site for his troops and improved it, has marshaled a formidable, ordered army. According to the conventions and manuals, he should win without difficulty, by virtue of the theater of conflict and by virtue of military might. But Alexander knows that every battle is the symbol of something and that one wins by controlling the enemy's mind. Darius had fled at Issus, preferring defeat to resistance, unable to gamble everything. He didn't know how to suffer.

"Alexander therefore planned the Macedonians' battle not in abstract fashion, but by betting on Darius's weakness. He pitched camp in full view of the Persians, and for four days he kept them awake, frightening them at night with the sounds of weapons, threatening a sneak attack that never came. On the day of the battle, Darius and his foot soldiers were troubled by their sleepless nights. In their weary, confused heads Alexander had already begun to win. The fray began at a fierce pitch, the first of October, 331. Darius's cavalry, made up of Scythians and Bactrians, let itself be dragged off to the west, in a fruitless chase. Thus a breach had opened up, just a few meters wide, in the mass of warriors at the center of the vast Persian front. A little thing, but Alexander immediately burst in with his elite cavalry, the faithful, ambitious Companions. With their swords they cut a swath to the Asian rear guard. The situation had been reversed. Alexander adapted to the developments. Darius did not: he had prepared himself to perfection, but in the abstract. He should now have called his cavalry back to the center, to surround the Macedonian wing commanded by Parmenio. At his disposal he had an enormous, powerful front, but no lucidity. If you understand this, you have grasped the foundations of strategy in life. Even before the battle has begun, Darius has lost his psychological wrestling match with Alexander the Great. Alexander risks his life by diving into the breach left open by the Persian horsemen, because he is betting that Darius is the same man he was at Issus, a coward. The mighty formation hides only his fear. Alexander is right. Darius whips the horses of the imperial chariot and flees again, psychologically broken once again. The enemy expects you to be intimidated by obstacles, you see. The right strategy, in such a case, is to command the enemy's mind, to move him without being moved by him. See now if you can tell me: What could Darius have done to win?"

"I couldn't say, sir."

"Come on, boy. If Alexander does something unexpected, charging into the breach at the risk of losing his life, what could Darius do that would be equally unexpected?"

Salvatore Dragonara shrugged his shoulders and looked at Terzo, smiling sweetly.

"Resist, that's what. If Alexander's so sure that the emperor is going to take to his heels, then Darius must remain on the field, at the risk of being hacked up by the enemy's swords. *That* would surprise the Macedonians. With that flexibility, he could have closed the breach, heartened his men, and crushed the enemy with the brute force of his cavalry and scythed chariots. As often happens with cowards, he didn't even manage to save his own skin. He took refuge in Bactria, in Afghanistan, where the satrap Bessus killed him in a palace ambush."

Dragonara looked at him, serene but in no way won over. "Time for a break," Terzo suggested. "Will it be coffee or a lemon ice?"

"Ice, if that's all right."

"So you *are* interested in something," said Terzo, going indoors. Raising a gray lever, he opened the wooden icebox, moved the thick blocks of ice a little man brought to him each day, and took out a little pot with the yellow ice chips inside. With this he filled a glass to the brim, put it on a tray with two brioches, and went back out to the terrace.

Taking care not to soil his notebook, Salvatore devoured the whole ice, dipping the soft brioches in it.

"Hungry, eh? When you want something to eat, don't stand on ceremony, at your age. And after all you've gone through in battle, that's no joke. Do you like poetry?"

The boy stood up all at once. "Poetry? Of course!"

"Lemon ice and poetry: we're on the right track. Well, listen to what the ancient Chinese master Sun Tzu argues in verse: 'The veteran of many battles moves the enemy, but is not moved by him. He leads the enemy to act naturally, he makes life easy for him: and then he strikes, confident of winning, because he attacks where the enemy has no defense.'"

Suddenly attentive, Dragonara saw Terzo invite him, with his hand, to repeat after him: "If you are so covert and subtle . . ."

"So covert and subtle . . ."

"As to have not even a shape . . ."

"As to have not even a shape . . ."

"So mysterious, so miraculous . . ."

"So mysterious, so miraculous . . ."

"As to make not even a sound . . ."

"As to make not even a sound . . ."

"Then you shall be arbiter of the enemy's Fate!"

"Then you shall be arbiter of the enemy's Fate!"

"Don't just repeat the lines. You must feel them inside. Adapt them to the situations of your life, your problems. They tell us that the enemy is our intimate; to defeat him we must think like him, live like him, breathe like him. Now if you're in a difficult situation, at an impossible pass, numerically disadvantaged, with inexperienced troops, the enemy will think, quite legitimately, that you are prey to anxiety. He will imagine you are in despair over the obstacles and, perhaps without wanting to, will end up feeling overconfident. At that moment, if you are able not to let yourself be intimidated, if you preserve your inner calm, before you have even made a single move with your troops, you will already have an advantage. The secret weapon is equilibrium. Do you know why?"

"No, sir."

"The enemy expects to find you frightened but in fact he will find you determined. Thus it is he who will have an unpleasant surprise. His presumed superiority will turn into a disadvantage. Disillusion makes the opponents fight with less vigor. 'We were supposed to be fighting an army on the ropes,' they'll say to themselves in puzzlement, 'and here they are resisting in orderly fashion. Why?' At the first response they will fall back, and if, at the right moment, you venture an intelligent move, they may even beat a retreat. Rule number one: never let yourself be intimidated. That way, you will enjoy the advantage of equilibrium, while the enemy will fight from a position of imbalance. Do you understand?"

"Yes, sir."

"So, do something unexpected. You know about the battle of Zama-Naraggara, don't you?"

"A little, sir, not much."

"Give me a synopsis of what you know."

Without enthusiasm, but with precision, Dragonara put together what he'd learned at school: "Second Punic War, second century before Christ, I think. Hannibal did not conquer Rome, despite his victories, and had to return to Africa to defend Carthage. There he found Scipio, who defeated him at the battle of Zama. That's it . . ."

"Zama-Naraggara," Terzo corrected him.

"Zama what?" the boy asked.

"Hans Delbrück: write his name down in your notebook. He's the military historian who explained the battle of Zama-Naraggara in 202 B.C. In Africa, Scipio had two choices: press on with the siege of the city of Utica, on the Mediterranean coast, and benefit from reinforcements by sea, or venture into the interior and confront the Carthaginians. These were the moves dictated by the common sense of the Roman senate, and even Hannibal, a strategic genius, thought them inevitable. Scipio, however, left the safety of his ships behind him and marched into the desert. He headed away from Rome and away from Hannibal, into nothingness, in forced marches, as if lost among the dunes. Nobody—not the senators, not Hannibal—knew what he had in mind. Today, thanks to Delbrück, we know that Scipio was making one of the most stunning moves in the history of humanity, and you, son, should etch it in your memory, so you can face your enemies in war and in peace. It is called the indirect approach, appearing where the enemy doesn't expect you. All of a sudden, in fact, Scipio changed route and occupied the banks of the Bagrada River. From that valley, known today as the Megreda Valley, the Carthaginians got their oil, wheat, fruit, game, staples, and goods necessary for day-to-day living. Scipio seized one city after another in the valley, commandeering the wheat, sealing the barrels, imprisoning merchants, destroying whatever his legions did not consume. Hannibal and the Senate expected him to make war on the Carthaginian army, but Scipio thought of life before death. He surrounded the supplies and flushed out the enemy. He starved Carthage by marching away from it. Throughout his Italian campaign, Hannibal, in his triumphs, had imposed his own tempo of battle on the Romans, luring them into traps and pitfalls. Now he was forced to give chase. On the day of battle, the armies drew up, as we say in military jargon, in an 'inverted front,' Scipio with Carthage at his back, Hannibal with the sea at his. Any and all retreat is precluded for the Romans; they must triumph or perish. We shall look at the battle of Zama-Naraggara shortly. For now, think: do you know why historians have named it after the village of Zama, near the coast? Because Scipio, in later relating the outcome of the campaign to the senate, would not admit to having strayed so far into the interior, sacking the Bagrada valley and disobeying orders. The battle was fought at Naraggara, in the desert, hard by black Africa. If Scipio had lost, the vultures would have picked the flesh off his legions. He won because he focused on life. Will you yourself prove able to think of life over death? Will you know how to recognize the roots that sustain the enemy, instead of vainly following his branches, fruits, and leaves?"

Terzo had the impression that young Dragonara was following more the flow of his words, their music, than the meaning behind them. *Maybe*, he thought, *I'm overdoing it. The Acad-*

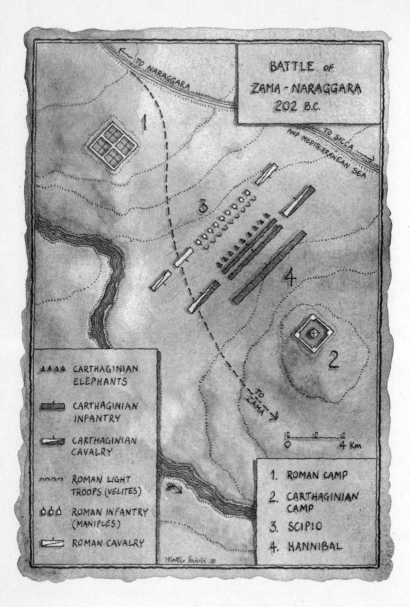

BATTLE of
ZAMA - NARAGGARA
202 B.C.

1

3

4

2

← TO NARAGGARA

TO SICCA
AND MEDITERRANEAN SEA

TO ZAMA →

0   4 Km

▲▲▲▲ CARTHAGINIAN
        ELEPHANTS

        CARTHAGINIAN
        INFANTRY

        CARTHAGINIAN
        CAVALRY

ꓩꓩꓩꓩ ROMAN LIGHT
        TROOPS (VELITES)

ΩΩΩ   ROMAN INFANTRY
        (MANIPLES)

        ROMAN CAVALRY

1. ROMAN CAMP
2. CARTHAGINIAN
   CAMP
3. SCIPIO
4. HANNIBAL

emy cadets were distracted and needed a bit of theater to rouse their interest. Maybe this boy's more attentive, and likes things cut and dried.

He changed tone: "So what can you deduce from what I've told you?"

This time Dragonara did not indicate polite assent, but merely shrugged: "Who knows . . ."

"You can deduce," Terzo patiently resumed, "what the Saracen prince Alamundarus observed when fighting the Byzantine general Belisarius: 'Victory never comes in a straight line.' If Scipio had kept a straight line—the commonly accepted logic—staying close to the sea as the Senate demanded, Hannibal would have torn him to pieces, reinforcing himself with the foodstuffs of the Bagrada Valley and playing on his tactical experience. All right then; give me a summary of what I've said so far."

The boy took his black notebook in hand and reflected: "Don't let yourself be intimidated, don't let your mind be governed by the enemy, move in an original way, not in a straight line . . ." He looked at Terzo, as if unable to find the words to express his thoughts.

"The boy's sharper than he seems," Terzo jotted in his logbook, an old habit from the Academy that now automatically came back to him.

"That'll be all for today," he concluded. At the door, he thought it polite to ask the boy: "And in what branch of the armed forces do you hope to enlist? The army? Air force? With the Americans now, there should be some very interesting developments in aviation. Speak freely, when I get to know you better I'll tell you what I think, if you care to know."

"What I really want to do is be a poet. I'm a pacifist and a Communist. I write poems, love poems mostly," replied Salvatore Dragonara, looking straight into his eyes from the darkness of the stairwell.

THAT EVENING, Terzo said to Princess Emma: "This student of yours wants to be a poet, not a soldier."

"So?"

"So what makes you think I can give him lessons to help him enter the Academy if what he really wants to do is write poems?"

"You yourself have always been a poet, not a soldier."

Colonel Terzo set his fork down next to the blue-and-black-skinned mackerel: "What do you know about my studies?"

"Have you forgotten that we met the day you enacted that lovely battle of Marengo for me, in poor Count Ciano's office? What do you think? I fell in love with a poet. You even sang an aria from *Tosca*. And then . . ."

"Then?" asked Terzo, embarrassed at the memory.

"Then, after I got sick and was confined to this house, I had a look at your manuscripts. Your principles of strategy are interesting: doing something unexpected in the face of a much more powerful enemy. Isn't there something unexpected I can do against cancer?"

"But . . ."

"You teach that one must be unpredictable to the enemy. And so I asked the doctor if I could have a child."

Terzo's fork missed the mackerel and fell to the floor. "And what did he say?"

"He said no. The medications I'm taking would kill it immediately. You can't fight cancer as you would fight an enemy. It's not an enemy: it's a part of me. You write that to win one must control the enemy's mind. And so, to win, I must control my own mind. To 'move the enemy,' as the Terzo doctrine says, I must move myself."

"What are you trying to say?"

"I'm trying to say I found you the Dragonara boy. We're going to have some young people about the house. You're teaching again. My mind should be governed by death, but I'm thinking of life instead. What do you think, my great strategist: have I won? There will be more new developments yet, I assure you. I'm going to perk up your life a little before leaving you, even though you still haven't managed to find out anything about the battle of my Ukrainian ancestor Svyatoslav. And if you think it's all a tall tale, you're wrong. Svyatoslav is a pure hero, darling."

Princess Emma said no more, but she often behaved in this manner with her husband, as if "perking up his life" were a conjugal duty. Colonel Terzo's devotion to her was a simple one: she was much too beautiful and refined for him ever to try to guide her.

There were no new developments for several days. Emma's illness was progressing; Dr. Pantera touched her rib cage with nicotine-yellowed fingertips and shook his head. Emma had read a great deal on the disease, with the avidity of an autodidact, and discussed time and cures with the aging doctor. "I feel fine," she would say, but she coughed and was losing weight. Without losing her beauty, like a forget-me-not closed between the pages of a dictionary, she was becoming dry and fragile. Only the colors of her hair, face, and eyes retained their charm, and Terzo never tired of furtively gazing at them, without her noticing. He was afraid she would mistake his tenderness for the look of concern one casts on the sick to see if they're getting worse. Emma noticed her husband's embarrassment but still derived a sense of comfort from it.

The colonel would give his lesson to Salvatore, alternating

mornings and afternoons, then work on the *Manual for Strategic Living*. After lunch he would rest and then run through the physical exercises Amedeo Campari had taught him. Every day, before the war, Amedeo had had him lie down on the library table and forced him, under the disapproving eyes of Marshal Puntoni, through an exhausting session of exotic exercises called calisthenics: "Home gymnastics, as practiced by American and English officers. If we don't do the same, we're sure to lose the war in a hurry."

Terzo, of course, no longer believed in the benefits of those bends, twists, and extensions of the muscles of his middle-aged body. Bending and panting, however, he managed to distract himself from his sorrows. There was something else, too, in fact, something the colonel intuited but could not bring himself to admit. Terzo felt responsible for the fate of his friend Amedeo. He believed Amedeo had rushed to the front lines to escape the dreary lot of working as a scholar for the military. Perhaps Terzo had overexcited him with all the hours spent talking about the attacks of the Mongols, the oblique order of the phalanx of Epaminonda, the theory and tactics of offensive-defensive battle. Amedeo might even have done something stupid at the front, playing the hero at all costs. Whatever the explanation, there was no trace of Amedeo Campari. And so Colonel Terzo celebrated his memory by bending forward, legs straight, to touch the floor, by twisting his torso, arms open, by hopping in place on tiptoe, one two three, one two three, one two three and four.

THEY LIVED in a small villa by the sea, with a terrace and garden populated by stray cats who had survived the famine of the war and now fruitlessly chased after a pair of ancient turtles. Rubbing his hair with a towel after a swim, Terzo watched the reptiles draw their heads into their shells and patiently wait for the mangy felines to grow weary. "An excellent example of the superiority of defense over attack, and the uselessness of besieging a stronghold without the support of heavy artillery," Terzo said to his wife to make her smile. "The cats are like Mongols: splendid light cavalry, but unsuitable for capturing fortresses."

He then went down to the street. The city seemed noisy to him, foreign. He strolled through a nearby marketplace full of kiosks and decrepit little shops. He never bought anything; the shopping was done by a domestic servant who would pray to the saint of the day while washing the dishes. And yet the merchants treated him with great respect, greeting him warmly and boasting of the freshness of the day's swordfish or the taste of a suckling goat. These were merely gestures of homage; they knew he didn't even have money for the newspaper in his pocket. Still he never came back home without having had the shopkeepers, in spite of his "No, thank you, I cannot accept," give him a couple of citrons or a packet of cured olives or cream puffs hot out of the oven. Terzo attributed their kindnesses to the manners of the princess, who treated these poor folk as if they were ladies of the court, and soon became a celebrity in the neighborhood, as famous as the smiling starlets in the posters at the local Cinema Italia.

Various rumors circulated about the new couple in town. Cosma, the barber who cut Terzo's hair very short, "King Umberto style," felt it was his duty, as an ex-soldier, to keep the colonel up to date on these. Cosma boasted: "I was in the Tuscan Wolves regiment, Colonel, the only Sicilian among all those Emilians. First Spain, then Albania, and then two years in a concentration camp in Germany to avoid breaking my oath to King Vittorio, God bless his soul." And then he bowed in homage to the king, who had escaped on the day of the armistice, September 8, 1943, while Cosma got used to eating potato skins in the Nazi *lager*.

"They say many things about you, Colonel, and a great deal

more about the princess. But the strangest thing is, in this neighborhood of backbiters, there's never a single bit of gossip. An amazing fact"—Cosma spoke as he sharpened his straight razor on a leather strap—"an unprecedented fact, and I was already a barber's assistant by '27."

Terzo, in the past, would not have bothered to ask what these stories might be, but now he needed some topics to entertain the princess at the dinner table. He was an abysmal conversationalist and it was usually she who did the talking. Now, however, with increasing frequency, Emma would remain gloomily silent, and the colonel felt it was his duty to lead the conversation. He would struggle and stammer, but his wife's will to live was so strong that, at the slightest amusing cue, she would go off into memories, observations, and plans until, after her pain shots, pills, and sedatives, she finally calmed down and was able to rest.

"Whatever do they say about us?" asked Terzo, in search of novelties.

Cosma dived right in: "According to Signor Lobianco, owner of Lobianco's butcher shop, you, Colonel, are really a general. Supposedly you drafted a perfect plan for keeping Italy out of the war, as that slyboots Franco did for Spain. A perfect plan. Il Duce studied it, summoned you to Palazzo Venezia, and said, 'Well done, Terzo. We are going to war all the same, otherwise we'll get eaten up by either England or Germany. Prepare me a different strategy.' And so you drafted another perfect plan, for winning this time. But some envious person said terrible things about it to the Germans. Hitler flew into a rage because he didn't want Italy to act on its own behalf, and so Mussolini was forced to reject the plan. Il Duce then called you back and said: 'Terzo, your plan was my own, but the Germans have tied my hands and I can't accept it.' The envious person, who was worried that Mussolini would change his mind, pulled strings with the General Staff and had you demoted to colonel for being a 'defeatist.' And do you know who that person was?"

"No," replied Terzo, his faced covered with white foam.

"Galeazzo Ciano. They say he was madly in love with the princess."

How do they ever come to know these things? thought Terzo. *Emma must have talked, or else the maid looked through the photo albums after saying a short prayer.*

"Ciano?" he said, incredulous. "Come on . . ."

"Ciano," the barber solemnly confirmed, "Ciano himself. Jealous of the princess, he sought to put her in a bad light and convinced Mussolini to attack Greece. Lobianco claims that Il Duce, shortly before he died in Dongo, confessed to his mistress Clara Petacci: 'If only I'd listened to Terzo! With his plan I'd still be in Palazzo Venezia, safe and in power.'"

"None of it's true," smiled Terzo.

"Try telling that to Lobianco. 'What do you expect the colonel to say?' he'd insist; 'Do you think he'd reveal secrets that no one would believe? Of course not: he remains silent and upholds the military code. But take my word for it: I was at el-Alamein, first and second battles, not to brag. And even on the African front they were already saying the king had been betrayed and there was talk of a perfect plan that was never used. On the eve of the last offensive, God help us, with boys dying by the bushel, Artieri, my lieutenant, a great nobleman and friend of the Prince of Piedmont, told me the secret face to face. "At least if we die you'll know, Lobianco, that they sent us to the slaughter. But mum's the word, understood?" ' And then Lobianco goes on to tell about your strategy, Colonel."

"But what on earth are you dreaming up?" said Terzo in self-defense, feeling embarrassed. With each stroke of the razor the fantasies grew larger.

"It was Sasà who told me—Sasà, son of Andragnosi, the ice man. Sasà is a Communist, because he works in the shipyards, but he's a good kid. He says Lobianco, one night, after playing cards, took a sheet of wax paper, the kind for wrapping meat, made some marks with indelible pencil, and explained: 'Look, Sasà,' he said, 'if Mussolini had listened to the king when he told him to adopt Terzo's plan, the Communists, today, would be out begging on the street, licking sardines for dinner, and you'd be singing the *Royal March* like a loyal little subject: Long live the king, long live the king, long live the king!'"

Terzo's war plan, according to the monarchist butcher Lobianco, unfolded in two stages. In the thirties, the colonel had suggested to Mussolini not to ally himself with Germany, but to place some armored divisions at the borders with Austria and with France, without explaining to Hitler what his intentions were. When Mussolini declared war on England, however, Terzo proposed an alternate plan: take Malta with a Pearl Harbor–style blitz, capture the Suez with a pincer maneuver, without foolishly straying too far from the Libyan bases, and provoke a revolt in Egypt, promising them independence. In the Balkans, follow a policy of anti-British friendship with the Greek dictator Metaxas. When Japan attacks the United States, do not declare war on President Roosevelt, but continue to conduct operations in our zone, emerging victorious in any case, with or without the Germans.

"A brilliant plan," Terzo admitted, laughing, "a bit reckless perhaps, but probably less absurd than the Fascists' strategy."

"But wait. That's not all. Sasà found out that you were an anti-Fascist, and that your best friend, a certain Aspani, no that's not it—what was his name? Campani, that's it, supposedly had secret contacts with the network of Communists who had infiltrated the army—"

"Campari, you mean," Terzo corrected him. It distressed him to hear his missing friend's name mangled.

"Well, one day Campari supposedly implored you. 'If you pass your plan for certain victory to Mussolini,' he said, 'the Fascists will triumph and the dictatorship will last a whole century. Let history take its course.' Unfortunately, however . . ."

"Unfortunately?" Terzo asked, happy to have so much to tell the princess.

"Unfortunately Lobianco, the monarchist, is married and Sasà, the Communist, has a girlfriend."

"So what's wrong with that?"

"Nothing at all, on the contrary. But wives and girlfriends talk," said Cosma the barber, raising his razor in warning.

"And so?" Terzo insisted, beginning to enjoy himself.

"The women say that the princess, on a dark, stormy night, persuaded you to pass the secret plan to the Allies, to make it unusable. Otherwise, according to Perla Lobianco, why would a lady of her station ever have come to live among us? To escape the mainland, where she might have been a target of vendetta, that's why. And there's more. Sasà's girlfriend is a student, Filia's her name, a proper girl, but she sees things the same way as him. Of course, I would never want my daughter selling newspapers on the street, but these are modern times. Anyway, Filia says the princess was a friend of the Soviet general Cujkov, back when it was still Russia, and that she had a spy in Stalingrad. Through that agent she was able to communicate your suggestions to Cujkov. How else do you explain that the Red Army took repeated beatings up to Stalingrad and after that never stopped winning?"

"It's because the Germans were spread out over too many fronts, were dying of starvation and following a maniacal strategy, with bad tanks stuck in the mud of the *rasputitza,* the mud sea of the Russian thaw. And because the Soviets fought with the determination of those who do not wish to be exterminated, were resupplied on a grand scale by the Americans, and had a tank, the T-34, that proved to be the best of the war. And there you are." Terzo cut the discussion short, becoming the Academy professor again.

"Filia doesn't give a damn about the *rasputitza* or whatever it's called, my dear Colonel. Filia says that Ruggero, the cabinet-

maker, came to your place to fix the garden gate—since the
bombing there's not a single door in town that moves properly
on its hinges—and that as you were giving your lesson to Totò
Dragonara, he saw some papers on your desk. He's a history buff
and decided to have a little look. 'Notes on the battle of Stalingrad, dated, with red and blue arrows and the positions of the
armies, Paulus's sixth division and Kleist's first Panzer division':
that's what he told Filia. Is that enough proof for you?"

Terzo remembered recently copying over the letters Amedeo
Campari had sent him from the front, in which he recounted
what he saw. They were desperate messages, which now entered
the town lore, thanks to the tactical memory of a carpenter.

"For these good people," Cosma concluded, carefully cleaning
his razor, "you, Colonel, are the real protagonist of the war. Forget Hitler and Churchill! You could have made us win! And for
this, they revere you."

Which, to Terzo, explained all the little kindnesses. Signora
Apollonia, the shirtmaker, had shown him a photo of her son,
killed by a mine, a portrait of an infantryman like so many he
had seen, too many, with hair slicked back and a gentle smile.
Making the sign of the cross, she had put that framed little picture in his hand, as if awaiting benediction. The widow Ganci, a
greengrocer, while preparing snails for the feast of the patron
saint, had pointed him to the photos of her twin daughters
killed in the bombing of the port: "The little girls were there by
chance that day, Colonel, sir, because their uncle worked at the
Arsenal and used to take them to get something to eat at the
sailors' mess. Everyone was evacuating, but where was I to go,
all alone? After the ship exploded, they didn't find a trace of my
girls. Did you know the anchor ended up on the bell tower of
the cathedral?"

*It was the bombing of the Arsenal that broke the city's resis-
tance,* thought Terzo. A warship loaded with munitions was hit
squarely by a bomb, a "direct hit" in the language of the Royal

Air Force manual, blowing sky high on March 22, 1943, the second day of spring. The flying anchor became the symbol of the surrender. Its absurd arc became broader with each recollection: "The anchor fell in the mayor's dining room"; "My cousin Saverio saw it in front of the painting of the Apparition of the Virgin, in the Church of the Theatine Fathers . . ."; "It crashed through the roof of the Charity House, killing all the orphans . . ."; "It flew all the way to the Capuchin Catacombs and the monks' bones mingled with those of the wretches killed . . ."; "It reached the church of the Admiral of Antioch"; "My wife saw it in Via Sedie Volanti, still encrusted with shells from the bottom of the sea"; "Do you know where the anchor landed? I'll tell you: on a whorehouse. A Fascist official was there that day, and they buried him without fanfare to avoid scandals." Every house seemed to have suffered the blow, and the city had surrendered to an omnipotent enemy.

Terzo tipped Cosma, who insisted on splashing him with cologne from a metal cruet and slipping a scented little calendar with sketches of pretty girls in bathing suits, dated 1940, in his pocket. "It's the last one that was printed," said the barber, "but you can still smell the perfume." Then Terzo went home.

Little by little, he grew accustomed to the legends, and the small favors, which he returned, soon legitimized the status of the colonel and his wife as monarchs in exile. For this reason, Terzo was hardly surprised when a girl, wearing the pleated blue uniform with white collar of the boarding school of the Sisters of Charity, stopped him on the street and said politely: "Colonel Terzo? My name is Fiore Mastema. I need to talk to you."

THAT A GIRL of good family would stop a total stranger on the street was already an event out of the ordinary. More than this, that an aristocratic young lady such as Fiore Mastema, Duchess of Malpasso and Fides, heiress to the Acquedolci estate, should be alone, unaccompanied, without an aunt or cousin as her chaperone, was truly unheard of. But Fiore seemed not to care a whit about such conventions. She had a light-hearted air about her, something unknown to the adolescent girls, severe and melancholic, whom Terzo had seen in church. Sure of herself and the world, Fiore had a gracefulness of gesture, which her black hair, cut short, also in contravention of the rules, and her blue uniform, worn with the nonchalance of a ball gown, communicated to passersby. That someone might find her alone and tell her mother, the stern, redoubtable, violent Duchess Luminosa Mastema, seemed a thought that didn't even enter her cheerful head and bright blue eyes.

On his rare visits to the Officers' Club, the colonel had heard talk of the Duchess Luminosa, née Fides. "She's really a man. What kind of man? A demon. I've seen how she keeps her laborers at bay: with a silver-inlaid rifle on her shoulder and a bullwhip in hand. Nobody messes with her, not even the Reds. She lords it over them from her horse and they scamper away." Now her daughter was smiling at him with the whitest of teeth, visibly embarrassing him. Terzo hadn't much familiarity with women; he had happened to marry Emma, but that was all. The only other women in his life had been his mother and his little sister, Teresa, who had died in a hurry, of an illness that today is easily cured with a few shots. Ever since, his mother had withdrawn into silence; polite, but always somewhere else. He would have ended up a bachelor, had Emma not decided otherwise. That was why he loved her and wanted to help her to the very end: because she had chosen him, had been the only person to have chosen him and no one else. Was it to escape? To hide from vendettas? Whatever the reason, she could easily have asked half of Rome for help, but she had chosen him instead.

"What can I do for you, young lady?" he finally said politely to Fiore, without stopping, indeed quickening his pace.

"I'll tell you at once," said the duchessina, taking his arm, "if you stop looking around as if I were pestering you. Just walk normally and smile, and they'll think we're father and daughter. If you keep twisting your neck to see who's behind us, somebody will finally notice. One has to know how to keep moving in this city."

Terzo stiffened and looked ahead, wishing the girl would disappear, just as she had appeared. "What can I do for you?" he repeated, erect.

"Do you know anything about Italian?"

"In what sense, may I ask?"

"The Italian language, the literature, Colonel, what other sense is there?" the girl insisted, then smiled, with a half bow, at an old lady passing by. "Damn! Just my luck, it's Signora Mirto-Nicolosi. A marchesa, a sourpuss and a gossip," she said, turning away. "It's a good thing she can't see beyond the end of her nose. She probably mistook you for my uncle Niccolò. Well?"

"Well, signorina, all I know of Italian is the little I speak, nothing more."

"What about Latin?" The girl wouldn't let go. "Greek? Philosophy? Mathematics? There must be something you know. Drawing?" she ventured, grimacing with hope.

"I can assure you, the only thing I know anything about is military history, which I teach, or used to teach . . ."

"Why, have you stopped teaching?" the girl stopped short, blushing.

"Yes . . . I mean, no," Terzo stammered. "I no longer teach at the Academy, I'm retired. Now I have only one student, a private pupil, who wants to try to get accepted at the Academy, or at least his mother wants him to."

"Salvatore Dragonara, you mean? I know. He's still your pupil, isn't he? Then listen, dear Colonel. You choose the subject you like best, since I'm very bad in all of them," and the girl laughed, as if to be a poor student for the nuns were a reason for irresistible mirth.

"I don't understand," said the colonel. He had no idea what the girl was talking about, and was bothered by the fact that she was leaning her body against his arm. He hadn't caressed a woman since Emma fell ill, and Fiore was throbbing with life and strength.

They left behind the main thoroughfare, with its shouting fishmongers and scent of chick-pea fritters, and turned onto a solitary street lined with very tall palm trees swaying in the breeze. They passed through an English garden with deserted lawns and waterless fountains and came out in a churchyard, the Baroque portal open wide onto the dark nave and aisles. The girl made the sign of the cross, recited a Hail Mary, with what to Terzo seemed sincere devotion even though she skipped the Amen, then whispered, "Please sit down. And stop looking around, you're making me nervous, too. I won't eat you, I promise. Now listen: tomorrow my mother will send for you to come to our house, Palazzo di Mare. The nuns I study with have said I need a private tutor, if I am to get my diploma in less than a preposterous number of years. It seems not even the family crest is enough to keep me from flunking, that's how remiss I've been in the eyes of those holy women. The superior said it loud

and clear to my mother: 'Duchess, only a professor, a male professor, can help your daughter shape up. A woman would only be
swayed by Fiore's willfulness. Look at my poor nuns, all victims
or accomplices of her schemes when she skips school. They even
lie to me, in God's name, just to protect the wretched girl. I send
them to confess at once to Father Isidoro and they smile all the
way, as if helping Fiore were a good work.'" Fiore pinched her
nose while speaking, to imitate the nun's shrill voice, and Terzo
smiled.

"When the Mother Superior reproaches me for being 'too vivacious,' what I think she means is that I'm too alive. She would
rather I was half dead, like the Mirto-Nicolosi cousins, with
faces the color of eggplants in oil. Anyway, my mother is going
to choose you as my private professor and tutor. That's because
my godmother Elena spoke well of you to Mama, said you're a
war hero, a conservative, a personal friend of the king, a military
strategist, married to a Russian princess . . . Actually the whole
thing is your wife's idea; she's a friend of my godmother's from
their days in Paris. Now this is what you're supposed to do—"

"Miss, I don't know anything about the humanities, I'm not a
friend of the king, I have never taught a woman before, and I
have no idea what my wife has to do with this mess."

"May I tell you the truth? I'm afraid you'll just have to put up
with me for a little while. Salvatore Dragonara and I are in love,
we want to get engaged and then married. He's fatherless, 'without a future,' as Mama would say. If she had any idea how much
I love him, we'd be lost. I am supposed to marry one of the
Mainoni boys, I can even choose which one, but those little
Duke's sons disgust me, they're like monkeys, all they can ever
talk about is tennis and car racing. Salvatore, on the other hand,
is a poet. Did you know? He's even written poems for me." And
the girl blushed again.

"Yes, a poet, I know," said Terzo, sighing, "it's not much help
in getting admitted to the Academy."

"My godmother's and your wife's idea is very simple. After-noons, you'll give me my lesson first, then Salvatore's. I'll pre-tend to be staying behind to visit the princess, to keep her company, but actually I'll spend a little time with him. Not even my mother will have any objection, and she's the most suspi-cious person in the world. She loves military men; she'll think everything's in order. Salvatore will come in by way of the ser-vice stairway, so no one notices him. Oh, please say yes, I beg you." She got so carried away in her entreaty that an old church lady gave her a stern look and brought a bony finger to her lips: "Shhhh."

"Isn't that the same lady as before, Mrs. Sirto-something-or-other?" asked Terzo.

"Yes, Mirto-Nicolosi," said the girl, keeping her composure. "But if she's being uncivil, it means she hasn't recognized me. She owes my mother a pile of money and would never dare act that way with me. She would play stupid, only to gossip after-ward." Protected by the darkness inside the church, Fiore stuck her tongue out in the direction of the impoverished noble-woman.

Terzo was confused: "But my wife hasn't told me a thing about all this, signorina. At least let me speak to her first."

"I know," said the girl. "She merely told you there would be some new developments. She's going to talk to you tonight. I had thought—I'm probably wrong and if I am, please forgive me—that it would be easier for you to say no to your wife than to me, since I'm so melodramatic about asking. Can't you see how desperate I am?" Fiore batted her eyelashes coquettishly, twisting her face in a playful grimace of pain. Still, her eyes showed the innocent fear that Terzo, in irritation, might reject the whole plan. "Oh, please. You're the only card we have to play. Salvatore told me you're very kind and intelligent. Don't abandon two kids who love each other. I wanted to speak to you myself, at the risk of being seen in the street, because it seemed the more honest way. And there you are."

"Are you sure my wife is in agreement?" asked Terzo, touched.

"It was her idea, I tell you . . . "

"I won't promise you anything, signorina, and I won't say anything, for now. If Emma convinces me there's no harm in it, then we'll see."

"Hurray! I knew it was the right thing to come and talk to you."

"Shhh!" repeated the wrinkled Signora Mirto-Nicolosi, searching in her shabby handbag for her silver glasses, the last relic of the wealth she had lost in the war, so she could get a better look at the bothersome girl. Before she could focus, however, the duchessina Mastema kneeled in a flash, to thank the heavens, and vanished into the Palermo sun.

Amused, Princess Emma confessed to her husband that yes, it was her idea "to help this postwar Juliet and her Romeo. Anyway, darling, with the monstrous store of knowledge you've got, you *could* help that plucky if unstudious girl. She wanted to talk to you herself, and I can see she's won you over. A sad story: the old colonel falls for the duchessina with the complicity of his dying wife."

SIGNORA ASTRACO had given the colonel, as a gift, a bottle of wine from her brother's vineyard in the country. To give himself a lift, Terzo drank a glass of it in a single draft. It was amber in color, unfiltered, and tasted of strong liquor: a comforting, warming flavor. He went to bed in a state of agitation. The flooring borne up by the flexible reeds, undulating under his footsteps, made him dizzy. In bed, to forget his ill-humor, he leafed through a copy of the daily paper, *Sicilia del popolo*. He was looking for the international news when his eye fell on a small item:

Duchess Luminosa Mastema has decided to reject all the demands of the peasants working on her lands. There is increasing dissatisfaction in Petranova and Navarino, untilled estates belonging to the Mastema family. A public demonstration will be held tomorrow with Parisi, Secretary of the Union. Meanwhile at Malpasso, a village in eastern Sicily, the population has risen up in a new "We Won't Go" revolt of the sort that struck Sicily two years ago. Youths and women have taken up arms, chasing the police and *carabinieri* from the town. They refuse the draft and declare they "no longer want to go with the army." If the rebels do not immediately lay down their rifles, the armed forces will have to intervene. The political parties, the Christian Democrats as well as the Left, have asked the inhabitants to reject all provocations and to protest only within the limits of the law. As in the earlier revolts in Comiso and Ragusa, the desire for peace cannot justify the use of weapons. These rebellions must therefore be condemned, because they stand in the way of national reconstruction.

The following day, the Duchess Luminosa Mastema called Colonel Terzo to Palazzo di Mare in words repeated by the porter she sent for him: "The duchess wishes to summon you . . . " There she explained the situation bluntly: Fiore inescapably on the verge of failure, masculine authority and the military discipline invoked by the nuns being her only hope for passing. She was willing to pay "a reasonable sum." Terzo accepted, without a fuss, the task of giving lessons in Italian, history, philosophy, and Latin, while declining the offer for payment.

"My wife and your daughter's godmother are friends," he said, "I couldn't possibly accept any money."

With a hasty gesture, the duchess immediately approved and made no more mention of payment thereafter. Terzo recalled having heard talk of her legendary miserliness. The colonel was then dismissed, as if Signora Mastema had a great deal to do. "I'm going away," she said, "I have to see for myself what the Communists are scheming on my lands, the wretched bastards. Excuse my tongue." Terzo was descending the red marble stairs, not at all happy with the situation, when he heard the duchess call back to him in a loud voice. He looked up and saw her white hair framed in the stairwell by the bannister: "Colonel. I beg you to inform me, as a man of honor, if you find anything improper in my daughter's conduct."

"Of course," replied Terzo, feeling even more unhappy about it all.

"Do I have your word?"

"Of course," he repeated, trying to think of a formula that would not tarnish his honor: "I'm sure there will be nothing wrong in it." Even to someone with his strict, conservative upbringing, the two innocent lovers seemed far from doing anything wrong. Or so he imagined.

 ALL PRETENSE of private lessons for young Fiore Mastema was soon dispensed with. She and Salvatore Dragonara would hold hands while politely listening to Terzo's lectures and then, for the period ostensibly to be spent on Latin translations, they would disappear into the study. The colonel accepted it out of love for his wife, for whom the distraction seemed to do some good, and because he had grown fond of the youngsters. So they wanted to be alone, far from the clutches of the duchess? Fine. His word of honor was on the line; he was hoping luck and her name would help Fiore at school. Meanwhile he was retrieving from the crates the documents he needed and, as long as the good weather allowed it, worked on his *Manual* in the garden, under the patient eyes of the turtles. Once summer was over, he withdrew to the kitchen, using the marble table after lunch. He would write while the maid recited the rosary, paying no attention to the coming and going of Fiore and Salvatore. When Emma asked him why he had been against the use of the living room for the kids' rendezvous and yet had no objection to giving up his study, he replied, in a serious tone: "There are only two hardwood chairs in the study. The carpet is covered with crates. They can't do much harm in there." Deep down he was hoping the maps of Ain Jalut, the meditative portrait of Emperor Leo, and the print of the sun of Austerlitz would intimidate the young couple. Less naïve than Terzo, the princess noticed, in the silences, the wrinkles in Fiore's dress, and their flushed com-

plexions, some very specific signs: clearly the temple of the strategy for living was not holding back the passions. Fiore ended up learning more about the use of artillery at the battle of Ravenna than about Catullus's sparrows, and soon she was blithely contradicting the colonel.

"War is culture. You, my dear children, keep mistaking it for a horrific bloodbath, a massacre of man against man, and indeed, war *is* bloodbath and massacre. It is an illness of human nature. But once you come down with it, nothing happens anymore without a reason. Every nation, every individual, fights according to his own culture and history. You win, you lose according to an ironclad logic, and yet luck still plays its role, as my friend Campari used to teach. Clausewitz's rule number one: 'In war, the only certainty is uncertainty.' The only way to oppose the rule of Fate is therefore to learn the rational method of combat. This paradox *is* war, and I shall teach you its secret."

Fiore Mastema dipped her spoon into her lemon ice, lazily pushing aside the jasmine flowers adorning it, and looked at Terzo: "And what would that be?"

"That, dear duchessina, would be that you never win, except in rare exceptions, by merely defending yourself. You must, sooner or later, resolve to attack."

"You always talk about victory and defeat, about precise rules and a perfect code we can take from war and apply to everyday life. Isn't that so?"

"Yes, but . . . ," Terzo felt confused; no student of his had ever addressed him in this manner before.

"How can you be so sure about it? Maybe the Cimbrians and Teutons, poor, simple folk, were looking for pastures for the cows and food for their children and they run into General Caius Marius—what more could you ask for?—and Caius Marius knows all these rules of war and slaughters them like lambs. What's so interesting about that?"

"In any case the Germanic tribes were not at all unwarlike or peace-loving, as you seem to think. Take Varus, for example, whose legions were exterminated in the autumn of A.D. 9 by Cherusci warriors under the command of Arminius. Led into the Teutoburg forest, the Romans fell into an ambush, having had no chance even to see the enemy. Arminius's men appeared and disappeared between the trees, attacking as though invisible. Three legions, eight hundred horsemen, twenty thousand legionaries, all annihilated by a phantom enemy with faces and arms the color of dead leaves. Varus committed suicide to avoid being taken prisoner. The tree-men won, and imperial Rome was forced to accept the Rhine as its boundary. But let's not get off the subject. I shall say again what I've already told you both a hundred times—and you, dear Salvatore, should at least pretend to pay a little more attention if you hope to gain admission to the Academy, though I already realize you don't care a fig about it. I explained the importance of defense to you: but one must be able to move from a defensive position to an offensive one. And here I need only quote master Delbrück. You take notes, Salvatore, and you, Fiore, listen well: I know you don't believe me, but sooner or later it will prove useful in your life."

Terzo read the translation of Delbrück painstakingly put together by Amedeo Campari: "Battle of Hastings, decisive for William the Conqueror's conquest of England. Think: nine centuries would pass, from 1066 to 1940, before another decisive battle was fought on British soil. Churchill triumphed over Hitler thanks to the air force. Back then, the Normans won. Let's hear Delbrück: 'The strength of the Anglo-Saxons was limited, of course, to the defensive; but battles cannot be won with defensive action alone. The defensive is purely negative, while victory is positive. With extremely rare exceptions, the only defensive that can finally lead to victory is one that goes over to the offensive at the appropriate moment. We recognized this point in the first historically confirmed battle, at Marathon, where the Athenians, who were likewise incapable of opposing the enemy on the open plain, chose a defensive position but were led forth from it into the attack by Miltiades at the proper moment. Harold was not capable of doing this. His housecarls and thanes were brave men, perhaps as individuals more so than the Athenian burghers and peasants had been, but they formed no phalanx.'"

This time it was Salvatore who dissented, gesturing "no, no" with his index finger. "But Colonel," he protested, "these examples are all out of date. Nowadays there's the atom bomb, Hiroshima and Nagasaki. Who needs strategies, tricks, forward and backward marches? You claim that, in war and in peace, we can derive some sort of living philosophy from your research. Please don't take offense: actually I think you're an excellent teacher and I'm very grateful to you for what I've been learning. But can't you see that the world is moving in the other direction? May I ask you a question?"

"Yes," said Terzo, resigned by now to the frankness of the kids who grew up during the War.

"Do you read the newspapers?"

"Do I? Of course, I also read the foreign press, and I have a subscription, the Italian mail permitting, to the *Pall Mall Gazette* of London, which has the finest military correspondent in all the world, Bob Wingate——" Terzo interrupted himself and looked out to the open sea. "What am I saying?" he whispered, more to himself than to his pupils, "the *Pall Mall Gazette* is defunct. Wingate died at Guadalcanal. Just last month I received his letters, which the censorship office had sent back to the General Post Office after war was declared . . . You're right. After the war ended, I stopped reading the papers. Just a glance at *The Stars and Stripes* every now and then. I hadn't realized . . ."

"You teach us to study the past in all its detail, but you forget the present," said the boy. "Let's have done with war, Colonel. It's a time of peace now, can't you see? Peace or nuclear destruction. Have you been to any of the peace demonstrations?"

"Demonstrations? For peace?"

"For peace, Colonel, peace. Bread, work, peace, and freedom. Land for the peasants. Do you really not know anything about them? The peasants have been occupying the landed estates. Sicily, in the next few years, is going to change more than it has in the last two centuries. You were an anti-Fascist, you know history: you should join with us, so you can be on the right side in the only battle worth fighting." Salvatore stood up, clenching his boyish fists: "The battle for peace," he shouted, as if at a rally.

Fluttering in the wind, Signora Astraco's sheets left Terzo's art nouveau terrace alternately shaded and unshaded. One minute Fiore was in sunlight, the next minute a gust put Terzo in the light and Dragonara in shadow. Their faces lit up according to the whims of the flying white screens. Terzo felt almost seasick from that shadow cinema: "And who will bring the reign of peace on earth?" he asked, more of the wind than the young couple.

"We will," Fiore Mastema solemnly replied.

"You?" said the colonel, glaring at the adolescents.

"Us," said Salvatore calmly.

"The Communists," concluded Fiore.

"Wonderful. Now you're Communists, too. I'm sure your mother will love that," said Emma, pulling tight the sash on her Chinese silk dressing gown. She had gotten out of bed earlier than usual, perhaps attracted by the clear morning air. When the sun shone on her Slavic features she looked transparent, her blue veins a filigree beneath the skin of her forehead and cheeks. She held the customary cigarette between her fingers.

Dr. Pantera had given her only a few months to live. She forced him to tell her everything; he had resisted, but then succumbed to the patient's charm. Afterward, alone in his office, he had tormented himself over having confessed the truth: "Why am I incapable of lying to that sorceress?" he lamented, striking his stethoscope against the charts that told the story of her illness.

"My mother doesn't know," Fiore replied proudly, "I saved up the money for membership myself."

"So you're Party members?" asked Terzo, concerned. Saying they were Communists was one thing, a kind of guarantee of good-heartedness; but being registered members, their names on a list of subversives, was something else for an old military man like himself.

"Can't you see, as a theorist of battle formations," his pupil, the aspiring poet, insisted with passion, "that the moment has come to take up sides? The twentieth century of war is over. Now the twentieth century of peace is beginning. You spoke to me about the French cadets who defended the bridges of Saumur with rifles against the Nazi tanks in 1940. The young are on the front lines again, but this time for peace."

"Perhaps, my two young Bolsheviks, you should ask someone who has had a little personal experience of Communism. A splendid theory, heaven knows—my grandfather was a friend of Trotsky and neither one came to a good end—but there are, I think, some problems in the application." Terzo looked at his wife in surprise: it was the first time he had ever heard her talk about politics. The sheets alternately shed light and shadow, shadow and light, on her. *In sunlight,* he thought, *she looks tired and sick, but the shadows preserve her charms.* And he sought to look at her only in shadow.

"Emma, for you and me it might be difficult to imagine that a laborer, a nobody who stinks of onions, a rude peasant of the sort Mama keeps at arm's length with her whip, is worth as much as the Mastema coat-of-arms: 'Sable on a glaive gules in fess spread eagle or.' We can trace our ancestors back to the Crusades—but no lectures, please, Colonel—while they can barely remember their grandparents. But they're better, they don't have our guilt."

"Real agitprop," said Emma, stroking Fiore's black hair. "Come on, Rosa Luxemburg, finish your ice, we're going for a walk."

"A walk? Together? Outside, with Salvatore? What a thought! The only time we get to see each other is at your house," said the girl, radiant.

"Don't you meet at Party functions?" asked Terzo.

"No," said Fiore, blushing: "I've paid for the stamps on my card, and I am a registered member, but I don't go to the local branch. How could I? I never leave home. Later, when . . . anyway, I'll start going."

"Later when what?" asked Emma, indifferent.

"When we get married," Salvatore firmly replied. "Once we've completed our studies we're going to teach the peasants. Fiore's going to be a painter, and I will write."

"You, a painter? Since when?" asked Emma again, with affection and a hint of irony in her voice.

"It was Salvatore who encouraged me. To read, to write, to paint, to express myself, in short. I draw all the little battle maps in my notebook. Mama has forbidden me to 'waste time with paintbrushes.' But according to my godmother Elena, Papa was actually a good painter. He painted watercolors in Tuscany, but I don't know what happened to them."

The godmother had summarized the story to Emma: "Francesco Mastema, born in Paris, a cultivated free spirit. Married, by family decree, to the sullen Duchess Luminosa, he withered away in her shadow and died of a heart attack when Fiore was still in primary school. One of his surviving gouaches, a melancholy profile of a Parisian mademoiselle, hangs in Fiore's room, where the duchess never sets foot."

"The aristocracy wastes the talents of individuals," Salvatore ventured to say, "the masses——"

"I didn't flee from Kiev to listen to political speeches by an Italian poet," Emma interrupted. "Enough. I'm getting dressed and we're going out."

Paying no attention to Terzo's puzzlement, Emma decided that Salvatore would walk with the colonel, several steps ahead, and she and Fiore behind, arm in arm, ready to break away if they encountered any source of potential embarrassment. At the gate Annuzza, the concierge, bowed devotedly to the princess. She took Emma's gaunt hand and drew her aside, into the cool of the stairwell. "You're going outside, signora? Today? Be very careful, there are disturbances in town. They're coming from the countryside."

"Who's coming?"

"The Communists. From the countryside."

"From the countryside? *Mamma mia!* Don't worry, Anna, they won't eat me." And looking more cheerful than Terzo had seen her in a long time, Princess Emma said in a loud voice, "Good Lord, Reds everywhere. We're taking Romeo and Juliet here to see their friends march, but please don't denounce me as an aristocrat or I'll end up in Siberia."

They went out, paired in their odd formation. The breeze lifted the waterlogged sheets and Colonel Carlo Terzo, Princess Emma Svyatoslava, Duchessina Fiore Mastema and the young poet Salvatore Dragonara were bathed in warm light.

DESPITE THE CONCERN that someone might see them, Terzo was relieved by their walk in the sun, the first they had all taken together, because his wife seemed so enthusiastic about it. Emma had wanted a child, he thought; at least now she had the two kids around the house. As for Terzo himself, better not to fantasize about a son. It would have been nice to re-create some battles for him with toy soldiers: Gettysburg, say; children always like the American Civil War, Gray against Blue. But the thought of how he would bring up the child, after Emma's death, disheartened him. *I wouldn't be a good father,* he thought. *Campari, yes:* he *would have always had the right answer on his tongue, and his son would have admired him as he leaped onto his horse. Not me.* As he looked at Fiore, his melancholy reflections became confused. And what if it had been a girl? How to live with a daughter, not knowing anything about women? The idea of having two girlish eyes in the house, however, proved very reassuring to him. He collected himself and, to distract himself from his gloom, turned his thoughts to the classics of war, to Bonaparte: when the situation was critical, Napoleon would hole up in his tent and study the campaign, reflecting for hours on end, until "the right idea" came to him. Thus he studied and took notes without respite, and as a result young Dragonara, a poet by vocation and an aspiring cadet to please his mother, was enjoying a course on strategy the likes of which not even the students at the Royal Military Academy at Sandhurst could have dreamed of.

"Tell me, then," Terzo said to Salvatore as, several steps away, Emma told Fiore about a fashion show at the Atelier Bresson before the war, "what did you come up with on the defensive-offensive theme I assigned you?"

"I prepared a presentation on the battle of the Golden Spurs," the boy replied, with a note of disappointment. He had hoped to have a peaceful walk.

"Let's hear it," Terzo approved. *Excellent choice*, he thought. *The boy detests war, but he's got a brain.*

"On May 18, 1302, the villages of Flanders rebelled against Philip IV of France, known as Philip the Fair. To stifle the revolt, the Count of Artois mustered a formidable array of noble French knights and Flemings loyal to the king and hostile to the revolt of the local bourgeoisie. They also had the support of Genoese mercenaries armed with crossbows and squadrons of German cavalry. On July 11, the royal army approached Courtrai—"

"Do you know the city's Flemish name?" asked Terzo, who had immediately become engrossed in the story.

"No."

"Kortrijk. Go ahead."

"The Flemish rebels were arrayed under the command of Count Guy de Dampierre. Their number included no soldiers, knights, or nobles, but only craftsmen, weavers, potters, tanners. It took many of them to hold up the long halberd—"

"What's it called?"

"It's called a *goedendag*." This time the boy was ready. "The French knights took one look at that ragtag army and laughed. They were confident they would put those peasants to rout with just a few charges—"

"And why's that?"

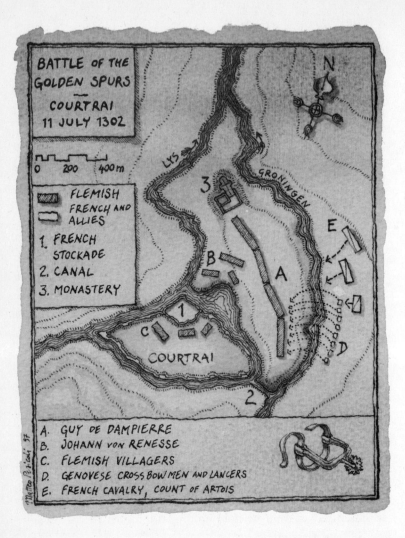

BATTLE OF THE
GOLDEN SPURS
—
COURTRAI
11 JULY 1302

0 200 400 m

FLEMISH
FRENCH AND
ALLIES
1. FRENCH STOCKADE
2. CANAL
3. MONASTERY

N

LYS

GRONINGEN

3

B

A

E

1

C

D

COURTRAI

2

A. GUY DE DAMPIERRE
B. JOHANN VON RENESSE
C. FLEMISH VILLAGERS
D. GENOVESE CROSSBOWMEN AND LANCERS
E. FRENCH CAVALRY, COUNT OF ARTOIS

"Well, after the fall of the Western Roman Empire and the barbarian invasions, the upper hand no longer belonged to the infantry—which, by means of the phalanx and legion, had brought victory to Alexander and Caesar; it belonged to the cavalry. Throughout the Middle Ages, knights prevailed over foot soldiers, who were considered little more than servants on the field of battle. Poorly armed, fed worse, and ignorant, the foot soldier could only flee when the knight, lance couched and plumes in the wind, charged at full gallop, with the blessing of king and Church."

"And so?"

"At Courtrai, however, Guy de Dampierre ignored the tradition favoring the cavalry—"

"Excellent."

"He adapted to the situation—"

"Perfect."

"He turned his own weakness into a strength and the enemy's might into a problem."

"Magnificent!" Terzo was so excited for his pupil that he dealt a swift kick to an empty tomato can on the street, sending it into a ditch surrounded by papyrus bushes. Startled awake, the frogs croaked in unison.

"Guy de Dampierre was twenty-five years old, and came from an aristocratic family. His father, the Count of Dampierre, had been imprisoned, in retaliation for Guy's rebellion, by King Philip. Guy took the reins of the rebel forces, showing himself to be a superb strategist."

"A clever tactitian," suggested Terzo.

The boy held his ground: "Strategist, Colonel, because Guy placed military strategy at the service of politics. And, if you'll allow me, I'll prove it."

Terzo gave him a puzzled look: "Be careful. You're starting to think like me."

"Guy knows he can't confront, in the open field, the flower of

French knighthood, who are furious at the affront of the revolt, with his laborers armed with pikes. It would have meant a rout and a massacre. In the battles of antiquity, fleeing meant death. Once the front was breached, the carnage began. Thus the importance of an orderly retreat, in the manner of Socrates, who at the battle of Delos withdrew with a group of armed companions, who ran away but were ready to defend themselves if attacked."

"Let's not get off the subject," advised Terzo, whose own lectures were continual digressions from one topic to another, and who had recognized his own style in his pupil.

"Sorry. Guy positioned his volunteers along the canals in the area. The Count of Artois was convinced that the mere appearance of the illustrious knights at Courtrai Castle, the monastery, the Groningen torrent, the Lys River, and the network of canals joining the two waterways would suffice to put the villagers to flight. In his arrogance he didn't notice that the Flemish rebels had drawn up at angles between the fortress and the river, protected in front by the Groningen, but with the turbulent waters of the Lys behind them . . ."

"What should Artois have deduced from this position?" asked Terzo.

"That soldiers who array themselves for battle without a path for retreat are ready to win or to die trying. When someone fights with a river behind him—like the Soviets at Stalingrad, on the Volga, in the fall and winter of 1942–43—his resistance will be fierce. The rebels knew that to gain their freedom they would have to win a pitched battle. Should they retreat, the monarchists would first lay waste to the countryside, then storm the cities: Bruges, according to Delbrück, was poorly fortified—"

"Save the politics for later. For now, let's look at the battle." Terzo, however, was impressed. *The boy,* he thought, *has easily grasped that military history is indispensable to the study of poli-*

tics. Perhaps I can get him to see the connection to our own lives and illustrate my method to him.

"The Flemish drew themselves up in a very dense front line of men-at-arms—"

"*Acies longa valde et spissa . . . ,*" Terzo quoted from the ancient *Annales Gandenses.* "Your turn, Fiore, please translate." This way, at least, he could slip in a few Latin exercises.

"A very long and dense line of battle," recited the young duchess, arm in arm with Emma.

"*Pariter adunati et densati lanceis adjunctis . . .*"

"All the men nearby, on all sides, pikes raised together . . ."

"*Brugenses unam solam fecerunt armatorum aciem praemittendo balistarios deinde homines cum lanceis et baculis ferratis alternatum postea reliquos . . .*"

"The men of Bruges gathered in a single formation, putting in front the . . . how do you say *balistarios?*

"Crossbowmen."

"Thank you. So, the men of Bruges gathered in one formation, putting the crossbowmen in front and the foot soldiers armed with lances and pikes behind, in checkerboard pattern . . ."

"And what did they hope to achieve with this formation?" A trolley passed in front of Terzo, but he didn't see the blue sparks falling from the rods connecting it to the electrical wires above. He was in Courtrai, on the morning of battle, the warm mist rising from the canals, the herons standing warily on one leg, alarmed by the movements of the soldiers and ready to take flight. The confident knights trampled the mud under their horses' hooves. The noble commanders pranced in front. The Count of Artois, veteran of six battles, wanted to humble the rebellious peasants and bring glory to his king. For the first time, villagers were telling an absolute monarch they wanted to do things their own way. A handful of potters armed with pikes made ready to confront the charge of noble paladins, the flower of knighthood, heirs to the *chansons de geste,* descendants of Roland and Reynauld. What, thought Terzo as he crossed the street, were they feeling? What were they thinking as they clutched the *goedendags*? How full of fear their souls must have been, in the face of the cavalry, how full, too, of humble courage, as they lay in wait, between the frogs and the cranes, with the waters of the river at their backs . . .

Dragonara continued: "Guy assigned the rear guard to a nobleman who had joined the rebel forces, Johann von Renesse—"

"No, no, no," Terzo interrupted, rousing himself and turning to face the boy, "you didn't answer my question. What did Guy hope to achieve with that formation?"

"A phalanx," replied Salvatore, self-assured: "a crude sort of phalanx. Sixteen centuries after Alexander the Great, the phalanx returned to the battlefield . . ."

Terzo slipped past a large crowd gathered in front of an ice cream shop, amid children holding brioches dripping with chocolate, and gestured to Salvatore to continue.

"Artois was an experienced man. After reconnoitering the terrain, he realized it was a much more complicated matter than he had thought. Instead of fleeing, the villagers were preparing to resist him. And so the Count of Artois waited."

"You can tell me later about Artois's tactical dilemma. Now for the conclusion."

"The knights are already in sight of the poorly armed wretches. Faced with Artois's hesitation, they protest, they rail, they openly accuse him of excessive caution, if not cowardice. Unable to resist his own men's discontent, Artois takes action and attacks. The Genoese crossbowmen rain arrows on the rebel phalanx, while the light infantry strikes from afar with their javelins. Since the Flemish are assembled very close together, the arrows and lances claim many victims. Panic grips the front line; Guy orders them to fall back. And the rebel craftsmen actually perform one of the riskiest of military moves: falling back under a hail of arrows, in proper order, without disbanding . . ."

"This in itself should already have struck the arrogant knights, for no maneuver in war is more difficult than withdrawing, in disciplined fashion, under attack," said Terzo as if in a trance, no longer knowing whether he was speaking to himself or to the boy.

"The Genoese bowmen can't very well pursue them on foot; without the support of the cavalry they would be massacred one by one by the Flemish. Their powerful crossbows are rendered useless by the distance. Artois, reasonably orders the Genoese to retreat and, convinced the morale of the rebels is in tatters, finally gives the command to the horsemen: 'Get ready to charge!' There's total confusion, as always happens in these instances. Under their horses' hooves the ambitious French trample a few unfortunate mercenaries who don't get out of the way in time. On the attack, the French reach the Groningen, but the stream proves difficult to ford on horseback, with all their heavy armor. Also, the steep, muddy banks are bristling with sharpened stakes planted by the Flemish . . ."

"So what happened?" Terzo asked impatiently.

"Without the details you can't understand the whole, Colonel; I shouldn't have to tell you that," Salvatore scolded his teacher, citing one of his own maxims. Then, calmly, he resumed his narrative: "What happens, at this point, is something that nobody has seen for sixteen hundred years. An infantry of craftsmen attacks the French horsemen, who are still stuck between the water and the mud. With a fury, the rebels deploy their *goedendag* pikes with a twofold purpose, using the point to unhorse the knights, and the edge to finish them off on the ground. The knights don't even have a chance to draw their swords, deprived as they are of their most formidable weapon: impact . . ."

"—the physical impact of the horse running at full speed, and the psychological impact of the plumes and the gleaming metal that blinds and terrorizes the foot soldier," Terzo finished the thought.

"With the force of their assault exhausted in the stream, the cavalry find themselves defenseless. The knights slip and slide in the foul mud, weighed down by their armor. The craftsmen stab their pikes into the interstices at the neck and the pelvis."

"Only in the middle of the front line—" the colonel interrupted him.

"Only in the middle do the king's horsemen cross the Groningen on the run, putting the Flemish phalanx to flight. But the reserves of Johann von Renesse, whom Guy had wisely left behind him—"

"Always have a line of reserves in life, boy, always! In peace and in war. You, too, Fiore, don't ever forget that."

"—the reserves close ranks and drive the enemy back. Each horseman stranded in the marshes is confronted by five or six armed foot soldiers. The *goedendags*, at the tip, have either a heavy iron cylinder or a hook, or sometimes an ax blade. With the hooks the rebels knock down the French knights like sacks of grain, then kill them with the axes. Against the whirlwind of swords, they wave the pike slowly in a circle, keeping the danger at bay. The rebels had sworn to Guy: 'Whosoever among us grants mercy to a prisoner, expecting ransom, will go to the gallows.' There was no need. No pity was shown the king's men. The brave Count of Artois, surrounded by foot soldiers with halberds, gallops toward a Flemish warrior-monk, William of Süftingen. In medieval tradition, a knight who surrendered to another knight in battle would be spared, welcomed into the enemy camp, and finally ransomed by offering sumptuous gifts to the victor. And so, using the pompous French of the royal court, the captain general, Count of Artois, brother-in-law of

Philip the Fair, declares his surrender: *'Je me rends.'* William, the rebel monk, looks at him askance and hisses in Flemish: 'What's that? Who are you?' 'I am the Count of Artois, and I surrender,' the knight repeats. 'There are no nobles here who understand your courtly French,' shouts William. He moves toward Artois, unhorses him, and tramples him to death. Sixty-three noblemen, French and Flemish loyalists, suffer the same fate in the fording."

"And why is Courtrai remembered as the battle of the Golden Spurs?"

"The Flemish were very proud of their victory. For a long time they continued to tell the story of the weaver who, armed with a *goedendag*, had confronted two knights all by himself— when normally one knight is enough to send a whole crowd of villagers running. Before darkness fell, the Flemish took seven hundred pairs of golden spurs from the armor of the fallen noble knights, as war booty. That's why Courtrai is called the battle of the Golden Spurs."

"Principal sources?"

Convinced he had made a good impression, the boy relaxed: "Now you're asking too much, Colonel."

"You're right. Take notes."

From his pocket Salvatore pulled out the notebook in which he alternately took down notes from his lessons and wrote poems. In disciplined fashion, he wrote, under dictation: "*Annales Gandenses, Annals of Ghent, Genealogia Comitum Flandrensium* . . ." but suddenly Terzo's formidable erudition seemed to falter, and, behind him, Emma's bright voice interjected:

"Ah, so the battle of my ancestor Svyatoslav is not the only lacuna in your learning, darling. You seem to be having difficulty even with the Golden Spurs . . ."

Rousing himself, Terzo resumed mechanically: "*Genealogy of the Counts of Flanders, Chronicle of Saint-Denis.* The principle work on the subject remains the Berlin doctoral thesis of Felix Wodsak, written in 1905. Sorry, I can't remember the publisher. But that's quite enough. Very well done, Salvatore."

"No, Colonel, wait, I haven't finished yet," said the boy, surprising him. "I haven't drawn the moral of the story. The tactical moral: for the first time since antiquity, infantry defeated cavalry and an army of artisans humbled the aristocracy. The strategic moral: inferior forces, if intelligently organized, can humble more powerful enemies. The political moral: one can prevail against armies of mercenaries and aristocrats with popular militias."

"I can't judge you as a poet, my dear Salvatore, but as a strategist you show a lot of promise," Terzo admitted.

"As a poet he's even better," interrupted Fiore. "Would you like to hear a few lines? I'll recite them myself, I know them by heart . . ."

"No, Fiore, please," said Salvatore, blushing.

"Nothing doing," said Fiore, who had made up her mind. "Are you a poet or not? Who ever heard of a poet who is embarrassed of his poems? So . . ."

As she was about to begin, her voice was drowned out by the clamor of a band. The brass section filled the street with sound and the crowd shouted: "Comrades! The land to the workers! Three cheers for Li Causi. Onward, brothers and sisters . . . Our ideal . . ." The Communist demonstration. Terzo and Dragonara, with the two women, huddled against the wall to watch. They saw hunched, elderly laborers with black berets pulled down over their foreheads, walking arm in arm with young men. The leaders marched at the front, chatting calmly among themselves. One of them, a gigantic farm-union leader, turned with curiosity toward the little group of bourgeois—Emma and Fiore in their white dresses, Terzo standing erect—and smiled. His white shirt was open at the collar, the cuffs threadbare but immaculate. Seeing his gesture, Fiore couldn't restrain herself any longer, stood up on tiptoe in her patent-leather pumps and raised a clenched fist. Her gold bracelets slid down her slender arm as she cried out: "Land for the peasants!" Salvatore applauded: "Hurrah!" The line of farmers on the march responded with applause.

"Who are those gents?" asked one laborer.

"Friends or bosses, I guess," said another. "Let's wave. We don't want to make a bad impression."

"Take a good look at them," said Terzo to Dragonara. "The foot soldiers of Courtrai were people like them."

"So do you understand what I've been trying to tell you?" said the boy, getting excited. "Guy had to put pikes in the hands of the laborers to gain freedom. Today the Party is turning them into a peaceful army to gain freedom and work. The commitment and discipline are the same, but without any blood being spilled."

As the procession streamed past, each new group of arrivals, seeing the fuss being made over Terzo by those in front, redoubled their enthusiasm. "Who is it?" "Can't you see?" "Is it Li Causi?," they asked; and: "Look, it's our leader," "It's him." "Hurrah!" "What a beautiful wife he has!" "Look at the daughter! A princess." "Look, he's saluting us with his fist." "They're with the Party." "Hurrah." Finally, Emma's Slavic features and blond hair led to the conclusion: "She's here from Moscow. Hurrah!"

Amid all the applause, the crowd thronged closely around the little group. Many were stopping to shake the embarrassed Terzo's hand, and the confusion grew. "Didn't I promise you some surprises? Here I am in triumph, among a crowd of Communists," Emma said to her husband, laughing at the absurdity. But her voice sputtered in her throat, she felt her knees go weak, and her face turned ashen.

"Emma, what's wrong?" asked Terzo, holding her up.

"Maybe the heat, I feel faint . . ."

Seeing her half-unconscious, the farmers shouted, "Stand back, stand back. The lady's not feeling well. Let's show some manners, bring us some water." A little boy with a flask slipped in between the legs of the adults; the union leader with the tremendous shoulders wet a white handkerchief and massaged Emma's temples with it. The throng was pressing. "Stand back," the giant begged, but he was unable to create any breathing room for the princess. He looked around to see if there were any open doorways to the nearby buildings, but all the homes and stores were bolted shut in anticipation of the demonstration from the countryside.

"Over here," cried Salvatore. Behind them was an old noble palazzo, gutted by the bombing of '43 and roofless, its ground floor windows boarded up. "Good work," said the large man, smashing through the plywood with one blow. Salvatore jumped over the windowsill and pulled out the last plank. Terzo took Emma in his arms and with a cautious step entered the palace. The crowd outside, unaware, filled the street with chants and hurrahs.

THEY WERE IN A ROOM just off the street, cluttered with debris and trash. Splintered, dusty bathroom tiles made it hard to walk. Where the tub and sink used to be were two holes with a bit of stagnant water. Terzo, who was steadying the princess, looked at the unknown man with uncertainty: "Maybe we should go back into the street and ask for help."

"No, there's no need, I already feel better," responded Emma.

Salvatore Dragonara, who had ventured farther inside the palazzo, came back and, balancing on the rubble, said: "Come over here, come."

He led them into the atrium of the ancient palace, a courtyard of white and gray pebbles, whose geometry got lost amid the marble columns, capitals, and the triton of a fountain gone dry. They laid Emma down on a shiny stone bench under the portico, which supported the balconies of the *piano nobile* above. From the triton protruded a black spigot, perhaps used before the war to water plants since stolen or dead. The only sign of them now was the large, dark circles on the surface of pebbles, where the large terra-cotta pots had sat for decades. The stranger reapplied the handkerchief, cool with water, to Emma's pale forehead.

"Thank you, I feel better now. A bit too much sun," she said, trying to get up.

"It's clean," he reassured her, indicating the handkerchief.

"Of course it is, thank you," replied Emma in her regal manner. "How nice and cool it is in here. It feels so good."

The courtyard had the fragrance of a cloister. The architect must have known what he was doing, because it was pleasant under the portico even in that heat. If the blue sky hadn't been peering through the collapsed beams of the ceiling, one might have forgotten the bombs of 1943 and imagined perhaps the imminent arrival of a carriage bringing guests to a princely banquet. Salvatore and Fiore started exploring the deserted palazzo, excited by the adventure.

"I'm very grateful to you, sir . . ." said Terzo to the man who had helped them.

"Not at all, I'm at your service. My name is Fernando Villa, leader of the farmworkers' union of Petranova. This is my first time in Palermo." Admiring the palace, he cast his eyes around and pointed to the central balcony. "Look, signora." A piece of shrapnel had mutilated a marble carving of a woman's face on the wall: an eye and a cheek were missing, and in the wound two peregrine falcons had made their nest. The male, suspicious of the intruders, was gliding in rapid circles, grazing the surviving eye and soft lips of the bas-relief. In the figure's hair the artist had sculpted spikes of wheat and flowers, perhaps to represent Demeter, the Sicilian goddess of the harvest, mother of Spring, now disfigured by war.

Salvatore and Fiore suddenly appeared joyfully on the balcony: "Come upstairs, quick," they said.

"My wife isn't able. The stairs . . ." Terzo protested, concerned.

"I told you I feel fine," said Emma, trying to stand.

"Do you really want to go up?" Villa asked politely.

"Yes, thank you. Just give me your arm; my husband will lead the way." But under the immense porphyry staircase, Villa felt Emma's grip weakening.

He looked at her, unsure. "May I?" he asked. But before the princess could answer, Villa spun her around and lifted her into his arms. And with a bound he carried her up the stairs.

"The last exemplar of chivalry. I guess it's not dead after all," laughed Emma. Her sickness, and the race upstairs in the stranger's embrace, made her head spin in a manner not altogether unpleasant.

"Over here," Fiore called to them. They entered a great salon with open sky. A patina of rain and bird droppings lay over a marble floor covered with inscriptions, its majesty intact beneath the filth. The doorways to the adjoining rooms were sealed shut with heavy wooden boards, as though the proprietors, before abandoning the skeletal, gutted house, had used the strongest planks to protect the rooms dearest to them, and had eventually resorted, as the undertaking proved prohibitive, to the flimsy plywood so easily removed by Villa in the rooms downstairs.

The last room, past a monumental fireplace featuring the Genie of Palermo protected by snakes, was barricaded with boards and rope. Looking around, Salvatore had discovered something and was now gesturing to the others to come and see. The first to put her eye to the crack he had found in the wall was Emma: "Incredible. An unbroken wood beam, obviously moved during the explosions, is holding up half a ceiling, sheltering furniture, some papers and books. Even the knickknacks are all in place. Very nice and tasteful."

"Why wasn't anything stolen?" asked Villa.

"The ceiling probably looked on the verge of collapse and nobody wanted to take the risk of being buried under an avalanche of roof tiles. The owners blocked the entrance, hoping to return as soon as possible. Something must have happened; maybe they died. And in the meantime the beam fell into place," Terzo explained. Any time the subject touched upon the war, however closely or remotely, his tone of voice turned pedantic. With a few shoulder thrusts, Villa dislodged the planks from the jamb, and they cautiously went in.

Under the architrave, what remained of the roof had formed

a kind of pagoda and an open-air skylight. The tiles deflected the rain. The books were dusty but dry. What must have once been a study now housed a wicker cradle and a painter's easel with a canvas on it: inclemency had faded the picture into a single opalescent stain. Atop a grand piano, shards of glass and sepia photos. Her head spinning, Emma imagined the scene: "Walking tiptoe under the Damoclean sword of the damaged roof, a thief, torn between greed and fear, steals the precious silver picture frames. The wretch—no doubt a manservant busy with the last-minute packing—could easily pocket the frames and take to his heels, but he prefers to brave the danger of the roof collapsing, breaks the glass to the photos and gives back, at least, those memories of the past. Mercury, the god of thieves, is touched by this respect for the Manes, the spirits of the dead, and so protects him."

Fiore Mastema picked up the photos. A young, dark-haired woman riding side-saddle on an Arabian horse; below, in green ink, the caption: "Giulia Farano on Gelsomino, at Forte dei Marmi, July '32." Then, two wan infant twins, "Paola (first born, June 24–July 7, 1936) and Maurizio (second born, June 24–September 21, 1936), children of Giovanni and Grazia Laurenti, photo by mother." Then there was a snapshot of an intense-looking young man, resting his motorcycle helmet on a Gilera. In the inevitable green ink, the caption read "Giovanni Battista on the eve of the 1939 Mount Pellegrino uphill race: Second Place." In a nervous, younger-looking handwriting, someone, perhaps Giovanni Battista himself, had added in pencil: "Because of broken gearshift."

Emma had sat down on a leather armchair which Villa had tried his best to dust off. Fiore was looking at the paintings: a languid young girl in the style of Hayez, two light cavalrymen reconnoitering, in front of a white wall. Salvatore was holding her hand: "What kind of room is this, anyway?" he said. "Look, there's even wine." Indeed, there was a small stock of wine in a

niche, only bottles of white, their labels now illegible. The room
must have become a kind of storeroom, before the evacuation.
Who lived there, and why had they saved, in the same place, a
carburetor, the scores for the Mozart horn concertos, a stuffed
fox, a Dervish saber, and a crystal alembic marked "University
of Heidelberg"? Terzo examined the shelves, nose pointed up, to
see if there were any books familiar to him. It was the library of
a Romantic: only volumes that promised love and adventure, in
the principal European languages.

"Let's go," Terzo said, suddenly concerned. "It might still be
dangerous here." Then he noticed a blue binding, swollen with
humidity, and recognized the title: "Look, Emma, it's the poems
you keep beside your bed."

Now feeling very tired, the princess forgot, despite the ruins,
that she was still in the house of other people. "Thank you," she
said to Terzo, then slipped the book into her ancient bureaucrat's briefcase as if it were war booty. "Baudelaire. Have you
ever read him?" she whispered complicitously to Salvatore.

"No," said the boy.

"What? And you want to be a poet? Starting tomorrow, you'll
spend ten minutes less on war, and you and Fiore will read with
me. In French," she ordered, gesturing to her husband. "Please,
let's go now."

"Should we inform the police?" asked Terzo as they descended the marble staircase.

"The police? Why would we do that?" asked Villa, seemingly
alarmed.

"We'll let fate decide," Emma said sternly. "That room
spared by war will either go to the descendants or be gnawed
to oblivion by mice. But we'll preserve it in our memories.
Does the boy still have a motorbike? Who still remembers the
days when those twins lived? Why on earth put a cradle in the
study? Was the owner a demented painter, his lair torn open by
war, like the homes of all us crazy Europeans? Or did harmony

reign in this house, before war imposed its chaos? There's no use trying to understand the past: like the petty thief, all we can do is make off with the silver, leaving truth and memory behind."

In the great courtyard, the breeze turned into a scirocco. From the open window one could still see peasants marching in the street, but the hurrahs grew fainter as their steps began to drag, one after the other, weary from a long day of doing their political duty. Emma was saying goodbye to Villa—"I want your address; I'll write to you"—when a strong gust suddenly blew a red kite in front of her, its tail of shiny yellow paper tangled together with the reel and string.

"A kite," said Emma cheerlessly, without surprise. She looked at Villa, her chosen cavalier: "Make it fly." Carlo Terzo was struck by the oddity of the wish and by the tone in which it was expressed, which lacked the seductive keenness she had used, a few minutes earlier, in enjoining Salvatore to read Baudelaire. Now there was an air of gravity, of penance, as if making the kite fly were some sort of liturgy to be celebrated with faith. Salvatore ran and gathered up the kite, Fiore untangled the string with her slender fingers, and Terzo studied the wind currents and the angle from which the paper rhombus might best rise above the remaining roof tiles, past the collapsed ceiling and into the open sky of Palermo.

"It won't fly," Salvatore grimly announced, "the main stem is broken."

"It won't fly?" repeated Emma, as if he'd said something blasphemous.

Villa inspected the damage, then went back toward a crater full of the sort of long, flexible reeds Signora Astraco used when hanging the sheets out to dry. He pulled a knife out of his pocket, clicked open the blade, and carefully carved out two strips of wood. He bent them into arcs, retying the string with his teeth, and opened his colossal hands; immediately the wind bore the kite aloft. Salvatore maneuvered the string amid the gusts of wind and the red silhouette soared gracefully through the open roof and over the parade of laborers.

"In Kiev, when we were children we used to send telegrams to kites in the air," whispered Emma, whom Terzo had persuaded to sit down. "Salvatore, take some sheets of paper. I want each one of you to write down a wish. Then puncture the sheet and send it up along the string. The wishes that make it to the top will come true. But don't read what the others have written or that will break the spell. Fiore will start; I'll go last."

Salvatore tore five blank pages out of his notebook and passed his pencil around.

"May Salvatore and I love each other until death," wrote Fiore.

"May I never betray my ideals, or Fiore," wrote Salvatore.

"Land for the peasants," wrote Villa.

"May Emma be saved by a miracle," wrote Terzo.

"May my husband, Colonel Carlo Terzo, lead a battle of his own, in the open field," wrote Emma, last of all. Villa threaded the fluttering scraps of paper onto the string, and the wind blew them up into the sky. Only one tore and fell off, coming to rest on the damaged statue of the woman with the spikes of grain in her hair. Only that wish, therefore, did not come true.

AFTER THE DAY of their outing, the princess's health deteriorated without further remission. Dr. Pantera suggested she be admitted to the hospital, and Terzo wanted to comply. But without hearing them out, Emma declared: "I will die in my own house," and neither of the men was able to convince her otherwise.

As he was leaving, Pantera said to the princess: "I can't force you to go to the hospital. You want to stay at home? So be it. I'll come by every day, at the end of my rounds. Not all the medications are available yet. The situation is not as horrible as during the war, when I was reduced to giving shots of sour milk for typhus. But it's certainly not good. I'll do my best." And he squeezed her diaphanous hand between his iodine-stained fingers.

Emma gestured to the colonel that he should pay the doctor what they owed him, but Pantera, seeing Terzo open his billfold, stopped him: "No hospital if you don't want to go, signora, but no money, either. Since you don't want to follow my advice, I'm resigning as your family doctor. I'll become your friend instead; I'll drop by as a courtesy. Of course, provided you will grant me the honor of considering you my friend."

Terzo looked at Emma, convinced she would reply with some witticism, appreciating the doctor's offer but distancing herself in her chic way. She, however, was moved, had grasped the fateful meaning of his words. For the first time in her life, Princess

Emma Svyatoslava was unable to smile. She squeezed the doctor's hands, trembling. She tried to speak but could not, smiling nervously, trying to find the old Emma, to relieve her husband's pain with a joke. Instead, she broke into sobs.

Pantera had seen too many people die. When a patient felt the presence of death for the first time, there was more comfort in a body's warmth than in words. He thus held Emma's hands and embraced her, as if he were once again the slim, dark Pantera picking up the wounded from the battlefields of the Isonzo in World War I, a younger, better Pantera. He tried to let her feel the large, familiar mass of his body, so that she might draw warmth from life.

The princess rested her head on the doctor's vest, her blond hair, dry from illness, hiding her face, so that Terzo did not see his wife in tears. She had not cried leaving Kiev as a little girl or quitting Paris as an adolescent, or even when scheming at Ciano's court between intrigues and antagonisms to save her own skin, her only weapons her fragile beauty and the skeptical air with which she blew smoke from her lacquer cigarette-holder directly into the eyes of the powerful. She had not cried during the months of the Nazi occupation, when it was a crime to have known Ciano and so many would have liked to get their hands on her in their search for Ciano's diaries and money. Now none of it mattered anymore. She could have explained her history to Terzo: the hasty marriage, the silences, the flight to Palermo. She *would* do it. She would ask Pantera how much time for lucidity she still had left. She would say goodbye properly. She wanted to throw her head back, to rearrange her hair, but it felt so sweet embracing the doctor. He smelled of cologne and phenol, the scent of old doctors, the smell of her father in the Ukraine. She stayed there without moving, quietly weeping, like a little girl before falling asleep to the *babushka*'s stories: "And the brave Svyatoslav saw destiny in the sky and said to his warriors . . ."

Dr. Pantera had heard Freud mentioned only once, by a Jewish patient fleeing to Lisbon in 1940, but he was a shrewd psychologist. Realizing the crisis was over, he helped Emma up and looked her in the eye: "Go and rest now. I'll come tomorrow, but I want to see a smile. One a day. That will be my payment." He mixed some yellow drops in half a glass of water, made the patient drink it, then left. Emma fell immediately asleep.

Left alone, Terzo felt dejected. There was so much that needed to be done in his life, what with the lessons, the love between the two kids, tracking his wife's illness and keeping her spirits up with town gossip, the work on the military Archives. So much that he seldom thought about the imminent end. Just as he'd been surprised by Emma's decision to marry, he now found it impossible to imagine living without her. Would he carry on with the lessons? Of course not: meeting with Duchess Mastema he would give himself away at once and create problems for the secret lovers. And why remain in Palermo, anyway? What, besides Emma, bound him to that sea of secret passageways, that sky with its hundreds of hidden, catalogued colors? Rome already seemed foreign to him now: he imagined himself in a cold house full of books and silence, and he felt terrified. *In war,* he thought, *nothing spreads so rapidly as panic, the mad fear that turns an ordinary troop into a mindless mob, when someone shouts "Every man for himself."*

Leaning on the terrace railing, Terzo was horrified. *Am I already planning my future?* he thought. *Emma is still here. I don't want to think of her dying. I have to think of her alive.* He washed his face in cold water, letting it run a long time in the sink. Then he did some calisthenics, bungling the back stretches. There was no Campari there to support his hips, to shout, "Look at the world upside down. Where are all your strategies now? The winner loses and the loser wins, dear friend, keep it up, that's it, let the blood wash your brain clean of all its theories. Don't forget chance, don't forget luck . . ."

Carefully balancing himself, Terzo would listen to his friend's mocking voice. It would have comforted him now to feel his strong hands guiding him like a colt. "Don't forget chance, don't forget luck"—the same irreverent words as Fiore's: "Chance is more important than your theories. Those poor Cimbrians . . ." Glimpsing Campari's portrait on the wall, he answered him in a low voice: "You were wrong, Amedeo, not to believe Sun Tzu when he said, 'Always disorient the enemy . . . Never engage stronger adversaries; maneuver instead, until your own men can strike an isolated part of the enemy forces. Thanks to this tactic, a small army can destroy a much more powerful one, squadron after squadron.'"

With a grunt, Terzo was back on his feet and confessed to his vanished friend: "I talk, but I've never seen a man die, Amedeo. Now I'm in trouble and I don't know what to do. I study and reason but I can't even control my own brain, let alone dominate the enemy. I fill my head with strategies because I'm unable to put even one into practice. Dr. Pantera gives morphine to Emma, whereas I drug myself with theories, which are just as powerless to cure me, just as indispensable to help me get by. I know the right maneuver for every desperate situation in war, but I don't know how to live. This is what you were trying to teach me when playing the madman on the cliff that day." Under the visor of his military cap, Campari stared at him ironically.

Having finished his exercises, Terzo washed up and went out. He was supposed to be at the Lolli station at six-thirty p.m. to meet a guest. His American friend Paul Gawain had written him a letter from Washington:

Dear Colonel Terzo:

My younger brother, Pilgrim, who has an engineering degree from Chicago, has changed his mind and says he wants to become a journalist. A small daily paper here is sending him around Europe to

write articles, paying him less than a sandwich a day. Do you think
you could help him out? He was kept very busy during the war,
doing what I don't exactly know, but he came out of it with
a serious case of nerves. Now he's better and wants to visit Sicily. I
would be immensely grateful if you could give him some tips and
keep an eye on him.

Terzo had thought of declining the request, pleading his
wife's illness, but Emma, who always, shamelessly, read his
mail, had accepted for him and within a few days had arranged
for Pilgrim Gawain to stay with Signora Astraco: "There's room
at my house, until my husband returns, and at my age I don't
care what people say." The few dollars the newspaper was paying him sufficed for food and lodging. Terzo, in the end, was
happy with the arrangement: it satisfied Emma's wishes and re-
paid Paul Gawain for his generosity and help when the colonel
was in prison.

Terzo arrived punctually at the station, but the train was late.
Hands in his pockets, he strolled around the square. At the entrance to the Cinema Dante, three boys were drinking beer and
chatting: "If Palermo ties Catania . . ." In the garden in front of
the box office, a group of beautiful palm trees provided shade
for the swallows and two ladies sipping their ices as they waited
to depart: "Padre Ferrauto said so to Mimma: you cannot explain to your husband that . . ." Terzo sat down on a bench but,
distracted by a headline announcing MAO OFFENSIVE IN CHINA
from a nearby kiosk, he didn't hear exactly what it was that
Padre Ferrauto had forbidden Signora Mimma to do. He
thought for a moment of leaving the palm trees to go and buy a
newspaper, so he could say to Salvatore: "See? I do stay up to
date." But the boys moved away from the cinema entrance and
pointed to something in the sky. Terzo looked up. A tightrope
walker, blindfolded with blue bandages, had strung his wire
across the square. Having climbed over the bannister, he now

ventured out onto the taut cable, balancing himself step by step
with a pole. Terzo wished he had his marine binoculars with
him. Could his eyes really be wrapped up like a mummy's? How
could he see where he was going? The rope was stretched at the
height of the third-floor windows; one false move would have
killed the acrobat. He must have been rehearsing for Sunday's
show, since there was no one here to collect coins, except for the
boys, who were egging him on and whistling. Terzo looked
around for a net, a safety belt, some sort of emergency system,
but saw none. Having now reached the center of the cable, the
man tested it with his foot and made it sway, patiently rotating
the balancing pole. Satisfied with the results, he stopped in his
tracks, let his blind gaze wander beyond the palms and the station, to the sea, the port, the ruins at the center of town. The sky
was a color that Terzo called Bright Silver. It reminded him of
the melting pot of molten lead in the printworks where together
with Campari he used to correct proofs of the *Military Archives
Bulletin. What can he see from there?* Terzo wondered. *How
much more can he see than we can?* For a moment, he thought of
asking the acrobat himself, after he had finished his practice.
Strange profession. What was the proper strategy: excess prepa-
ration or taking one's chances? An impossible battle: one mistake, and no chance to right it. Not even General Desaix could
say, "This battle is lost; there's still time to win another." You
lost and that was it. *Maybe,* thought Terzo, *I could buy him a cup
of coffee and a baked iris; he mustn't make much money on a day
like today.* The station's irises—small sweetbreads stuffed with
ricotta cheese—were famous throughout the city. The funambulist, however, unconcerned with the beer-bottle toasts the
boys were honoring him with below, did not finish his passage.
He steadied his balancing pole, moved his feet along the rope—
first the left, in a slow pirouette, as in a tango, then the right, in
a precise leap—and changed direction. For a moment, one very
brief moment, he was airborne, elegantly twisting his body

about, the pole parallel to the asphalt. His bandaged feet landed on the rope, his knees bent to absorb the impact, and he began to walk nonchalantly back toward his railing.

The change in program displeased the boys below. One stuck two fingers in his mouth and blew a shrill whistle. His friend took aim and launched a beer bottle labeled "Falcon" into the air. But the man was too high up and the dark glass soon lost speed and shattered on the pavement.

"What are you doing?" shouted Terzo, intervening, as the frightened ladies took shelter in the lobby. The funambulist stopped, to avoid making any false steps, balancing high above the square without looking down, eyes fixed on his balancing pole.

Terzo approached the small group of boys. "Leave him alone," he said. They were hardly more than children, despite the beers and the cigarette butts in their mouths. The third urchin guzzled down the rest of his beer and then casually hurled his bottle as well, unconcerned about the broken glass. Before the colonel could stop him, he extracted a dirty slingshot from his pocket, put a stone in the sling, which had been cut out from a bicycle inner tube, and fired. The women screamed, and Terzo's stomach tightened. The acrobat stiffened, as if wishing to anesthetize his body before impact. The stone passed right in front of him and struck a swallows' nest in the palm shoots. The man headed toward his balcony. He had lost his graceful step and was now waving his pole like a blind man's cane. The cable vibrated with a metallic sound, while the terrified swallows flew in circles above the station.

"Let's see if he has wings," shouted the boy. He closed one eye to take aim and pulled back the sling. Terzo jumped on top of him and managed, with his wrist, to divert the shot. The knife that then appeared in the young hoodlum's hand didn't make him look any less a child. "You gonna back off now, buddy?" he said, coming toward Terzo. A train whistle filled the square, as the news headlines rustled in the wind. The boy was skilled, and he leveled an expert slashing stroke at the colonel, who was still on the ground. The blow, however, was blocked by a military boot. The boy whimpered as the same boot dealt out precise kicks to the other urchins. Cursing, they all slunk away toward the gardens of the Noce district. Green duffel bag in hand, the young man wearing the boot helped Terzo to his feet, panting from his effort, clicked his heels smiling, and said, in decent Italian:

"Pilgrim Gawain, Colonel. Sorry to have been needed in such circumstances."

"Not at all, you have my heartfelt thanks. You got me out of quite a pickle. How did you recognize me?" asked Terzo, dusting off his jacket.

"My brother Paul is a stickler for detail. He even gave me a photo of you. Who were those crazy kids?"

"Children of the war."

Carlo Terzo looked around for the funambulist. There was no one on the rope. From the balcony railing, his face, now freed of its bandages, reappeared for a moment. He was not a young man, and had straight black hair and the saddest eyes Terzo had ever seen. Hands joined, he bowed in thanks to the strangers below and went back into the room, which was protected by some icon or other.

"Strange city, indeed," muttered Pilgrim Gawain, while the swallows twittered around him.

PILGRIM GAWAIN, too, became inte-
grated into the routine of the Terzo home.
In the morning he would go around town
for his articles, interviewing the leaders who dreamed of independence for Sic-
ily—"We'll be the forty-ninth star on the American flag," they'd
say—or fantasizing a trip to meet, clandestinely, Salvatore
Giuliano, the famous bandit. Dragonara acted as interpreter,
though everyone found Gawain's Italian amusing and efficient.
Exactly what sort of investigation of Sicilian life he wanted to
conduct was unclear. He explained to Terzo: "If the separatists
and monarchists want to organize a revolt against Rome, they
need to start here. If the Communists want revolution, they also
have to win here. And if democracy is really to take root, it must
take root in Sicily. Don't you agree?"

"I don't know much about politics," Terzo parried, and it was
true. Little by little, however, Gawain seemed to give up jour-
nalism. He sat in on Terzo's lessons more and more often,
chatted with the princess, promised Dr. Pantera to get him med-
icines and a new stethoscope from the United States. He no
longer went out in the morning, preferring to stay in and question Signora Astraco as to the customs of the Palermitans. After
breakfast he would go down to the Terzos' house. The seminar
on the terrace thus became a kind of strange academy. The
colonel continued to prepare Salvatore Dragonara for the un-
likely competition for entry into the Military Academy. Salvatore wrote poems, and read them afterward to Fiore, Emma,

and Pilgrim. The colonel always refused to listen to them, as though lending an ear to those lines would have meant betraying his commitment as a teacher. Salvatore, on the other hand, followed Terzo's course with keen attention. At first the colonel thought he was doing so out of politeness; after all, if he had any time alone with Fiore, he owed it to Terzo. Soon, however, he noticed his pupil had a genuine intellectual interest. Salvatore considered war the "oppression of peoples," but the mental game of strategy thrilled him.

Fiore meanwhile was promoted to the third level of the Teacher's School. In exchange, the nuns had asked the duchess to have her continue her private lessons through the summer vacation. "Since she's been studying with that colonel, Fiore is another person," they said. By thus spending her afternoons with Emma, Duchessina Mastema was slowly beginning to take on the princess's manner, impressing Terzo with her wit, playfulness, and skeptical airs. When she casually rearranged her hair, it was as if Terzo saw the old, healthy Emma again. She would amuse herself by teasing him: "But how do we know that the Swedish knights, at Visby, were exhausted from the heat? Who can assure us of this? Why do we doubt certain sources and believe others?"

Only Pilgrim Gawain, who had just turned twenty-five, had actually been in a war. When Terzo asked him in what units and on what fronts, he got only vague responses, such as "I was a stretcher bearer for ambulances, as a conscientious objector," or "The war is better forgotten, dear Colonel." Finally he admitted: "I was even in the special services, doing research more than anything else." Terzo decided it was inappropriate to ask any further questions; the war had just ended, and the young man was a former enemy. Gawain asked Salvatore for the notes to the lessons he had missed and studied them at night. A friendship was born between the two, and they passed the time reviewing English and Italian. When Fiore had to go back home in the late afternoons, they would go to the cinema. What with study, romance, and the need for company, everyone, just about, had moved in with the Terzos.

THE SUMMER went by in a hurry. From the terrace, Gawain saw the swallows fly away. Behind the blue of the sky a more placid tint shone through: Empty Sky, in Terzo's taxonomy. The menu Signora Astraco was serving changed: no more spaghetti with tomato sauce and eggplant; now it was soup of broccoli, saffron, raisins, and pine nuts. The young American, survivor of the secret war, spent the month of September stirring tomato sauce and quickly bottling it in green jars, endlessly swatting the flies that were attacking the tomato paste laid out to dry on wooden scrub boards with a copy of the *Herald Tribune* rescued from the Hotel delle Palme. Whatever the real reason for his journey to Palermo, the city had effortlessly swallowed him up, and he hung about, neither happy nor unhappy, pointlessly busy as the insects he tried in vain to keep away from the tomatoes.

The day finally arrived when Terzo was to present his lecture on the mysticism of Alexander the Great, a subject that, at the Academy, had aroused the objection of his colleagues and the enthusiasm of the students. The colonel was a man of method. He knew he was a failure, a strategist without a battle, a warrior without a war. But he would not have given up his *Manual* for anything in the world. Whatever humiliation life might still have in store for him, he would continue to show, scientifically, how it was possible to derive a code of proper personal conduct from war. "I am useless, beaten," he said to Campari's portrait while doing his calisthenics, "but I'm not going to change. Such is my life, and I'll be true to it, Amedeo. You used to say you believed in nothing, but you, too, you, deep down, remained true to what we studied together."

It was the second of November. The previous day, All Saints' Day, Emma and Fiore had talked a great deal. Terzo was unable to make out much of it, however; he only heard mention of some "festivity" and saw some packages disappear from atop the armoire. Fiore asked him: "Colonel, could we begin the lesson a bit later tomorrow?" Terzo said no: he might turn a blind eye to the furtive kisses of the precious young couple, but changes in schedule horrified him.

"Please," the girl implored, "it's a surprise."

"You can show it to us during the hour you normally spend by yourselves in the study," said Terzo, and this time he wouldn't budge.

It was cold now during the day, and so classes were no longer held on the terrace. Since the study was too small, they gathered in the dining room, with French doors looking out onto the garden. Around the table sat the students and teacher and, when she was well enough to get out of bed, Emma, too.

"To understand the political and military strategy of Alexander the Great," the colonel began, "one must get to know his mother, Olympia. Does anyone here know anything about her?" Amid a tide of negative responses, Terzo resumed: "I didn't think so. Well. Alexander the Great was the firstborn son of Philip of Macedon and Olympia. The same name, you'll notice—*nomen omen,* there's destiny in names—the same name as the mother of Prince Eugene of Savoy, another great strategist. The royal couple had met at a rite in honor of the god Dionysus on the island of Samothrace. The secret ceremonies called for wild dances, rich libations, prophesies of the future, and, deep into the night, carnal relations among the participants. During the religious orgy, Philip and Olympia fell in love, coupling for the first time in the Dionysian frenzy." Terzo broke off instinctively; at this point he was always forced to glare at the cadets who were elbowing each other in jest, not being accustomed to hearing mention of "sexual orgies" at the Academy. What he saw instead was Fiore's beautiful oval face, and it was he who blushed, thinking: I have to lecture in front of a girl!

"Philip considered himself a descendant of Heracles, the hero of the twelve labors. Olympia was a princess of Epirus whose family boasted Achilles as an ancestor. The night before the wedding, Olympia had a dream, which she confided to one of her priests: 'I am alone, wearing a white tunic, laying my bridal trousseau out on a meadow, awaiting my groom. A sudden wind sends the linen flying. I try to gather up the sheets, but the whirlwind even tears away the light dress I am wearing, leaving me naked. The sky turns dark with black, low clouds. I am afraid and want to run away, but there are no houses nearby. A cloud descends over me, and in horror I see a violet lightning flash. Terrified, I cover my sex and my breasts with my hands. The lightning strikes me, embracing me in light, and consumes my body.' King Philip also had a dream, after his first wedding night with Olympia, which he told to an old comrade-in-arms: 'Olympia and I are lying on the tall bed, still naked. Love and passion burn so hot in me I take some red sealing wax and, in perpetual remembrance, I let it drip onto my bride's sex. The heat of the molten wax does not hurt her; on the contrary, she smiles, drunk, throwing her head back and biting her lip. Blood flows onto her white teeth. Then I take the royal bronze seal, I plunge it into the sealing wax and into my wife's sex, impressing my brand, a proud lion's head, forever into her vulva.'"

Terzo looked at the kids, who were astonished by the lecture, so different from all the rest. He noticed that even Emma, leaning in the doorway, was listening, with Dr. Pantera at her side. "The court soothsayer, Aristandros, was summoned. Bowing deferentially to Philip, Aristandros predicted: 'The seal, Your Highness, is your sperm. You branded it into the flesh of the queen, and now she is pregnant. A boy with the bravery of a lion shall be born.' Having spoken, Aristandros left the royal palace and fled into a nearby wood sacred to Dionysus. But Olympia was unsatisfied; her dream had not been interpreted. And so she waited for night to fall, and then ordered Melissa, her lady-in-waiting, to send again for the soothsayer. By way of secret passages used to bring in lovers and spies under cover of darkness, Aristandros returned to the royal palace. His head bowed, his hair and beard white, the old man asked: 'Why have you summoned me, my queen?'

"'Why did you say nothing of my dream today, old man?'

"'Because I was so commanded by the god.'

"'And what did the god tell you?'

"'To answer the king. The king asked me to interpret a man's dream, and I answered him. He did not ask me about women. Nor about gods.'

"'What do you mean?' Olympia insisted, impatient.

"'I mean what I said. May I go now?'

"'No, you may not, not until you have told me what destiny is concealed in my dream. Ask the god to speak of the dream of a woman. And of gods.'

"'The god has already spoken to me, and ordered me to answer you, but only if you dared to question me in person. You dreamed the night before the marriage, Philip the night after. The lightning that struck you is Father Zeus. Your maidenhead was consumed in his amorous orgasm. You were already pregnant on your wedding day. The child you bear in your womb is not Philip's, but comes from the hallowed loins of Zeus.'"

Terzo had slipped into that teacherly trance from which he could not be roused until the end of the lecture: "We cannot even conceive today of what Alexander the Great—a man, not a hero of Homeric mythology—managed to achieve in his lifetime. Caesar, Attila, Genghis Khan, and Napoleon always acted from the center of their political power, making forays into Britain, Europe, Asia, Africa. Alexander, however, between twenty-two and twenty-three years of age, controlled Macedonia and Greece, the then known world, and dominated the legendary Africa of the pyramids and Asia as well, Cappadocia, Mesopotamia, Armenia, vast Babylonia, the invincible land of the Parthian archers, all the way to India. Had it been up to him, he would have gone all the way to China and Japan. He was not only a commander. No, he would take the field himself, sword in hand, riding his stallion Bucephalus, his battle steed for twenty years. Imagine General Eisenhower, commanding the Allied invasion of Normandy, stepping off the first assault craft and into the blazing inferno of Omaha Beach. Or Churchill parachuting over el-Alamein. That's the kind of leader Alexander the Great was. He designed a global strategy, led his army through unknown worlds, and risked his life, in the attack, like a common foot soldier. At the battle of the Granicus River, for example, in 334 B.C., he breaks his lance. As he asks for another, Mithridates, son-in-law of Darius, is bearing down on him. Alexander digs his spurs into his horse, sidesteps, and strikes Mithridates on the face with the stub of his lance. Resax, another Persian noble, draws near, swings the ax with the silver handle and strikes the Macedonian king on the helmet. The metal bends amid sparks, blood, and locks of blond hair, and Alexander falls to the ground. Backing up and kicking, the beast saves its master. Stunned and blinded with blood, Alexander thrusts his lance forward, at random. And he impales Resax. Without his guide, however, the horse changes direction, sidestepping toward the enemy. Spithridates, one of the bravest Persian warriors, sees him and moves away from the front line. He wants the highest honor, that of striking down Alexander the Great. He lets the black Bucephalus run past him and attacks from behind. Without hesitating he goes straight for Alexander's naked neck. Clitus the Black, a Macedonian veteran, pulls up at a desperate gallop. Spithridates has waited too long to deal his blow. Clitus strikes with such fury that he severs the Persian's arm at the shoulder. The silver scimitar that was to have beheaded Alexander ends up under Bucephalus's hooves."

Some sharp noises, as of gunshots, rang out in the street, then screams and the rat-a-tat of a machine gun. Surprised, Colonel Terzo interrupted his monologue, opened the window, and scrutinized the garden.

"It's the kids, Colonel," explained Signora Astraco, appearing between her sheets, "they're playing cowboys and Indians, like in the American movies."

Terzo shook his head, closed the shutters, and resumed:

"Let's make a few things clear. First: there is no hero, in military history, braver than Alexander. Second: with the sole exception of Genghis Khan, nobody has conquered an empire of comparable size in one lifetime. The Mongol leader, however, limited himself to fighting on two continents, whereas Alexander invaded Europe, Asia, and Africa. Third: his military, tactical, and strategic decisions were always rational. Can we deduce, from all this, that Alexander was the ideal warrior, the model from whom we should, in our search for adventure and victory, draw inspiration? Not so fast. That's what Campari used to say when I pushed my argument a bit too far. But certainly the ancients idolized him. Gnaeus Pompeius considered himself Alexander's heir. Julius Caesar broke out in tears when he realized his deeds would never equal Alexander's. Emperor Augustus used to meditate over his tomb. Napoleon wrote: 'Only by studying Alexander does a general know war.' And he himself always considered himself the greatest. His mother convinced him he was the son of Zeus. And I repeat: the mysticism Alexander inherited from Olympia was the source of his great deeds. Before advancing into Asia to fight the Persians, Alexander made two stops. First at Troy, to pray at the foot of the fortress besieged by his ancestor Achilles. On the altar of a temple there, he found a breastplate sacred to the Achaeans. He stole

it and used to show it to his troops before each battle, like a
relic.

"Then he lands in Egypt and stops at the Siwah oasis, at the
sanctuary of the god Ammon, the most revered in Africa. He
asks the oracle his destiny. Imagine the scene: desert, palm trees,
temples, the high priest of a religion already a thousand years
old, receiving the young warrior. I have always believed the
meeting was planned beforehand, as military propaganda. But
to the Macedonian warriors setting off on a campaign beyond
the confines of the known world, it must have seemed a miracle.
The high priest shook the tabernacle of prophecy and invoked
Alexander as 'Son of Zeus Ammon.' The gods of Olympus and
the gods of the Pyramids were incarnate in their heir. Alexander, son of Zeus and Ammon, from that point forward fought as
if he were immortal. I've told you about the injury sustained at
the Granicus; but Alexander was wounded eight times in all, in
battle and in hand-to-hand combat.

"When, war-weary and homesick, his veterans incited one
another to mutiny with the cry, 'Let's go home!' Alexander tore
off his tunic, shouting, 'There's not one part of me that isn't covered with scars. There is no weapon, lance, arrow, ax, or catapult
that hasn't opened my flesh.' And it was true. At the Granicus, at
Issus, in the sieges of Tyre and Gaza, under a city's walls and in
the open field, Alexander fought as if he weren't mortal. No
chronicler—not Arrian, not Curtius Rufus, not Plutarch or
Diodorus Siculus—ever mentions a single moment of fear in
him. But the army's refusal to follow him beyond the Hyphasis
River, which was too far from Macedonia and too close to the
unknown ocean, broke Alexander's spirit. At Chaeronea, when
only sixteen, he had defeated the veterans of the Sacred Theban
Battalion. He had humiliated the fierce mountain-dwelling
Thracians and Celts with ruthless guerrilla warfare. In the attack
against the Trojans at the Wolf's Pass, he clambered along unassailable mountain trails and learned that in war you can surprise

your enemy by taking the hard path. He defeated the Greek mercenaries at the Granicus, bested Darius twice, at Issus and again at Gaugamela, and finally vanquished the Indians of King Porus. To say nothing of the sieges. Write this down, Dragonara, twenty sieges: Thebes, Halicarnassus, Tyre, Gaza, and the cities of India, always without fear. And yet for every enemy over-come, another one appeared before him, still more mysterious and elusive. He vanquished them all, but he could not ford the Hyphasis River and bathe in the ocean because his obsession had exhausted the soldiers. The great Alexander was defeated only by his chimera: to fight, each day, a new, invisible enemy."

The crackle of gunfire from the street became denser, and Terzo waved his hand as if to silence it. "On the way back a hor-ribly tired Alexander watched his soldiers besiege the fortress of Multan, in India, in 325. They fought with catapults and arrows, but wearily, without commitment, just trying to save their own skins. Only the gods know what ocean of disillusion and nostal-gia was engulfing the general who had conquered the world. Without waiting for his officers, without asking the foot soldiers to cover him, Alexander climbed the walls of Multan, alone. Just like that: he propped a ladder against the defense wall, raced up it and attacked the formidable Indians of the Malli tribe with his sword. Peucestas, the lieutenant charged with watching over the sacred armor stolen from Troy, tried to rescue his comman-der. Too many foolhardy soldiers followed suit: the wooden lad-der gave way and flew to pieces. Left without companions, Alexander hurled himself from the wall and into the enemy city, fighting off arrows and swords as best he could with his shield, and by making a screen from the branches of a fig tree. The Indians surrounded him. That demon with gleaming steel helmet, plumes cut off, sword covered with blood to the golden hilt, meted out blows and picked up rocks that he launched with the same ardor as the urchins firing at the tightrope walker at the station. Surprised, the defenders withdrew to the shelter of an arcade; from there they hurled rocks at him, trying to stone him to death, shouting, 'He's a ghost!' Finally, scaling down the wall onto a heap of dead, three Macedonians arrived. One was immediately run through by an arrow. Another shaft struck Alexander in the chest, puncturing his lung. The blood gushed out mixed with air bubbles—a *sucking wound,* as you Americans call it—a hopeless injury. Alexander kept on fighting, until the hemorrhage bent his knees. In the fray, the surviving Macedonians managed to carry him on his shield and hurl themselves over the enclosure wall, taking shelter in friendly hands. To remove the arrow from his ribs, the surgeon enlarged the wound with a razor. The blood gushed out; Alexander was now fighting for his life. By some miracle he survived; but he would never recover. Walking and riding became a torment for him: he was an invalid soldier. None of his veterans, however, would ever know. Stoically, he bore the pain in silence, saving face, saluting the troops on parade from his tribune; he attended the banquets, followed the work of the council, pressing his chest with his hand. What lesson, Dragonara, can be drawn from the episode at Multan? Don't forget: after having pursued his enemies to the far ends of the earth, Alexander was forced to turn back because his soldiers didn't want to fight anymore. In defiance of all military logic, he leaped into the besieged city, attacking his enemies by himself. Why?"

"Because he wanted to commit suicide."

Terzo looked up. After twenty years of teaching, for the first time, somebody gave the right answer. But it wasn't Salvatore's voice he'd heard. It was Dr. Pantera, spent cigarette butt between his fingers. "It's obvious," the doctor went on. "Alexander's mother had convinced him he was not Philip's son, but the child of Zeus. Being in love with his mother Olympia, he traveled the world seeking a father to strike down, seeing him in the thousand enemies he encountered. When, because of his soldiers' desertion, he could no longer search for him beyond every

frontier, he sought death in the siege of . . . that Asian city, whatever it's called . . ."

"Multan, Doctor, Multan—at least that's what the English
call it. You're right, in any case. Write that down, Dragonara.
Historians believe that Alexander hired an assassin to kill
Philip. He feared being disinherited, if his mother were repudi-
ated. A parricide, therefore, in league with his mother. Olympia
would have the infant son of Philip's second wife strangled
when still suckling at his mother's breast. So much for Clausewitz, friends: Alexander's strategy can only be understood
through Greek tragedy, *Oedipus Rex,* myth, religion. That
would have been a bit much to expect of poor Darius. Having
won all the battles, having found the limits of his life at the ac-
cursed river Hyphasis, which the troops refused to cross, having
returned at the head of a vast empire that to him was narrower
than a cell, Alexander, stabbed with each breath by the pain of
his wounds, underwent a change of character. His fellow soldiers no longer recognized him. Finally, during a banquet in the
imperial tent, Clitus, the cavalry commander who had saved his
life at the Granicus, disgusted by the Oriental rites that Alexander, like a satrap, now imposed on his courtiers, told him brutally to his face: 'I didn't save you to see you become a caricature
of an effeminate Persian, all scented with unguents and covered
with silks and brocades. We didn't defeat Darius only to ape
him.' Offended by the truth, drunk with wine, Alexander seized
the lance of one of his guards and ran through the friend to
whom he owed his life. For the next three days, he wept and
fasted in his tent, wailing, 'I am the lowest of men,' sobbing,
'Clitus's sister was my wet nurse.' What do you think, Doctor?"

"I'm sorry a certain client of mine, an expert on Freud, can't
be here to hear you. First Alexander the Great kills his father,
then the man who had saved his life, brother of his wet nurse. In
every war, this same young man seeks to avenge himself on his
parents. He hated them, not Darius."

"That's stretching it a bit, Doctor. We are now certain that Alexander never once demonstrated any fear. That no general ever took the risks he did, battered, bruised, run through, wounded and lacerated no less than eight times." Terzo looked around as the shots in the street grew still more intense. "Why was Alexander not afraid? Because the mystical Olympia had convinced him that the immortal son of Zeus and Ammon could never feel fear? Well, on the day of the battle of Gaugamela, as the dawn shed its light on Darius's magnificent front line, superior in length and power, Alexander was called upon to sacrifice victims in the propitiary rite. 'To which god shall we devote the offering?' asked the priests. Alexander, who had cut the Gordian knot with the edge of his saber, did not hesitate: 'We shall sacrifice the victims to the goddess Fear.' To Fear, mind you, the goddess every soldier venerates, since every soldier is possessed by her. The goddess Fear, who torments, terrifies, and paralyzes, in war and in peace. Fear, who puts Darius to flight, making him abandon his wife, the most beautiful woman in all of Persia, and his loving daughters, leaving them the defenseless prey of the Macedonians. The goddess Fear, who deprives us of reason, turning us into animals, like the goats, rams, and oxen terrified by the knives of the priests. Why did Alexander offer his sacrifice to Fear? Was he not a fearless commander?"

"The other soldiers sacrificed to Fear so that she might not blind them in the fray," said Emma. "Alexander, instead, invoked her in order to know her. He wanted her to turn his insides out with panic terror, to liberate him from the divine thunder that impregnated his mother, to free him from the heroic seal of his father. Possessed by the goddess Fear, Alexander would no longer be the scion of Achilles and Heracles, son of Zeus and Ammon. He would be a man again. Was Alexander married?" she asked, in a calm tone, without doubts.

"Yes, but we do not know if he was ever in love, either with a man or a woman." In his fervor, Terzo had forgotten all modesty and spoken of homosexuality in front of Fiore Mastema.

"Alexander prayed to Fear because he wanted her to possess him, to vanquish him, to soften and weaken him till he was fragile as a girl, timid as a maiden," Emma continued. "Hadn't Achilles himself dressed up as a girl to flee from the Trojan War? Alexander prays that he might become one of us. No longer a great general, but a living, trembling person, capable of feeling emotion when the blood of children reddens the sewers of Thebes."

Colonel Carlo Terzo understood that decisive detail for the first time. The lecture on the mystical strategy of Alexander the Great was his showstopper, but it had been missing this one detail. *That* was why Napoleon and Hitler, and all those who wanted to remake themselves in Alexander's image, had covered the continents with corpses. Because, not knowing fear, forsaken by that terrible, moderating goddess, they didn't hear the cries of their victims, didn't see the horrors of their own actions. No longer experiencing fear themselves, they sowed it everywhere.

"And so?" he asked Emma, unsure, as if he were the student.

"When Darius ran away in terror at Gaugamela, Alexander sensed that his fate was sealed. He would never be afraid; he would have to go forward forever, toward new enemies, new frontiers. But when Fear descended on his soldiers and made them withdraw at the Hyphasis River, it was all over for Alexander. He was not looking for death at Multan; I disagree with you, Doctor. He was looking for fear, in the paroxysm of a war waged by him alone, against an entire army. He didn't find it, and had to content himself with that. He would die sterile, never having known love or terror. He was not a god, but neither was he a man," the princess concluded.

"I, ladies and gentlemen," said Terzo, standing up and carefully enunciating each word, "I believe that classical strategy, such as it is taught in the military academies, signifies nothing and explains nothing. Today we can easily see why, after the atomic bombs of Hiroshima and Nagasaki, it has become sheer folly to speak of artfulness and culture in war." Pilgrim Gawain had taken a cigarette from the doctor's pack and lit it, puffing hard. "But, as in the case of Alexander, we can also see why we have such difficulty grasping the symbolism that drives one man to conquer and another to flee. Alexander the Great, to whom the goddess Fear never granted an audience, never knew hesitation. His thoughts were always clear, his boldness was limitless, his victories overwhelming. When he died of a fever in Babylonia, on June 13, 323 B.C., his empire dissolved in an instant. He had broken up the Persian empire without building anything in its place. His conquest was empty, his power meaningless. He did not fight to change life, his own or that of others. He was driven by a longing to prove himself different from others, better, more powerful, less fragile, less ridiculous. What drove the Germans, and us, their allies, to destroy the peace of Europe? The same mania for control. This, then, is what the new art should be: winning by absorbing the point of view of the enemy, and never forgetting fear. The new strategy of life cannot begin with Alexander. Where it should begin I have no idea; but I do know it cannot begin with the strategy on which I have spent most of my years. Perhaps Fiore is right, that one cannot in the end deduce, from the battles in my *Manual*, how to live and how to fight. Amedeo Campari would have an alternative answer. I don't, and I am sorry. Thank you."

Colonel Terzo sat back down, covering his face with his hands in exhaustion. Fiore slipped into the kitchen, then put something in front of him. "Surprise!" Terzo opened his eyes and saw a medieval knight, with lance in its rest, silver-studded plumes, shining breastplate and shield with the royal eagle, intent on subduing his frisky horse. "It's for you. Today is All Souls' Day, Colonel, and the custom here is to leave these knights of sugar and marzipan around the house for the children to find." Fiore placed a multicolored tray before him, full of little bananas, strawberries, cherries with green leaves, prickly pears, and shiny tangerines. A gift from the hereafter, like the pomegranate seeds Hades gave Persephone.

"Thank you," said the colonel, admiring his sweet warrior and the colored fruit. "But why on All Souls' Day?"

"Because in this city, Colonel, it's the souls of the dead who bring presents to the children. There are no stockings for Epiphany or Christmas trees. We go to the cemetery to ask the dead for toys. Can't you hear them shooting?" Fiore opened the French doors and they all went out into the garden. The turtles were enjoying the city's somnolence, but in the street the little children were killing one another in a bloodless war with Winchester rifles, Colt revolvers, and Sioux bows and arrows, gifts from the dead.

"Strange city indeed, eh, Gawain? Gifts from the dead!" Terzo joked, concerned that the discussion might upset Emma.

But the princess was happy with the lecture and the oddity of All Souls' Day, which they called the Day of the Dead. Dr. Pantera had brought some soft rolls and stayed for lunch. "They should be stuffed with oil and anchovies. They're eaten in memory of the Manes, the spirits of those who are no longer with us."

After the ritual repast, Fiore and Salvatore had to go home. Gawain said: "I'm going to walk around a bit. Maybe I can get an article out of the souls who deliver marzipan in the night."

"*Pasta reale* we call it," said the monarchist Dr. Pantera, "the paste of the king."

It had been a fine day, one of the last. And it would have been so to the end if, shortly after lunch, Gawain had not come home with a black eye, chest covered with bruises, labored breathing, and shirt all torn. The beating made him forget his Italian. He spoke to Terzo in English: "I went to the Botanical Gardens. When I came out, by the lions' cage of Villa Giulia, three hoods came up to me, knocked me down, and started punching and kicking me."

"Have you still got your wallet?" asked Terzo. There were thieves circulating in the city who would strip their victims of everything, money, bicycle, clothes, leaving them naked, at night, and trembling in fear of the bands of stray dogs.

Gawain touched his ruined jacket: "It's still there."

"Watch?"

"Right here. Under the hail of blows I didn't grasp much of what was going on. They were speaking in dialect. One of them said: 'The girl . . . ,' yes, 'she's not yours . . .' But I don't have a girlfriend. Ouch . . ." Gawain protested, as Pantera applied disinfectant to his cheek.

"Do you want to report them to the police?" asked Terzo.

"Perhaps it's better to wait," Emma interrupted. She opened the doors to the balcony and then immediately closed them again. It was cold, and those sweet fruits had given her nausea. "It's better to wait," she repeated distractedly. She felt overcome by fear. She put the marzipan sweets on the sideboard, letting the sunlight from the garden shine on them. *I hope it's not too late to make votive offerings,* she thought.

DEAR COLONEL TERZO,

I hope this letter reaches you, since the mail is a little strange these days. I also hope you are well, and your wife and our young friends are, too. The demonstration went well, but things are still difficult. A few landowners have given in, and now Comrade Gullo is preparing a law that should be favorable to the laborers. But there is discontent here in Petranova. Not far from us, at Malpasso, they have declared an Autonomous Sicilian Republic, as the populations of Comiso and Ragusa did two years ago with the "We Won't Go" movement. That is, the boys no longer wanted to go do military service because for them, they said, the war was over, after so much suffering, and that's why they called it "We Won't Go." The towns were forming a republic, and they didn't want to wage war for Italy. The Party and the union were against it, and after 1944, the worst seemed over. But now we have this renewed attempt. I understand the rebels, because life for them is not very good, between the postwar situation and the landowners. But the right path is the struggle for land and unity. Whereas at Malpasso they have raised their own flag and declared themselves independent. I have written to the Party to ask what we should do, since at Malpasso there are only kids and women and old people, because the men were with the Division the Germans massacred on September 8. They want freedom, but I, and Luca Moliterni, a schoolmaster here from Turin for work and a member of the Party, who is helping me write this letter, we think those good kids are mistaken, and I hope they don't end up dead or in jail. However, I am writing you for a more pleasant reason, to invite you, your wife, and your young friends to come visit us out here for the feast of Santa Lucia on December 13. We're going to make *cuccìa*, a cake of blancmange and wheat. Master Luca tells me it's a sacred cake, ancient as Demeter, goddess of the harvest and of Sicily. The spike of grain is the symbol of the peasants, and for this reason the Malpasso peasants have put it on their flag (as a symbol of Sicily, that is, because we don't support their struggle). Aside from the *cuccìa* we want you to taste our quince jam and mustard, which is made in fact from grape must and ash (but it's good). If it's not asking too much, could you please remind Comrade Dragonara to stop by the Regional Federation office in Palermo and see if there's a response for us, and if there is, to bring us the letter so we can spare ourselves the surprises of the postal service? If you do come, we'll meet in the square, I'll be waiting for you there with Master Moliterni. You can get there by bus or train, but if you come by car, please travel by day, because at night there are bandits who prey on travelers, and if they find a comrade among them, they certainly won't let it slide. There's one gang that operates around Malpasso, in the pay of the monarchists. A few weeks ago Comrade Matteo Riga was murdered, and I and Master Moliterni think it was the gang that killed him. Their leader is a young man with a white scarf around his neck, a spy or mafioso. His name is Angelo but he goes by the nickname of Famine, because he's skinny as a snake. So it would be better if you traveled by day.

Affectionately and respectfully yours, Villa and Master Moliterni.

Colonel Carlo Terzo read the letter, distracted by his many troubles. Dr. Pantera had been very clear: "The princess will not live long into the new year. Stay close to her. I will not let her suffer, I promise. Her heart is strong. As for the rest of her . . . well, you can see for yourself." Emma was all skin and bones. At night, when the effect of the doctor's yellow medicine wore off, she would moan. It was a thin wail she let out, a barely perceptible whimper of pain, as she stretched her legs under the sheets.

Terzo would remain motionless to avoid disturbing her, unsure whether or not to offer help. And he would remember, incongruously, the time when she had first wanted to make love. For months after the wedding, they hadn't even slept in the same room. Nor had it occurred to the colonel that marrying that beautiful woman meant he had the right to possess her. He lived under the illusion that Emma needed him and that it was already an honor, for a loser of his caliber, to have her by his side. On the eve of their first anniversary, it was she who had entered his room, covered his eyes with kisses, silenced his questions with her fingers, and let herself be possessed. Emma noticed his inexperience, his desire to let himself go in the excitement, his embarrassment, his holding back in shame. She didn't say a word. She climbed on top of him, draping the sheet like a cape over her naked body and grazing his chest with her small round breasts. Terzo became immediately aroused, to the point of orgasm. His eyes half shut, his head buzzing with pleasure, he whispered, "Forgive me, I'm not very good. It's my first time. I'm sorry." Emma calmed him as if he were a sobbing newborn: "Shhhh . . . don't talk . . . shhhh . . . it was beautiful." Hiding his face in her hair, she let him fall asleep. But in the middle of the night, she woke him up again, poking her sharp knees into his back. She seized him and kissed him, plunging her tongue into his mouth, wanting to be taken at once, and again and again, until dawn, spurring him on with whorish incitements until she finally climaxed, screaming raucously and scandalizing the neighbors. Then she pulled the sheet between her storklike legs and fell asleep. Terzo watched over her as if she were a little girl. And she really did look like a little girl, naked, with her ash-blond hair, her Cossack face, her cherry-nippled breasts. Their love continued in this fashion. Long periods of abstinence, then nights in which Emma alternated between sweetness and passion. Now the pain of her illness made her whimper as she once did in pleasure, and in Terzo's mind sorrow mingled with nostalgia. He was once again watching over the sleep of his child-wife, until the late autumn dawn finally invaded the bedroom.

The colonel hadn't the least intention of going to Villa's place, given, among other things, the difficult situation he had described in his letter. Emma, however, said: "That Villa's such a dear. We must go. Even if it's the last thing I ever do."

Why, thought Terzo as he prepared notes for his forthcoming lesson, was Emma so attached to that man? She had seen him only once, on that strange morning of the bombed-out house, the demonstration, and the kite of wishes. But she wrote to him, and he wrote back. She, of all people, who had had to flee the Communists. Who knows? Had she been struck by the simplicity of the man, shepherd of some sort of political Arcadia where a tired lady will let herself be spun round in one's arms and away, up the stairs? Perhaps. Emma herself had no doubts: "Do you remember," she asked her husband, who was stung by a pang of jealousy, "with what mastery he cut the bamboo reeds to repair the kite? Villa's a true gentleman. We must go. We'll have to find a car, however. I don't think it would be a good idea to go by train."

Gawain leaped up. "By car? On those roads? Not on your life. Listen. I know an American pilot—don't ask me what he does for a living because I don't know and don't want to know, but we used to work together in the States and we've remained friends. He flies to Catania twice a week in his plane, a Caproni 133, war surplus. He showed it to me once: wooden benches for seats, not very fancy, but he's here in two hours and then leaves the same evening. He's already asked me once if I want to see Mount Etna, which I really don't care much about, I've had enough of explosions to want to see a volcano. But the Republic of Malpasso is something else; I should get a good article out of that, don't you think? We'll ask him to give us a ride: round trip, in a single day."

To Terzo, flying into an area crawling with guerrillas seemed like madness. He would call Dr. Pantera and ask him to forbid it. But as soon as he lifted the heavy black Bakelite receiver, Emma called to him: "Do you think Pantera can stop me? Do you consider me already finished? I'm not dead yet, darling." And the colonel had to accept it.

Gawain invited Salvatore to come along, and Terzo told him: "At least you'll get to see the battlefields on the slopes of Etna where the German General Hube stopped Montgomery's Allied forces in 1943." The boy dropped in at the Federation office to ask for directives for Villa regarding Malpasso and tried to console Fiore: getting the duchess's permission for such an excursion was impossible. Gawain borrowed a Jeep and assured everyone he was a brilliant chauffeur, showing Emma and the more skeptical Terzo an army driver's license bedecked with bright official stamps.

Despite Terzo's doubts and the excluded Fiore's long face, the imminent excursion created a good mood. It was therefore with disappointment that, on the eve of the expedition, the colonel received a note from Duchess Mastema that said: "I must see you at the palazzo at once; I have something urgent to tell you," followed by the bombastic signature and the ducal seal.

"Are you going to go?" asked Emma.

"The tone makes me want to write her back and say: 'Dear Duchess, since I left the army I no longer take orders.' But with this whole business we've created here, it's probably better not to take any chances." He looked at his wife, fearing she might feel he was reproaching her, then corrected himself: "You know how I am; I'm not very good at deceptions."

Emma looked back at him: "I don't like that witch. I've heard too many stories about her. Are you afraid of her?"

"Afraid? Of that stuffed shirt?"

Emma didn't reply and gave him a hug. Signora Astraco, leaning out her window and speaking in a low voice, had told her a few things about the duchess: "Haven't you seen her name in the papers? She's a big cheese in the party that opposes agrarian reform. Cosma the barber knows everything about her." Cosma, honored to have Princess Emma stop by his shop, had given her his customary scented calendar, "View of Trinacria," as a gift, and said, with an air of importance: "The opposition press claims that Duchess Mastema finances the bandits, those half-guerrillas, half-highwaymen. She hates unionists, labor associations, and Communists." Cosma lowered his voice as if to reveal a secret: "Have you heard the story about the whipping?"

"No," replied Emma, as the young men on the street smiled at the sight of such an elegant woman chatting with the white-coated barber.

"When she was young she once whipped a disrespectful laborer in the face. At the inn, the poor bastard's friends teased him about it, and in his pride he said, 'I'll run into that noble whore some night'—pardon my language—'and then . . .' The usual toadies reported the threat to the Circolo dei Nobili; the duchess played dumb, as if she didn't notice the peasants spitting on the ground when she passed on her mare. Then one day the laborer disappeared together with his fifteen-year-old son; they were both found at the bottom of a well. The magistrate in charge of the case was a Neapolitan. He listened, investigated, spoke with the parish priest, questioned the victims' relatives alone, without even the court clerk being present. Then he summoned the duchess herself to appear in court, creating a scandal that required the intervention of the archbishop. He accused her outright. But it was useless. Under pressure from Niccolò Fides, the duchess's uncle, the Neapolitan was forced to close the case. But since he was a man of honor and convinced that it was Mastema's thugs who'd killed those poor peasants, he requested a transfer and ruined his liver ruminating over the injustice. Duchess Mastema came to live in Palermo and now oversees her domain from here. How a woman like that ever gave birth to a lovable girl like Fiore, nobody can figure out," Cosma concluded.

"Do you really have to go?" Emma asked her husband again.

Terzo did not have a sixth sense. "Yes," he replied, "but I'll be right back." And he was off. The appointment was for three o'clock. It got dark early those late autumn days, and on this day the sky was particularly dark, and of such a charged and lowly color that Terzo decided to label it Gunpowder in his classification system. It hadn't started raining yet, but it was hard to see; the clouds rumbled in the wind, and the few people out walking hurried their steps, staying close to walls in anticipation of the storm. The streetlights shone dim. It was no time to be out on the streets in the dark.

The main entrance of Palazzo di Mare had a double door that rose to the level of the first floor. Through a glass peephole, a toothless old lady eyed the passersby, pouring lentils onto a plate and rummaging through them with her fingers to remove the pebbles and bits of dirt before pouring out some more. She gestured to the colonel that the duchess was waiting for him, then continued her sorting.

The stairway was cold and open onto the courtyard. Now some thunder could be heard, around the Addaura district and Mount Pellegrino. At the end of the last flight of stairs was a gate, left ajar. Terzo felt a shiver: *I ought to have worn an overcoat,* he thought. *It gets cold in the South, too.* He passed along a long, empty corridor, directing himself toward a light, but it turned out to be a votive candle under an icon of a monk. He took a few more steps and called out: "May I come in?" No answer. *They could have sent someone to meet me,* he thought. Fed up with this reception, he decided to leave. At that moment, from the back of the dark hall, the voice of Duchess Mastema rang out: "Over here."

It came from a small wood-paneled study, a dark, damp room.

The skylight was already casting shadows on that gloomy day. The duchess was working, occasionally leaning her head forward to see better. A nearly spent ember was the only source of heat in the room.

"Everything all right, Colonel?" she said, without greeting him.

"Of course. And you?" replied Terzo. Always polite, the colonel was surprised by her discourteous manner.

"One does what one can, what with the disrespect for the Crown and the riffraff in the street. Do you read the newspapers?"

That made two, with Salvatore Dragonara: "I study the history of war. Ancient texts."

"You're wise to do so. Better to take refuge in the past when the rabble knew their place and the nobles ruled for the common good."

"There were peasant wars in the Middle Ages, too. And Spartacus led an army of slaves against the Romans. Today's demonstrations are strolls in the park by comparison." Terzo surprised himself by talking in this manner, and a smile came to his lips. Was it because of his pupils' ideas or the antipathy he felt toward the duchess?

"I wanted to talk to you about Fiore," said the lady of the house, looking up from her documents.

"With pleasure," Terzo replied. "Shall I remain standing, or may I sit down?"

"Do sit down. The only people I ever receive are tax collectors; I'm not used to having guests."

"You were saying about Fiore?" said Terzo, sitting down. His voice took on a particular military cadence he detested but which proved rather useful in life—a nuance in tone that a soldier might use with a sergeant, to let him know he was a boor, or a lieutenant with a captain, to say, "I know a thing or two more than you," or a colonel with a general, to send him to the devil, all within the bounds of a perfect respect for protocol. Terzo thus used a weapon that in a barracks sufficed to convey insult, derision, or censure. The duchess spoke only to nobles who were her social equals, or else gave orders to intimidated subordinates. She was surprised by the tone of a man who was nobody's boss but didn't serve anyone, either.

"How are the studies going?"

"Fiore is an intelligent girl. She's vivacious, spirited, full of *joie de vivre*."

"I asked you about her studies."

"And I am answering you. Nothing in her intellect or character should prevent her from excelling at school. Perhaps she doesn't like the nuns and should go to a public school, to the *liceo classico*. The girls' section of the Liceo Meli is supposed to be magnificent. It's right nearby——"

"The girls in our family have always received a religious education. The sisters tell me Fiore is no longer rebellious; she seems happy, at peace. She's nice with her friends and her teachers. She's often smiling, even when praying."

"The change is not owing to my private lessons. Maybe the girl has matured, maybe her talks with my wife cheer her up. My wife really understands people."

"I've heard about your wife," said the duchess, and her tone was not one of approval, "but something about my daughter worries me. Those smiles . . ."

"You're worried about her smiles?"

"Yes, I'm worried about her smiles. She's rebelling against the upbringing I've imposed on her, isn't she?"

Careful, Terzo told himself. "Signora, I accepted the task of giving Fiore private lessons because my wife asked me to. I refrain from passing judgment."

"Nothing has changed in Fiore's life, at least in appearance. So why is she happy? The only new thing has been the lessons at your house."

"It was you who requested them. If you think they're no longer necessary—" Terzo bluffed, but the duchess interrupted him with a wave of the hand:

"That's not the point. I am a widow . . ."

A widow. The word made a grim impression on Terzo. *And I,* he thought, *will soon be a widower, I'll wear black like the duchess and live in an untidy house. I'll turn yellow like her, with that sickly gleam in my eye . . .* He nodded, without speaking.

"I'm a widow, Colonel," the duchess repeated, as if sensing the unpleasant effect the word had on Terzo, "and Fiore's future is in my hands. I have no male children. If I marry her well, the family will, of course, lose the name, but not the estate, so long as the peasants don't usurp it. Fiore must behave in a manner befitting her station. Do you know Elena, her godmother?" The duchess spoke of her daughter and her estate with the same bookkeeping tone.

"My wife introduced her to me. They're old friends, from the days in Paris."

"Do you think she might have a bad influence on the girl?"

This was a strange question, coming from the duchess. She usually only asserted confirmed realities when she spoke, or else asked ambiguous questions, to take her interlocutor by surprise.

"I don't know Signora Elena very well," Terzo said, pronouncing his words very distinctly, "but if she's a friend of my wife she couldn't have a bad influence." *That's not a lie,* he thought: *the godmother and Emma influence the girl with nothing but the best intentions.* Despite the duchess's rancor, he simply could not feel guilty.

"You're a man of honor, Colonel, a military man. I have to go away for a few weeks. The rebels have occupied one of my estates, and that riffraff is calling it the Republic of Malpasso. They won't let the tax collectors onto the property, they won't pay the tithes, they've chased away the Marshal of the Carabinieri. What's more, the peasants of the nearby town are

threatening to steal my untilled land, as if it belonged to everybody. But now the soldiers are on their way and will put them in
their place, the way they did in Ragusa two years ago. And there
are also some local boys, thank God, who have maintained their
respect for authority. But I have to go there in person to assess
the damage, since all the men have taken to their heels," the
duchess concluded. Soldiers and estates were the cornerstones
she feared would be torn away by her daughter's smiles and the
peasants' revolt. She wanted an alliance with Terzo, in the name
of tradition. What answer would he give her?

It's true, the colonel thought, *that I've believed, even more than
she, that one can draw a timeless lesson from the past. Yet here I
am, hiding her daughter's sweetheart to please my wife, and I
don't know if it's right or not.*

He preferred to remain silent.

"On your word of honor as an officer of the king, tell me: Do
I have reason to suspect anything improper in my daughter's
conduct? Some illicit meetings with a young man, perhaps? If
you suspected anything of the sort you would tell me, wouldn't
you?"

Terzo would have liked to reply that to invoke honor, king,
and country for an innocent love was blasphemy. But he'd never
seen combat, never seen a man die, and it would have seemed
hypocritical for him to play the moralist. He who doesn't know
war is polite. In that usurer's study, he and the duchess were
equals: neither had the right to speak. It would, he thought, be
too complicated to explain the failure of her own life to a suspi-
cious mother, and so he remained silent.

The duchess continued: "If I found out Fiore was compromis-
ing the family name, I would know how to tame her."

In the dampness of that house and the shadowy atmosphere
of this meeting with a sinister interlocutrix trying to win his
solidarity, Terzo felt truly unhappy. He was tempted to speak
frankly with the duchess and tell her that times had changed,

the war had been lost, and young girls would now go about with their arms around their boyfriends just as in Paris and New York. We've got the atom bomb now, he wanted to say, how can you think of locking your daughter up in the house? Once again, however, he feared giving away the young lovers.

"Fiore is adorable," he said, "and you should be very proud of her. If I had a daughter, I would want her to be like Fiore." And he stopped there, because he was about to add: "And if I had a son, I would want him to be like Salvatore Dragonara, even though he prefers Baudelaire to the Battle of Lützen."

"Is there a foreigner staying in your house?" the duchess asked out of the blue.

"No," Terzo dryly replied. So that was it. And the beating Gawain had taken was not a pleasant thought.

"Are you certain?"

"Are you interrogating me?" Terzo answered in irritation, forgetting his prudence. "I've already told you. Do you trust me or not? If you want to cancel the lessons, please do so. They've been given as a token of friendship and can be halted whenever you like. I realize whom you're referring to. There's a young American, the brother of an officer who's a friend of mine, but he's not staying at our house. I'll answer for him. He's a serious young man, he fought in the war. And now I really must go. I am sure Fiore has told you my wife is very ill."

"Fiore and I do not speak much," Mastema confessed, and for the first time during their twilight conversation, there seemed to be a quaver of feeling in her voice. "I am sorry for your wife. If my husband had lived, Fiore might be different."

She did not offer to shake his hand, nor to see him out. She merely picked up her papers again. The colonel headed into the dark corridor. It did not seem possible that Fiore lived in that icy, enclosed world. He understood now why her godmother and Emma, cheerful, sunny women, were trying to pry the girl away from her mother, and he was happy to have been their accomplice. His visit to Palazzo di Mare dissipated the nagging uneasiness he had felt about the furtive meetings in his study. He had given the young lovers a little happiness, nothing more. Having arrived at the little monk with his votive lamp, the only feeble light in the hall, he turned around and walked back to the little room. Sticking his head inside the door, he said: "I'm new in town, and I thought perhaps you might help clear something up for me. That Mr. Gawain, the American we were just talking about, had a very bad experience. He was beaten up. He doesn't know anyone here, and they didn't rob him. What do you make of that?"

What Duchess Mastema made of that was not visible in the face that looked down at her papers. Her only comment was: "Tell him to mind his own business. And if he doesn't like it here, let him go back to America."

XIV

THE APPOINTMENT with Gawain's friend was at six o'clock in the morning, at Boccadifalco airport. When the alarm went off, Emma was already almost finished applying her cosmetics. She hadn't made herself up for a long time, and the lipstick and powder did her no good. In the yellow light of the lamp, she looked even paler than usual, the dark circles under her eyes more visible than ever. Still, Terzo was pleased to see her in front of a mirror; it meant she felt a little better. He made her coffee, and then they waited for Gawain to appear, looking out the window into the garden still in darkness. He arrived punctually, at fifteen minutes to five. They went to pick up Salvatore, whose mother made the sign of the cross and begged them: "Please be careful, God preserve you. An airplane!"

Gawain might have his army driver's license, but he still drove like a madman. Always placid and contemplative in manner, he let loose behind the wheel of the green military Jeep. He passed a truck, riding on two wheels along a soft dirt shoulder, did not respect a line of ancient, vegetable-laden carts on their way to market, and, spotting from afar a convoy of vehicles of the newly reconstituted Italian army, stepped on the accelerator, passing truck after truck, until he reached the head of the column. When he finally overtook the front car, he blared the horn like a child.

The colonel clung tightly to his strap. Salvatore was writing poetry in his notebook, scribbling the lines as best he could.

Emma seemed thrilled at the ride. "Do you always drive this way?" she asked their senseless guide.

"Even worse," Gawain replied, laughing in the wind. "During the war they used to say to me, 'If the wounded aren't already dead, you'll kill them yourself.' I was an ambulance driver, a conscientious objector and a pacifist. To show I was an idealist and not a coward, I would drive even when the bombs were falling, then tiptoe through minefields to save a few soldiers. I would find them broken in two, half dead, mutilated. Does it bother you to hear these things? No? You're a brave woman. War's a bitch, or better yet, a whore, a *puttana*, as you Italians say. We all curse war and call it a whore. But I say: What have whores got to do with it? They just do their job. You ever seen one tear people to shreds? No. Whores are just women. It's war that's disgusting. And since I was a brave kid—because when you're twenty years old you don't think you'll ever die, not even when a grenade explodes at your feet"—Gawain slammed on the brakes, the Jeep skidded, Terzo grabbed onto the seat, Salvatore did not look up from his notebook, and Emma gave a little cry of surprise—"and since, as I was saying, I was too stupid to realize that I might drop dead at any moment, I was promoted to triage. You don't know what triage is? On the front we couldn't save everyone, and so on the days of wholesale slaughter I had to decide which of the wounded to attend to immediately, which ones to send to the doctors for later care, which ones to give a shot of morphine and hope they could wait, and which ones were without hope, for whom the chaplain would have to suffice. I would write in chalk on their jackets, and when it was raining I would write it in blood on their foreheads.

"Some would let the officers through, or their friends, or their platoon companions. Sometimes the soldiers would scream at us because a particularly brave sergeant, a real friend, was wounded and we couldn't care for him." Gawain narrowly missed a blue bus, and the driver cursed in dialect. "Anyway, all

I could do was catalogue the wounded according to regulations. Seeing shoot-outs, mines, nose-diving airplanes every day, do you know what the infantrymen start to think? The infantry are all young because, believe me, nobody can send a foot soldier on the attack too many times, because he gets wise and stops taking chances. On the front line you have to use adolescents, young guys who are afraid to look bad. The kids arrive at the front thinking 'I'll never get injured, it's not possible, my mother loves me too much, my sister gave me this lucky necklace and Bobbie promised to go salmon-fishing with me in the rapids when I come home.' A foot soldier, when he's eighteen, has his memories—the leather football his father gave him, the job at the coffee shop, school, the church choir, the blessings of Father Dmitri. The others, yes, *they* can be shot, in the chest, the head, the arm, the leg, the stomach, but not him, not him, not with those memories."

Terzo was listening in fascination. For weeks, Gawain had said nothing about the war, and now, racing along in the car, he was unburdening himself, forgetting the secret torment that had made him ignore the colonel's questions. Stepping on the accelerator along that narrow road had made him relax: "In a few months that kid sees his friends fall, dead or wounded, or taken prisoner. In infantry, companies and batallions are remade in just a few weeks; yesterday's faces disappear. But then the rules change. No more 'I can't be shot.' Now it's 'I *won't* be shot if I'm careful.' The boy is no longer the first to jump out of the foxhole; he ducks for cover shamelessly at the whistle of the incoming bomb." In the excitement of his story, Gawain was talking half Italian, half English: "He's now a mature foot soldier. He thinks before obeying an order, faithfully follows the good officers but bides his time with the inexperienced ones and the blusterers. And then that boy notices that all the guys who came to the front with him, now veterans and experts, begin to fall, one by one. The boy who is loved by Bobbie and blessed by Father Dmitri, now all alone, makes one final rule for himself: 'If I don't get out of here, soon it'll be my turn.' I worship your husband and I listen to what he says because he makes me see military intelligence at work. But the only rule that counts is this one. Usually, shortly after understanding it, the boy is wounded or killed. I have seen him die a hundred times and every time he had the same face, every time he had the same rules written all over him, those eyes that said 'It won't happen to me,' or 'I'll make it if I'm careful,' and, at the end, those eyes of resignation, that said 'I knew it.' They're the eyes of a dead boy with all those things inside, Princess. It was too much, I was no longer right in the head, and still they made me go fight my pacifist's war somewhere else. In '41 I wouldn't have gone, I was an absolute pacifist. But this was 1943, and so I accepted."

"And where did you go, Gawain?" Terzo ventured to ask.

"Here we are," was all Gawain replied. He braked on the gravel of the small entrance road to the airport, and all confidences stopped with the speed of the car. He went back to being the old Gawain, polite and reserved. As they boarded the commandeered Caproni 133, Terzo noticed a black sedan, of the sort used for bishops or ministers, approaching the tail of the aircraft; the door opened, and as he was trying to find out if there were any other passengers, he entered the cabin and could no longer see outside.

The airplane had wooden seats, and all along the fuselage were hemp straps, where the spring-clips for backpacks and parachutes had once been inserted. The pilot, a small red-haired man wearing sunglasses despite the gloomy weather, rumbled onto the short runway of Boccadifalco, shouted "OK," and they flew off toward eastern Sicily. Terzo had been on an airplane a few times. Gawain asked Emma: "Is this your first flight?" and she just smiled at him. Gawain could see it was the smile of someone concealing things she doesn't want to tell, not even to those she loves, and he winked at her in understanding.

"But what are you doing?" Emma said to Salvatore, reproachfully. "You're flying through the air, where you can see the clouds, the sky, the snow-capped mountains all around you, and you only sit there bent over your poems? You're just not interested in anything else."

Salvatore was a polite boy, but this time he protested. "That's not true, Emma," he said—after the day of the kite the princess had asked him to use her Christian name—"I'm in love with Fiore. And I follow the colonel's lectures with a lot of interest. And I'm also involved in politics. As you know, I'm carrying Comrade Villa a letter from the Regional Federation about the Malpasso affair. Here it is." And Salvatore proudly pulled a grayish envelope out of the inside pocket of the blue jacket his mother had made him wear for the journey. In the same movement, a photo of Fiore fell out onto the seat, but he quickly picked it back up, dusted it off with the back of his hand, and religiously put the snapshot and the letter back in his pocket.

"He wouldn't have the time to enjoy the landscape anyway, Emma," said Terzo, "because we have a lesson scheduled for today. Santa Lucia or not, I made a commitment to your mother, dear Salvatore, and I intend to keep it. By spring you will be a serious candidate for the Military Academy, especially if you remember every now and then to do the bending and stretching exercises I prescribed for you. If on the other hand you prefer poetry and politics, that's your business. We're free, aren't we? Well, long live freedom!"

"I like it when you play the old-fashioned gentleman. Careful, though, or you'll end up like la Mastema," Emma teased him. She was worried, however: her husband had told her nothing of his conversation with the duchess.

The colonel continued, unfazed: "Today I will speak of oblique order in battle. We have already said what oblique order is: rather than confront the enemy in front lines that are parallel, like train tracks, one of the two strategists decides to turn his formation forty-five degrees, thus attacking the adversaries at only one point, usually on the right. If a breach is achieved, oblique order makes it possible to effect a quick encirclement. But careful, Salvatore, don't think of this as a mechanical maneuver. Using an oblique order in the open field flies in the face of the logic that would have you match each man with another man. You have to know how to take chances, how to be dialectical, mentally mobile." The plane hit an air pocket and the jolt distracted Terzo from his train of thought. But he had repeated and contemplated his lessons so many times that he could go on by rote, letting his mind wander. In such cases he could observe himself teaching, looking for cues, reasoning things out, contradicting himself.

"I've not been able to live in accordance with the principle of oblique order," he thought aloud, "I'm afraid of spontaneity, of naturalness, of living as one should, of confronting risks and hopes without caging myself in a strategy, without taking protective cover in my obsession with Hannibal and Clausewitz. The horror of battle would have swept away my theories; I would have had to reckon with myself, with fear and bravery. Alexander prayed that the goddess Fear might visit him once at least, to make him human. Well, I should sacrifice to the goddess Life, so that she might finally possess me, force me to choose, to think, count, and decide without letting myself be carried away by chance. Even Emma, who has made me so happy, just happened to me, without my deserving it. Had I had to say even one word to win her, I would not have been able to utter it. I know the rules of victory and defeat, not the reasons for fighting. Salvatore has no idea of how to fight. He doesn't know the difference between a defensive-offensive battle, as at Marathon, and a battle of annihilation, as at Cannae, and yet he is committed to the future. To poetry, to Fiore, to the peasants. He's a better strategist than I, because he has understood that strategy does not exist outside battle."

"That's not true, Colonel, you fight, too, when you try to explain life to us through your theories," replied Fiore. Terzo roused himself; he'd been distracted; perhaps the altitude, in the poorly pressurized cabin, had confused his thoughts and words. He'd been expressing his musings out loud. And here was another surprise. Fiore was smiling from the rear compartment, where the machine-gunner used to sit during raids. The colonel was not happy about this new development. First, he was irritated for having lost the thread while speaking to everyone. But then to see Fiore there, on their excursion, for whom he felt concern and to whom he had said yes only to help his wife—that was too much for an orderly man like him.

"What are you doing here?" he asked her.

The girl noticed the irritation, so unusual in the colonel's manner of speaking, and blushed. "Actually—"

"I arranged everything myself," Gawain laughed, also feeling embarrassed by Terzo's tone, "if the duchess gets angry tell her to take it up with me. In America we don't have noble titles and I won't give her the time of day. But don't worry. Even if we stay the night, Giles will take the plane back to Palermo before dinnertime, isn't that right?" The little pilot shifted his leather goggles for greater comfort and gave a thumbs-up. "You'll take her back to the palazzo in the Jeep, right?" And again the pilot raised his right thumb from the control stick to say "OK."

The colonel's face did not relax, and so Gawain took cover: "I told the princess."

"Is that true, Emma?" asked Terzo.

"Yes, and please don't be upset. I want to have a day of happiness. With an airplane, we can even do the impossible and come back from Catania in a few hours. When we left her at home, Fiore cried. The day of the kite had been so beautiful, I was sorry we couldn't be together one more time, we and Villa. It seemed impossible, I felt too sick, Fiore's life was too complicated. And yet, here we are, see? Isn't that just beautiful?"

Terzo thought again of the duchess's grim face, looked askance at Gawain and stroked his wife's cheek: "Beautiful, darling."

"Anyway, Colonel, Mama's going to be away for quite a few days. The help won't tell on me: I'm wise to too many of their thefts," Fiore said cheerfully.

Giles shouted: "Everybody look! On the left! Now!" Emma looked out her window: the crater of Mount Etna, which they were circling while waiting to land at the military airstrip, was spewing lava, ash, and white-hot rocks into the sky without interruption, while a red stream slithered toward Misterbianco. They couldn't hear the rumbles and explosions of the eruption below them, but in fact the spectacle was more impressive drowned out by the engine's monotonous roar. The lava spread downstream as tongues of fire rose in the air, only to lose strength and fall back into the dark of the woods.

While Fiore and Salvatore were admiring the view, Emma took Terzo's hand in her own and said: "Isn't it marvelous? We've given a bit of life as a gift. It's the only thing that makes me feel better: to give life, of which I have so little. Promise you won't be angry. I love you, Carlo. I love you and thank you." She passed her emaciated forefinger over his eyes and pointed it heavenward. As Giles was pulling up for the final landing maneuver, the moon had reappeared in the sky. The reflection of the sunrise and the glow of the volcano had turned it a dark red. "The day my ancestor Svyatoslav went off to the battle that you, Carlo, are unable to trace, it is said that a blood-red moon rose in the sky. Everyone saw it as a bad omen. Returning to the encampments, Svyatoslav confided to his squire: 'A soothsayer told me that I will fight under a red moon, and that I will win, but that before the moon sets, my life shall end. The price of victory,'" Emma whispered into her husband's ear.

Colonel Carlo Terzo looked at the red moon in the sky, frightened by its perfection, and said nothing.

THE BAND struck up a little march with brass and percussion, and a small girl dressed in white approached the ladder, holding out a bouquet of wildflowers to Emma. Villa had arranged things on a grand scale, greeting his friends with the municipal band, the elementary school chorus, and a procession that accompanied them all the way into town. Then, as if they were some sort of august delegation, he invited the crowd to applaud them one by one, as he called them to his side: "Colonel Terzo, his wife, who is from Russia, Comrade Dragonara . . ."

Terzo looked around without understanding, already checking his watch to make sure they wouldn't be late getting Fiore home. He wanted the plane to depart at five.

From the little square they moved on to the home of Master Moliterni. His wife, a young woman with raven-black hair held up in a complex system of pins, offered them a breakfast of milk fresh from the cow and barley coffee: "It's all we have, forgive us. But taste the homemade bread, it's excellent." Salvatore took Villa aside and, trembling with a sense of the importance of it all, handed him the envelope from the Federation. Villa turned it over to the schoolmaster, to let him read it. Moliterni was showing Emma his infant daughter and, honored with the task appointed him, left her in her mother's arms. Donning a pair of reading glasses, he opened the envelope and extracted two small pages, each bearing a blue stamp. Suddenly overcome with concern for political discretion, he looked at Villa, furtively motioning in the direction of the guests. Villa nodded to him and, reassured, the professor read:

Dear Comrade,
As I am certain you already know, many other Sicilian centers were previously involved in the 1944 revolt, declaring themselves "autonomous republics," refusing the draft and the harvest tax. Behind this protest against the draft—called "We Won't Go"—lies the real dissatisfaction of working masses disillusioned with Fascism and the war. However, the Party reminds you (and we have received precise instructions from Rome in this regard) that in no way are you to participate in actions or demonstrations of a subversive nature, and that the political activism of the Communists must always remain within the sphere of legality and respect for existing law. The negative experience of Comiso and Ragusa, where the "republics" were defeated and so much energy was wasted, confirms our position, in terms of avoiding useless bloodshed as well. We are, however, aware that many young men and many women are taking part in these revolts, driven by a justified desire for equality and social liberation. I therefore invite you to preserve contact with those elements you judge to be good for integrating into our Party, while discouraging them from taking part in armed actions. Our program remains that of winning autonomy for Sicily and returning land to the peasants through occupation of the estates.

Certain that you will correctly interpret these instructions of mine, I send you my warm regards,

Giuseppe Damasco, member of the Regional Secretariat

Villa was not thrilled with what he had just heard. He looked at Moliterni, hoping to see some dissent in his eyes, some doubt that might justify the restlessness he was feeling inside. Leading the occupation of the estates was Villa himself, who was an organizer, a spontaneous orator, and a brave soldier when the police attacked. But when he was confronted with a written text, the leadership passed to the schoolmaster. Villa sympathized with those boys who refused to return to military service, those women who set fire to the town halls and draft registries, demanding bread, peace, and work. He had an anarchist's heart, and a Communist membership card in his pocket, like so many peasants.

"What I appreciate about the Communists is their science of organization," he said. "Wherever there are two Communists, there is a Party section in the making. Organization is the only thing that can overcome centuries of aristocracy in the countryside. But I just can't help it, Luca: when I see the flag of Malpasso with its spikes of wheat, deep inside I have to applaud."

He put the letter in the pocket of his fustian jacket, thanked Salvatore for having brought it to him, and announced to Terzo: "My dear Colonel, there's been a change in plan, I hope you don't mind. You may have read in the newspapers about the Autonomous Republic of Malpasso that has been proclaimed at the border with Petranova. Well, I can't support it, as the letter also confirmed." Villa touched the pocket over his heart, as if to reassure himself he was on the right side. "We're fighting for agrarian reform and the end of the feudal estates. And the Mastema estate—yes, Fiore, your own mother's land—is right there between Petranova and the Malpasso Republic. Today we are going to occupy those untilled lands; we will claim them in the name of those who work the land and, again if you don't mind, we will ask Fiore to march at the head of the procession. When the Malpasso rebels come running to see us occupy the land— which they will certainly do, since I sent a town crier with a drum into the town to spread the news, and I intend to have our municipal orchestra at the front of the march—they will realize that ours is the proper line of conduct, and they will follow us. That way we will prevent the army, or the gangs of brigands, from attacking them and creating a massacre. The demonstration was planned for next Sunday, but the developments at Malpasso have forced me to speed things up. But there won't be any problems. It'll be a fine country outing for all of us."

Terzo was aghast. But before he could open his mouth, Emma intervened: "We'd love to come. But the girl will stay by my side; she won't march at the head of the procession. It's better this way. And don't forget: before nightfall, she has to be back at the airport, so she can get home in time for dinner. Do I have your word?"

Villa was a man of honor: "Even if it means carrying her in my arms," he joked.

They set off, followed by the band and the trail of laborers and their families. On their mules, protected from the cold by the traditional hooded cape that sloped down to cover both rider and mount, the peasants rode along the Dittaino River. The children ran ahead, sending flocks of crows flying, then sat down on the black rocks to wait for the adults to catch up. The union leaders, Villa and guests, went ahead, followed by Emma and Fiore on a little cart drawn by a mare whose reins were held by Moliterni. Then came the poorest laborers, wearing broken boots and military overcoats turned inside out: Terzo recognized Italian, German, American, and even a few English uniforms. Then came the women. The old ones would bend over now and then and, with a small billhook, gather bitter herbs for the evening's dinner. The married girls, happy to be going somewhere but ashamed of their broken shoes compared with Fiore's shiny pumps, wouldn't look the outsiders in the eyes. Alongside Emma's gig, there passed a blond young man wearing an altar boy's tunic. When Moliterni asked him: "What are you doing here, Pepe? Did Father Inguardì give you permission?" the boy seminarian, without answering, ran to join the others his own age. The dogs followed behind him, rolling around in the dust and accompanying the band with their yelps. The musicians knew only two political songs: "*Bandiera rossa*" and "The International," so they soon were striking up other numbers in their repertoire, such as "Rosamunda," "*O Sole mio*," and even the Fascist "*Tripoli, bel suol d'amore*," which after a dirty look from the schoolmaster was quickly changed to the "Hymn to Garibaldi": "*Si scopron le tombe e si levano i morti . . .*"

The light on Santa Lucia's day, eve of the winter solstice, cast short shadows. Colonel Carlo Terzo was tense, and Emma's pale smile was not enough to reassure him. Feigning interest, he asked Villa: "Where are we?"

"Etna's right behind us, Colonel. It's erupting, though we can't see it through the fog. Once the sun comes up you'll see the reflection. Over there are the rivers: the Dittaino, the Gornalunga, and the Simeto. We're almost there, don't worry, and we'll leave the fields right after the occupation. I have to get back to wire the Party and tell them everything's all right. Moliterni will take you by car; the Misterbianco branch lent us one for the occasion. In exchange I promised our band would play for them when they occupy their lands on the twenty-eighth. They say Li Causi's going to speak that day, but I don't believe it. Look, there's the Primosole Bridge . . ."

"Salvatore, Gawain, quick, come here . . ." shouted Terzo, forgetting his worries. "You, too, Fiore, and Emma, look, past the orange grove, you see? That's the Primosole Bridge. There, on July 13 and 14, 1943, the Germans of the Goering Panzerdivision fought the British Eighth Army of Marshal Montgomery, hero of the African desert. First the English paratroopers took the bridge; but then the Goering division, made up of elite airmen of the Luftwaffe, took it back during the night. On July 31, Montgomery tried to overcome the German resistance to the west of the volcano, near that grove of oak trees." Terzo pointed toward a dark thicket in the cold. "German reinforcements arrived, under the command of General Hube. The Goering and the Fifteenth Panzergrenadier gave the Allies fits. The Italians brought six infantry divisions without vehicles and four endowed with a few trucks and tanks under General Guzzoni. The

offensive came to a halt at the Primosole Bridge. Hitler sent reinforcements: the First Parachute and Twenty-Ninth Panzergrenadier divisions. The Allies made new landings on the
eighth, the eleventh and the fifteenth and sixteenth of August,
this time to the north of the volcano, to isolate the Germans
with bridgeheads. They entered Catania on August 5. The battle
of the Primosole bridge allowed Guzzoni to evacuate sixty
thousand Italians, while forty thousand Germans, including the
paratroopers of the First Division, crossed the straits of Messina
with ten thousand motor vehicles and tanks following behind.
The Allies would have to fight those same Germans, up and
down the Peninsula, for the next two years. The Italians' capacity for resistance, on the other hand, was spent. The Fascist government fell on July 25. This bridge, dear Salvatore, has an
important place in Italian history. Take a good look at it."

The procession had come to a stop. Mules and horses formed
a circle round the colonel, while the women crouched down on
broad pumice stones and the children gnawed on crusts of bread
in silence. Pepe the altar boy, paying close attention, had returned to Emma's side. The musicians in the band, having set
down their horns and drums, were passing cigarette butts back
and forth, the gray smoke condensing in the cold air. The last
circle of the audience was made up of laborers. They were all
listening to Terzo as if he were a street singer. An old man, a
scar on his forehead half-hidden by his woolen beret, said to the
colonel: "Down there, Colonel, a German is buried. I've got his
helmet. I asked the English if I could keep it and they said yes."
The altar boy also seemed to want to say something, but the
dogs started barking, the laborers started moving again, and the
semicircle around Terzo broke up.

Little by little—first three or four, then half a dozen, then finally a small crowd—armed guerrillas began to show up. There
were boys with regulation army pistols and old men with
Mausers or 91 carbines, a popular Italian rifle, on their shoul-

ders. Some were gripping the butts of Bren machine guns. The Second World War had heaped its wreckage onto that group: there were German *Maschinenpistole,* a pair of black Thompsons, a few American Winchesters. Those who hadn't managed to get their hands on a real weapon aimed for dramatic effect, wearing cartridge belts strapped across their chests, as in the movies. Others had large, curved knives dangling from their belts. Many had bandanas around their necks, embroidered with images of Trinacria, the symbol of Sicily, with the spikes of grain in her curls.

"We're from the Republic of Malpasso," said a tiny white-haired woman, wearing widow's weeds, from the neck of which protruded the tip of a white shirt. "Welcome, brothers and sisters of Petranova. The border of our Republic starts at the Primosole Bridge, runs along the river and mountain, down the slopes of Etna, from the Cave of Ashes to the Little Craters. The oak groves belong to us, but you are allowed to pass through and use the wood. We knew you would come, and we welcome you."

As if to punctuate the woman's words, one of the Malpasso guerrillas shot a short burst of machine-gun fire into the sky. The dogs took shelter between their owners' legs, yelping, but once the echoes of the shots had stopped, they began to bark in compensation. Villa was not pleased with that show of bravado. The letter in his pocket minced no words: "In no way are you to participate in actions of a subversive nature . . ." Without smiling, but courteously, the Petranova union leader replied: "I've heard about you, Donna Marena. I appreciate the spirit of your protest, even though we do not share any borders. We are Italians. Fascism is dead. We must rebuild the country and give the land to the peasants."

"And I have heard about you and the union," replied Donna Mareno. "Have no fear. There won't be any disputes between us. We are from Malpasso. They want our children to get back in uniform and we say no. If you want, I'll tell you where the best of the boys I brought into this world ended up: rotting in Russia, Germany, and Africa. I've been a midwife for forty years, and I've seen a lot of them. The United States of America is a country made up of many small countries, right? Well, we are Sicilians, and we are also Italians. I speak Italian, but we belong to the Republic of Malpasso: here we live, and here we'll die. Together." The young man with the machine gun wanted to repeat his noisy exclamation, but Donna Marena stopped him: "I don't think we should be wasting bullets to create confusion. Listen, Villa, could we talk for a minute, alone?"

Villa didn't quite know how to deal with the armed rebels of Malpasso. The letter was burning a hole in his breast pocket: "Preserve contact with those elements you judge to be good"— yes, but how? The legend of Donna Marena had been circulating in the area for months. One story told of an English paratrooper thrown onto a cluster of prickly pears by the scirocco before Donna Marena found him and hid him in her cellar. When a captain of the Goering division, drawn by suspicion, came to question her, she had a child-bearing woman spread out on the trap door, blood streaming down her legs. She shrewdly stood up to the German: "Would you like to help this child to be born, sir?" With the same firmness she was now leading the draft-dodgers of Malpasso. *Yes*, thought Villa, *we can talk, but there should be witnesses.* "Of course, Donna Marena," he said, "but let's not offend my guests."

Donna Marena looked at Terzo, then at the American Gawain. She didn't trust anyone, but this was no time to be fussy. Nearby was a ruined hut in which the laborers had lit a fire of dried branches, chewing their bread, olives, onions, and *ricotta salata* in silence. Donna Marena entered, and Villa introduced everyone, rubbing his hands in front of the fire. Pepe the altar boy and the young man with the machine gun brought in two saddles, which served as chairs for Donna Marena and Emma. To Fiore they passed an army blanket, which she transformed into a poncho and used to cover herself and Salvatore. Master Moliterni looked in from the doorway, a little jealous for not having been invited to this meeting of the General Staff.

"I tried to warn you, Villa, but they chased away my courier with shotgun blasts. You're here with your brass band, but the situation is very dangerous. I lied to you out there, to avoid spreading panic. Last night two squadrons of Italian soldiers surrounded the town on the Etna side. A coal stoker working the furnace ran into them and was told they want to come into town and arrest the armed rebels, plus the women leading the revolt. We wanted to flee to the mountains and then, little by little, go into hiding in nearby towns and bury the weapons. Between here and the bridge, however, down by the river, near the old flood troughs, bands of mafiosi, brigands, and tax enforcers have moved in. Duchess Mastema's people. She has lands in Malpasso and Petranova and is trying to get somebody killed; maybe she'll order her men to fire on the soldiers and then blame it on us. She's had our escape routes cut off. Every path is being guarded; not even a goat can get through. We were able to come in at night, circling by way of the Cave and the Brazier to the northeast. My people are tired, I can't make them march anymore. I'm not asking you to join us; I know how your Party sees things. We'll figure out some way to get through this. I'm only asking you to take the women and children with you; mix them up with your own people, then carry on with your demonstration. By sunset you'll be back in your town, and we will have saved these poor souls from the bullets. Only you can prevent a massacre."

The wind made the fire crackle loudly. A crow cawed as it flew over the hut's caved-in roof. Villa was thinking of the dangers surrounding Malpasso, and how he might help those people without disobeying the letter from the Federation. Fiore thought of her mother, whose name had stung her like the crack of a whip. *Everything I have,* she thought, *was paid for by her:*

*the clothes that all these women admired, school, everything. My
mother is arming the bandits.* Salvatore put his notebook back in
his pocket and held her hand under the blanket. For the rest of
his life, Colonel Terzo would remember his pupil this way: a
young poet, a diligent student of strategy, in love with his girl,
holding her tight under a blanket as everyone around spoke of
war, real war this time, while he consoled his beloved and remained calm. Emma had lost the pallor of her illness, her
cheeks now flaming red, and Terzo's anxiety faded. In the end,
he thought, things between the kids will turn out all right.
Elena, the godmother, will intervene; we'll work it out. If only
Emma could live: she alone has no power over her troubles.
Gawain offered a Camel to Donna Marena, who politely refused.

Villa took the American cigarette and lit it with a twig.
"Donna Marena," he said, "I respect you. My Party does not approve or support demonstrations of armed violence; in fact, it is
involved in a struggle against armed gangs of mafiosi and brigands. Our occupation of the land is open to the people and the
workers. I don't approve of violence; I repeat this so these witnesses may hear. The draft must be respected. But a demonstration is not a herd; I don't count people the way one counts goats.
Anyone who wants to join us is welcome, as long as they're not
armed." He stood up, passed in front of the circle of stones surrounding the hot embers, and held out his hand to Donna
Marena. "We'll hide them for a little while. You lay down your
weapons and try to convince yourself that unity is the only way."

They left the hut. Donna Marena climbed up onto the gig
and shouted out: "Everybody listen. The soldiers have arrived,
and there are bands of mafiosi nearby. Whoever has weapons
and wants to keep them, come with me. Whoever does not, or
wants to give them up, will go with Villa, along with the old
people and the women and children." Hers was the voice of a
woman accustomed to being listened to. Gawain helped her

down from the carriage, and the group of armed guerrillas formed around her. They carried their weapons like tools, the youngest brandishing them threateningly at an enemy they imagined was hiding behind every tree, the grown men holding them with care, as if they might go off on their own. Colonel Terzo whispered to Emma: "They're not very experienced fighters. I'm going to ask Villa to take us back immediately."

Villa in turn climbed aboard the cart turned into a makeshift podium: "Friends and comrades, we raise the flag of peace and work on the untilled Mastema estate. And in peace, just as we came, we will now return to our homes. The demonstration is over. Orchestra first."

Master Moliterni felt he needed to explain things to Gawain, who didn't understand the reason for all the bustle: "We're going to content ourselves with a symbolic occupation. Usually we till and sow the abandoned lands. Maybe Villa fears some kind of provocation."

Donna Marena was discussing with the young guerrillas whether to pass west of the bridge, where Marshal Montgomery had already once attacked to no avail, or to attempt to negotiate the treacherous sheep trail that ran along a gorge, high above the torrent. She gave her order: "Marro, go to the women and have them give you whatever bread they have. We'll need it more than they will." Marro, the boy rebuked for firing his weapon a bit too cheerfully, walked away irritated at having to perform so domestic a chore, with his automatic rifle in hand. He whispered to the women, who were holding children, and quickly returned to Donna Marena.

"They said no," he said, agitated.

"No?" replied Donna Marena, drawing their route in the ashes with a knitting needle.

"No," he repeated proudly: after the infantile assignment, he was now negotiating with the president.

"Would you like to explain, boy?" asked the woman, without losing her patience.

"They say they're not going with Villa. They want to stay. They say they won't go, not even if we shoot them. If somebody has to die, they want to die with the men."

Donna Marena went over to the women of Malpasso, whose eyes were downcast. "I'm the president of the Republic," she said, "you elected me the way the Americans do. There's an American right over there; ask him. When you elect a president, you must listen to him. Go with Villa, we'll meet up in a few days. There are soldiers and bandits around here. Think of the children."

"Donna Marena, if the men stay, we stay," said a girl with braids. "They're our fathers, our husbands, our brothers. It will be as God wills." The peasant women with sunburned faces, a mother with a newborn clinging to her shawl, little girls and grown women, all nodded in agreement. An old woman made the sign of the cross, and the girl with the braids began to recite the Rosary: "Hail Mary, full of grace, the Lord is with thee. Blessed art thou among women . . ."

There was no time for the chorus of Malpasso women to respond, "Holy Mary, mother of God," for Pepe the altar boy came running back to Donna Marena, shouting: "The soldiers are at the bridge, the soldiers are at the bridge!" Terzo looked toward Primosole. A patrol of light infantrymen was mounting a machine-gun nest, blocking not only their road back to their airport, but the peasants' road back home and the only possible path of retreat for the rebels out of range of the bandits' weapons. The colonel turned around, surveying the area to the west of the volcano with Campari's old marine binoculars: "We should have known," he said. He handed the glasses to his wife, who saw first the December sky, and then, out of focus, the branches of a large carob tree. Terzo gently directed the lenses

toward the mountain pass called the Furnace: the bandits' bonfires could be seen glowing through the mist. Following the
flood troughs that Donna Marena had hoped to cross, a long line
of horsemen was zigzagging down the mountain slope. Emma
studied the volcano and saw soldiers, turned back to the gardens
and saw mules and rifles, then pointed the binoculars at the
stagnant swamp alongside the river and a group of houses cut
into the mountainside and saw bandits, bandits everywhere,
with rifles slung across their chests, moving about, swift and
well organized.

Villa asked Donna Marena: "Do you think the soldiers will
let us through? I'll bring the women and children with me, if
you can persuade them to come." There was no need for her to
answer, however, because a convoy of open trucks, flatbeds, and
prison vans could be seen arriving from the valley. They were,
no doubt, to be used to carry away prisoners, and who was going
to explain to that portly officer barking orders at the awkward
soldiers from the rocky riverbank that the demonstrators were
peaceful and followed a different political line from the armed
rebels? They were surrounded.

"What are we going to do, Colonel?" asked Villa. "I'm very
sorry. I would never have expected this. It was Santa Lucia; we
were expecting a celebration, a peaceful march."

Terzo wasn't listening. He was measuring, with his eyes, the
length of their right flank, rather exposed, with respect to an escarpment that could easily be fortified. To the left, he tried to
calculate the distance between the shore of the river and the
embankment of the bridge. He identified the machine gun: a
Breda. From that angle, he thought, there might be a slim
chance to get past.

"Salvatore and Gawain," he shouted, "write this down. Uneven terrain, bridge occupied by conscripts. Mercenaries behind.
Doubly surrounded. Salvatore, formulate the situation in terms
of the classics of war."

BATTLE AT THE ABBEY
OF S. GIOVANNI
13 DECEMBER 1946

0 50 100   200m

A

B

1

2

3

1. ATTACK
OF VOLPE
2:30 P.M.

2. RAID OF THE
BANDIT
FAMINA
2:45 P.M.

3. COLONEL
TERZO'S
STRONGHOLD
3:00 P.M.

A. OAK
GROVE
B. ETNA

"Stonewall Jackson, American Civil War—"

"I don't see any railroads, Salvatore, and I'm not sure the adversaries are willing to die for their cause."

"Battle of Bannockburn, in . . ."

". . . 1314," Terzo completed the thought.

"Anglo-Scottish war. Marsh in front, escarpment, dense woods, river on the right. A place for ambushes . . ."

"Not bad, Salvatore, but neither Robert I nor Edward II was surrounded. We are. Try again. Here's a hint: think of pure theory."

"Sun Tzu?"

"Sun Tzu," repeated Terzo with a tone of approval, "that's the one: old Master Sun, fourth century B.C. Go on."

"Dialogues with the King of Wu," said Salvatore, consulting his notebook and immediately continuing: "The king asks Master Sun, 'How should one proceed when one's army is caught in an area from which there is no path of escape? Lines of reinforcement are cut off. The enemy lies in wait along rocky, difficult terrain. There is no chance of attack or retreat. What is one to do?'"

Before Terzo could say whether Salvatore had finally cited the canonical example for their predicament, a shot was fired from the slope of the volcano and whistled through the air toward the occupied lands of Duchess Mastema. Marro fell to his knees, fired a useless burst of machine-gun fire into the ground as a reflex, and was dead. The bullet had hit him in the temple, leaving him wide-eyed, no longer humiliated by his banal chores nor proud to be negotiating with the president of the Republic. "Hit the ground! Take cover!" shouted Terzo. Salvatore and Gawain repeated the order: "Hit the ground! Take cover!" The battle had begun.

"FIRE!" From the Primosole Bridge the soldiers shot a few bursts from their machine gun, but too high to endanger the Malpasso rebels. "Cease fire! The shot came from the mountain," shouted a sergeant. The Breda kept the slope in its sights, the troop resumed its defense operations more warily than before, and the portly officer continued to wave his arms about, barking out orders.

"Are you all right?" Terzo asked Emma, who was lying on the ground beside him.

"I've got everyone into a fine mess, with my stubbornness."

"Don't worry. We've got nothing to do with it. In a little while we'll carefully make our way back down to the bridge. I'll present myself to the commanding officer with my identity card. I'm a colonel on leave; he'll let us pass," said Terzo to calm her down. But he didn't like the tone of his words. Meanwhile Marro lay there dead as a doornail, while two companions tried to crawl over to him and the women moaned in terror. *They can't leave*, Terzo thought.

Villa came running up. Despite the cold, he was sweating. "Colonel! If I go toward Etna the bandits will fire on us. If I go toward the bridge, how will I ever explain to the soldiers that we were only here to occupy the land and that we're not with the rebels? We're caught between a rock and a hard place. What should I do?"

Donna Marena ran her hand through her gray hair, and

Emma noticed she was wearing a wedding band of iron, not gold. "We'll attack the mafiosi ourselves. We'll force our way through, and you, Villa, will take your people by way of the Furnace. By the time the soldiers manage to climb up there, you'll already be back in Petranova."

Unsure, Villa looked back at the colonel. "Tell them what they should do, Carlo," Princess Emma Svyatoslava said quietly. "You know."

Colonel Carlo Terzo spoke, without pausing to think: "Donna Marena, the soldiers have a heavy machine gun and could hit you if you move away from here. As for the bandits, to judge from what they did to that poor boy, they obviously have a few marksmen among them. They are safely perched up high, they can calmly take aim, as if shooting target practice. Let me say your plan is a bold one, but it is destined to fail." He used the same tone as Dr. Pantera with Emma's disease, one of resignation to a bad prognosis.

"What do you advise?" asked Emma.

"I have no idea, darling. I'm not familiar with the terrain, I don't know what sort of forces we're dealing with, and we really must catch that plane on time. Fiore—"

"I will stay here until these people are safe," Fiore interjected. "Please help them, Colonel. You've been talking to us for months about battles. You know how to win." She was holding Salvatore's hand tight. Defying her faraway mother was her first adult act, but the excitement made her face glow and turned her back into a little girl.

"I don't think you appreciate the gravity of the situation," said Terzo, with uncertainty in his voice. His loved ones were in danger, the terrain impossible, the formations on the ground unknown. Weapons, tactics, the stuff of his whole life now suddenly appeared before him, as well as Marro's blood, the morale of the rebels, and the range of the Breda machine gun that the officer was positioning at the bridge. The dead boy. Terzo turned to look at him, but instantly a bullet screamed over his head and struck a wooden rafter in the hut. "Get down, everybody get down," he repeated. On his hands and knees he reached Marro's body, turned him over, felt his neck. Dead. *The first I've ever seen in battle,* he thought. *That's what I told Ciano that night: I've never seen a man die. What kind of strategist could I ever be, if I've never seen a man in the flesh fall lifeless to the ground, a useless, dust-covered sack, killed by some wrong move or incorrect strategy? The citizens of Malpasso think they can fight by making a show of their picturesque weapons, and here are the results. But I know where we are, I know all too well. Dragonara's right, he's right, good kid: we're in Sun Tzu's discussion with the King of Wu. He and I alone know the meaning of that ancient dialogue.*

Terzo had seen his dead man, and was now surrounded on half a hillside, with the bridge below and a treacherous river on which to lean his right flank. He risked ending his life in dishonor, arrested as an accomplice to a revolt he was not part of and knew nothing about. But the old intensity had returned to Emma's face. He saw her alive, full of excitement. He turned back, slithering along on his elbows. A pair of bullets followed him in vain.

"Stay down," begged Donna Marena. "Didn't you say they're good shots?"

"I'm against the sun. They're unable to aim at me. They've got the glare in their eyes," said Terzo. That simple trick of the trenches, which had come to him spontaneously, aroused the admiration of the rebels. A bright sun had just then emerged from the fog. His legendary account of the Allied invasion, his rank of colonel, with which they all heard him addressed, the fear of being surrounded, the trust that Villa demonstrated in his regard, all combined to make the peasants look at Terzo as a miracle-worker.

"What do you want me to do, Emma?" Terzo asked.

"Help them," she said, "take them away from here. Save them."

That was enough. Terzo calmly asked Villa and Donna Marena: "Will you let me try to get us out of this predicament? Without your absolute trust we're not going to make it. If you have any doubts, state them now or forever hold your peace. Rule number one: if political leaders don't have confidence in a military strategy, defeat is assured. Look at the disasters of Hitler and his staff during the Russian campaign in '42 and '43."

"You have my full confidence," said Villa. "Inviting you here has turned out to be a real blessing."

"I will listen to your advice, Signor Terzo, but the militia of the Republic of Malpasso remains under my command, so long as the Republic lives," objected Donna Marena.

"That's fine, signora. Send the women down the slope, behind the hut. It's shielded from the snipers, and also from the machine gun, at least for the time being. Have somebody check how much food we've got, and how much water. Then I want an exact count of weapons and ammunition, down to the last cartridge. Can we be certain that no one is keeping provisions or ammunition for himself?"

"Absolutely."

"Villa and Donna Marena will be my General Staff. You, Moliterni, are responsible for provisions. As soon as we have an exact count of everything I'll tell you what the rations will be. I also need you to give me the exact number of noncombatants."

Here Terzo turned to the crowd and, shielding himself behind an oak tree, said: "Women, old people, and children will now follow Master Moliterni to a safe place. The men who want to fight should remain here, but move behind that rock. The bullets won't reach you there."

There was a quiet stirring of people forced to creep along the ground, fearing a sniper shot; the only ones left on the plateau in front of the oak were now men, the hundred or so who had followed Villa, and an equal number of militiamen of the Republic of Malpasso. "Those of you who have served in the army, go to the right, those of you who haven't, to the left." The crowd again began to move, and Terzo immediately spotted a new problem. Villa's unarmed laborers, most of them veterans, went to the right. Donna Marena's youngsters, weapons round their necks, revealed, by moving to the left, that they had never worn a uniform. His authority was about to be put to its first test.

"Who here has been trained how to shoot?" The peasants timidly raised their hands, while the armed boys looked at the ground, disappointed.

"Any NCOs among you?" Two came forward.

"Sergeant D'Oro, sir."

"Corporal Curatolo, sir."

"Where did you fight?" he insisted on asking, fearing empty boasting.

"Isonzo, August 1917, Colonel," replied D'Oro.

"What unit?"

"Third Army, Duke of Aosta."

"Good work," said Terzo: they'd been sent on the attack in an impossible position and had managed to push back the Austrians, inflicting surprisingly heavy losses, risking everything without artillery cover or provisions.

"Corporal Curatolo, Colonel, sir," called out the laborer with silvery spikes of grain on the bandana round his neck, standing at attention in textbook fashion. He had a tanned, Arab face, with narrow, decisive eyes. "Third Savoy Regiment, General Carnimeo."

"At Cheren?" Terzo asked, surprised.

"At Cheren, Colonel, sir. I fought with General Lorenzini, God rest his soul, and then with Lieutenant Guillet and the Eleventh African brigade. I made it back home by luck: Lieutenant D'Andreis got his hands on a Siai S-82 aircraft, and we reached our lines after flying over the African territory held by the British." Curatolo's eyes were sparkling.

Villa and Donna Marena did not understand why Terzo was looking at him with such respect. But then the colonel did something else, like someone his wife had never known: "Tenhut!" he shouted crisply into the December air, and out of military instinct, and the mental effort that serving in uniform demands, the old soldiers leaped to attention. The young militiamen, the children, and the women all heard a different timbre in Terzo's voice and tried as best they could to stand up straight.

"At Cheren, the soldiers under Amedeo Guillet, under Carnimeo and Lorenzini, held their own against Platt's English soldiers. If those idiots in Rome hadn't divided the forces, as you, dear Salvatore, know one should never do, if they had sent a few planes instead of serving the Germans, they would have pushed back the front. Guillet, with a cavalry charge, then broke through the lines surrounding him and resumed the guerrilla war dressed up as an Abyssinian: *Cummuntàr as Sciaitan*, Commander Satan, the askaris called him. But tell me yourself, Curatolo, what you and your fellow soldiers did at Cheren."

"We did our duty, Colonel, sir."

Villa was speechless. Curatolo was a very docile laborer and a committed comrade. Everybody knew he had served in the war, had even been wounded, but he had never said a word about what he had done. Now he was compelled to speak, and the colonel could only look on him with admiration.

"We are lucky," said Terzo, after making sure the trees sheltered them from the snipers. "We have an assault expert in D'Oro and a veteran of broken encirclements in Curatolo. Listen to them, and you'll come out of this alive. If we let ourselves give in to fear, we're finished." As he pronounced the word "fear," he listened to his stomach to see if he could detect any there. No. It was calm. If things went bad, he would die with

Emma and avoid loneliness and old age. He was the only hope these people had left; he had no time for fear.

Just how good D'Oro and Curatolo really were became immediately apparent. They mingled with the rebels and persuaded them to turn over their weapons to more experienced soldiers. In less than thirty minutes, what in the bandits' telescope still looked like a country outing come to a bad end had become instead a passable military redoubt. On the slope behind the hut, sheltered by the thicket of oaks, were the women and children. The elderly and adolescents had decided to stay with the fighters, as had a group of younger women as well. Terzo had objected, but Donna Marena cut him short: "In the Republic of Malpasso, defense is the prerogative of the citizens, without distinction as to sex." Curatolo, with a guerrilla intelligence acquired from having fought behind enemy lines in Africa, put the women in charge of defending the hut.

"You should see how women fight when their children are watching," he said. "They are tigers, Colonel, tigers."

To confront the enemy, Terzo lined up the veterans with the most experience and put them under Curatolo's command. For their protection, he had small holes hurriedly dug by the old peasant who had kept the German helmet as a souvenir. "I thought I would be breaking ground on the Mastema estate," he laughed toothlessly, "and here I am a soldier again." Master Moliterni estimated that, with strict rationing, there was enough to eat and drink for two days. As for ammunition, there was actually too much. To D'Oro, Terzo assigned command of the smaller group checking on the soldiers in the rear, and positioned the young rebels there.

"Know your enemy," Terzo said to Villa and Donna Marena. "Who are these soldiers? What do they want? And what sort of people are these bandits? Also, I want you to describe to me every road, every path, from here to the nearest town where you think you'd be safe."

"The soldiers want to arrest us, the Malpasso people," Donna Marena calmly explained, "but they have orders not to kill, as long as we don't shoot at them. Their officers disdain us because we no longer want to fight, whereas they are just back from the front. They're not too particular. A lot depends on their commanding officer: if he's a decent man he'll spare us; if he's cruel, some will die. The bandits are in the pay of Duchess Mastema and want to terrorize Villa's laborers, who are occupying the land. They shoot on sight."

"In short," Terzo observed, "on the one hand, soldiers of the regular army, who are fighting against civilians and are therefore unsure whether they should act as warriors or policemen. It would be nice to know who's in command, what he has in mind. On the other hand, highway bandits, who are ferocious when they feel safe, uncertain when they're threatened. What we need now is a map."

Master Moliterni handed him one drawn up by the Military Geographical Institute. A native of Turin sent to Sicily to teach school, he did not know the mountains and meadows the way the peasants did, and so he carried the map around with him whenever he left his village, in case he got lost. He kept it hidden, feeling ashamed of it as of some sort of bourgeois tic; but now he was proud as ever to be able to show it off. He became even more puffed up when Terzo looked at it and, seeing trails and mule paths traced with microscopic precision, said to him, in Piedmontese dialect, "Thank you, fellow citizen. This will be worth more to us than a rifle." With the map unfolded before him, Terzo felt calm and strong. He took some pencils from his breast pocket, carefully arranged them on the band's bass drum, now transformed into a precarious work table, and called to Salvatore:

"Write this down: December 13, 1946, on the slopes of Mount Etna, behind the Primosole bridge, with the Dittaino and Gornalunga rivers in view. Apparently surrounded by regular forces of the Italian army equipped with a Breda machine gun, and, farther up the mountain, near the areas known as the Oak Grove and the Old Furnace, by irregular formations of well-armed bandits supposedly affiliated with the mafia and at the command of large landowners. The purpose of our mission: to avoid bloodshed among the civilian population in our care by defending ourselves from attacks and attempting to find a way out of the pocket in which we find ourselves. A serious situation, which the presence of civilians makes even more serious."

And you, he thought, *are the strategist for these poor people, you who have just seen your first man die and will search through the books lost in your own mind for the way out of this mess. Just like Flavius Vegetius Renatus, who wrote the* Epitoma rei militaris *in the fourth century, bringing together in one book the military knowledge of the Romans, but had never fought in battle or seen a man die. As Austrian Field Marshal von Ligne noted, "Vegetius says a god inspired the legions, but in my opinion a god inspired Vegetius." And how would Vegetius have fared, had he been called upon to command a platoon of peasants, giving orders to kill and be killed? Will his god inspire me, too?*

In silence he recommended himself to the unknown god of weaponry, and felt immediately ashamed: *Enough! Try to concentrate! These people are counting on you, and you act like a library scholar? If the soldiers open fire, or the bandits suddenly attack, how are you going to react? With the digests of Geoffrey Plantagenet?*

"IT COULDN'T HAVE turned out any better than this." Up at the Old Furnace, Famine, ringleader of the band of brigands besieging Terzo and his people, smiled with satisfaction: "The soldiers have plugged up their rear. Now they'll never escape," he said in dialect. "Villa's hotheads are in there, too. No escape. We'll go down the hill and teach them a lesson. Now listen. The peasants are unarmed. The Malpasso rebels have weapons, but they can't even kill flies. Did you see how I laid out that pansy who was popping off his gun?"

Famine had singled out Marro for his celebratory salvo and killed him, taking aim from above with a high-powered rifle. "You know the orders: no more occupation of the lands. We bump off the union workers and frighten the women, so they'll keep their husbands and sons at home. Kill 'em real bad, aim at their eyes, drag them under your horses, lash the women with your whip, make it leave marks on their skin. Understood? Now we'll trickle one by one down to the wall of the abbey, by the river. Then Volpe will go ahead with his team. Shoot from the road. They'll get frightened and run down the slope, and Taddarita and Sgobbio will gallop there and head them off. Watch out for the ones with weapons; you never can tell . . . At the first gunshot, they'll get on their horses and run away, you'll see. If anything should go wrong, if the soldiers, for example, begin to move, I'll fire a smoke bomb and we'll meet back up here. The soldiers would never venture this far. If you catch Donna Marena, the whore who calls herself the president, I want her brought to me alive. On your horses now, lads."

The bandits set off without haste, first those on foot, pistols in their belts, then the squad on horseback, rifles slung over their shoulders. Leaving the river behind them on the left, they followed the path as far as the deserted Abbey of San Giovanni. Abandoned by the monks during the Allied invasion, the ancient monastery had been fortified by German soldiers and converted into a theater of ferocious battles. The bishop of Catania had not yet had occasion to reconsecrate it. In the silence, the horses' hooves sent out sparks from the paving stones of the churchyard. Once at the volcano, they began climbing up the ash-gray mule path.

Terzo, having left Curatolo on the lookout, suddenly heard him call to him. "They're coming. From San Giovanni."

"Salvatore, look," said Terzo, keeping the binoculars trained on the bandits, "infantry in front and cavalry behind. As they get closer, the foot soldiers will tend to fall more and more behind the horses, looking for protection. They don't want to be alone when they arrive in front of the enemy. The horsemen can easily run off at a gallop. Not the infantrymen."

"Some of my men are excellent riders," said Villa, "champions of the September Joust of the Saracen. If we send them down there through the woods, we can take the bandits from behind."

"Let my boys have their guns back. They'll attack those pigs and tear them to pieces," suggested Donna Marena.

Terzo wasn't listening: "Take this down, Salvatore. You, too, Gawain. Villa, order all those on horseback to dismount. Round up all the mules and horses and put them in a safe place. We'll fight on foot, all of us together."

"Why, if we've got all these good horsemen? Don't you have

faith in them? I've seen them ride at the Joust, I tell you, at full gallop," Villa insisted.

Terzo paid no attention.

"Are we going to line up in the middle of the road?" Salvatore ventured.

"I'm surprised at you. Are we theoreticians of the frontal assault, in the tradition of General Lee? Absolutely not. Look at the map—no, actually there's no more need for it, look down below. What do you see? River, abbey, road, wood to enemy's left. What battle is it?"

Villa and Donna Marena thought Terzo had gone mad, ordering people to give up their horses. But young Dragonara diligently picked up his notebook and, as he customarily did on the art nouveau terrace in Palermo, consulted the little maps Fiore had drawn up, one for each battle, his own handwritten notes, and Terzo's corrections: "Marathon? No, that's on a plain. Trasimeno? No, there's a lake there. Well, let's see . . . Ah, incredible, Colonel! Look, Villa, it's the battle of Crécy."

"Date?" asked Terzo, while Donna Marena was thinking: *We are in the hands of a lunatic.*

"August 26, 1346, the Hundred Years War. The flower of French knighthood, on the order of King Philip VI, rose up to attack Edward III's English army," said Salvatore in amazement, as Villa showed Donna Marena the sketches of the battle of Crécy in the notebook: "Incredible: forest, mountain, river: exactly the same landscape we have here before us."

"If you get any more astonished, we'll have the enemy down our throats and you can tell *them* about Crécy," said Terzo curtly, in a voice Emma had never heard him use before. "Curatolo, draw the veterans up in a rake formation. Do you know what a rake is?"

Salvatore translated it into Sicilian for him, but Curatolo was already nodding.

"Good," Terzo resumed. "Draw the men up in front and behind, like the teeth of a rake, but slantwise to the road. Not crosswise, understand? Form a square of soldiers and one of the younger boys—I noticed they've got slingshots: tell them to aim at the horses. They'll say it's kid stuff, but you tell them they're traitors if they don't obey. They'll take the position of the English archers at Crécy. In the formation, mix the novices together with those who have combat experience, to keep morale up. I'll be there with you. D'Oro, you will bring up the rear with the reserves. Gawain, you're a pacifist, but you can certainly keep an eye on the Italian army unit out there. If they move, let me know."

"I'll keep my eyes open, sir," said the American.

"Fiore, tell the women to cut up some aprons and make bandages from them. Nobody fire until I give the order."

"And where do I go?" Salvatore asked anxiously.

"Where did the Black Prince go at Crécy?"

"To the right flank."

"Bravo. You, too, will go to the right. And you're exactly sixteen years old, the same age as the Black Prince, son of Edward III."

It is *the battle of Crécy,* Terzo thought incredulously, *and now the bandits will come up the hill like the French, bold and self-assured.* Around the bend the first shadows of the enemy, weapons in hand, were beginning to appear. *It's them, it's the Genoese crossbowmen. They're expecting the cavalry, but here we are, instead, all together, on foot.* The Malpasso rebels, upset because the rifles had ended up in the hands of the farmworkers while they could only take up slingshots, were nevertheless overcome with the sense of order and fear that precedes a battle. No longer individuals, they were now part of an army. And as an army they would win; if the army scattered, massacre awaited them. The bandits were near, behind the oaks; one could hear them cursing the climb and the imminent danger. Some of those marching cautiously had pulled up, for safety's sake, closer to the horses, closing ranks.

"Your colonel really knows it all," Donna Marena whispered to Villa; "he's either a devil or a madman."

Volpe appeared round the last bend. "Square one, fire," Terzo ordered, and the first line of bandits was caught in a burst of crossfire. "Square two, slingshots," and a hail of rocks pelted the horses, which panicked and threw their riders. *Crécy*—thought Terzo—*arrows like snowflakes, as the witnesses remembered it.* The bandits, under the barrage, forged ahead, firing pistols and rifles and certain they could overcome the resistance. But Terzo had lined up his rake at an acute angle to the road. Pointing his index finger, he explained to Donna Marena: "To hit us, the bandits have to turn to the left as they continue to go uphill. At the top of the road they will therefore be without defense and we can eliminate them one by one. It's a brilliant idea, signora, but it's not mine—it's Edward III's. Delbrück explains it well, but I'm sorry, I really don't have time to go into it right now. These guys are certain they're going to slaughter us, and after the frightening welcome we've given them, they're going to want a final confrontation. Corporal, nobody leave his post. D'Oro, on your guard."

Volpe had seen the two Monastero brothers, his long-time partners at the card table, fall in the fusillade. The bandits on horseback tugged hard on the reins, pulling up to a halt, and those on foot fell to the ground cursing: "The bastards are shooting!"

Volpe and Sgobbio insulted them: "What are you cowards doing? Come on, let's go thrash the beggars. They've killed the Monastero boys. They're scum."

To get their horses out of the slingshots' range and avoid being exposed to the bullets, Volpe, Sgobbio, and Taddarita applied their spurs. That was what Terzo had been hoping: just as at

Crécy, six centuries earlier, there was confusion between the frightened foot soldiers and the attacking horsemen. Each group took turns slowing down. Those who bravely charged ran into those who hesitated. The battle turned into a mêlée. Sgobbio stuck his spurs into the flanks of his mare, jumping right into a square of rebels. As he fired twice, Taddarita, just behind him, bullwhip strapped to his wrist, made it whistle in the air. The Malpasso boys scattered, overwhelmed by the enormous animal and Taddarita's lashes. They backtracked toward the hut, some defending themselves, some turning and running. Curatolo's square, holding ground, continued to fire round after round. Donna Marena ran up to those fleeing and ordered them:

"Back! Malpasso back! This is no time to be afraid." Finally, heartened by the cover provided by the rifles, the boys resumed their position.

In the tumult Terzo shouted to Salvatore, who was far away: "Rule number one: always try to raise the morale of your troops. That's it, boys! Let's go!" In the confusion, D'Oro coolly took aim and killed Sgobbio's horse. A large crowd immediately set upon the bandit but, swift as the devil, he escaped and was soon among his own. Bullets and stones were hitting their mark with precision. Terzo's formation, to the side of the road, provided a magnificent defense: the bandits were on top of one another in an infernal commotion that raised dust from the mule path and left men and horses on the ground. In the fray Marro's brother struck left and right with a large hunting knife, slashing and mutilating as he went.

Famine, from his position, was horrified. At the first round of gunfire and stones, he had sneered, re-wrapping the white scarf around his neck: "From the side of the road? They can't even line up." But then he saw how much trouble his men were having firing even a single shot, advancing each time, defenseless, only to turn to the left and find themselves faced with Edward III's ingenious rake formation, reduced to an impotent mob. He had been thinking of how he would boast to his chief that night and ask for a special reward, and here a dozen bandits had already fallen, with the survivors retreating. He hastily looked for the smoke bomb. He'd thought he wouldn't have to use it; he'd brought it with him only in deference to the cut-throat's eternal reflex: always to keep an escape route open. Cursing to himself, he took the bomb out of a haversack and released the safety with a sweaty hand. As it shot into the sky, it traced a sharp parabola from the mountainside and fell into the woods. The soldiers at the bridge followed its path, the rebels dropped their slingshots for a moment; already the bandits were taking to their heels. Marro's brother raced after them, giving chase, but D'Oro blocked his path.

Only to the right, where Dragonara had bravely held his position, were Volpe and a group of horsemen still furiously fighting. Fingers to his mouth, the student whistled like a goatherd to Pepe the altar boy and sent him off to ask Terzo for reinforcements. The colonel ordered D'Oro's rear guard to charge, and Volpe was forced to retreat.

Crécy, thought Terzo: *the sole example of a decisive battle won only by defense. The dead numbered twelve hundred French knights and eighty-three troop commanders, drawn up in columns with the vassals behind their banners, as well as King Philip's brother and nephew, the Counts of Alençon and Blois . . .* The rebels surrounded the bodies of the dead bandits in the dust, looking for weapons. Terzo watched them and thought of those who had fallen six centuries earlier: Raul, Duke of Lorraine; Louis, Count of Flanders; Jean, Count of Harcourt; Simon, Count of Salm; Louis, Count of Sancerre; Jean, Count of Auerre; Jean, Count of Grandpré. Also among the fallen was John of Bohemia, Count of Luxemburg and father of Emperor Charles IV.

Pepe was shouting at the top of his lungs, bent over a dead man in a leather jacket: "Look who it is!" It was Taddarita: a bullet had pierced his skull, just as the ancient arrow had struck down blind King John.

Put to rout, the bandits retreated, driving their horses at a gallop downhill, firing a few shots at random.

"We won!" screamed Villa.

"They're running away," Donna Marena said calmly. Actually, she couldn't believe her eyes: that man there, with his "rake," using slingshots in imitation of the longbows of the English archers, and his slantwise, not crosswise, formation to the side of the road, had defeated the bandits who had been terrorizing the Catanian plain for months.

"Have we won?" Salvatore anxiously asked, arriving breathless at his teacher's side.

"Do you think the Black Prince abandoned his post before receiving a clear order? Who told you to come here? How do you know those imbeciles don't have a reserve force? What if they break through on your side?"

The boy blushed.

"Anyway, to answer your question: we haven't won," Terzo continued, "they've lost. They thought they'd come and take us like a pack of blockheads. Now what idea did we borrow from Edward III at Crécy?"

"To have the horsemen fight on foot."

"And what did that move mean, tactically and psychologically?"

"It assures you the protection of the archers, the slingshots, that is, for us. Without their horses, the horsemen know they must win or die. They can't escape, and this instills confidence in the foot soldiers. In the first battle against the Helvetii, Caesar ordered everyone to fight on foot and had their horses taken away."

"So you can even attack with dismounted cavalry?"

"Yes, sir. I believe that's what Henry V did at Agincourt, sixty-nine years after Crécy. Will you use the same tactic?"

"I don't think so. The bandits were taught a lesson and they'll be more careful now. They'll try to kill us in an ambush. They need to avenge their dead. They can't go back to their bosses empty-handed, having received a drubbing by a mob of peasants. We were surrounded and we're still surrounded. Curatolo, go around with the rations and change the sentries."

Colonel Carlo Terzo returned to the hut, unfolded the little map, and started to think aloud. "Write this down, Salvatore." It gave him a feeling of security to dictate his thoughts to the boy, though he could never forget he was in the middle of a real-life shoot-out, with real dead and their own lives in danger. He feared that panic might spread; by posing the problem in the abstract, as with Campari at the Archives, he felt a great wave of calm come over him. "Let's summarize: what are the principles of strategy?"

The pupil slowly recited: "According to Sun Tzu, the best strategy is not to win a hundred battles, but to bend the enemy without fighting."

"And how does one manage that?"

"By defeating not the enemy's army, but his strategy."

"Which means?"

"Instead of attacking the soldiers, one should strike at the reasons why they are fighting."

"And what is the strategy of these bandits?"

"To cut our throats," replied Donna Marena in Salvatore's place.

"Right," Terzo approved, "but to what extent are they willing to risk their own necks? Judging from how they fought this morning, I'd say only up to a point. Now they've gone back up the mountain to lick their wounds. They'll be careful. They realize we're ready and waiting for them. They're going to be craftier next time around. So let's think this out and prepare for the worst. We'll never get out of here only by defending ourselves. At some point we'll have to attack." Terzo looked at the encampment: he saw boys munching on bread and onions, their slingshots now hanging proudly from their waistbands, and armed peasants comforting their women. They had escaped with no dead, a real miracle; only two rebels had sustained serious injury, and Gawain was now bandaging them up as best he could.

Up on the mountain, Famine was greeting his men with insults: "Well done, gentlemen, very well done. Thrashed by the bumpkins. What on earth am I going to say to you-know-who? Sorry, we ran away when we saw the women and children."

Humiliated and frightened, the bandits dragged their feet along the ground. "First we see Taddarita and the Monasteros wiped out in that pandemonium," they muttered to one another, "and now we have to put up with this abuse."

"They may be children, Famine, but they shoot like furies. They weren't even in front of us, they were along the road, shooting from the side. They frightened the horses with their slingshots . . ." said Volpe, defending himself.

"With slingshots, *mamma mia*, how terrifying. And did they make ugly faces to scare you away? From the side of the road? And couldn't you turn around?"

Once a battle is over, anyone can fight it again from an armchair. If poor Volpe had read as much as Terzo, he would have known that even Hannibal, exiled to the court of King Antiochus after his defeat at Zama, had to put up at dinner with the philosopher Formio, who explained to him in detail how easy it would have been to defeat Rome if only he had followed his plan. Volpe could write his own name, if only barely, thanks to an old aunt of his who was a nun, and certainly knew nothing about Formio. But he learned this lesson well that day, chewing on half a cigar.

Famine felt cold and wrapped himself in his oilcloth cape. The weather had changed again, the weak sun had vanished, and a gray fog began to rise from the river valley, thickening around the slopes of the volcano and the forest of oak. Within an hour it would envelop the hut and conceal Terzo's men from the soldiers' view.

"All right, so they turned us around," he said, scratching his head. "But we have to go back. Leaving Taddarita and the Monasteros down there is like putting our signature on the attack. The boss is going to be here soon and I don't feel like telling him that the bumpkins with their slingshots lined up on the side of the road. We're going to split up now. One group will come with me down to the woods, to flush them out. You, Volpe, go with the horses down to the riverbank, so they don't see you. The instant they show up, we attack with all we've got. This time we've got to put a lot of them away, so the boss won't know what happened earlier. Remember, we're still owed half our pay."

Famine put a revolver in his belt and led them through the woods. They moved slowly, in the humid shade of the oaks, a group of armed men who killed for money, offended by the deaths of their companions and fearing their gangleader's wrath. Eyes open, they held pistols in their hands or rifles on their shoulders. Volpe's group proceeded on the white pebbles of the riverbank. When the fog lifted, the bandits dismounted, leading their horses by the reins, so they wouldn't slip. At the end of the bank they would remount, hidden by the shrubbery, and make ready to head off the fleeing peasants and rebels. They had lost their air of arrogance; Volpe glanced back and forth at the mud-swollen waters and the dampened bushes. All at once the underbrush opened up with a rustle; the rifles nervously cocked. It was two lynxes, stopping there to stare at them with yellow eyes.

"Lynxes?" Volpe whispered. "I thought they'd all been killed."

"Maybe they're the ghosts of the Monasteros," Paredes muttered. He'd been to America, and on his way back he'd seen phantoms dancing on the ocean.

"We were the hunters, and now we're the hunted?" Volpe said, worried. With a shudder he took aim at the pair—let them hear the shot downstream—but the big cats disappeared.

To distract himself from his worries, Colonel Terzo meanwhile dictated to Salvatore: "During his campaigns, Napoleon used to shut himself up in his tent, studying. 'Nobody is more fearful than I am when preparing the battle plan,' he said. 'I exaggerate the dangers in my imagination, and try to paint every situation in the worst possible light. I work myself up into a state of painful agitation, but when I present myself to the General Staff, I must be serene and confident. Once the decisions have been made, I forget everything and concentrate only on what may bring me success.' Let's do like Napoleon; let's imagine the worst. Though evoking panic can paralyze you, we have to look at our worst fear and continue to think rationally. Do you know why total fear is called panic?"

"No, sir."

"You can write a nice poem about it. The god Pan, a foster-brother of Zeus, was busy defending Olympus from the siege of the Titans. In order to win, he aroused 'panic' in Typhon, the cruelest of the giants. We must look panic in the eye: the worst that could happen would be for the bandits to burst into our camp. Or for the soldiers to attack us in the meantime. Imitating the battle of Crécy will have been useless if we can't break the siege. The man we really need is Campari, my old friend. He was in the pocket of Nikolayevka, on January 26, 1943; he knows what it means to attack to break through an encirclement. We have to think, Salvatore, think. Guicciardini . . ."

Terzo stopped, no longer able, in the cold, to call to mind the strategic plan he was looking for. Salvatore, by now, had learned how to unblock the colonel when his formidable erudition jammed up:

"Guicciardini . . ." the boy calmly repeated.

"Ah, yes, thank you, Guicciardini praised Prospero Colonna

for 'fighting with his brain before fighting with his sword.' We can't accept an uneven battle and risk being hacked to pieces. What might Frederick the Great be able to tell us? Let's see . . . *Generalprinzipien von Kriege*, chapter entitled 'When and How to Give Battle.'" Drawing from his memory, while his pupil continued to write, Terzo recited: "A reasoning man must never make a move without having a good reason to make it; even less should the general of an army engage in battle without knowing his objective. But even the great Frederick of Prussia did not always win. And do you know who it was that defeated him? Field Marshal Count Leopold von Daun, in the service of Empress Maria Theresa of Austria." As he spoke, Terzo nervously unfolded Master Moliterni's map, tracing their movements in pencil. "Frederick invaded Moravia in 1758, during the Seven Years War, and surrounded the fortress of Olmütz. Von Daun reviewed the options of someone under siege: sortie or classical resistance. He rejected both. Always look for a choice different from what is expected of you, Salvatore. Remember von Daun. Immobilized for seventeen days at Leitomischl, he suddenly set out and took up strong positions around Olmütz, to the east of Gewitsch and to the south of Dobramilitsch and Weischowitz. In a forced march, traveling fifty kilometers a day, he covered the left bank of the March River and reached the walls of Olmütz in good shape. Frederick wasn't expecting him and was forced to withdraw. Von Daun was able to resupply the city and defend it at the same time. He denied Frederick the chance for both open-field battle and siege, and he won. Understand? When Typhon seeks revenge and gives chase to Pan, do you know what the goat-god does? He turns into a fish and jumps into the river. And in that form, half fish, half billy goat, Zeus put him in the firmament: the Capricorn of Pan, my astrological sign, is also the symbol of strategy. Be always half fish, half goat, half panic, half courage, a crossbreed, never one single thing, as the enemy would have you. Alexander sacrificed to the goddess

Fear so that he might be possessed by panic and become a hybrid, as every great strategist must be. Damn!" Standing up in a fit of inspiration, Terzo shouted: "Villa! Signora Marena! Curatolo! D'Oro! Everybody come here! Messenger Pepe! Quick!" In just a few minutes the entire camp came alive.

FAMINE WAS CROSSING the grove of oaks. He passed an abandoned windmill and, trying to find his way in the increasingly dense fog, stopped behind the slope that hid Carlo Terzo's troops from view. He stuck his head out to see if Volpe and his men had completed their march along the riverbank. Not seeing them, he was about to light a cigarette but had second thoughts and put it behind his ear. He looked at his watch; he felt hungry. He reached into his haversack: there were a couple of cheese rinds. He chewed them slowly, as his companions watched with envy. They had breakfasted at dawn and since then had only shared a few canteens of water. Time passed. At last, somebody waved a hat down on the riverbank. Volpe. The trap was set. Famine felt like running and shooting. Running to counteract the cold in his muscles, running to dispel the hunger, shooting to teach those bastards a lesson and be able to meet the boss with head held high. Running because he was afraid, afraid to die like Taddarita, afraid to fail in his mission and be exposed to reprisals from the soldiers. He heard a faraway, rhythmical thumping, muffled and regular, thump thump thump: could his heart possibly be beating so loudly in his throat? *Come on,* he said to himself, *what am I thinking? I'm going to make them pay. I'm going to take Taddarita away, bury him in the woods, and as soon as we can, we'll give him a proper Christian burial. Tonight the money, tomorrow we celebrate.*

He whistled, ran past the last tree trunks, and came out into the clearing firing his pistol. Once past the posts where the horses were tied up, the men leaped onto the bare grass, firing at the hut, and hurled two TNT sticks in the direction of the still-red embers of the bonfires. Still shouting to spur themselves on, they made it as far as the road, where Terzo had earlier lined up his veterans sideways. Overlooking the mule path, they suddenly stopped, uncertain.

"Famine?" A horse's head appeared, then Volpe's contrite face. Thrown sideways and barefoot, Taddarita's corpse dangled from the saddle. The bandits were meeting in the appointed place; the plan had been executed to perfection. The only negative detail: the enemy had disappeared. Everyone, Donna Marena's rebels with their ammunition slung across their chests, the entire Malpasso army, the laborers of Villa's union, the army veterans, the women, the elderly, Marro's brother, who was wearing the oiled leather boots he had stolen from Taddarita, as well as the guests, the American Gawain, the lovers Fiore and Salvatore, Princess Emma, and the municipal band of Petranova, were marching in silence, with mules and horses, behind their bookworm strategist, Colonel Carlo Terzo. Copying Count von Daun at Olmütz, Terzo had abandoned the spot where he was supposed to be under siege, disengaging himself as well from the battle. As Famine was still trying to figure out what had happened, the colonel was already leading his people into the safety of the abbey. In single file, through the fog, the rebels and peasants had carried out a textbook disengagement and now dominated the valley, the river, and the Primosole Bridge. They had left the bandits behind them and put them between themselves and the soldiers, like a buffer. Donna Marena had had her doubts: "Along a mule path, in silence, in the fog? We'll get lost and walk right into the bandits' hands." But Terzo had given the order for the drummers in the band to go at the front, in the middle, and at the end of the column, so that, by striking the skins of the bass drums ever so lightly, they would give everyone a beat to follow. And it was this muffled sound which Famine, in the fog, confused with his own heartbeat. As they cheered entering the empty halls of the Abbey of San Giovanni, Emma, now pale as a ghost, said to her husband: "You've won."

"No, I haven't. We are no longer surrounded, but we're not free yet either. All I've done is reproduce two battles, Crécy and Olmütz."

"But the drumming in the fog was a stroke of genius," exclaimed Salvatore.

Colonel Terzo looked at his pupil with affection. "When Napoleon's Grande Armée was advancing into Russia in the heat, in June 1812," he said, "the cloud of dust kicked up by the march was so thick that the lieutenants ordered a drum major to beat the rhythm at the front of the batallions, so nobody would get lost. Write it down."

THE GENERAL blew his nose, cleaned his glasses and binoculars, and ordered the attendant to pass him a coffee in a tin cup. He looked at the military map, checked the fog and the position of the machine gun, looked haughtily at the young lieutenant in front of him, and said: "It's all clear, isn't it?" The general's philosophy was a simple one: he understood things, and others did not. If others tried to understand, he amused himself by pointing out that there was a subtle connection that escaped everyone's notice but his. And he liked to ridicule the unfortunate. For this reason Lieutenant Ferba, not long in the service, had thus far learned nothing, in his campaign against the "Sicilian rebels," about the art of warfare, but a great deal about diplomacy.

"All clear in what sense, General?" he asked.

Grateful for the opportunity, General Nasca, of the Fifth Aosta Infantry Division, explained, without undue hostility, as though resigned to having to live in a world of idiots: "You see, my dear Ferba, the rebels have enlisted the help of sympathetic elements of the population, hoping to create an obstacle for us. The sly devils think they're going to stop me by putting women and children under my nose. A typical tactic of guerrilla warfare. Do you know where the rebels are now, Ferba?"

"No, sir," said Ferba.

"The shoot-out was a trick, Ferba, don't you see? First a single shot to convince me to send in a scouting patrol." He was talking about the shot that had killed poor Marro. "Since we didn't take the bait, they want to pull us in. Think, boy. Now they're hiding along the slope and waiting for us to file in there so they can slaughter us. Let's let them stew in their own juices. And speaking of stew, I think it's time to distribute rations." General Nasca loved plays on words, especially his own, and laughed heartily.

And so the soldiers ate, while Donna Marena had rations distributed from a combination of her own provisions and those of Villa's peasants. In an attic of the abbey, Villa found some mattresses and cots left by the Germans, and he assigned these to the older people. The women lit a fire in the kitchen and the braziers in the cells, and soon people were warming up. Terzo gave orders to Curatolo: "Make sure all the doors are covered. Get good marksmen to take turns. If they see the bandits coming back, sound the alarm at once."

But Famine's bandits had other things on their minds. Having come down for a certain ambush, a turkey-shoot against a handful of peasants, they now felt hunted by an elusive adversary who was ready when they thought he was oblivious, aggressive when they expected him to be docile, well protected when they were preparing to deliver the coup de grâce. Moreover, they had nothing to eat, the weather had taken a turn for the worse, the fog was dense, and they would soon have to be at their appointment with the boss. Famine had Taddarita's corpse brought into the shelter of the hut. He looked at it and shuddered; a few insects were already creeping along the dead man's threadbare jacket.

"Where are the Monasteros and the others?"

"We couldn't find them," Volpe confessed.

Rather than cover him with insults, Famine gave him a worried look, and his dejection made Volpe even more frightened. "We're in big trouble," he said quietly, so the others wouldn't hear, "big, big trouble. We've got the soldiers behind us, I have no idea where those bastards have gone, and I don't want to find out as they're gunning us down. You stay here. I'll go get the boss. He'll treat me like a doormat, but it's better than continuing to make our own decisions. Wait for me here."

He didn't wait long. Soon a mortified Famine reappeared from behind the hill, followed by two dozen horsemen wrapped in long, dark-blue capes. Each was carrying a rifle over his shoulder. Closing out the squadron was a sullen figure, who descended from his horse without a word and handed a bandit his rifle, the butt of which was decorated in silver. The new arrivals passed around a few loaves of bread and cornets of olives, while Famine, Volpe, and Sgobbio went over to report to the leader. In silence, the caped men stood guard.

"You let yourselves be beaten by peasants. I shouldn't have trusted you." The boss struck the ground with his whip, raising ashes.

"It's like they know what they're doing. They never are where we expect them to be—"

Silencing him with a gesture, the boss said: "That's enough. Call everyone together. Everyone. I've paid a great deal of money, and you tell me that when it's time to fight the riffraff goes and hides? But when *you* were hiding in the bushes you felt braver than Roland in France, didn't you? Brave enough to shoot a laborer. Everybody back here, in an hour. On foot, on mules, by carriage, or however the devil they get here, I want them all here in an hour. I'll flush out those peasants."

"The soldiers are out there, too. Now we're the ones stuck in the middle," Famine said mournfully.

"The soldiers won't intervene. General Nasca is just another imbecile. Go, stop wasting time."

He raised the hood above his eyes and went out. One of the bandits standing guard tried to see who this mysterious man was who promised money, weapons, and ammunition and treated the cruel Famine like a sniveling dog. He tried to get a glimpse of his face, without attracting attention, stretching his neck as if tired from getting up so early. The boss jerked the blue cowl back down, and the bandit, terrified, turned his head. None of the men had ever seen him, and nobody wanted to. A passing glance, perhaps, but to look him in the eye, no: that was a privilege they gladly left to Famine. The memory of that kid Firriolo curbed their curiosity. With every night they spent around a bonfire, the Firriolo legend became richer and richer in detail. But no matter what the real story might be, it was enough to make them keep their mouths shut. Having just arrived among them, and being neither a mafioso nor a brigand but just cunning, the young Firriolo had let slip: "Me? I know who the boss is." And when Sgobbio and Volpe laughed, he insisted: "I saw him get out of a black Lancia sedan, and I won't say in whose company."

"I suppose he even asked you for advice," Sgobbio mocked him. "And what do you think of the situation, Mr. Firriolo, Your Excellency, sir?"

At that point Firriolo had blurted out: "If you knew who he really is, you'd all be running around like chickens with their heads cut off. But I'm not going to say. When the moment comes to talk, I'll make a mint. Want to bet?" They bet a bottle of Cerasuolo wine, but Sgobbio was never able to demand payment because, a few days later, the loose-lipped Firriolo disappeared. "He went north," said Famine, but nobody believed him. "Firriolo in northern Italy? The only mainland he found was under a heap of stones, and the crows have already pecked out his eyes. So much for the chicken with his head cut off." Such was the obituary pronounced by Taddarita, while spitting tobacco into the fire. Ever since then, the bandits had decided it was wiser to look the other way on those few occasions when the hooded figure passed among them.

After the two failures, Famine was very quick to follow orders. In the neighboring villages and valleys, in vineyards and cellars, he rounded up, by means of whistles, shouts, promises, insults, threats, and a few lashes of the whip, every last brigand, two-timer, strong-arm, hit man, bad cop, lowlife, and cheap hood who had ever received a farthing from the boss. Many came on horseback, others on mules, and those who didn't have any borrowed them or made do. All were armed. When Terzo sighted them in his binoculars, they looked less bewildered than during the morning's attacks. Fear held them together, and they rode in orderly fashion. "Devils in capes," Villa muttered. It was a congregation of assassins and cheats, scoundrels made more dangerous by Famine's warning: "Boys, our bread is at stake. Either we beat the bumpkins, or the boss will withdraw his protection and we'll have the soldiers to deal with. Keep that in mind."

TERZO LOOKED BACK out the window with his binoculars, more as a compensatory gesture than to reassess what he already knew. Famine's horsemen were advancing at a slow trot; on the bridge, General Nasca's lookouts were on the alert. The colonel summoned Curatolo and D'Oro to give them the latest orders. Then he went back to watching the bridge and the horsemen. In less than twenty minutes they'd be within range. "We're in an abbey, the enemy is attacking us head on, and behind us is an occupied bridge. What battle is this?" In the progress of that improvised cavalry there was an air of calm that disturbed him. "This morning they came forward like bullies and brutes only good for picking on the weak, and I wasn't impressed," Terzo explained to Salvatore, handing him the binoculars. "Now they're coming up all silent and grim. More afraid, less self-assured, yes, but more dangerous, too. Take a good look, Salvatore. They have scouts, do you see them? Those two men on horseback leading the way, prancing back and forth. They're protecting the rear. Now look downhill, there's a patrol of three gorillas checking on the soldiers' movements. They must have a commander, someone who recruited the new arrivals and is keeping them in line.

Do you see anyone in fancy clothing, I don't know, maybe carrying a more valuable rifle, or with more elegant trappings on his horse? No? We have to try and find out who is doing the thinking for them. Usually officers like to have some sort of ornament." But the leader of the bandits, riding between Famine and Volpe, was wearing only the simple, dark-blue hood over his face, indistinguishable to Terzo, and a mystery to his own men.

"They're trouble, Salvatore," Terzo muttered, and looked at the peasants chewing their bread. It seemed strange to him that he'd made it this far merely by quoting his battles from memory. He tried to think. Imminent attack. We're holed up in a monastery. Frontal clash. Are these elements of some past battle? He couldn't remember. He went back into the church to look for Emma. She was lying down on a cot, wrapped in a blanket. Fiore was sitting next to her.

"How do you feel? Do you need anything?" he asked her.

"Are they coming back?" was all she said in response.

She was very pale. Terzo had never seen her look so exhausted; yet it seemed the outcome of the battle was the only thing that truly mattered to her, as though the common danger freed her from the thought of her own agony. Terzo decided not to lie.

"Yes," he said, "and this time they won't run away."

"I know you'll find a way to defeat them."

Emma smiled with such serenity as she said this, that Fiore repeated, with assurance: "I don't know how, Colonel, but you will defeat them."

Salvatore was asking him something, and Donna Marena and Villa were awaiting explanations, but Terzo did not answer. He went back to watching the cloud of dust approaching from the mule track, calculated the range of General Nasca's Breda machine gun, and turned to his wife and whispered: "If only I could think with their leader's mind. If I could make him think what I want him to think, control his mind, then we might

make it. I haven't figured out what the battle is that we're facing, Emma. Perhaps I should do as Stonewall Jackson did with
the Union's General Banks, who felt too ashamed to fall back
and therefore lost. Jackson attacked and retreated in a circle,
confusing poor Banks. But I don't see any railroads here, and
we're not in the Shenandoah Valley in 1862. Write this down,
Salvatore, write: *Mystify, mislead, and surprise*: that was Jackson's credo. But I don't know what battle this is, Emma. And the
enemy is right in front of us. Look for yourself. Genghis Khan
crossed the Kyzyl Kum Desert, traveled six hundred impossible
miles to catch the shah's soldiers from behind. What was the
key, Salvatore? His soldiers' struggle? That, no doubt, was magnificent, but if he hadn't thought of it, what good would the
struggle have done? None whatsoever. And we're not in the
desert."

"But don't you see?" said Emma in a hoarse voice.

"What should I be seeing?" Terzo turned, in surprise, toward
his wife.

"The battles. Fate has put you face to face with your books:
the *Manual for Strategic Living* and the *Encyclopedia of Battles*.
In a few hours you'll be called upon to fight them all at the
same time—to interpret, with the wretched soldiers you've got,
the campaigns you've been studying all your life. It's what I
asked of the kite, my wish in the courtyard of the bombed-out
house. Now I can tell you. And now you must fight, Colonel
Carlo Terzo."

Terzo looked at Emma without understanding. "Your wish?
Kite? *Encyclopedia of Battles*? . . . No, no, not now. I have to decide where we are. The eighth battle for Jerusalem, in 1187? After the defeat at Lake Tiberias, Balian defended Jerusalem for
twelve days, arming adolescents like Salvatore, but finally Sal-
adin's army broke through. The inexperience of the peasants is
similar to that of Balian's troops, but this morning we actually
won, unlike King Guy, who lost at Lake Tiberias. And so?" But

however much he tried to remember, however much he turned
the binoculars from the volcano to the valley, to the river and
the bridge and then back to the ancient monks' cemetery on the
hill, protected by a low, whitewashed wall, however many notes
he dictated to Salvatore, he still could not call to mind what battle it was he was about to fight.

The bandits' horses were now within range. Famine, gaunt
and nervous, looked up toward the abbey.

HIDDEN BY HIS HOOD, the leader of the bandits said to Famine: "Now you're going to get them. You will lead the attack. If I see you hesitate, I'll shoot. Once you get there you'll do as much damage as you can and then turn back. Their only choice will be to go down toward the bridge, at which point the soldiers will be all over them. They won't distinguish between the peasants and Donna Marena's rebels; it'll be a massacre. There must be no survivors."

Famine was a highwayman. If he could steal a traveler's purse or extort money from peasants without bloodshed, he was a happier man. But the death of his companions that morning, the assurance he felt having his boss nearby, and the throng of horsemen pressing all around him, made him more aggressive. He had no choice, in any case. Defeat meant losing his commission, becoming a cutthroat, leaving the island.

Following orders, he scattered the horsemen along the thicket on the hillside, where the greenery blended with the red ash of the volcano. Then he gave the signal to Sgobbio, who lazily approached, set up a small howitzer on a tripod and took aim, all the while smoking a clay pipe. Closing one eye, he calculated the distance, grimaced twice, and when he thought he was ready, grumbled: "The boys are in position." The blue hood gave a slight bow, Famine winked, Sgobbio took a bitter puff on his pipe and let out a shrill whistle, like a buzzard. It echoed on the mountain behind the Abbey of San Giovanni, and the shelling began.

The first shells landed behind the churchyard, frightening two horses tied to an olive tree. Donna Marena leaped up. "What is it now?" she cried.

"Hit the ground," shouted D'Oro, "take cover." Chaos filled the makeshift camp. The soldiers of the Republic of Malpasso left the wall where Terzo had positioned them and ran to their families. The musicians in the band, cocky from the morning's successes, had gone to the front lines, but now they were fleeing, scattering sheet music everywhere. There wasn't even time to give an order.

"Don't be afraid," Terzo shouted. "They're aiming too low. Look: only the ground downhill is blowing up."

But Sgobbio had the right idea. The explosions, however harmless, terrorized those poor people. The shells would not do much damage: the churchyard was large and lined with trees, and the massive walls of the abbey protected the civilians inside. The blasts and shrapnel, however, sent Villa's peasants and Malpasso's militiamen running. Some ran down the slope behind the church, which was enclosed by a torrent and by the mass of the volcano. They held one another's hands, sinking their feet into dried lava and ash, stunned and frightened. Moliterni's wife lost her hairpins in the rush, her beautiful black hair now covering her face, blinding her as she fled down the hill, clutching her newborn in her arms.

There were those who claimed afterward to have been the first to see the sticks of dynamite flying down from the mountain. Some said they were orange, some said they were yellow, some even said they could read the letters TNT on them. For years each had his own story. But in his binoculars Colonel Terzo found the two snipers who, perched upon a rocky bluff, were taking target practice with the explosive. The first stick exploded at the feet of Master Moliterni's wife and baby daughter, Lucia, and blew them to pieces. From her paneless window, Emma saw the woman running, then a reddish mist, then the sand absorbing the blood.

"They're shelling us, so they can come and slaughter us or force us down to the soldiers," Terzo thought aloud. "I have to figure this out. What battle is this? There is a monk's cemetery, the defense wall, and then? We'll only save our skins if we can hold the wall and flush the gunners out from the hill. In the meantime, Donna Marena, for God's sake, tell your people to come back. They'll kill them all with their dynamite."

Donna Marena, the midwife and president of the Republic of Malpasso, ran fearlessly onto the slope, planted herself in front of the fleeing peasants, and spoke calmly. Fear dries the mouth: Terzo knew that during the Spanish civil war those condemned to death used to spit in front of the firing squad to show their courage. Speaking in battle, in a clear, loud voice, meant you had guts. Donna Marena did more than this: she opened her black-clad arms and shouted: "Malpasso back! Now! Don't go past this cross." Famine's men saw her from the mountain, lit a fuse, and fired. But the dynamite struck a lava formation and fell down into the torrent, where it exploded in a crater of mud and water.

The crowd was hypnotized by Donna Marena's courage, as she stood over the blood of Moliterni's wife and daughter. Nobody went past that red borderline. Another stick fell from above. Spinning in mid-air, the fuse hissed like grease in a frying pan until the blast went off, deep in the volcanic ash. The two bandits had taken cover behind the bluff, awaiting the explosion, but when they resurfaced they saw only the gown of Pepe the altar boy, who had been the last to take shelter. Donna Marena had stopped the rout.

Sgobbio, smoking, calmly adjusted the aim on his howitzer. The shells were now landing inside the abbey walls. Terzo had to persuade his men to resume their positions along the wall, where they risked being struck by shrapnel. "We have to defend ourselves from attack," he said, "the horses are on the hillside and approaching."

"To your posts," Curatolo shouted, and D'Oro, the former sergeant, dealt out kicks and slaps to the more fearful of the men. Donna Marena, still breathless from her dash down to the torrent, climbed into the pulpit and, taking advantage of the echo in the church, pantingly called out:

"Where are you running, citizens of Malpasso? Do you want to go back to living like animals? What kind of example are you setting for your children? Do you know who it is that is slaughtering us like pigs? It's Mastema's thugs. They killed Marro. There's nothing left of Moliterni's wife, nothing left of the baby Lucia. I brought that little girl into this world with these hands. Do you want those men here raping your wives and butchering your daughters like lambs at Easter? You run away. What are you, a bunch of chickens? I thought I was commanding the free citizens of the Republic of Malpasso. I thought you were sick and tired of fattening the nobility. I guess I was wrong. You're worse than chickens: at least they have the courage to defend their chicks. Do you like being slugs? Snails? Nitwits? So be it. Malpasso will be defended by its women. Ladies, leave the children with the men, they've got no balls. You had the courage to bring them into the world, to go through the pain of labor; you won't let them be slaughtered before your eyes."

Donna Marena stepped spryly down from the pulpit, grabbed a shotgun from a man's hands and rested it on her shoulder. That was enough. Blushing with shame, rebels and peasants shouted, "No, no" and "We'll go." Some women would not give up the idea of taking up arms themselves. There were quarrels, with brothers and sisters fighting over the same rifle, but within minutes Terzo's line of defense was reconstituted, denser than before. The defenders dug holes to protect themselves from the shelling, while downhill Sgobbio seemed to be running out of ammunition. The explosions became more infrequent.

"What battle is this? Attack from a central position, with an arrogant enemy and tired, frightened defenders. And a cemetery behind them. How can I not remember? Artillery . . . Salvatore, Salvatore . . ."

The cannon began firing hard, and the horses set off along the hillside, commencing the attack, kicking up red sand. The bandits were wearing long hooded capes that hung down over the horses' flanks; this made them look like centaurs, monsters who, by leaps and bounds, to shouts and whistles, were eating up the distance between them and the white wall. Shrapnel and rifle shots again sowed panic among the defenders. Terzo thought of General Hancock: to keep them at the wall he had to show them he was not afraid of the shells. Standing up, he said: "They're just tickling us, boys, let's stay put."

A woman shouted to him: "You take cover, Colonel. What would we do without you?" He heard himself answer as Hancock might have:

"In moments such as these, signora, everyone's life is of equal value."

A rabbit darted along the wall, terrified by the explosions. It ran belly to the ground, halting for an instant to sniff the chaos. Laughing from fear, Pepe the altar boy cried out: "Run, rabbit, run. If I were a rabbit, I'd run too." The rabbit seemed to hear him: it turned its pointed muzzle around a moment, then disappeared into the woods. Terzo understood. *What an idiot I am*, he thought. *How could I not have thought of it earlier? The Union bluecoats also said "Run, rabbit, run." It's Gettysburg, by God, three days of hell, July 1 to July 3, 1863.*

"Salvatore," he shouted, "go watch how they come up after the shelling. They're Pickett's men, this is Pickett's Charge at Cemetery Ridge, the most extraordinary attack of the War of Secession, led personally by the Confederate's General George

Pickett. If General Lee had succeeded in beating the Union's General Meade on July 3, 1863, at two-thirty in the afternoon, the European powers would have intervened in the war, and the South would have succeeded in defending slavery. The fate of the world would have been different. But the Confederate tide was extinguished in Pickett's Charge, which left three brigadier generals, thirteen colonels, and nineteen regiment banners on the battlefield."

Terzo looked in the direction of the church, where the women had taken refuge. A shell exploded near them, the shrapnel cutting down two men who were still standing. The first fell face forward and did not move, while the second rolled on the ground from the impact then sat right back up, like a puppet, ashen and muttering, "I've been hit, I've been hit." D'Oro whistled, and Fiore and Gawain carried the wounded man into the church. Terzo untied a horse and jumped into the saddle.

"Nobody move, or shoot, until I give the order. Stay in your foxholes. They're going to stop shelling us now, they're too close. Curatolo, get ready. It's your turn. D'Oro, on the alert."

FAMINE AND THE OTHER BANDITS came up below the wall. The shelling stopped and the shouting and shooting began. The Malpasso boys stayed on the ground; the shelling had achieved the desired effect. Still, spurred on by Terzo's cries of encouragement, the peasants kept firing with regularity. "Over here, over here," Famine barked, spurring his horse toward the rear of the abbey, where the monks' orchard once grew. As a little boy he used to steal peaches and almonds there, and he remembered that the enclosure wall was surrounded by a little moat. More than once he'd leaped across it with his shirt full of fruit and the cellarer at his heels. Now he led a group of about twenty noisy bandits. His childhood memory proved right: one had only to flick the reins and the horses leaped over the little stream and galloped through the soil. Now only the guest house, where itinerant pilgrims used to stay,. separated the invaders from Terzo's defense. "We'll take them from behind," shouted Famine. A woman saw them from the window and sounded the alarm. Volpe shot at her, and she fell forward.

The horses leaned into the gravel-covered turn, and Famine was already savoring the surprise attack on the enemy. With instinctive caution, the bandit barely touched the reins; he didn't want to be the first to burst into the churchyard, where a shootout was raging. He let a young thug, Moschitta, known for his long reach when peasant girls passed by, go in front of him, along with Papola, the killer of young Firriolo. At the first blast of flames, Famine was able to pull on the reins and step aside. The blaze enveloped Moschitta instead, whose cries became confused with the neighing of his horse. Then, as if on the rebound, the fire struck Papola. His mare kept on running, no longer directed by the bandit on her back, who was waving his flaming arms about.

"Stop, goddammit, stop," Famine cursed. Curatolo's third Molotov cocktail crashed against a pile of firewood, and the barrier of flames had finally isolated the attackers. Donna Marena's militia had been carrying a few tins of gasoline, which Curatolo had used to prepare the guerrilla fighter's most ancient weapon. The effect of the crude firebombs was extraordinary. Their raid a failure, the aggressors jumped back over the moat and disappeared into the fields. Better the boss's wrath than burning alive, thought Famine, fleeing with the rest. As for the dynamiters up the mountain, they, too, seeing the danger, dropped their explosives and scattered.

Along the front line at the wall, the offensive continued into the evening's first shadows. Bandits attacked and fell, but now defenders, too, were falling, in great numbers. Gawain and the women came to their aid. "Aim, fire," repeated Terzo. "They expected to surround us. If we can hold out until Famine turns tail, they'll call off the attack. Fortresses always have the advantage in sieges." On his horse, and with his erudition, so incongruous amid the carnage, he was going about encouraging the defenders when Pepe the altar boy approached him.

"Look, Colonel," he whispered.

A procession of old people, women, and children, all with hands in the air, was silently filing out of the abbey and into the churchyard, without turning around. When the last person had come out into the cold, Terzo saw a bandit following behind, pointing a machine gun at them.

"He must have slipped in through the little window in the shed," said Pepe, making the sign of the cross. *At Gettysburg, too, the Southern squads made it past the first trenches*, thought Terzo. *But later they were forced to surrender. Or am I remembering it wrong?* Pepe tugged at his jacket, and he saw Emma and Fiore among the hostages.

"Throw down your weapons, if you want them to live," hissed the bandit. The peasants ceased firing.

"That's Diotru, he's really evil. He'll kill them." Having served Mass daily for so long, Pepe had learned how to speak without moving his lips.

"Throw down your weapons and open the door." Diotru's eyes sparkled strangely, one blue, the other green. He had long aspired to Famine's position. He'd seen him running away, as he was bravely lowering himself in through the embrasure. If he could force the peasants to open up, the boss would make him leader of the gang. He shouted loudly to his companions outside: "It's Diotru. I'm going to open the door now. Don't shoot. We've screwed 'em. Move, bastards." To lend strength to his threat, he twisted the arm of the girl with the braids, who fell to her knees in tears. Beyond the wall, the bandits, no longer held back by the defenders' fire, warily approached.

"All right," said Terzo. "Don't shoot. We'll open up." Without

turning around, he was following D'Oro's movements. Balancing on the damp roof tiles, the sergeant was positioning himself
behind Diotru, making ready to jump on him and disarm him.
"Don't shoot," Terzo repeated, to gain time. Curatolo, hand on
the bolt, awaited the precise order. With a loud creak, the rusted
gutter collapsed under D'Oro's weight. Diotru quickly turned
around, firing immediately. The old sergeant slid off the roof,
struck the portico lifeless, and fell back onto the pebbles.

Terzo had told Salvatore the story of the Confederate's General Nathan Bedford Forrest: in four years of war he had killed
thirty men and had seen his horses killed in battle no less than
twenty-nine times. Now it was his own turn: frightened by the
machine-gun fire, his mare started and Diotru killed it instinctively, sending the colonel tumbling. With the barrel of his
weapon still hot, the bandit pushed the braided girl toward the
door, making Curatolo stand aside. "Open the door, witch." The
bandits outside were already beating on the door with the butts
of their rifles.

"We're here, Diotru," they shouted.

The girl groped at the bolt that held the double doors shut,
but it wouldn't budge. The bandit nervously shoved her aside
and tried to open it himself. The peasants watched him defenseless, the pride in their weapons now gone. They had lost all hope
of escape. Salvatore's eyes sought out those of Princess Emma
Svyatoslava in the first line of hostages, to try to see what was
going through her mind, and he was astonished. She was pale
but unafraid, as if waiting. The boy absorbed her sense of calm
and looked at his teacher. "This is certainly not the end," he
whispered to Gawain. "The colonel always has a strategy for
winning."

He was right, but this time the secret lay not in memories
and ancient tomes. Rising painfully from the ground, Colonel
Terzo reached into his pocket for the regulation pistol he always
had with him and promptly killed Diotru, firing two shots into

the bandit's shoulders as he was fiddling with the door. "Never aim at the head, an elusive target, only for the foolhardy," Campari's voice echoed in his head. "It's much better to try for the chest, which makes a good target. You may not kill the aggressor, but you'll certainly stop him." Diotru was a ferocious man, and Terzo understood killers well. Not for a moment had the bandit suspected that this stuffy gentleman might have a weapon and be capable of shooting someone in the back like a brigand. "Always confound the enemy. Always."

It was the first time Colonel Carlo Terzo had ever killed a man; indeed, it was the first time he had ever shot at anyone. They were all looking at him, Emma dumbfounded, the peasants incredulous, the girl with the braids weeping, her arm dislocated. He reloaded his pistol and said calmly: "I don't believe I ever ordered a cease-fire. Hit them now. They're propped up against the wall like cod left out to dry. Fire away."

Master Moliterni, who from that day on never stopped wearing black in mourning for his wife and daughter, always said: "I, too, started shooting, even though I'd never touched a rifle. We were all shooting like madmen. To us the colonel was Alexander the Great."

With a "hurrah!" Curatolo returned to the wall, and whoever had a weapon started shooting. The bandits' surprise at the counterattack was overwhelming. The women bombarded them with roof tiles, dirt clods, and stones, until someone dug up a cross from a monk's grave and aimed it at the back of the last fleeing bandit.

"Cease fire," Terzo finally ordered. He had his right hand in his pocket to hide the trembling. *I fired just as Amedeo taught me,* he thought. *"Aim at the body. The head is a target for the foolhardy." I didn't even order the man to stop and drop his weapons. I shot him in the back, as one does in war, to kill and to survive.* He was searching inside himself for a reaction but couldn't find any, other than his trembling hand. He now understood the silence of veterans. You do what you can and, once the war's over, you can't explain it to those who weren't there. You can't talk about war. *What should I do? Tell Salvatore to write this down? Shoot the enemy in the back? At the movie theater, people would boo, but here it was the right thing, the reasonable thing to do. Strategically perfect.*

He looked up at the dark sky on the evening of Santa Lucia. Now they could breathe again. In primitive warfare, one fought only by the light of day. He told Villa and Curatolo to take turns standing guard and entered the church. He hadn't eaten a thing since dawn and bit into some homemade bread and salty white *tuma* cheese that the women were cutting into thin slices. Emma smiled, lying down on her cot: "You're slaughtering them," she said.

"We have to get out of here. We've been lucky so far; the next time it will be a massacre. People are tired and afraid. We've had a lot of victims. I've given the order to have the wounded cleared out. Pepe knows the goatherds' trails, along the side of the volcano. But it's not possible for all of us, with the old people and children, to leave at night. If the bandits don't leave, we're done for. Unless we surrender to the soldiers."

"I'm sure you'll come up with an idea."

"Speaking of ideas," said Terzo, "what are we going to do about the kids?"

"The kids?" Looking down the aisles, Emma understood her husband's concern. The women were laying out shawls and blankets along the church's benches, creating makeshift beds for the night. The pale twilight of the solstice filtered through the stained glass, illuminating a breast-feeding mother and an old couple huddled against the cold inside a confessional. A woman dressed in black was reciting the Mysteries of the Rosary. The families had been reunited, and Salvatore and Fiore were busy arranging two saddles as pillows, getting ready to spend the night together. No one paid any attention to them.

Becoming again the traditionalist he was, the colonel objected: "In church, and they're not even married! Let's go. The Duchess—"

"—and by tomorrow morning they may be dead," Emma interrupted him. "Is it really a sin? God will be pleased by their love, after all this war around His deconsecrated church. Leave them alone. Try instead to get some rest."

The colonel loved his wife as a man rarely loves. One loves an adventurous mistress, a new girlfriend. But Terzo was one of those men with the good fortune to remain in love with his wife, to lose himself in her, to listen to her with confidence. The old soldier in him turned a blind eye to the scandal. He went out to check the rear lines, and as he passed by the young lovers, he gave them some leftover bread and wished them goodnight.

As Salvatore was about to share it with Fiore, Pepe the altar boy jumped in front of him: "Are you mad? Do you want to go blind? Eating bread on the feast of Santa Lucia is a sacrilege. Here, I brought you something else. We'll save the bread for tomorrow." He spoke in a low voice, as if in front of the altar.

"Do you really believe you can go blind from eating a little bread?" Salvatore smiled and looked at the bowl that Pepe was holding out to him.

"Oh, yes. Blind. Didn't you know? Padre Inguardì told me. Hundreds of years ago there was a famine in Syracuse. People were dying of hunger, dropping like flies in winter. They'd eaten everything, even the last hosts in the churches. They'd boiled book covers to make broth. They'd melted the glue from the furniture to make soup. There was nothing left. The bishop retired to this room. He barely had the strength to say a prayer to Santa Lucia: 'Have mercy on us,' he said, 'don't condemn us to death,' and he fell to the ground in exhaustion. At dawn on December 13, he was awakened by the wind whistling through the rigging of ships in the bay. Dragging himself to the window, he saw a boat without sails, docked at a roadstead. A fisherman summoned his remaining strength to climb aboard and beg the sailors for some biscuit. But there was nobody there. No crew, no helmsman, no captain. The bridge and the hold were loaded with barrels. The fisherman opened one and found it full of wheat. He threw a gangplank onto the pier and cried out: 'Bread, bread!' The ship was unloaded as best as was possible; people boiled the wheat and immediately devoured it, without taking the trouble to grind it into flour for bread and noodles. And the bishop decreed: 'To thank Santa Lucia for the miracle of the ship, on her feast day, December 13, we will no longer eat foods made with flour. Only dishes made with whole grains of wheat.' Try it: it's called *cuccìa*."

In the bowl were solid wheat grains, with their dark incision down the middle, mixed together with a pudding of sweet must. Salvatore took some with his pocketknife and held it out for Fiore:

"Careful, it's sharp," he said.

The girl cautiously put the blade in her mouth and chewed the grain. "Very sweet," she smiled, "try some." And she held out a mouthful for Salvatore.

"*Buon appetito,*" said the clever altar boy, and he disappeared into the pitch darkness of the abbey.

Salvatore was hungry, and the porridge was excellent. The hard grain opened up between the teeth, while the spicy must numbed the tongue and the head. They were still passing the penknife back and forth, emptying the bowl, when Fiore turned the little blade clumsily in the dark and cut Salvatore on the lip.

"Did I hurt you?"

"No, no," he replied, but Fiore put her fingers on his face and felt the blood.

"I cut you. Forgive me. Wait, I've got a handkerchief." And she stanched the cut, holding the batiste cloth to his lips, but she couldn't see whether the wound was still bleeding. Like someone blind, she touched his mouth with her fingers. Salvatore took her hand and they kissed.

Alone together in the large, icy nave, with the taste of sweet wheat, wine, and blood in their mouths, Salvatore and Fiore embraced, lying down on the blanket the peasants had given them. Her lean body didn't even feel the hard marble beneath it. He felt awkward and embarrassed: in Terzo's study he could be bold, but now the sacred atmosphere, the darkness, the danger made him unsure of himself. Fiore, without a word, removed her bodice, and the cold air hardened her nipples.

Covering Salvatore's face with little kisses, she opened his arms to make a cross and stroked his soft hair, saying to him: "You are my man, you are my husband, it's not a sin because you're my husband and you're going to give me children and we're going to leave Palermo, we're going to go away, aren't we? Where will we go, my love?"

"To Paris," Salvatore whispered, as Fiore was kissing his neck.

"Paris? How boring. I'd rather marry little Duke Mainoni," and she removed Salvatore's jacket and shirt.

"America, then. We'll go to America with Gawain. He promised me I could study at the University of Indiana."

"And there aren't any nobles there. Perfect." The more clothing they took off, the tighter they held each other and wrapped the rough wool blanket around themselves. They couldn't see each other in the dark, but Fiore's hands reminded both that they were making love.

"Now," she said.

"Here?"

"We'll get married. My mother won't be able to do anything about it."

Salvatore turned Fiore gently about. His heart leaped into his throat, and he didn't quite know what to do because he was a virgin like her, hot in his embraces but uncertain in love. "Recite a poem as you're doing it," Fiore murmured, but Salvatore was unable, unable to find her body and remember his poems; and so she guided him, with modesty and passion, under the blanket and with the cold on her shoulders, made room for him inside herself and felt him there. To avoid moaning, and to forget her mother's cruelty, the shadows of the peasants nearby, the mystery of the church, and the problems of the day to come, Fiore began reciting one of Salvatore's poems herself and it seemed beautiful to her and she felt him move inside her with passion and apprehension, but instead of crying out as she would have liked, she said quietly, "I conceived the finest verses of a century of sadness, but before I wrote them I forgot them."

Salvatore wasn't listening; he felt his own heart beat and her breast quiver. He was panting. Fiore, like a little girl wrestling with a boy in kindergarten, flipped him onto his back and climbed onto his chest. Letting the blanket fall off, she made love to him, continuing softly to repeat lines of poetry to him, not only his but also those they had read on the albatross, in the book of the bombed-out palace:

> The poet is like this prince of the clouds,
> familiar with storms, unruffled by archers;
> an exile on land among jeering crowds,
> he has a giant's wings, and cannot walk.

Salvatore moved his head back and forth, eyes closed. The wind blew through the windows long stripped of stained glass, but he was very hot. He held her tight, but Fiore broke away and continued to make love to him freely, saying, "My companion, my friend, my man, you're mine and only mine and they won't take you far away from me, never, never, never." And then her voice broke, seeming perhaps too loud in the darkness, and fell into little girl talk. She fell silent and still covered Salvatore's face with her hair and kisses, and he felt lost, felt she was stronger and freer than he, and that he would never be as strong and free as she. Then he arched his back to raise his woman up and celebrate her in the dark, to love her all the way, and she recited verses, forgetting whose they were. Then they fell asleep in the dark. This was their wedding night.

Everyone slept in the besieged abbey, except for the sentinels guarding the black slopes of the volcano, Terzo, who was thinking of what battle he would be fighting the following day, and Emma, who was restless with pain and fatigue. Her husband had whispered to her: "We're in church. Pray. Your prayers are rare, and therefore precious." The princess prayed, commended the young lovers to God, forgave them for their innocent audacity, asked for wisdom for her husband, relief for herself, and salvation for the poor people around them. Then she closed her eyes.

The last to fall asleep was Pepe the altar boy. That basilica of refugees seemed to him more solemn than a Mass sung in the cathedral. The gown he was wearing, which he had previously thought of as a uniform for play, good for throwing stones and pilfering incense in the oratory, weighed heavy on his slender shoulders. He shuddered and recited the Pater Noster, ". . . Thy kingdom come," as if he were hearing those words for the first time. Before the freezing bodies, before the dead assembled in the churchyard and the wounded moaning around a flickering candle stub, he repeated, "Thy kingdom come, Thy kingdom come," and crossed himself devoutly, deeply moved.

Terzo decided to sleep for an hour, but first he wanted to go up to Curatolo on the bastions to oversee the changing of the guard. Feeling his way, he found the ancient stairs and went out into the cold. The terrace roof was short and ringed with battlements. He looked down into the darkness of the valley. Seeing Pepe absorbed in his prayers, the prayer of Sir Jacob Astley, on the dawn of the battle of Edgehill in 1642, came to his lips:

"Lord, Thou knowest how busy I must be this day. If I forget Thee, do not Thou forget me." There was not a single light burning on the plain; the soldiers had extinguished their bonfires. He did, however, think he saw a brief flash, a spark, dot the ridge of the volcano. "Tired eyes," he said to himself, but suddenly there was another little flicker, then another, followed by ten more: a string of fireflies descending in orderly fashion, side by side and overlapping in the distance.

Without fear, Curatolo's voice reached him in the darkness: "Do you see them, Colonel?" The fireflies were now a constant strip of light, a violet wound on the mule paths. Terzo raised Campari's binoculars, but he already knew that those lights were horsemen with torches, in a number he had rarely seen in his life: ten, one hundred to one for his poor peasants, horsemen guided by a hidden leader and now determined to settle the battle once and for all. The north wind made the flames quiver for a moment, then the flow of armed men came back together in the darkness, continuous, powerful, unbending along the footpaths.

A LIVID DAWN was rising. Curatolo, wet with dew and scratched by brambles, returned from his scouting mission.

"We're finished, Colonel," he said. "They're going down onto the plain and drawing up in battle formation. There are a lot of them, an infinite number. They've summoned the men from the Forcade fief. I recognize them by their horses. We're going to have to fight."

The fog lifted slightly, and before Terzo's eyes an enormous front appeared. Horsemen to the sides, riflemen in the middle, rows and rows of bandits. Too many for his remaining forces. Donna Marena came up to him. "We will fight, and we will die. You go back and surrender to the soldiers."

"The bandits have a brain now," Terzo observed, "and it was careless of me not to realize it. Hans Delbrück, *Geschichte der Kriegkunst*, Book One: 'If you don't eliminate the enemy, peace will not return.' That was clear yesterday. It was the battle of Gettysburg. We won, like the Union forces, but we were unable to destroy the Confederate army." He looked down at the ashen plain and ordered: "In the middle we'll put the Malpasso boys and the women who feel like fighting. Anyone who still has a horse or mule will go on the right flank. Curatolo's veterans will go to the left. Let's move."

Curatolo was about to obey, but Donna Marena protested: "The women in the middle, with the boys? But didn't you see what happened yesterday at the wall? My people have no expe-

rience, only good will. They'll be overwhelmed. They'll surround us. Let's put the men in the middle."

Villa nodded: "Sounds reasonable to me."

"There's still time before they attack us, signora," said Terzo.
"We'll talk to the boys. Can they hold out for five minutes?
That's all I ask, five minutes. You, Villa, and I will be there with
them, we'll fire them up."

The woman shook her head. She still could not quite believe
in that old-fashioned gentleman, even though he had thus far
succeeded in confounding the enemy. Curatolo, on the other
hand, had rediscovered in Terzo the leader he'd lost with the
end of the war. In Africa he had felt proud of the resistance that
Amedeo Guillet had put up against the English. Returning to
his life as a farmer, it pained him to hear people speak ill of the
Italians: "Terrible soldiers, good lovers," the Americans would
say, smiling good-naturedly. To their struggle for land, Curatolo
brought the same discipline and spirit of organization he had
learned in the army, and that was why Terzo appreciated him so
much. On that day of action, his two separate lives seemed finally to come together. "Donna Marena," he said, "listen to the
colonel. You can argue in a democracy, but in war you must
obey. Give them the sign, and they'll follow you."

The president of the Republic of Malpasso bowed her head.
"Goddamn war. The more I run away from it, the more it's on
my back. We rebelled against it, and now we have to fight to
save our lives." Her ragamuffin army was quickly roused from
sleep and arrayed in front of the abbey, cold and trembling, with
a handful of nuts and a crust of bread in their bellies. Donna
Marena climbed up onto a black lava formation shaped like a
podium and shouted: "Brothers and sisters of Malpasso, friends
from Petranova. The thugs of the landed estates have been trying to slaughter us for two days, but we're still here. This is our
final test. If we stay together, we'll make it. Everyone must do
his duty, without moving or firing, until the orders are given.

Look at those close to you, think of the women and children, and think of the land. Colonel Terzo knows what he wants to do. He will free us. You are brave, and I'm proud to be your president. God willing, this will be the last day of the war on Malpasso. Now listen to what the colonel says."

Terzo was broadly gesturing "no." He had never given a public speech before, except in the quiet seminars at Saint-Cyr. But the crowd lifted him up bodily to the makeshift dais of lava, and he had to speak.

"I . . . ," he began, "we . . . ," but he didn't know what to say. He looked up in despair and saw a pair of falcons flying in circles, high in the early morning sky. "Friends," he said, "friends. You know about the Romans, about their magical powers in war. Before a battle, our ancestors would look for omens, predictions of fortune, by observing the flight of birds. They would try to read their fate in the sky. And so I say to you: Look at that pair of falcons. See them? They are the proof that we will win. Look at them, my friends, they're flying eastward. They're veering toward the dawn, toward the sun. It's a good omen, believe me. No battle has ever been lost that was heralded by a pair of birds of prey flying east. Do not leave your companion's side. Stay together, like the falcons, come what may. Do what you're told. Don't be ashamed of being afraid. But don't run away. Donna Marena will carry the flag of Malpasso, Trinacria with the spikes of wheat in her hair. And my friend Villa will hoist the union flag. Don't abandon those banners, friends, your lives depend on them. Where they go, you go, too. Defend them, and we'll go home."

A strange thought crossed his mind and he felt ashamed and stammered, pausing awkwardly. But Emma gestured with her hand for him to continue, and he resumed speaking: "Fifteen hundred years have passed since a Roman general last looked into the future and read the omens before a battle. That was in A.D. 439, when General Litorius predicted victory for his legions.

He read destiny by studying sheep bones, but I prefer to observe the free flight of birds. Be brave; I am honored to fight at your side. Trust in the falcons, trust in your own courage, and may God bless you."

Thus his pep talk ended. He blushed and climbed down from the lava formation muttering insecurely: "A bunch of peasants are trying to save their skins and you talk to them of Litorius and scapulomancy. Poor fools, a fine leader they've chosen." But Villa shook his hand. Emma, Fiore, and Salvatore were applauding loudly and Gawain escorted him through the crowd. And his soldiers, armed and unarmed, poorly dressed and hungry, shouted "Long live the colonel, long live Malpasso, land for the peasants, to arms!" The only ones who remained in the abbey were the most seriously wounded and the children, together with a small guard. When everything was ready, Villa took Terzo aside.

"There's a problem, Colonel."

"What is it?"

"I realize we need to have a flag to keep us organized in battle. But I can't raise the union flag. Even if I die, I don't want to disobey the command I was given in the Federation's letter: not to get involved in revolts or participate in acts of violence. We've ended up here by chance, it's true, to defend ourselves, but I'm still a disciplined militant. If they kill us and find our banners among the weapons, the Party will be implicated. It wouldn't be right."

"I have no other flag, Villa, and I need a banner for the people to gather under."

"I've got one," said Curatolo, appearing between the two, "and I would like you to be the one to carry it in battle, Colonel, sir." It was an Italian tricolor, folded up like a handkerchief.

"Thanks, but—"

"We had it in Africa. Lieutenant De Andreis gave it to me as a souvenir. I always bring it with me when we occupy lands. I'm a socialist, but I did my duty in that bloody war. It's a good flag, it's seen some good men die."

"I can't carry it, Colonel, it has the Savoy coat of arms," said Villa. "My comrades wouldn't understand. But in your hands, it's not a problem."

"Thank you." Terzo took the flag and unfolded it in the morning twilight. Curatolo saluted, hand to his cap.

Villa entrusted the union banner to Fiore. "Guard it well, please," he said, and already they were opening up the great door and heading into the field. It wasn't yet eight o'clock.

The flags split up. To the east, Salvatore Dragonara and young Marro with the Malpasso flag, Trinacria with the golden spikes. To the west, Curatolo with the horsemen of the Saracen's Joust. In the middle, Terzo with the tricolor, Villa, and Donna Marena barely had time to take their positions with the boys and women of Malpasso when the enemy charge began, horsemen in front, bandits on foot behind. They were from the Forcade domain, riding their San Fratello horses bareback, like mustangs. They squeezed the animals' flanks with their boots and raised their rifles with both hands, holding the reins between their teeth. Whenever Forcade men came around, there wasn't a single peasant who didn't wish he was back in his hovel, not a single girl who didn't commend herself to Our Lady of Tindari. When the charge had covered half the dusty distance separating the two front lines, Curatolo spit on the ground and clenched his fist, urging the others on, shouting: "Children of tomorrow, let's get the scoundrels."

Spurring on his fighters, he broke away from Terzo's front with the left wing, crossing in front of the enemy horsemen, engaging them in a skirmish, then continued on at a gallop toward the oak grove. The Forcade cavalry followed them wildly, riding away from the battle. They were shooting and shouting, "We'll cut your throats, you shepherds!" The first line of bandits on foot hurled themselves on Terzo's central formation. The Malpasso boys, to make up for their embarrassing retreat on Santa Lucia, fought to the death. The women fired their guns as though possessed, praying. It was a fierce battle of knives and fists and rifles firing point-blank and leaving bluish splotches around the wounds.

Pepe the altar boy tore the revolver away from a fallen bandit and, kneeling as he had seen done in comic books, he fired one shot after another, left eye closed, teeth clenching his tongue in the effort. Terzo shouted, "That's the way! Good work!" Donna Marena was helping a wounded fighter. Villa was shouting "Freedom!" Many fell. A certain Paredes, who had been a gangster in the United States before enrolling in Famine's band, was disposed of by 'Nzinga, Fugazza's cross-eyed girlfriend. But Fugazza didn't have time to shout "Look out!" before Sgobbio grabbed her by the hair and cut her throat. Fustaino, who dreamed of becoming a land surveyor, was dispatched to the next world by a rifle butt, bashed to the ground. Anga, his cousin, tried to protect the body from the crush, firing as long as he could, then slid to the ground, stabbed to death. The rebels of Malpasso fell, the peasants of Petranova fell. But bandits also fell, forgetting now why they were fighting and who was paying them, as they raged in the fray simply to survive. Terzo had hoped for five minutes of resistance, but the boys and women had held firm for ten. Then they fell back. The colonel's shouts, Donna Marena's encouragements, and Villa's large body held them together. They did not flee but remained united until the bandits' fury bent them into a semicircle under the pressure and terror.

"They can't go on, they can't go on!" shouted Villa.

"They're just women and kids, Colonel. Give the order to retreat. Let's take cover inside the abbey," said Donna Marena. Only a small group of peasants armed with pistols protected the three from the bandits. They were in the heart of the battle. Volpe aimed at Terzo, but his horse sidestepped and he had to aim again. Villa fired at him with his carbine 91, but the weapon misfired, the click seeming to resonate louder than the surrounding clamor. Roaring with rage, he seized the gun like a cudgel and clubbed Volpe's skull, knocking him from his saddle.

Colonel Carlo Terzo watched it all and saw nothing. He was unarmed, having given Salvatore the pistol with which he had shot down Diotru. Out of the corner of his eye he studied the wall of the Abbey of San Giovanni behind them and calculated the degree to which his slender line of defense had already given way, then looked toward the oak grove to which Curatolo had raced off with the Saracen's Joust cavalry and computed: "Mixed-breed horses, heavy terrain, a paste of dampened ash: be careful estimating speed. These boys have only a few moments of fight left in them . . ." He looked at his steel chronometer and at that moment a bandit lifted Pepe the altar boy off his feet, shouting: "I'm gonna cut your throat." But Master Moliterni cut him down with a shot from his revolver, then readjusted the glasses on his nose.

Now, he thought. *Or do we have still another minute? Deciding, thinking: that's what Napoleon's two-o'clock-in-the-morning courage means: withdrawing to reflect in the heat of battle, to correct one's mistakes, react to new developments, pray for good luck. To be at war and also far away, to be among the dying and think of a way to save the living. Just one more second,* Terzo was thinking, when he felt the barrel of a pistol against his temple. It was Donna Marena.

"Give the order to retreat or I'll kill you. I don't want to see them die. They're slaughtering us."

But what was Carlo Terzo thinking? Had the moment to act finally come? Where were his books now? What would Sun Tzu and Giovanni da Pian del Carpine suggest? What volume of Delbrück should he have consulted? Could he avert a rout by the analysis of fear in battle conducted by Ardant du Picq in *Etudes sur le combat?* Or by the prudence of Emperor Maurice as expressed in the *Strategikon:* "It is pointless to try to overwhelm the enemy in hand-to-hand combat. Even if it appears you are winning, it is absurd to seek a victory so brutal, which costs blood in exchange for useless glory."

"Order them to surrender," insisted Donna Marena, though she realized that Terzo would rather be killed.

"Just a few seconds more," he said indifferently, "a few, very decisive seconds. How can you not understand, Donna Marena? This is a classic battle: one dies only in retreat. If we flee, not one of your boys will live to see the abbey. They'll stumble over one another, and each bandit will kill ten of them. Don't you realize? Retreating in orderly fashion is the most difficult maneuver for a soldier to execute. Might that not be also true in our lives? Isn't that what I taught? Socrates, when retreating at Delos—"

"That's enough, clown," Donna Marena pulled back the hammer. "Order the retreat or I'll blow your brains out."

"Sound the horn, and God save us!" Terzo shouted to the bugler of the band. The boy blew the notes that he thought sounded most like a charge. Fear dried out his lungs, but he played his cornet tirelessly. The bandits, sensing that the front was giving way, climbed over one another to strike, cut, push back, yelling, "Run, you cowards and girls!" They were aiming to win, driven by their disdain for the peasants, stubborn yokels who stood between them and their pay. Terzo brushed away Donna Marena's pistol as if it were a horsefly, and repeated: "Sound the horn, there's a good boy!" The bugler blew again into his old cornet, and as his heart was bursting he remembered the story his grandfather Ruggiero used to tell him on snowy nights, about Roncesvaux, the ambush set by the traitor Ganelon of Mayence, and Roland the paladin, who blew on the horn Oliphant to call back the army of Emperor Charlemagne and warn them, blew on it until his temples exploded and spurted blood. The boy blew on his cornet the same way, and he would have blown until his temples burst, but at that moment Curatolo, racing at full gallop with his horsemen, heard the distant horn, turned his head slightly and saw the tricolor, hoisted high on a shotgun barrel, being waved by Terzo.

"Now, Curatolo! Now, my friend!"

At the agreed-upon signal, Curatolo pulled on the reins and reversed direction: "Come on, boys, back to our own through Hell! *Communtar as Sciaitan*, charge!" Surprised by this maneuver, the Forcade horsemen kept racing forward through the oak trees and scattered, now useless for battle. A few managed to return alone to the field, but became easy prey to Petranova's rifles. Until that moment, Villa's union had been left relatively unengaged, on the right wing. But when Terzo began to wave the flag, they all sprang forward in disciplined fashion. Donna Marena lowered her pistol and watched the maneuver in astonishment. Falling back at the center of the front, the Malpasso rebels had drawn the bandits into a curved pocket, which first Curatolo on the left, then the Petranova farmers on the right, sealed shut. In a flash, the bandits were surrounded. Crowding together under their own forward rush, they didn't know which way to turn. In front of them were the Malpasso boys, using the fallen horses as a shield and firing under cover. Behind them, Curatolo's demons and Villa's peasants fired into the pile, every bullet finding a victim. Mad with fear, the enemy became a mob, throwing off their weapons, looking for an escape route or hiding under the corpses. Mammarau, Forcade's tax enforcer, realized the day was lost. Sticking two fingers in his mouth, he whistled and led his horsemen away from the fray.

Salvatore had been fighting with the right flank. The heat of the press now brought him next to Terzo: "I've figured it out, Colonel!" the young poet shouted in his excitement. "It's Cannae. Hannibal put the Gallic mercenaries, the weakest fighters, in the middle, to pull the Romans into the trap, which the cavalry closed up. Use your own weakness as a weapon!"

Of the surrounded bandits, only Famine, white scarf over his face, and a few other thugs kept firing, to avoid falling into the hands of the rebels. Terzo was looking for the enemy leader. He wanted to capture him and turn him over to the soldiers, so he could negotiate free passage for his people. Looking at the handful of enemy men still holding out, he spotted the figure in the blue hood. High atop a beautiful bay gelding, he was cracking a small whip at anyone who came within range, as if he believed himself invulnerable to bullets.

Inside the abbey, the women had the impression the battle was won and spilled festively out onto the meadow. The Malpasso boys turned around to stop them, a few of them running up to them.

"Go back," shouted Curatolo, "it's not over," but the confusion had opened a breach in Terzo's line. The blue-hooded figure shouted:

"Over here, Famine." He spurred his horse through the tired peasants, who were now out of ammunition, and fled.

"Stop!" cried Salvatore, planting himself in front of the huge animal and grabbing the reins. The hooded figure's whip whistled through the air and a bloody furrow opened on the boy's face.

"Get out of the way," cried Terzo, running up, but the injured student stubbornly held onto the reins, trying to unhorse the enemy.

"I'll kill you," roared the bandits' boss, raining blows on him and trying to drag him under the bay's hooves.

Fiore, too, had quit the abbey wall to celebrate, but instead saw the terrible duel. She started running, her feet sinking into the ash, and shouting, "Let him go! We've won!" The bandits still on horseback took advantage of the impasse and fled into the woods. Suddenly Famine appeared behind his boss and, without saying a word, shot Salvatore. Leaping over the wounded, Fiore reached her beloved, who had fallen to his knees. The hooded figure raised his whip to strike the girl and flee from the last circle of enemies, but his raised arm stopped in mid-air.

Salvatore was gasping, Fiore bending over to assist him, when the hooded figure swooped down on the girl and hoisted her up into the saddle. Fiercely spurring his horse, he ran off at a gallop. Famine provided cover for the abduction by firing.

"Fiore! No!" shouted Terzo. Recovering the pistol from his pupil, he aimed, hands joined, at the abductor while he was still within range. Not the head, but the torso, a large target . . . But the wind of the gallop had blown back the hood of the bandits' leader, and the white hair of Duchess Luminosa Mastema appeared in the pale light. The colonel threw the pistol down into the ash, as Fiore twisted wildly in the saddle.

"Let me go, Mama, Salvatore is hurt," she cried.

The red flag Villa had entrusted to her slipped out of her bodice, flew up into the air, proud as a kite, then fell back to the ground, where it was quickly reduced to tatters by the horse's hooves. Mother and daughter galloped into the horizon and disappeared behind the flood troughs of the Old Furnace.

Salvatore Dragonara breathed his last before the sun had reached midday.

COLONEL CARLO TERZO awoke at six, put his Neapolitan espresso pot on the stove, and ended up forgetting about it as he did his calisthenics, the water sputtering all over the shiny aluminum. He had not improved at his exercises, and continued to huff and puff to no avail. Head down, cheeks red, and neck swollen, he thought back on his afternoons with Campari as his trainer. "What is the world like upside down? What is reverse strategy? Does the loser win and the winner lose?" He remembered prewar Rome, the Fascist regime he despised but did not fight, the hours spent in the Archives poring over books. Even as a young man he had already considered himself a total failure, a warrior without a war. Now those distant days seemed precious and bright to him. He reread the notes he had scribbled and actually found himself intelligent, precise. He had been clever, but indecision had condemned him to obscurity. "One cannot win without attacking. Rare is the purely defensive battle."

He stepped out onto the terrace and watched Signora Astraco maneuvering her eternal bedsheets. He seldom went down into the garden, which was invaded by weeds. The stray cats, less emaciated thanks to the leftovers, had given up their trench warfare against the turtles. Terzo now had a radio, which Pilgrim Gawain had given him as a gift before returning to the United States. He used the shortwave band most of all, to listen to the BBC news, but at a certain time of day Signora Astraco would ask him if she could listen to a music program, *The Seven-Pearl Necklace*. Dr. Pantera had prescribed him the usual yellow pills that he bought from Manetti the pharmacist on Corso Olivuzza. He would take one with a gulp of water and sleep a deep sleep without nightmares. The ritual of the pill helped him forget he was sleeping alone. During the day, however, never, not even when engrossed in the endless writing of his *Manual for Strategic Living*, was he able not to sense, with some fiber of his body, that Emma was dead and he was alone, forever.

The princess had died a few days after the peasants' war. Her brief happiness during those hours of action, when she had seen her husband put years of study into practice and fulfill the wish she had made to the kite, had vanished in the instant that Duchess Mastema abducted Fiore. Terzo had managed to conceal Salvatore Dragonara's death from her. He told her he was injured and in the hospital. On their return to Palermo, Emma was at the end of her rope. Pantera let her slip into death with gentle care and morphine.

Pilgrim Gawain spent all his money and the newspaper never published a single one of his articles. He went back to America to teach at the University of Indiana at Bloomington, where he had wanted Salvatore to study. The boy had asked him, "Is an American allowed to marry anyone he wants, without asking for the family's permission?" And Pilgrim had answered: "Yes, if he's white." He now wrote to the colonel from the United States, urging him to transfer to Bloomington to teach military history. Terzo, however, wanted nothing anymore, neither to travel nor to stay put. He was once again the Colonel Terzo he had been at the Historical Archives of the General Staff with Campari and Marshal Puntoni: without hope, and with no interests other than strategy. But now he no longer believed that one could deduce, from Raimondo Montecuccoli's victorious maneuvers against the Turks in 1664, a strategy for how to face life's troubles. He would complete his *Manual*, but only because he had promised his wife.

That war with its dead and wounded, which saw the brains of his sole pupil, Salvatore Dragonara, spattered on the ashes of the volcano, the war that saw him shoot Diotru in the back, did not seem to him compatible with the exercise of reason. "Strategy is useless," he wrote to Pilgrim, thanking him. "Alexander the Great, after conquering one enemy, saw another arise and chased that chimera to the ends of the earth before dying alone in Babylonia. I, in my nothingness, have been chasing the chimera of a perfect *Manual* for living and making war, a method for always winning, for never making mistakes, a rational criterion for finding one's way out of the most dramatic situations. As I was preparing myself for every battle, with my invincible strategy, life ignored me and passed me by. I am like the Russians surrounded during the German invasion in 1941: I have every weapon at my disposal, but they are no longer of any use. When I had to fight, I won by applying what I had studied; but I lost, in an instant, the people I loved. I would not be useful to your students, dear Gawain, soldiers in a world with the atomic bomb. What could I possibly teach them? That the Mameluks, a century before defeating the Mongols at Ain Jalut, had slaughtered the Knights Templar, with patience and discipline, in Transjordan, in May, 1187?

"It's too late. Strategy doesn't pay. Napoleon, in the end, admitted: 'After so much study, I have no plan in mind.' And Frederick the Great? 'There is nothing to know about war, except that one must march ten leagues per day, fight, and rest.' You have to prepare your plan, of course, but what becomes of it once the first shot is fired? Do you remember the Prussians' Field-Marshal von Moltke? 'No strategic plan lasts beyond the first skirmish with the enemy. Only the ignorant believe they

can discern, in a military campaign, the meticulous execution of
an initial idea developed in great detail and ending in victory.' Is
a good strategist therefore no more important than a donkey, as
Tolstoy seems to believe in *War and Peace*? On the contrary, and
the war we Italians lost proves it. A good strategist lays down a
general plan, aware that life and war will tear it to pieces. His
skill lies in being able to act on those fragments, in mixing them
up, making them shine. Strength and weakness, victory and
defeat, might and futility are the elements of life to him. He
always acts, whenever and however he can. By instinct and education, he knows how to react to every unforeseen development,
drawing out of thin air all the signs that nobody else sees. From
the faces of the enemy, he gauges their endurance. From the silence of a spy, he gathers information. He prepares the battle in
his mind and fights it with his intuition. I, on the other hand,
was able to keep Mastema's militia at bay, only to see Salvatore
killed and Fiore abducted. I relived the greatest battles of history over the course of one day. But is that really how it went,
Gawain? Or did I make it up in my frustrated imagination? Was
it really just a country skirmish that nobody else witnessed and
whose martial importance I alone recognized?"

THAT AFTERNOON, after a month of solitude, Terzo went back
to Cosma for a shave. He bought stamps for his letter to Gawain
to mail at the Lolli station. The barber welcomed him with a
great snapping of white cloth and immediately began to chatter:
"My condolences, Colonel, my condolences. The princess, bless
her soul, was a great lady. We're going to miss her. You're one of
the family here, you know that, don't you? Anything you need,
I'm at your service. I'm so happy to see you again. Time flies,
unfortunately. I've been wanting to ask you for a long time—if
you don't mind—but weren't you giving private lessons to Miss

Fiore? What's become of her? Did you know that on the Mastema lands there was a battle between mafiosi and peasants?
You didn't?"

The colonel stared straight into the mirror and let the shav-
ing cream mask his reaction.

"This time, however, the peasants didn't let themselves be
slaughtered," Cosma resumed, stirring his brush in a tin basin;
"they were organized and allied with the rebels of a nearby
town. And they whacked those wicked mafiosi good. You know
what Sasà Andragnosi, my friend from the shipyards, told me?
You remember Sasà? He's the son of the ice man, the one who
slips into everybody's house and knows all their secrets. He
heard the uncle of Duchess Mastema, Niccolò Fides the judge,
say that the Malpasso rebels were under the command of a Soviet general who had come to Sicily through Yugoslavia, traveling a thousand kilometers on a mule and in a boat. And it was
thanks to him they beat the mafiosi, you see. A great strategist—nobody knows his name, but maybe you'd be familiar
with him. Can you imagine those bandits? They didn't know if
they were coming or going." Cosma continued lathering up
Terzo with his feather brush and went on: "The soldiers who'd
been sent there to arrest the rebels also ended up breaking up
the gang of the famous 'Famine'—famous, that is, in the newspapers. To me he's a hellhound. After a week they were all set
free, excuse me and no questions asked. Even in a democracy
the little guys weep and the rascals laugh. Sooner or later Salvatore Giuliano will end up the same way. They'll put him in the
cooler just for show, big headlines and all, then he'll be out with
money in his pocket. Mark my words. Anyway, the leader of the
revolt was a certain Donna Marena, and she ended up in jail, in
Naples, and she'll stay there, you can bank on it. My cousin Giovanni, the boatman, went out one night to fish for squid and saw
her being boarded onto the mailboat. Four carabinieri, hand-
cuffs and all, but she stood tall, Colonel, so tall that Giovanni

said to me, 'Even with the cuffs on her wrists, it was like she had arrested the carabinieri, and not the other way around. The Madonna of the Chains, you know? Tall and silent, silver hair, people paid their respects as she passed by. My brother Nardo took off his cap—it was cold, but I took mine off, too. The carabinieri gave us a dirty look, but everybody was taking his hat off: porters, sailors, dockers, the shipyard workers getting off their shift. Only the carabinieri kept their hats on. And this Donna Marena saw us salute her but she didn't say anything. She just kept walking and that government ship, she boarded it like it was her yacht.' And now they're keeping her in a cell under the sea, God forbid!"

As the razor swept over the colonel's face he thought of the woman who had held a pistol to his head, of her hair coiled like the Medusa's, of the valor with which she had heartened the fragile central formation of their reenactment of the battle of Cannae.

He imagined her in her cell, in the dilapidated Neapolitan prison, far from the rebels she had brought into the world. She had given herself up to the soldiers to save her people and Villa's farmers. As she was being interrogated, the officers were so astounded to find a woman leading the revolt that Pepe the altar boy was able to lead everyone else to safety along the goat paths. The newspapers had given the credit for the defeat of Famine's gang to General Nasca. But it was only Hannibal's maneuver, as reproduced by Terzo, that had saved the peasants from massacre and the rebels from being court-martialed for desertion. Not knowing what had really happened, Nasca had gone back to Rome, where he was considering running for political office. The first elections since the war were supposed to be held in a few months, and to have victories against subversives on one's résumé was certainly a good thing.

"That Nasca's going to become a big cheese," warned Cosma. "You know him, don't you? He entered the war as a captain and now he's a general. Actually, I need a recommendation; my son is looking for a position."

Terzo thought again of his duel with Campari in 1940. Crossing back over the Primosole Bridge, he had not even recognized in Nasca the haughty officer who had delivered Ciano's letter to him on that beach in the Maremma. Gawain had taken care of everything: he showed Nasca a few of his mysterious credentials and convinced him to help them: "We're tourists, and our friend Salvatore is gravely injured." A sergeant drove them into town and nobody asked any questions.

The shave completed, Terzo crossed the Capo market, took a very brief glance at the headlines on the newspapers hung outside the kiosk, strolled about, had an espresso, "No sugar, thank you," and headed at a brisk pace to the station to mail the letter to Gawain. Then, instead of returning home, he went to Palazzo di Mare. It was cold and rainy; the sky was Gunpowder Gray. The electricity in the air gathered around the dark blue clouds and already some lightning was flashing in the mountains, around Castello Utveggio and Monte Cuccio. The colonel wanted news of Fiore, whom nobody had seen since the battle. She hadn't appeared at any of the Christmas celebrations in the city, or even—though Terzo didn't expect it—at Emma's funeral or at the mass commemorating the thirtieth day since Salvatore's death. Terzo had asked the barber, nonchalantly, how it was that the girl hadn't danced with the Dukes of Mainoni at the New Year's Eve ball. Cosma had looked in the mirror to make sure they were alone.

"It's better not to know, old friend, better to keep quiet. Didn't you notice? The battle was fought on Mastema land and the newspaper didn't once mention the name of Duchess Luminosa. And what about poor Dragonara? Not a word in the articles, just a little sidebar: 'Mafiosi Kill Young Leftist Sympathizer.' And that was the last of it: case filed away by decree, under 'Incident,' no trial. What do you think? Does it help that the inquiry was conducted by the duchess's brother, Judge Paolo Fides, under the supervision of her uncle Judge Niccolò Fides? Believe me, Colonel, they'll be talking about the revolts at Comiso and Ragusa, and about Giuliano's exploits, for a long time to come, but nobody will remember Petranova and Malpasso. Like it was a battle of ghosts."

The colonel pushed open the heavy double door and headed toward the icy stairway. The old concierge stopped him.

"Who are you looking for?" she asked.

"The duchess. I'm Colonel Terzo."

"Go away," she muttered.

Normally Colonel Terzo, a very shy man by nature, would not have insisted. But anyone who loses a beloved spouse ends up assimilating a few of the deceased's personality traits into his behavior, out of habit, out of memory, and to keep her still alive. Terzo remembered his wife's passion for Fiore, the complicitous charm with which she had organized the girl's love affair with Salvatore, the conversations on the terrace. He thought of how Emma might behave in his place, how she would have ignored the rude concierge with smiling indifference. And so he acted like her: he continued up the stairs. After two flights, he felt someone grab him from behind.

"Go away. You're not welcome here," said a man with large hands and a beret pulled down over his forehead.

A man can dress in civilian clothing as much as he likes, but anyone who has spent his life in the armed forces will recognize an ex-corporal even in the next world. Shoulders straight, face composed, close-cropped hair, deferential tone with an officer, even when threatening him. The man towered a full head above Terzo, but still the colonel commanded: "Ten-hut!"

Unsure of himself, the stranger released his grip, then stiffened, muttering: "You can't go inside . . . Colonel, sir."

"Lay your hands on an officer, you wretch? What's your unit, anyway? In what company did you learn to play the bully with your superiors?"

"Me? I, sir, I fought in the war, and how. I was with the Third Mechanized Division, Eighteenth Bersaglieri batallion."

"Well, then, answer me this: How did you spend the night of Christmas 1941?"

The corporal looked at Terzo. A moment earlier he had nearly tackled him, and now his eyes were misting over. "If you're asking me, it means you already know the answer, Colonel, sir. I don't lie, that I can swear on my daughters' heads. If I was with the Eighteenth, how else could I have spent that Christmas? Freezing and shooting, sir, that's how I spent it. The Russians attacked us at Ivanovski, we resisted, we fell back, and then reinforcements from the Pasubio and Torino divisions arrived and we took back our stronghold."

Terzo took Salvatore's notebook which now he always carried with him, out of his pocket. "Did you have machine guns?" he asked.

"No new equipment till the summer of '42, sir."

"What about 47/32 antitank guns?"

"Yes, sir, but they were useless against even the smallest tanks."

"Mortars?"

"The 45-millimeters were useless, a burden, but the 81s were good. But we had little ammunition."

"Any 75/27 artillery?"

"Wrecks, with all due respect."

"Did the 20-millimeter anti-aircraft guns work?"

"Yes, sir. It's thanks to them that you see me here."

"Well done. I won't report you, then."

The corporal saluted, raising a taut hand to his blue beret.

Terzo climbed the last few flights, walked through the long, gloomy corridor, and burst into the duchess's study.

She was, once again, busy doing accounts. She barely looked up. "Go away," she said. "I'm going to fire the incompetents who let you in. Go away or I'll call the police."

"How is Fiore?"

"Don't utter that name again in my presence. My daughter is dead, as far as you're concerned, and for me as well. The living person is a puppet, kept only to preserve the family's honor. My daughter is dead, and it was your wife who corrupted her. Go away."

"What did you do to her?"

Duchess Mastema rose, pushing her papers aside with her knotty arms. She was seething with hatred, the hatred that had given her the strength to fight with the rabble and hoist her daughter into the saddle and flee.

"I should have flayed her with the whip, but I had to content myself with seeing the little pig, your pupil, killed instead, right before his teacher's eyes."

"My wife is dead. I want to see Fiore. Otherwise I'll denounce you to the police for the murder of Salvatore Dragonara."

"Well, then, you'll have to explain to the President of the Court, my brother Paolo, what you were doing with the rebellious peasants and what my daughter, a minor, was doing with you at night. You kidnapped her. Then at the Court of Appeals you'll have to explain, to my uncle Niccolò, why you killed Diotru. Do you really think you can send a Mastema to jail? The dregs may govern, but blood still counts for something. It's only to avoid scandals that I haven't had you arrested. But if you push me, I'll hunt you down."

"I'm perfectly willing to go to jail. But you can't keep Fiore imprisoned."

"Fiore is not here. And your ridiculous strategies won't help you find her. You want to go to court? Go ahead, we live in a democracy. I'll send these notes to the newspapers. Here, read them. I just received them from a cousin of mine in Rome. As you can see, I was expecting a visit from you."

Terzo caught a glimpse of a few lines on the crumpled sheets of paper. "Dear Emma, In gratitude for your services I attach payment for your expenses. Ciano." "Dear Emma, The appointment is for 12 o'clock. I'm trembling with anticipation. GC." And: "Emma, Pavelic fell for it like a fool. Could you see him again tomorrow and make him talk more? You're worth more than a whole squadron of destroyers. When this is all over I'll take you to Punta Ala. Galeazzo."

"They're just old papers," said Terzo, "a world that no longer exists. Emma used to laugh at the gossip when she was alive. Imagine now, when nobody can hurt her anymore. Just let me see Fiore and I'll go away. I don't like to leave fellow soldiers in the lurch."

"You won't report me, I'm certain of that. You cherish the memory of your no-good wife too much. Would you like to see Fiore's room? To make sure she's not in Palermo?"

The duchess led him furiously by the arm through the corridor and threw open the door. The room was empty, cold, and had not been used for weeks. In the middle was a wood-frame bed, its mattress folded in half over the metal springs. Out of a tear there appeared, like a cloud, a tuft of white wool. There was a suitcase half filled with clothes, and two dolls embracing each other on a side table. On the floor, a portrait of a lady with a book in hand, head bent, eyes half closed in sleep or sadness. On the rectangle of wall where the painting had hung, now darker than the rest of the wallpaper, Fiore had scribbled in pencil: "Freedom for the people." Terzo recognized her schoolgirl handwriting, round and pleasing.

"She's dead as far as I'm concerned. If you want her things, be my guest. There'll be less for me to pay the junk man." And with a kick, Duchess Mastema sent those wretched, forgotten things flying through the air, summer blouses Terzo thought he'd seen Fiore wearing, underwear with monograms sewn in dark blue cotton thread, a few sheets of paper, a small bag with dried lavender flowers. The clothing fell back down onto the damp mattress and seemed already old, like the garments of a plague victim, abhorred by all. The colonel feared that Fiore might really be dead.

"Tell me she's alive or I'll break your neck," he said.

Cruel men and women, imprisoned in their cynicism by hatred, egotism, lust for power, and resentment, develop one sole instinct. They are able to recognize immediately when a tranquil person abandons his usual timidity and, by some chance, turns fierce. The duchess understood that Terzo might indeed strangle her, and so she admitted: "She lives far away from here. She won't be back. We're going to marry her off to someone who'll take her—ruined as she is—in exchange for a dowry and, of course, a great deal of wealth. Satisfied? Now get out and don't ever set foot in here again."

Terzo turned his back on her and noticed the desk, above which was a small, art nouveau mirror. Stuck inside the frame was a snapshot of Emma and Fiore smiling in the garden, in the shadow of the philodendron. Salvatore had taken it on Saint Rosalia's day. Fiore was eating a melon pudding, her mouth dirty with red custard and grimacing, with three jasmine flowers between her lips. Emma was fluttering her fingers to say "Ciao," the way she used to say goodbye to people dear to her, whether they were old friends or casual acquaintances with whom she had become immediately infatuated. Terzo pulled the photo out and kissed it slowly, as he had the silver trinket that marked General Desaix's position at the battle of Marengo on Ciano's desktop that night in 1940.

"Do you want anything else, fool?" the duchess shouted, and with her hand she swept away the few things remaining on the desktop. Terzo grabbed a small, canvas-bound book on the run and put it in his pocket.

He descended the stairs and, raising his collar against the cold, walked back across the Capo market. He came out in Piazza della Rivoluzione, letting himself be swept along at random by the crowd, in front of the fish shops with their octopuses slithering viscous in baskets, the blue sardines on white marble slabs, the red mullet covered with algae and ice. After the *Ecce Homo* altar, he sidestepped the church of the Theatine fathers, demolished by the bombings. A street kid offered him Camels and condoms, a sailor asked him for directions to Piazza Croci. He bought nothing and answered nothing. He walked and walked, pushing on toward the port, where the streets turned into trails of beaten earth between the ruins. He saw an avenue blockaded with wood planks and a sign saying, "Danger: Unsafe Structures. Entry Forbidden." He hopped over the barbed wire and found himself in a courtyard covered with plaster flakes.

A woman shouted a warning: "Turn back. There are unexploded bombs in there." But he forged on, through the already thick weeds. There must have been a church there once, or perhaps an ancient temple. He saw columns and aisles, a gutted roof; the remains of a large baptismal font made it impossible to enter the apse. Pieces of mosaic were scattered about, like the loose change a drunkard lets fall from his pockets at night. In that disorder of disfigured capitals, vaults, and hands of shattered porphyry, an inscribed stone had fallen face down. Terzo turned it over with his foot and read, in very black lettering, the words: ITALICA VIRTUDE.

Leopardi's *Brutus Minor*, which he'd studied in high school, when his father was still alive. To himself he recited, teeth clenched: ". . . and buried in the Thracian dust, vast ruin, lay Italic virtue . . . ," and then his memory betrayed him. *Here indeed*, he thought, *lies the virtue of Italy, denigrated by historians, and with good reason; for the courage of her soldiers, their patience and suffering, went to ruin with the craven strategies of Il*

Duce and the vanity of his officials. And I, too, am guilty, he thought, *since I knew we were headed for tragedy and didn't dare raise my voice and say so. Reserve and discipline? No. It was cowardice and stupidity.*

From a low stone wall, Terzo hoisted himself up into a mullioned window with the center column missing, and saw, sheer below him, the sea. Gray waves, strong undertow, a land wind forcing the multicolored boats to stay ashore, dry-docked far from the water. At the bottom of the hill of rubble, a fisherman was mending his net, sewing with a wooden needle. Terzo shouted: "What is this place, sir? Where am I?" But the roar of the waves drowned out his voice and the fisherman kept sewing without answering him, holding down the net with his naked big toe.

"It's called the Agony, the Church of Our Lady of the Agony of Sicily. It was first a fortress, then they turned it into a hospice for the incurable. The bombs reduced it to its present state. There used to be a Raphael painting, but the Spanish took it away."

Terzo turned around. It was the survivor of the Russian campaign, employed at Palazzo di Mare, who had answered him.

"I have something to tell you, Colonel," he continued.

"To tell me?"

"Yes, sir. I know where Miss Fiore is, God bless her."

"Where?"

"In Naples. Pregnant."

The night of the battle. With Salvatore. Emma was right.

"Where in Naples?" he asked.

"With some nuns. One day her mother beat her, and Miss Fiore started bleeding. I went and called the doctor. The concierge later read the pharmacist's prescriptions: Miss Fiore's pregnant, she said. That's why they made her leave."

"What are they going to do about it?"

"She's going to marry Duke Mainoni, who hasn't got a penny. In exchange his father will get the Primosole lands. A beautiful spot."

"Are you sure?"

"Yes, sir. When they took her to the mailboat, I helped her on board. She seemed drunk as she went up the stairs, the poor thing was trembling, her knees buckling. I'm telling you this because Miss Fiore was always very good to us; it was a joy having her around the house. I even used to work for her father, God rest his soul."

The land wind blew hard, carrying gloom and rain out to sea, perhaps to northern Europe. Terzo thought the clouds would pass over Naples, where Donna Marena and Fiore were being detained, each for having desired a different destiny. He remembered his lessons with Salvatore: "Never accept reality as it is presented to you. Always look for a different position. Never act as others expect you to act." Donna Marena and Fiore had adopted this philosophy and fallen into disgrace. Life dissolves clever strategies into cruelties.

"Is there any way to help her?" he asked the corporal.

"I don't think so. She may already be married by now. Let's hope she can accept her fate."

"Let's hope not," Terzo surprised himself by saying, as if it were Emma speaking through him, "let's hope she has strength and good fortune." And the voice inside him made him add: "Let's hope that in the goddamn prison in which her mother has locked her up she has with her the sayings of the Chinese master of war, Sun Tzu, who was summoned by the King of Wu and asked: How do you get out of an impossible situation, when you are surrounded and all you can do is prepare for death? And yet in doing so, you still must try to find a way out? Do you understand, Corporal? You're done for, the enemy is already celebrating victory, and yet hidden in your funeral rites is a strategy invisible to all except yourself, a strategy that will take you, like a ghost, outside the encirclement. Do you know what the trick is? Do you? You die of exhaustion in the pocket, leave your ghost behind, and come out alive and different. As Campari must have tried to do in Russia—*he* knew Sun Tzu, even though he pretended to be bored when we studied him. Let's hope Fiore remembers him, let's hope God grants her luck." He fell silent and shuddered: "Thank you, Corporal."

"Just doing my duty, sir. But now I have to go; the neighborhood is full of gossips. If the duchess learns that I've spoken to you, she'll sack me. I'd be happy to leave her, but I've got my daughters to think of."

"Go."

The corporal leaped over the rubble of the Church of the Agony, and passed under a broken arch, supporting himself with one hand on a truss, but before disappearing beyond the wall, he asked: "Do you know General Monroy?"

"Yes."

"He was our commander in Russia, a good, brave general."

"Yes, he is."

"Is he alive? Do you ever see him?"

"I last saw him in June of '42. He came to Rome from Russia to persuade Mussolini not to send another expeditionary force to the steppes. If he'd listened, thousands of boys would still be alive, including my friend Campari," said Terzo, thinking: *And I wouldn't be alone in the world.*

"May I give you a message to convey to him, Colonel?"

"Yes, of course."

"Give General Monroy my regards. Tell him they're from 'the Palermitan *bersagliere* of Ivanovsky.' He'll understand. On the morning of Santo Stefano, after the Christmas Day battle, he gave me a bottle of grappa to give to the medical officer who had been left with the wounded who couldn't be transported.

The Russians had surrounded them, and we *bersaglieri* went to liberate them. We arrived December 27, but they were all dead, the medical officer and the wounded. Tell that to the general, if you see him."

Colonel Carlo Terzo saluted the corporal, and for the first and only time in his civilian life he was sorry not to be in uniform. He wished he could be in full regimentals and salute the corporal with saber and blue sash, making the dark air hiss with the gleaming steel. He had studied the ordeal of those men, meter by meter, on his maps. Monroy, a former noncommissioned officer, tried to prevent the massacre of the Alpine Troops in Russia, but Mussolini's only reply was: "Italy can't have fewer soldiers in Russia than Slovakia does." He remembered the maps Monroy had shown him, after the rout on the Don: the secretaries' handwriting had replaced the proud names of the divisions— Pasubio, Mechanized, Turin—with the macabre expressions: "Mortal remains of the Pasubio," "Mortal remains of the Mechanized," and so on. The mortal remains of an army, of a country, of the Church of the Agony, of this city. *We're all just remains*, he thought, upset, *like all the people frozen, crippled, burned, wounded, maimed, and murdered by war, from the poor medic with his immovable wounded to Salvatore, my only pupil.*

Dejected, he sank down onto the large, rain-worn head of a Roman hero. In the past, in the face of so much unhappiness, he would have reacted by turning to the wisdom of Montecuccoli, the oblique order of Epaminondas, the retreat of Gustavus Adolphus. But he no longer hoped to understand life or strategy. From his pocket he extracted the little book he had grabbed on the run in Fiore's room and opened it at random. The wind started turning the pages rapidly, first back, then forth, until it stopped at a page on which Fiore had translated, in pencil, something about an albatross:

The poet is like this prince of the clouds,
familiar with storms, unruffled by archers;
an exile on land among jeering crowds,
he has a giant's wings, and cannot walk.

The corporal had left, seeing Terzo sit down on the monumental stone. But after taking a few steps he turned around. The name of the young medic killed in the Russian izba had come back to him. Reentering the open-roofed church, he stopped, silent. The colonel was weeping, sobbing like a child, twisting a book in his hands, wailing hoarsely in the storm.

COLONEL CARLO TERZO went to the Capuchin cemetery every day to clean the tomb of his wife, Princess Emma, and decorate it with flowers. He was uncomfortable with manual work, but little by little he had learned to rinse the white marble surface with a large sponge, let the water run over it, and then dry it with a deerskin rag. He always chose red flowers: roses, tulips, carnations, even poppies, which he would pick around the canals of the Papireto. The caretaker knew him by sight, and would keep his tools for him. The colonel thought he had seen him before.

"Were you in the service?" he asked him.

"No, I change jobs often," the man parried. "Here the work is calm and the pay is decent. I buried your wife myself. I remember because you gave me a tip, which nobody ever does. They turn their backs on us, with good reason."

Terzo would sit at the edge of the tomb and briefly tell his wife the things that had happened that day. He knew Emma would love to hear gossip: who was marrying whom, how the new leaders of Italy were making out, perhaps some news of the Savoia court in exile. She would have laughed heartily at the television, with its ballerinas wrapped in tasteless costumes and stockings heavy as those of a country nun. But the colonel knew very little about all that, since he spent his days on his useless *Manual for Strategic Living*, copying into the text the index cards he and Campari had written, the notes he'd taken on the Second World War, the lectures he'd prepared for Salvatore

Dragonara and, finally, the solitary work of these years. Thus he always ended up talking to her about strategy, telling her about, for example, Giovanni da Pian del Carpine, "a Capuchin monk whom Pope Innocent IV sent on a mission to the Mongols, in Karakorum, a two-year journey on foot, in 1246. Upon his return he wrote *How to Fight the Mongols*. A mild-mannered friar of Saint Francis, of the sort you see around you here, penned a deadly treatise on the art of war. And do you know what that devil of a friar suggests as a way of countering an army on horseback?" But then he stopped and excused himself: "But what do you care? You like to talk about other things."

He did not go to the cemetery on All Souls' Day because he wasn't used to seeing little children running and playing among the tombstones. Celebrating the dead with sugar dolls and gifts requested from those beyond the grave seemed to him to explain a lot about the city with the Bright Cobalt sky. He had stayed in Palermo out of inertia. *Napoleon had the courage of two o'clock in the morning,* he thought; *I don't even have the courage of midday*. He now understood why his wife had opted for the hidden calm of the Sicilian capital; Duchess Mastema's threat of blackmail was unambiguous. A request to the Office of Classified Information, where two of his former students now worked, had sufficed to confirm to him that Emma had spied for Minister Ciano during the period of the Albanian invasion, and had perhaps been his mistress. She despised Fascism with the same snobbish distaste with which she scorned Communism in her native Ukraine. But she had to survive in that world of battles, and had done what she could, in her silent, elegant way.

"I know you married me because I was a good cover," he said to her, crouching on the gravel, "but I do believe you liked me in the end. You grew fond of me and for that, I shall always be grateful." Walking back home, he remembered his last night with the princess. Dr. Pantera had warned him: "She has only a few hours left." He gave her a shot of tranquilizer and, ignoring

Terzo's insistence that he go home and rest, he laid his huge body down on the sofa, wrapped in his overcoat, and waited.

Emma was pale, her breathing labored, her eyes closed. She gestured for some water, managed to drink a sip, but couldn't speak or move. Only the white batiste sheet, barely rising and falling, attested to the life remaining in her. Terzo sat in a chair, a sheet of paper in his hand. The dawn filtered through from the terrace. As soon as the darkness of the master bedroom began to dissipate, Emma asked: "Take me out on the terrace. I'm suffocating."

"It's cold, Emma, it's winter," the colonel said in a low voice, standing up. The doctor, however, who had come running when he heard voices, said:

"Do as you wish, Princess."

Terzo took his wife in his arms, and Pantera covered her with her old bearskin coat, a relic from Kiev, and opened the door to the terrace. The air was cold, the city dark. The sea, however, was already suffused with a bluish light, the jacklamps echoed the stars, and the last of Orion was setting, pursued by the Scorpion. Emma breathed hard; the cold numbed her throat, like cognac. They sat her down in an armchair.

"I have a surprise for you," murmured Terzo.

"A surprise? Now?"

"I've found out about the battle."

"The battle?"

"Your ancestor Svyatoslav's battle. Yesterday I read about his deeds in a Ukrainian chronicle, and today I was able to reconstruct the campaign on a map. I was waiting for you to wake up to tell you." Terzo clutched at a sheet with notes on it.

"You certainly took a long time, Colonel. But how will you explain it? We don't have Ciano's desk, the way we did for Marengo."

"My blackboard will be the sea. Your ancestor Svyatoslav was Duke of Kiev. In A.D. 969, he left Russia, crossed the mountains, and conquered Philipopolis, the city that today is called Plovdiz."

"Plovdiv," Emma corrected him.

"Plovdiv. Now, see that string of fishing boats returning to port? They are the lights of Svyatoslav's column. The Slavs are advancing, confident of victory, pressing the Byzantines hard. See the three little red lights at the top of Castello Utveggio? That's Plovdiv. Svyatoslav leaves a garrison there, which allows him to retreat. He marches through the Maritza valley. There, past the fishing nets: look at the flat current: that's the Maritza, the valley that leads straight as a road to Constantinople. Svyatoslav's Russians march with enthusiasm; there are sixty thousand of them, a formidable army for that era. Imagine every light you see as a regiment."

"I don't like your tone. When you say an army feels confident, you're usually about to announce their defeat."

Terzo pointed to the sea: "See where the first lights of Mondello are shining? That was how Constantinople, with its golden spires, must have looked to Svyatoslav in his dreams. He had forded the Danube, leaving the Black Sea to the east, to storm Adrianople and conquer Constantinople. The booty would be great, every squire would go home richer than a king. Adrianople is there, offshore: it's the shoal confining the jacklamps in a circle. Do you see it?"

"I hadn't noticed it. A life spent paying no attention to shoals," Emma said, trying to make a joke. She felt oppressed by the air and fell silent.

"Do you want to go back inside?"

The princess shook her head.

Terzo squeezed her hand. His throat was dry, but he went on: "Adrianople is the bloodiest city in history. A crossroads between Asia and Europe, it was the theater of seven battles. The first was won by Emperor Constantine in 323. The second saw the Visigoths pitted against the Romans, in one of the most decisive battles of the millennium. Fritigern's barbarians massacred twenty thousand legionaries and ensured the superiority of cavalry over infantry for the next thousand years . . ."

"Tell me about Svyatoslav."

"Forgive me, I'm incorrigible. So, Svyatoslav's sixty thousand soldiers arrived in Adrianople."

Emma started coughing. Pantera supported her shoulders, gently massaging them. When the coughing stopped, her breathing was labored.

"Svyatoslav is marching on Adrianople. There, waiting for him—see the offshore dike?—is John I Zimisces, the valorous tutor of Emperor Basil II."

Emma was wheezing and Terzo took her face in his hands: "In a brilliant battle, Svyatoslav encircled the Byzantines around the line of the dyke I showed you, defeated John Zimisces and, a few days later, entered Constantinople in triumph."

Emma opened her eyes, looked straight at her husband: "Don't lie to me. Tell me what really happened."

No longer looking at the faintly brightening sea, and holding his wife close, Terzo told her about the battle of Adrianople, Wars of the Byzantine Empire, A.D. 972, when the energetic general John attacked the Russians twice, first with a hail of arrows, "in the direction of the lighthouse," then in a brutal cavalry charge, "along the front of the offshore dyke." Taking to the Danube, allied ships surrounded Svyatoslav, forcing him to retreat toward the Ukraine. There were few survivors. At their own doorstep, and utterly exhausted, the Russians were set upon by primitive tribes and massacred. Duke Svyatoslav was the last to fall, arms crossed over his sword, never seeing his holy Kiev again. Colonel Terzo went on and on, his arms around his wife's emaciated body.

Emma Svyatoslava did not fall for her husband's comforting version of the story, but neither did she learn of her ancestor's bitter fate. As she was dying she murmured, "If only heaven would give us a battle with no dead, like a fable on the sea, with lights and Orion, with no pain but only the story, Carlo, only the story. A hundred years of war in tales but not a day of battle." Pantera noticed but said nothing, as the colonel was pointing to the Kiev of his fantasy, far out at sea. When the story was over, he picked up his near-weightless patient and carried her back to the bedroom. The dawn was tinged with pink, and Dr. Guido Pantera, a Darwinian atheist, whispered the prayer for the dead for the first time since his afternoons at the oratory of the Piarist fathers, in May 1889.

LINGERING longer than usual at the cemetery one Tuesday, the day sacred to Tiw, Teutonic god of war, Colonel Terzo didn't realize the main gate had already been shut. He tried shaking it, but it was made of solid iron and wouldn't budge. He walked back to the caretaker's cabin to ask him to open up. In front of the entrance he saw two posts of pale wood planted in the gravel, a good distance from each other and linked, some ten feet above the ground, by a thick, taut rope. He stopped, disconcerted. The caretaker then popped out of the skylight of the toolshed. With great care, he crossed over the cement roof and leaned out toward the rope. With a little leap, he found his balance and began to walk along the rope, arms outspread in air. One step after another, without looking. He moved quickly, like a professional acrobat. And yet, despite his mastery, he seemed afraid. A fall would certainly not have killed him, but still he brought to his training session the caution of someone venturing out over an abyss.

Without calling attention to himself, Terzo watched him go back and forth and, feeling embarrassed, tried to beat a retreat. He would ask the monks to open the gate for him. The gravel crunched under his feet. The man stopped and, with a blind man's intuition, without turning around, said: "Is that you, Colonel?"

"Yes. Now I remember where I first met you. The day they shot stones at you, at the Lolli station. I tried to help you."

"Was that you? You saved my life. I lost my balance, and only instinct kept me from falling. It was impossible to dodge the stones without moving. One more and I would have fallen." The caretaker balanced on one foot and said more softly: "I haven't stretched the rope high since then. I won't be giving any more performances. I'd be looking for the boy with the slingshot in every crowd. He doesn't realize it, but he actually did get me that day. But what happened to you? Were you locked in?"

Before Terzo could answer him, the tightrope walker had made a graceful leap onto the enclosure wall. He stood up on tiptoe, elegant as a ballet dancer, opening and closing his arms, which he unfolded like wings, fingers extended, as though flying. He looked at Terzo as he proceeded along the narrow wall with silent steps. He paused for a moment on the pitched roof of a chapel, then advanced along the cornice, between two angels. Still gazing at the colonel, he crossed the cemetery airily, poised himself on a broken marble column and, with a final somersault, disappeared on the other side of the gate. Left alone, Terzo headed toward the exit. The gate was wide open, but there was no sign of the caretaker acrobat. Behind him a fresh female voice rang out:

"Just a minute, please, I'm going out too."

Fiore. Terzo hadn't seen her yet but already he knew that Fiore was behind him as his hands grew hot on the cold metal.

"Thank you," she said. "I hadn't realized it was so late."

"How are you, Fiore?"

"Colonel?" Fiore put her hand to her mouth, surprised, and dashed to him and embraced him, holding him tightly in her arms and stroking his hair. She didn't weep, but breathed in sobs, as he was saying, "Fiore, dear Fiore." She took his hand and they went out into the street. Fiore rested her head on the shoulder of his overcoat as they walked, and spoke softly to him. "We're alone together, like the first time, when I stopped you at La Zisa. It wasn't that long ago, but it seems like a thousand years to me. I really liked you then; you were so upright, so calm. The war had just ended, people were walking around either subdued and humiliated, stoop-shouldered, or triumphant and too self-confident, hiding their defeat with disdain. But you were neither. During the lessons I understood why. For you it was only the latest war, one among so many."

Terzo liked that the girl was speaking to him so informally, but it wasn't really accurate to call her a girl anymore. Fiore had grown; she was tall and supple, still beautiful, a woman with two lines on her forehead, two razor cuts, which her youth could not erase.

"Tell me about yourself," he said. "What do you do? Where do you live?"

Fiore threw her head back and smiled: "Well, offer to buy me a coffee at least."

She had copied that gesture from Emma. The charming tone hiding the melancholy, Fiore had learned that from the princess, during those afternoons on the terrace. In his heart, Colonel Carlo Terzo felt two different emotions at once: sorrow for the death of his wife and an equally indestructible happiness that such a woman had lived, and that he had loved her.

"Of course," he said, "excuse me. Uncivilized as usual, as Emma would have said."

They crossed the street and Terzo, nervous, held Fiore's arm as the cars, oblivious to pedestrians, raced down the avenue.

"I just can't get used to the traffic," he commented.

"Really? Well, I just got my license. I like to drive. One day I'll come to pick you up and take you to the beach at Mondello. I have an English convertible. You should see how the men grumble when I overtake them on the roads."

"You shouldn't drive so fast." He accompanied her to the Mazzara café, which he'd heard Cosma say so much about: "Totally modern, Colonel, the most chic café in town."

They were the only customers, except for a corpulent gentle-

man smoking a slender cigarette, book propped against the remains of a copious snack, a hot chocolate and countless crumbs
of brioche scattered across page three of the *Corriere della Sera.*

They sat down in front of him, and a little boy, not more than
ten years old, in black trousers and white shirt, came up to
them, adjusting the shock of hair on his forehead:

"What would you like to order?"

"A Courvoisier, double," replied Fiore.

Surprised, the colonel muttered, "A coffee, please," and, in
imitation of Fiore's odd request—a woman ordering alcohol
in the afternoon—added, in a low voice, "make mine a double,
too."

The boy, unruffled, nodded and communicated the order to
the headwaiter, who put the cognac and coffee on a tray, then
placed the glass in front of the colonel and the cup and saucer
in front of Fiore. "It's the other way around," she said, smiling
at the mistake. Raising the brandy with two fingers and looking
at Terzo, she said: "To our loved ones. May they be as happy today as on the day of the kite." She drank two long gulps, closed
her eyes, and shuddered.

"Don't stare at me like that, Colonel, or I'll start calling you
sir again. I'm not an alcoholic, don't worry. But for a meeting
like this, I need a little pick-me-up."

"Where do you live? Why didn't I hear from you? I went
looking for you at Palazzo di Mare, but to no avail."

"Yes, I know. One of the servants told me. My mother kept
me in the country for several weeks after the battle of the peasants. We were hiding in the Mirto-Nicolosi house. Do you remember that nasty old lady who was spying on us in the church?
Then we went back to Palermo by bus. I told my mother I
wanted to see Salvatore and speak to Emma. She slapped me,
then slapped me again. She said nothing; that was the real tor-
ture. Locked up in my room, I started vomiting. I thought
maybe it was fear. Then I got a fever. She thought I was pre-

tending and started slapping me again. I fainted. The maid saw the blood-stained underwear and begged my mother to take me to a doctor. Mama said: 'It's probably just her period.' She didn't want me to go out of the house, but then resigned herself."

Terzo, at the word *period*, turned slightly around, to see if their neighbor had heard. It appeared not; the man had set aside his tome and was now writing on large sheets of foolscap.

"This little doctor, just out of medical school and plied with money to keep him quiet, took one look at me and said, 'The lady's expecting a child. Congratulations,' and then disappeared into the clinic. I was dragged onto the first boat for Naples. At night, complaining of seasickness, I was allowed to go out on deck. I wanted to throw myself into the sea, but I still thought Salvatore was alive and I could avoid marrying Mainoni until I came of age. My escort was that shriveled-up mummy, Signora Mirto-Nicolosi. In fact, when my godmother Elena had tried to help me, Mama sent Mirto-Nicolosi to threaten her: 'If you get mixed up in this, we'll get the lawyers after you and charge you with kidnapping.' The old hag couldn't believe how much importance she'd been granted: she didn't speak to me once during the entire journey, but stayed locked up in her cabin the whole time. 'Don't overdo it, ma'am,' the doctor had told me, pretending I was married out of respect for my mother. 'You're strong,' he said, 'but you've had a mild hemorrhage.' I'm going to have this baby, I thought, and I'm going to wait for Salvatore. In Naples, we went straight to the convent, where the nuns were all nice to me except for the mother superior, who never had a good word for such a sinner. I was imprisoned. Not a single letter from home, no news of Salvatore or you. Daylight hours I spent in the cloister, evenings I slept, as soon as it got dark. Sleep? Actually, Colonel, closing my eyes in that convent was utterly impossible for me. I would look at the lights of Naples out my little window, through four iron bars a century old. I cried and cried, trying to remember Salvatore and our child. But nothing could console me. Finally a nun, a wrinkled little thing whose gown was so full she seemed to walk above the ground as if held aloft by a hot-air balloon, came one day to say the rosary with me, and after the Sorrowful Mysteries, she shook her finger at me and said, in Neapolitan, 'That's enough of your crying,' and then left. But from God knows what secret pocket of her gown she had taken out pencils, a pocket knife, a notebook, and two books, and left them on the bed. Thereafter I spent my days writing. I wrote to Salvatore, to Emma, to my godmother. I would relive our afternoons, trying to convince myself that Salvatore had recovered."

Fiore gestured to the waiter; "Another cognac, please," she said, then resumed her story. "Then everything came crashing down. The mother superior summoned me to her office, where my mother was waiting for me. She informed me of the day I was to be married, and how much this reparative marriage was costing her in lands and dowry. The family was losing its Primosole lands. I thought of stalling, making excuses, pretending to be sick, but as I was about to leave, my mother said: 'That boy, Salvatore, is dead. Forget about him. I'll make his very name disappear. You will stay in Naples; the scandal hasn't died down yet." All I remember is the nausea, not the pain, no, not the anguish, just the nausea, the dizziness, the need to vomit up my soul. On my knees I begged my little nun to find out if it was true. She was able to obtain a note from my godmother, and that dashed all my hopes. If it hadn't been for the baby, I would have thrown myself down the stairs. But I couldn't; I was pregnant with Salvatore's child. At times I thought maybe my mother was having me drugged, because I couldn't react; I was spent. On my wedding day they dressed me up in beige and took me to the church. Mama didn't come. Just the two of us, the priest, and the witnesses, a lawyer and the sphinx, Signora Mirto-Nicolosi. I went to live with my husband, Mainoni, who didn't even try to enter my bedroom, and remained polite and absent."

Fiore drank her cognac. "This is the first time I'm telling this story," she said. "Who else could I have told? I lived as a wife and a widow, pregnant and unhappy, always under the watchful eye of a maid. I would write to Salvatore, letters I would never mail, my belly kept growing, I was in a fog. The brief happiness I'd known in your house seemed like some sort of joke, a bad joke just to make me feel worse. I would wake up, sit up in bed, and go out on the balcony and watch the sun rise over the bay of Naples. The pain was starting to descend deep inside me and nothing could stop it, nothing. It invaded me like a liquid, pene-trating my brain, and I would think 'This can't be. Why me? How can I feel so bad? Will it never end?' I prayed, but it seemed meaningless. Then I thought of you, Colonel. I started ruminating about your lessons: 'The importance of having re-serves, in war and in life.' The wisdom of Hannibal: use your weakness as a weapon. The sun beat down on the sea, and in the distance I could see the rosy shape of Capri. I started sketching in the notebook the nun had smuggled in to me; I drew an imaginary line, my mother in front of me, and me surrounded. What reserves did I have? And what weakness? It was total, that was clear, but where was the hilt by which I might grab my sor-row and turn it into a weapon? That night I dreamed of Emma, it was a peaceful dream, we were on the terrace eating can-taloupe ices. You and Salvatore had gone into the study to get a map, and the princess leaned over to whisper in my ear— remember how she used to do that? And very softly, so you wouldn't hear, she whispered: 'Fiore, take good care of your man, but don't let him know. By himself he'll only get into trou-ble. Listen to him and guide him, but don't let him know, for heaven's sake. They're very sensitive and fragile, like Sicilian puppets.' And she laughed heartily.

"I hadn't slept for months. I woke up with an aching heart, but I understood where I'd gone wrong. By withdrawing into my grief, I had forgotten Salvatore. I no longer remembered

him, his words, his face, his hands. I lived with my sorrow, not
with him. I was the only person in the world who remembered
his poems and the afternoons we spent flirting in your study.
But I was about to forget the colors, the details. Those were my
reserves: my memories of Salvatore were the hidden strength I
would bring into battle. But how could I, a prisoner, ever surround the enemy? It was hard to imagine. The old nun's smuggled notebooks were similar to those little things Salvatore used
to write in. Do you remember them? God only knows how he
ever managed to fill them with his precise, careful handwriting.
For every battle he would ask me to draw a map. I concentrated
on his sentences, his thoughts. He was an amazing boy. He
didn't care a whit about war, but he learned a lot from you. I
would get discouraged and say things like: 'We'll never be
happy. My mother will force me to wait till I'm twenty-one to
get married, and you'll get tired of all our secret arrangements
and leave me.' But he would calmly reply—he was so calm, even
in battle, do you remember?—'We have to fight, like young
Kellerman at Marengo. Didn't you hear what the colonel said?
One must always have a reserve. I am yours, and you are mine.
Let them separate us, but let's not underestimate our capacity
for resistance. So they think we're children? Well, the Romans
thought the center of Hannibal's formation at Cannae consisted
only of feeble mercenaries. We'll use our weakness, and we'll
surround them by continuing to love each other.' I wouldn't listen, and he would kiss me—he was a very good kisser, you know.
He'd look in his little notebook and say: 'Swear on our love that
if they ever take you far away from me, you will remember the
dialogue between Master Sun and the King of Wu. Swear it.' Do
you still remember Sun Tzu, Colonel?"

Fiore took out a cigarette, rummaging through her purse for
matches. But the man at the neighboring table flicked a silver
lighter and lit it for her:

"*Prego, signora,*" he said.

Terzo repeated the ancient lesson: "The King of Wu discusses strategy with Master Sun: 'How should an army in dire straits fight, an army that's surrounded or put to rout?' Sun Tzu always has the right answer, and so the king imagines a desperate situation. 'We've crossed the border and invaded a hostile nation. Now we're surrounded by vast numbers of enemy troops. From our tent we can see lines of regiments and trenches extending, impenetrably, all the way to the horizon. We look for a breach through which to flee, but all escape routes are blocked by fortifications. How does one save oneself, master, when all hope is lost?' Sun-Tzu, or Master Sun, replies: 'The path is simple, Your Majesty, but complicated, like life itself. If you hope to come out of the pocket the same man you were when you fell into it, you will die. If instead you are able to consider yourself dead, if you resign yourself to losing your life, and can imagine yourself a cold corpse like your companions struck down by arrows, you are already transformed. One part of you ends up among the piles of the dead, but the other part will spring out of the trap and see home again. He who cannot accept losing his old life must resign himself to dying. Do you think yourself capable of such conduct? Then order your men to dig deep trenches and build parapets from tree trunks and bundles of sticks. The enemy will realize that you're prepared to die to defend your encampment. They can conquer it only by sacrificing the cream of their warriors. You yourself, my sovereign, will speak to the troops and officers: "The final battle awaits us. Slaughter the oxen, distribute provisions. We will fight on a full stomach. Whosoever has debts to pay must pay them, and if the debtor has no money, then the creditor must pardon the debt. Nothing must remain unsettled." After speaking, shave your head as a sign of mourning, burn your royal bearings, give up all hope of living. As a commander, you no longer have any strategy. Your soldiers and officers are armed with the vow of death. The surrounded, defeated army no longer exists. You are aiming a deadly weapon, one willing to die in combat. Have your armor polished, your swords and daggers sharpened; unite the soldiers in spirit and strength and attack on opposite flanks. Let the drums roll ferociously, let the soldiers shout at the top of their voices, as if it were the final scream of their lives. The enemy will be surprised. They were waiting for us behind their trenches dug with care and ostentation, expecting to find us fearing for our lives, and instead we appear from two different directions, hardened by resolve. At that moment of uncertainty, order your assault troops to go to the enemy's rear lines, striking them from behind and opening up the siege. You will thus have snatched life and victory from the jaws of defeat.' So said Master Sun, Sun-Tzu."

Fiore extinguished her cigarette in the ashtray and lit another: "To start another life I had to admit that the gentle Fiore of the jasmine flowers, of Salvatore, of the kite, was dead. To regard her as lost, left to rot by her cruel mother. That's what I did. I didn't think I had the strength, but I closed my eyes and thought of myself as dead, day after day. I would clasp my fingers around the widest tree trunk in the lemon cloister and say: 'My hand will surround you.' One afternoon I slipped away undetected and went to a barber, paying him with a pair of earrings to give me a crew cut, as a sign of mourning. Then my baby girl was born, and I devoted myself to her. At night I would study and write. On the day I turned twenty-one, I sent a letter to Mr. Ripellino, a lawyer in charge of my father's interests. At first, no response. My mother was intercepting my mail. Then Ripellino came to see me in person, after threatening to denounce Mama to the courts for illegal confinement if she didn't allow him to speak to me. He assured me that now that I was of age I had come into the possession of more than enough money to support myself and my child, assets that my father had left in my name. Ripellino, a real gentleman, and a clever one, too, negotiated with my father-in-law. If they tried to keep me, he told them, he would appeal to the Rota and plead forced marriage and lack of consent, which would mean certain annulment. And a lot of gossip about town. Wouldn't it be better to annul the marriage discreetly? He pledged to leave the Mainoni family the Primosole estate, since nothing could have made me go back to the place where Salvatore died anyway. The Mainoni got their land, and my ex-husband was more than happy to find himself suddenly rich and unmarried at the baccarat table. Giulio Dragonara, Salvatore's younger brother, has legally recognized my daughter's paternity, and so now she has her father's name. Meanwhile I've enrolled at the university, done some traveling. Next month I'm moving to London."

"And your mother?"

"She got sick, with a strange illness the doctors don't understand. She's alive, but has no memory. She started by forgetting who I was. 'Who are you? What do you want?' she would say. Then she forgot my father. Finally she forgot to manage her lands. She still insists on holding onto her papers, in that dark little room you've seen. She clutches them in silence, looking up at the skylight. She's unable to feed or dress herself. I go to see her on my father's birthday, for his sake, and also out of pity for the poor thing, who can't even remember where the bathroom is. 'I don't know who you are,' she says coldly. 'Tell me who you are.'"

"Why didn't you call me?"

"I wasn't strong enough. I had to become another person to survive. I found out about Emma in Naples, from the first card my godmother sent. I adored her. What's become of Villa?"

"He turns up on the anniversary of Salvatore's death, when the Communists get together. He tells me about new political developments in Sicily, sends me photographs of their rallies. He never says a word about our battle. He fought bravely, out of love for those poor people of Malpasso, even though the Party was against it. Thanks to Donna Marena's sacrifice, everyone was spared. He prefers to keep quiet."

"Thanks to her and to your strategy, that is. Without you, the whole thing would have turned into a massacre, like what happened to Salvatore Giuliano at Portella della Ginestra. Give my regards to Villa. He's the only one left who remembers the kite of our wishes. He and the two of us, who ran into each other in the cemetery. Strange, today's visit will be my last before England. I wanted to go to America with Salvatore. Instead, dear Colonel, I'm leaving without him. And now you'll have to excuse me, I have to go say goodnight to my little girl. It was my memories of you that saved me in Naples, you know."

Before Terzo could protest and ask her to stay a little longer, she gave him a kiss scented with smoke and cognac, passed her hands over his eyes, and exited without turning around, as if fleeing.

Colonel Carlo Terzo looked up at the ceiling and thought: *So Salvatore Dragonara actually listened to my lecture. So by ordering Fiore to study Sun Tzu, he saved her. So we can indeed turn suffering into a weapon. Those two kids, crushed by a war of hate, did not go to the slaughter like sheep. They fought. Salvatore is dead, but he passed on his precious wisdom to Fiore, and she freed herself, at a bloody price, from the siege in which she was trapped. The strategy that would make us invulnerable, and always victorious, does not exist. Chaos can defeat us at any moment, but we can also save ourselves at any moment. And so my* Manual for Strategic Living *is not a total loss.*

"What an amazing story. Excuse me for taking the liberty of listening in. I, too, am a military history buff. And you are someone I would like to know."

Terzo turned around in surprise. It was the elderly gentleman at the neighboring table who had spoken.

"I don't mean to be a bother. It's just that, at my age, one becomes curious."

"Not at all," said Terzo, and asked for the bill.

"The Prince of Lampedusa has already taken care of it," said the waiter, bowing. With a gesture of the hand, the stranger begged Terzo to accept. Expressing his thanks, the colonel left a sizable tip for the boy, slender in his white shirt.

"Shouldn't you be in school?" he said to him.

"Me? I'm a worker, Your Excellency."

Putting on his overcoat, Terzo looked back at the solitary prince. He had resumed writing, and the café light fell slantwise on one of his lines: "*Nunc et in hora mortis nostrae.*" "Now and at the hour of our death."

Dear Carlo,

I hope these lines reach you in Italy. I am writing to you from the cockpit of a Fieseler Storch, the little German airplane they call "the Stork," which is the envy of all of us soldiers in Russia. It rises and descends like a stork, lands on the snow, leaves orders and mail and then flies lightly away to a place we'll get to only after a week of marching in the cold.

The question is a simple one, dear friend. I, Captain Amedeo Campari, of Novara Lancers, liaison officer with the Wehrmacht (congratulate me, I'm a captain now, promoted three weeks ago), have in my possession, spread out on the instrument panel of the Fieseler Storch, a well-written and even better-stamped order in the hand of General Hans von Hobstfelder. The general has decided that, having fulfilled his obligations, Captain Campari, liaison officer between Italy and Germany, has leave to quit the front and immediate access to the rear lines, Karkov or Lyublin, at his discretion. Countersigned by Colonel De Blasis, Italian Army in Russia. What this means, dear Carlo, is that my old friend, lieutenant and pilot Nicholas Walter, is about to go home, and I can go with him. A separate peace for yours truly, and for Italy, hopefully to study with you. Nicholas has read your works and is a great admirer and hopes to meet you some day. A good deal, eh? And so why, instead of saying a quick goodbye to Mother Russia and heading off, am I here writing to you while Nicholas is performing the final formalities in the Command barracks? Because I've seen war. I've lived through the

battles we used to study. I've seen the corpses in the mud at
Passchendaele, the massacres of innocent prisoners at Agincourt, the
death in the summer sun at Visby.

Every time I've saved my own skin, dear Carlo, I've thought back
on our last meeting in Tuscany, when we dueled. Who was right? Is
war the domain of the madman, as I maintained, or were you right in
saying that there's a lesson to be drawn from the slaughter? In hopes
of finding the answer, I reconstructed, in detail, the two defensive
battles on the Don and at Stalingrad, where General Monroy sent me
in October: "Campari, the Germans are telling me every day that
they're about to take the city and then they don't move forward an
inch. Go and have a look and tell me what the hell is going on."
Unfortunately I lost my notebooks last Tuesday, when I had to choose
between hastily jumping aboard a truck full of corpses or crawling to
pull them out from the underground refuge we were ingloriously
abandoning. I'm writing from memory, so please forgive me if this
letter is confusing. I've had a fever for the past week, my teeth are
chattering like a kid's. Do you remember the exercise we used to give
the cadets at the Academy? We would divide the class in two parts, an
entrenched platoon of "enemies" and an attacking platoon of "our
boys." What to do? The classic solution: the commander of "our boys"
should fire on the enemy and send part of the troop around to the
enemy flank, to surround them. An exemplary maneuver. It came
back to me when the Germans, who weren't exactly happy at the
arrival of this little Italian asking so many questions, took me to the
front.

The city is no longer there, just rubble. In the daytime the
Luftwaffe drop their bombs, at night the Russians resupply
themselves with rations and weapons from across the Volga. The
wounded are sent away, and today the new arrivals will be wounded.
The only light comes from the houses still burning, or from the river
when a barge capsizes and the oil bursts into yellowish flames. By
way of welcome, I was sent on reconnaissance (never fear, I
conducted myself well, standing when they were standing, on my

belly the next moment). We went warily down to the old warehouse by the station, which the Russians call the Pavlov House, a small four-storey building transformed into a bunker. On one side is the silo, with a grain elevator. Hundreds died trying to capture or defend it. I walk on the dust of ruins bombed repeatedly for months, a dust now finer than the delicious face powder of Laura d'Attimis. The sergeant setting the pace signals a halt. Whatever it was he heard, only he knows. Too many days underground have given him the ears of a mole. To me the silence seemed total. An instant, then a bullet tears through the neck of the German officer who had deigned to utter a few, cold replies in response to my questions. I hit the ground, without waiting my turn this time. Grenades from the floor above, snipers on the ground floor. Where is the enemy's right wing, Carlo? Behind the Sadovaya station? Perhaps, but it's difficult to judge if you're pressing your face into the dust. And the left flank? At the Red October building? "Yesterday it was ours, today it's Russian, tomorrow it will be ours again," I'd been told by the German officer now imbuing the brick-dust with his blood. Which way is south? In the direction pointed by the open-handed teenaged Wehrmacht boy, blue eyes gaping at the gray sky at the surprise of finding himself, so young, with the top of his skull gone? Immobile until the 24th Division artillery allows us to get away, I have time to reflect. Problem: what constitutes the flanks in a vertical battle, with the enemy fighting on alternating floors of an empty building? Which way is south when you're fighting underground?

In the evening, as the Russians fire their Katyusha rocket launchers, in a machine-gunner's nest I run into Nicholas Walter, the Catholic Luftwaffe pilot from whom I won, at poker, in '38, the marine binoculars I hope you still have. He appoints himself my guide at Stalingrad, and I present our dilemma to him: "Method or madness?" He's a veteran of the most horrific battle of the century and his opinion means a lot to me. But instead of answering, Nicholas drags me to a boarded-up window. "See where the Katyushas are coming from?" he says. "That's where the tractor factory used to be,

on the riverbank, where the flames are flickering from the barges
that have been hit. Calculate the position." I was stumped, and do
you know why? The ramps were in the water, Carlo. The Russians
had so little terrain on the bank that in order to fire on us they
installed their missile launchers in the Volga. "A war of water, earth,
fire, and air. The four elements against us. Between dead, wounded,
and prisoners, we soon will have lost 800,000 men, 1,000 tanks, 2,000
cannons, and 1,400 planes. If you can get it past the censors, tell
Terzo," sneered Nicholas, "but maybe not even he will be able to
draw a lesson for living from Stalingrad. Tell him: there is no moral
in massacres. Not even we, the best soldiers in the world, can win
with a strategy of death."

Massolo, a carabiniere of the 66th Section, a fellow Milanese who
became my good friend, asked me one day, "Lieutenant, who's going
to win the war?" I didn't know him too well at the time, and so I said:
"What do you think, Massolo?" And he answered in dialect: "Not the
Germans, Lieutenant, sir. Too wicked, those guys."

I told this to Nicholas Walter, who wants to take me away in his
Stork, before the Don becomes the largest pocket of surrounded
soldiers in human history. He laughed, the way people laugh here, in
grimaces: "Go tell the Führer that terror is not a strategy. My heart
weeps: isn't that how you Italians say it? I've fought in France, Africa,
and Russia. Fighting on equal terms, we've always thrashed the
bloody Allies. But we will lose the war. In the face of death, we are
the best, but in battle, as Professor Carlo Terzo teaches in his study on
Zama-Naraggara, the winners are those who think of life, not death.
The best strategy aims at peace, not conflict."

This is a confused letter, Carlo, but I have too many things to tell
you and fever does not help one to think clearly. The wind is making
the Stork's wings sway, the windows have fogged up, but I feel
protected here, and rather warm. A fine name, Stork. In a few
minutes I'll hear the snow crackling under Nicholas's boots and I'll
have to decide: do I stay behind with my soldiers or do I go home? I
could go with honor. I've done my duty, I have my new orders, I've

been with the Hobstfelder command since 1941, since the time of the
Italian Expedition Corps in Russia and General Messe. Still, I have a
strange feeling. If I could know which of us was right that day in
Tuscany, I would also know whether to stay or leave. But by myself,
without arguing with you, it's too hard.

What follows are two episodes from my lost notes, reconstructed
from memory. Then we'll see what I decide. We're in Cerkovo, minus
thirty degrees centigrade, which the wind against our overcoats turns
to minus fifty. With me is a kid soldier, a glassblower from Venice,
family name of Angeli. We're still in the Valley of Death, in a pit of
woe, and we can't see one step ahead of ourselves in the snowstorm. A
Katyusha is blocking our advance. Nobody knows what to do, what
orders to give, and this Angeli goes off on his own toward the enemy
rockets, armed with an antitank rifle stolen from the Russians. The
gunfire is so heavy that the Germans point their fingers to their heads
and say "Crazy Italian. Kaputt." But Angeli instead crawls forward as
in a commando manual, aims like a sniper, and takes out the soldiers
manning the rocket launcher. He's severely wounded by a burst of
machine-gun fire as we encircle the artillery post and mow down the
Russians. Angeli's hurt, but he's breathing. I order him to be taken
back to the rear lines, and room is made for him on the sleigh of a
little Fascist officer just arrived from Rome, named D'Aiello. Poor
bastard, he's dragging his bags behind him and he's already itching to
go back home and saying he's sick. He protests when, to fit the
wounded kid on the sleigh, he has to leave some trunks behind. I
don't even listen to him and go back to the front line. A week later I
run into a furious Massolo, who tells me: "Lieutenant, sir, as soon as
you left, that sonofabitch D'Aiello picked up that brave kid Angeli,
bloodstained bandages and all, and threw him off the sleigh to freeze
to death, just so he wouldn't have to leave his baggage. It was the
Germans who saved him."

This is war, Carlo. But this, too, is war: listen. At Arbusov,
December 22, General Lerici's Turin Division falls into a trap.
Among the reserves are the carabinieri of the 66th division and a

handful of my light cavalrymen; we'd lost our beloved horses and for a while had used those splendid little Russian horses that are accustomed to the cold, but now we were fighting on foot, like the English at Agincourt. 120 mm mortar fire, Katyushas hissing. There we are, dying, in an immense valley without defenses and no way out. The only road, leading to Cerkovo, is blocked. I see our men split up into groups, attack, and turn back. General Hobstfelder orders us to "resist," because we're the rear guard and it's all right with him if we're the ones taking the hits. The retreat to Mankovo is blocked by the courageous advance of the Russians, armed with Parabellums, an excellent weapon that never freezes up, unlike ours. The Germans take cover, and it's the Turin Division's turn to fight. We put up little resistance. The last 149/40 cannons are blown up, the Russian T-34 tanks arrive.

Now I'll tell you what happened in that terrible confusion, what I managed to see from my hole and what, not trusting in my senses, I had other soldiers confirm for me. Now it seems as if the entire Italian Army in Russia was witness to the episode. I hear the story told each day by a different infantryman, and in the end, it's only right: whoever is still here has a claim on the unbelievable. As far as I'm concerned, I might already be a clean skeleton up on that hill. We looked at one another furtively. If one fled, we would all flee. As Ardant du Picq warned, "Every man for himself" is the cry that scatters an army.

Nobody had the courage to advance, nor to be the first to flee. I was thinking of you, Carlo. I was trying to keep a cool head, to find a way out, a plan, an idea. I'm not much of a strategist, nothing ever comes into my head, either by madness or method. I shouted out orders, threw some grenades, sent the wounded back, but back where, if we were surrounded? I didn't dare shout "Forward, Savoia!" as I should have done, but neither did I shout "Let's get out of here!" I thought of the enemy's flank: that's where I should attack. But I don't even know where I am. All I knew was my dirty overcoat, the companions I could see if I craned my neck, and the bullets flying over my head. Nothing more.

A Russian horse that had thrown its rider came up to us. We must have still smelled of hay. He had a thick coat of fur, and pranced blithely amid the chaos. Massolo, the gentle carabiniere from the Bovisa quarter of my hometown, went over to him on his hands and knees, grabbed the reins, calmed him down and, speaking to him in Milanese, jumped on his back, grabbed a large Italian flag, and shouted "Forward, Savoia!" as we officers were supposed to have done. "Forward!" and then he charged the enemy. When I used to suggest such episodes for your courses at the Academy, you would say: "No bluster. We're not educating a generation of blowhards."

All this stuff is true, Carlo: death is raining down on us, the wretches scream "Mama" when they're disemboweled, and carabiniere Massolo grabs the flag and yells "Forward!" Without savagery. "Forward!" means "Home, in Italy, in the sun, with the family, no more snow, no more chickenshit, no more of the bastards who brought us here, no more Germans, no more Russians, no more robbing the poor peasants' izbas and hens, no more dying with your face in the snow." "Forward!" and Massolo rides on, silver braid on his chest. While we deadbeats, terrified, deafened by the rockets, resigned to death, we deadbeats get up off the ground and hoarsely reply "Forward!" running in snow knee-deep, paying no attention to those who fall, "Forward!" as if we'd be home in a flash. We run our bayonets through anyone who appears in front of us and suddenly we're on top of the 120 mm cannons. A T-34 cuts us off. Holding up a magnetic mine, Morganti, a Blackshirt volunteer skinny as a nail, confronts the tank. He lets it run right over him, the crawler-tracks crush him into the snow. The T-34 advances. Morganti turns around, alive! attaches the explosive and flees, the track-marks sharp as a tattoo on his face. The mine explodes, the tank stalls and comes to a stop. "Forward!" I run after the little horse and the Italian tricolor: that Risorgimento picture will save us. The Russians think we're mad: how can anyone charge that unassailable defensive position? But there's no time to answer and now it's their turn to retreat.

I could say: I'm right after all. Why, if not out of madness, did Massolo act the hero, and why did we follow him like medieval paladins? And yet, in this my last Russian meditation inside the peaceful Stork, I feel you have a point. During the Russian shelling at Arbusov, on my hands and knees, there wasn't any strategy I could see. But then the taciturn Massolo charged with the flag, embodying Clausewitz's "enlightened audacity," which is able to overcome simple courage. A carabiniere determined the outcome of the battle, because we had no choice but to follow him. When you are one of many, it's easy to be brave. To be the first to flee, however, takes guts. We followed him because his gallop told us, "If we stand still we'll die, so we might as well attack." With typical Milanese common sense—We can't sit around here all day, Lieutenant, sir!—he offered us a strategy for returning home, reason enough to make us kill. Which Mussolini was unable to do, leading Italy to ruin.

What, then, is war, Carlo? Is it the Fascist D'Aiello consigning Angeli the glassblower to an icy death simply to save his embroidered underwear, or is it Massolo saving a division? Is it insanity or reason? If I can figure it out, then I'll know what to tell Nicholas Walter when he comes: springtime in Rome or retreat with the boys. I wish I could consult with you, as I always wanted to inside the shitholes next to my butchered companions. We would have been afraid together, we would have screamed, but at least you would have helped me to understand. Instead I'm here alone, in this little airplane that soon will fly to safety, with or without me. When the war is over, please explain in your *Manual* that: 1. Germans make the best soldiers, but you cannot win with a strategy of death; 2. the Allies are fighting reluctantly, but in the end their numbers will prevail; 3. the Italian soldier is a good soldier, when he has a serious reason to fight; 4. no General Staff, of all the ones you condemned me to study, has ever been as cowardly and ignorant as ours. Show why, Carlo, and you will have honored my good, brave boys slaughtered in Russia.

Nicholas has opened the hatch and the snowflakes are falling inside.
Give my regards to old man Puntoni and don't forget to do the
exercises I prescribed.

Farewell, Carlo. Respectfully, your disciple and friend, Amedeo
P.S. Nicholas sends you, as a gift, the small book here enclosed, by a
certain Detlef Holz. It is entitled *Deutsche Menschen. Eine Folge von
Briefen.* It is a fine collection of letters . . .

Colonel Carlo Terzo set down the letter, with its scribbled
"Amedeo." The light of the Palermo spring shone bright in the
study where Salvatore and Fiore used to play their love games.
Those yellowing pages were the last memory he had of Amedeo
Campari, the last argument advanced in their unresolved debate. Methodically, Terzo would reread it every day, after his calisthenics ritual. That afternoon, after setting down Campari's
farewell, he felt once more the same confusion that had come
over him when he'd held those pages for the first time in the
winter of '43. Galeazzo Ciano, no longer foreign minister but demoted to ambassador to the Holy See in the reshufflings of a
desperate Mussolini, had summoned him "with utmost urgency," sending a messenger to his office in Villa Ada. Sitting at
his desk, Count Ciano received him without ceremony, without
even a greeting, in their second and final meeting, holding out
the letter like a threat. He gave him only enough time to read it,
then said imperiously:

"Well?"

"I hope Amedeo made it to safety. He's a very brave young
man."

"Is that all you have to say, Colonel?"

"What else could there be?"

"The German military censors intercepted your correspon-
dence. Berlin demands that you and Captain Campari be court-
martialed."

The colonel felt like telling him to go to hell, together with the German censors who could presume to interrogate Amedeo, soldier of a routed army in flight, but he refrained out of military instinct, not wanting to compromise his friend. As Ciano had not yet sent the letter to the Italian Military Tribunal, it was better to see what his intentions were. He merely said, "I don't understand what the Germans want."

"Would you like something to drink?" asked Ciano, stalling in turn.

"A coffee, please," replied Terzo. Normally, he would have muttered an embarrassed "No, thank you," but it was 1943. He hadn't had a decent coffee for months and was certain His Excellency's would be good.

"Coffee," said Ciano distractedly, and rang a bell. The door opened slightly and a hoary head peered in. "Furzi? Two coffees." The war years had taken their toll on the old secretary. He was gloomy, submissive; his suit, flawless three years ago, had stains on the vest. He greeted Terzo warmly.

"Good to see you again, Colonel. Doing well, I trust?" he said, as if to make up for the ambassador's coolness.

The coffee's delicious aroma filled the office, but when it came time to drink it, Ciano bolted out of the room in anger. In haste, before he returned, Furzi whispered to Terzo:

"When is this war going to be over?"

Terzo said nothing.

"Don't worry. One of my sons is a prisoner in India and the other's in Greece. I could have kept them out of the service with a recommendation from His Excellency, but they volunteered."

He seemed sincere, but Terzo remained cautious. "The news from Russia is not good," he said. "Our men are surrounded, and Marshal von Paulus and the Sixth Army have been lost."

Furzi arranged the coffee pot and cups on a silver tray and said: "Every month you send us your analysis of the battles for the encyclopedia Count Ciano asked you to write. At first he used to read your comments carefully. I even heard him quoting them to Generals Messe and Cavallero. But ever since Il Duce removed him from the ministry, and the Germans, especially Ribbentrop, have taken a dislike to him, all he does is fret. Did you see the state he's in? All pale and nervous, a shadow of the man he used to be. I hope he doesn't do something stupid. But I still read the things you send."

Surprised by the secretary's interest, Terzo was about to reply when Ciano came back into the room, rearranging his shiny hair. Furzi was right: the count was puffy and anxious. Paying no attention to the secretary, he again picked up the letter bearing Campari's messy writing and shook it in the air.

"How can anyone write such things?"

"Three years ago I asked you to let me go to the front, precisely because I had no direct combat experience. Instead, you decided I should work on the *Encyclopedia of Battles*. If I had fought on the front lines, I could give you an impartial answer. Unfortunately, I am unable to pass judgment on a friend who is tired and ill, shut up in the cockpit of a Stork under the Russian snow trying to decide whether he should come back home or stay and die with his men."

Ciano leaped up from his chair. "Are you so sure he will die?" he asked, alarmed. "Are you already sure they've been routed? The bulletins are not good, but Il Duce is convinced that the Germans have more men and means to right the situation."

"Men and means, I don't know," Terzo said softly, "but even if they did . . ."

"Even if they did?" Ciano pressed him. His menacing tone seemed to be demanding reassurance from Terzo.

"Mr. Ambassador, I don't think Hitler will win the war. And I'm not even talking about the theaters of operation, which are terrible in Africa, not good in the Pacific, and bad in the East. I'm worried about something more profound."

"Go on."

"My information confirms Lieutenant Walter's impressions. Fighting on equal terms, the Germans have always beaten the Allies. But the terms are no longer equal; America is strong. After coming very close to victory, the Germans will lose the war. And Italy, God help her, will lose with them."

"How can you be so sure?" Ciano was an intelligent man; he understood that Terzo's logic was irrefutable.

"All my life I've been trying to prove that a good strategy is based on life and not on death. Hitler was a good soldier in the First World War, wounded several times on the front lines. But what sort of Europe does he want to build? Telling a Russian: Die or I'll make you a slave, is the best way to convince him to resist. Analyzing the charge of the Imperial Guard under the command of the Grand-Duke Constantine, at Austerlitz on December 2, 1805, I wrote to you: 'The Russians will fight with discipline, resignation, and ferocity.' In war, Mr. Ambassador, those who are most capable of suffering emerge the winners. But to suffer for a long time requires means and reasons. You haven't given our soldiers any. It's a miracle they've held out for three years. The war is lost."

Terzo's tone was grave. Amedeo's story, on first reading, as in the hundreds more that would follow, had put him in a grim frame of mind. The timidity Ciano had inspired in him in 1940 was gone. Amedeo was forcing him to tell the truth.

"I'm beginning to have my doubts about you, Colonel. Perhaps Captain Campari is right. You can be a cold calculator, but you know nothing about courage, valor, and morale—decisive assets in battle," Ciano exclaimed.

Hearing himself called a coward by the man who had denied him his much awaited chance to fight, Terzo turned red: "You're right. I've never seen a man die. But what I've learned in preparing my *Manual* will suffice to show you that you're wrong, Count Ciano. If I could have a sheet of paper . . ."

Furzi diligently handed him a white pad and a red-and-blue pencil.

"Thank you," Terzo said dryly and, showing a page to the pale Ciano, drew two precise lines. "There is no doubt that the debate over strategy can be ultimately traced to the question raised during the duel in Tuscany mentioned by Amedeo. 'War is a duel,' Clausewitz summarizes. But what is the key to it? Is it method or madness? I take the liberty of quoting Churchill's judgment, from when he was still our friend, in 1931: 'Human affairs are governed far more by mistakes than by strategy.' The best soldiers and the finest weapons cannot make up for an erroneous strategy. Now follow me closely . . ."

Treated like a student, Ciano didn't breathe a sound.

"One or the other: either I am right, and there is method in war, or Captain Campari is right, and there is only madness. If the former is true, the Allies will win because, as Napoleon acknowledged in exile on St. Helena: 'In the end, English gold was able to defeat my battle plans.' The efficient British fiscal system won the war by paying for the rifles and cannons of Waterloo. The current war was lost in the trenches of Russia and the factories of Detroit. 'To make war,' Montecuccoli used to say, 'three things are needed: money, money and money.' But since you, like the propaganda, seem to believe that we shall win through irrationalism, I will explain to you why, on this front as well, which Campari was so fond of, the Axis will lose. I quote Hitler, Mr. Ambassador. The rumor reached me all the way from Germany, and I'm sure you yourself are aware of it. In November 1941, when he saw the Wehrmacht offensive bogged down outside of Moscow, he admitted: 'Wars are decided by economics, by the production of cannons, tanks, and ammunition.' By method or madness, the Führer knew he had lost."

"If you understood things so well, why did you waste your time explaining Marengo to Princess Svyatoslava that evening instead of warning me?"

"An unforgivable mistake. I tried, but you started waving at the Fascist Students' parade outside the window. I was talking, but you weren't listening."

"And what were you telling me that was so important?"

Terzo heard again the words he'd said three years before, and they rang hollow, like an outdated newspaper article: "War is not an end but a means. Clausewitz teaches that the strategist must measure his objective against the tools at his disposal. That night, I merely suggested that you organize a seminar with the officers of the General Staff. None of them had ever read a word of Clausewitz, like the Germans. Leo Geyr von Schweppenburg, tank officer and former military attaché in London, once said to me, 'We consider Clausewitz a snob, stuff for little professors, not soldiers.' I tried to save you from the same sin of pride. The strategy of reviving Roman imperial pomp with our wretched rifles was wrong. The German strategy of believing that blond hair is enough to prevail over American factories is equally wrong. It's all there in Clausewitz, sir: 'The first, highest, most basic decision the statesman and field-commander have to make is to choose which war they will fight, without trying to turn it against its nature. This is the fundamental, and most complex, theme of strategy.' We should have reflected before destroying Europe."

"In Berlin there's talk of secret weapons."

"Let them talk. The Germans are fighting from inside a pyramid. Every report from the field has to go up to the Führer and then descend back down with orders. Too complicated. The Allies' war is chaotic, but their chain of command, split between politicians and generals, is better at intercepting errors in operations. Who's going to explain to Hitler and Mussolini that managing information well is more important than tanks?" And Terzo traced his long lines on the sheet of paper.

"But Il Duce—" Ciano ventured hoarsely.

"If Il Duce still thinks he can win, try—as I know you can—

try to dissuade him. In every way. This is not the battle of Marengo. No General Desaix is going to appear this time. The war is lost, and there's no time to win another."

"Mussolini believes in the Germans. If you give me your word as an officer that you will keep it secret, I'll tell you what Colonel Battaglini, head of the General Staff of the Third Mechanized Division in Russia suggested to me."

"To aim for a separate peace."

"Have you also spoken with Battaglini?" Ciano asked, astonished.

"No. I've studied the war, as you ordered me to do in 1940."

Galeazzo Ciano had the same feeling as back then. This Terzo was not a typical military man. His quiet strength was disturbing. He was tired of listening to him. With the most unpleasant of tones, he dismissed him: "The Germans are furious. They're talking about sabotage. They're asking why a captain, granted the honor of reconnoitering the front, would divulge information about casualties and defeats. I will try to keep Il Duce in the dark about it. It was I, after all, who gave you the assignment of writing the encyclopedia, and I don't want to make a bad impression. You, meanwhile, clear out of here. Go to Sicily to survey the terrain, since people are talking about an invasion these days. By the way: your friend's letter was found inside this book. The Germans are obsessed; they consider it proof of guilt. Burn it."

He handed him the volume and resumed writing. Furzi had opened the door. Before leaving, however, the colonel turned around.

"Your Excellency?" he asked.

"Yes?" said Ciano, surprised he hadn't yet left.

"You didn't tell me whether Captain Campari finally left or stayed behind at the front to fight."

Galeazzo Ciano hardly looked at him: "The Germans recovered only one body, that of Lieutenant Nicholas Walter, from

the charred ruin of the Storch, not far from Staraya Kalitva. The
passenger's seat was empty. The last available news on Captain
Campari had him at the side of General Reverberi, during the
decisive attack of the battle of Nikolayevka."

Colonel Carlo Terzo opened Amedeo's book and translated
Holz's epigraph aloud:

> "Of honor without glory
> Of greatness without splendor
> Of dignity without mercy"

EPILOGUE

THE LETTER from Amedeo Campari you have just read has been in my possession for some time. It was sent to me by Colonel Carlo Terzo, whose story I, Pilgrim Gawain, an American pacifist who saved a tightrope walker in Sicily, have just told you. Those scribbled-over notebook pages are now in the care of the University of Indiana at Bloomington, together with the documents, ancient maps, and the rest of the Colonel's archives, which were sent to me in 1964. I had long insisted to Colonel Terzo that he move here to Bloomington, but he didn't want to accept our offer. He wrote me the following letter instead:

My dear friend Pilgrim,
I can't imagine what will become of my papers in a city where I live all alone and don't know anyone. The Italian government doesn't seem interested. The deed of title to the Amedeo Campari Study Center was lost in the postwar chaos, if in fact it ever really existed and was not the last creation of Emma's imagination. I wouldn't know who else to entrust them to, and I'm told American universities excel in archival management. Since you've been courteous enough to insist on my coming, I've decided to send you my papers instead. They're worth more to you than I am. When working on the *Manual for Strategic Living* and, during the war, on the *Encyclopedia of Battles*, I collected materials of the highest quality. If nothing else, my files have documentary value. All the principal battlefields in Europe and the Mediterranean have been measured and surveyed, with the help of Campari and the late Puntoni, and their current geography compared with the traditional sources. The repertory of

maps is invaluable. Please consider that of Marengo a personal gift in exchange for the trouble of finding a home for these reams of paper. It's the map Emma had on her lap when she asked me, before the war, to tell her about the fateful charge of my hero, General Desaix, in Ciano's office. It was originally a gift from her, and I want you to have it.

I am well, but I suffer from loneliness more than I would have expected. I thank you again for your repeated invitations, but by now I've become a Palermitan and don't want to leave Emma. So please accept these papers, old sport, they are much more valuable than Colonel Carlo Terzo.

With much affection,

Carlo

I wanted to write him a telegram to protest, but I noticed another letter in the envelope, written in an unsteady hand. It was from Signora Astraco, queen of the sheets, Terzo's neighbor from across the way:

Dear Professor Gawain

whom I had the honor of having as my tenant, I, Consolata Astraco, have asked my barber friend, Signor Cosma, who sends his affectionate regards, to help me write this letter. Which is a sad one because on the thirteenth of June, when I went to give Colonel Terzo, who was unwell, his shot, I found him on the floor, sick. He was taken to the hospital but died, all alone, poor man, during the night. He gave me this letter for you and directed me to please send you his boxes of papers, which were his life, as you know. I am keeping my promise, because I made it with the sign of the Cross. Cosma will help me to send them, but as for the money, don't worry, the colonel covered every expense with his pension. Now he is buried with Princess Emma, God rest her soul, and lies under our sky, whose colors he used to count, but he can't see it anymore. God will keep him close, because I think he was a good man even though he didn't go to Mass. He was the only tenant who never complained about my sheets. In fact, when I apologized, he would say, "What sheets, signora? Those are theater curtains. When they open I can see the cities of the sea." Take good care of his papers, Professor, and if you ever pass through our beautiful Palermo, don't forget to come and see your fond landlady,

Consolata Astraco

I held the page in my hand, feeling faint. Professor Stuart Fogg, my roommate, asked me in his perfect British accent:

"Bad news?"

"Yes," I replied, "terrible news. Terzo is dead. He was so at home in ancient history I ended up thinking he was immortal." I left the study in silence, but Fogg, who had been in the war, knew how to behave in these cases. He put on a strange Greek sailor's cap and followed me outside. We walked aimlessly about the campus, then he bought two beers at a convenience store and we sat down on the grass.

"I've never understood why this Italian means so much to you," he said skeptically.

"Because he knew the secret of victory and defeat."

"What are you talking about? If I remember correctly, we thrashed the Italians not too long ago."

"His country lost the war, but he knew how one wins and how one loses, in everyday life and on the battlefield. Have you seen the file boxes recently delivered to our office? They teach you how to act in peace and war. You mock the Italians, but on your night table you have the Loeb editions of the *Iliad* and the *Odyssey*. Do you remember when the Achaeans assemble the alliance to besiege Troy? Odysseus, to avoid having to fight, pretends he's mad and sows the fields with salt. Achilles dresses up as a girl, with silk peplos and blond curls, and hides in a harem. So, Fogg, the two most celebrated heroes of Classical Greece, the wily Odysseus and the magnificent Achilles, are deserters. Better mad and girlish than a warrior. And you know why? Because fighting without a valid reason is for fools."

Fogg took a long swig from his bottle, burped, and stood back up, adjusting his cap. "Strange people, you Americans, former subjects of the throne. You're masters of the world, while old England licks her wounds. And you, instead of feeling proud, you brood over some little Italian who spent his life studying the war while his countrymen were losing it. See you in the cafeteria." Fogg guzzled the last of his beer, politely tossed his bottle in a waste bin, and headed back toward the faculty buildings.

I should have explained, but explain what? How could I confess to the eccentric Fogg what I was unable to reveal to my teacher Carlo Terzo? That I, Pilgrim Gawain, a graduate in Engineering, conscientious objector and stretcher bearer, had worked on the Manhattan Project? Disturbed by all the dead I had gathered in battle, I had spent months shut up inside a desert barracks, resolving aerodynamics problems, helping to construct the atom bomb before Hitler's scientists did. A government bureaucrat appeared one day in my office, accompanied by my brother, whom I found standing silent at attention. The official said only: "We know you hate war. There were some who warned me against inviting you into our project, thinking an objector must be some kind of spy. But that's nonsense. You showed a lot of guts under fire, and your brother vouches for you. I'm told you're a genius with aerodynamic algorithms. An old professor of yours, Mike Berman, recommended you. 'Gawain is a wizard with numbers in the clouds,' he said. You'll be working with the best minds in the world. The choice is simple: it's either the atom bomb in our hands, or in the hands of those who want to make us their slaves. You choose."

So I went. Some nights I wake up in a sweat, thinking I would have done anything to bring the war to an end. You know the rest of the story: nuclear bombs dropped over two Japanese cities, thanks to my numbers in the clouds. Having saved thou-

sands of soldiers from the massacres of an invasion is no conso-
lation. I used to listen to Terzo in anguish. He had, among his
papers, the secret algorithm that makes it possible not to lose,
even when defeated, and not to become arrogant, even when
victorious. The simple man Fogg calls "that little Italian" knew
how to weave our existence into the tapestry of history. My
conscientious-objector friends would consider him a fatuous
warmonger, but they would be wrong: Terzo redeemed the suffering of battle, and from it drew wisdom useful to all.

I haven't got the education to analyze his studies properly,
and I am sorry if memory has betrayed me in my account of
them. My silence and regret are useless now. I should have told
him I was one of the engineers of the atomic bomb; he probably
had some suspicion. Once I was close, very close, to telling
Princess Emma, strange creature, enchanting, tender spy. It was
the day we went to Etna, when my dear friend Salvatore, whom
I loved and still love, met his end. Carlo Terzo would have explained to me how to graft that experience of death into my
life. And in exchange, he would have understood how nuclear
weapons have transformed classical strategy. But I said nothing.
Hidden inside me, the truth overwhelmed me. Fogg recently
read me a passage from the Gnostic gospels that says: "If you express the talent of your soul, your talent will save you. If you do
not express it, it will destroy you." I beg of you, do not make the
same mistake.

I was thinking of all this when, without any reason other
than nostalgia, I returned to Sicily. The ship docked on August 31, under a sky that Terzo would have catalogued as Italian
Blue. I went and put orange blossoms on Emma's and Carlo's
graves; they were the princess's favorite, for their intense white-
ness and scent. I put carnations on Salvatore's and went to see
his mother, who looked tired and weak. The Party had named
the "Salvatore Dragonara" branch office after him, and she fre-
quented it daily, just to reread her son's name painted in red on

the wooden sign. She never asked either me or Terzo to explain or even recount what happened on Etna that day. The war had just ended, and violent death was considered a fact of life.

Signora Astraco invited me to taste her cantaloupe pudding with jasmine flowers. While she was in the kitchen filling two small bowls, I leaned out the window and pushed aside the eternal white sheets with a reed. The pomelia bushes, which Emma would save from the frost in winter by putting eggshells over the buds, had been removed. In their place was a table, with a portable record player on top. A girl in black slacks was sitting on the railing, looking out at the panorama, oblivious to vertigo. The sea was very calm, scarcely rippled by a stream of current about which Terzo surely would have fantasized some field battle between General Sea and Marshal Coast. The girl was wearing a striped, close-fitting T-shirt of the sort that people wore in Europe that summer, and took deep puffs on her cigarette, her small chest heaving. She looked up, saw me, and turned back toward the sea-roads, now bereft of their strategist. Sitting over the emptiness, she smoked freely, in peace, as though centuries had passed since Fiore Mastema's courtly love had been humbled by tragedy. The telephone rang from inside, and her mother appeared in the doorway: "It's Paolo," she said. The girl pulled on her cigarette, stole a glance at me, and said in a bored voice:

"Tell him I'm not here."

I went back inside. The telephone book was still on the corner table with the white center-cloth. There was only one listing under the name "Mastema."

"Miss Fiore, please?" I asked.

"There's nobody here by that name" was the response, and they hung up.

Signora Astraco had overheard; she always heard everything from the kitchen. "Are you looking for Miss Fiore?" she asked. "She moved away from Palermo long ago. Didn't you know? She lives in London now. With her daughter. London, *Madonna mia.* What a beautiful lady she's become! Look: she wrote a book and sent it to me as a gift, with her signature."

The day before my return to the United States, I went to the Libreria Flaccovio, behind the Quattro Canti quarter, and asked for Fiore's book. "The last copy," said the young boy working in the bookstore, and he wrapped it in thin white paper. I read it on the boat on the way home, crossing back over the ocean. The cover shows a drawing of a wave and the title, *Prince of the Clouds.* On page three there is a dedication: "In fond memory of Salvatore Dragonara (1930–1946), father of my daughter, Chiara. This life's battle is lost, my love. But I hope we, too, shall have time, like General Charles Desaix, to win another, in another life." I truly loved her book, and I hope you will read it, too.

Bloomington, Indiana
October 17, 1967